Red Souls Series

Red Souls

Wall of Unknowing

States of Being

RED SOULS

By Susan F. Banks

DEDICATION

To Michael and the usual suspects.

Special Thanks for the wonderful writers of the Raven's Keep on Scribophile for helping me get this story off the ground.

Check out **susanfbanks.com** for a music playlist that accompanies this book.

PROLOGUE

Our world is only one of all possible worlds that are allowed by the fundamental principles of quantum physics and that exist simultaneously in probability space. – Yasunori Nomura

The Guardian of the Astral Gate in Los Angeles is 170 years old. Jat the Deceiver is older than the world. Guardian and Deceiver have been locked in battle for the Soul of L.A. since the city began. Now Jat is mounting a new attack. The Guardian will need a Circle to help her drive the Deceiver back to the Underworld. The Circle of Augustus is an ancient fighting force forged in love and fire that can resist Jat's deceptions. The Circle must rise again in the modern age.

Chapter 1: Worlds Collide

Willet Du Place did not normally go out walking by herself, but she did today, enjoying the early morning light of the desert where she lived. She wandered farther out than usual. Even in the desert there were noises. A truck driving by on the freeway, a particularly loud squawking bird, or a barking dog – any spiking sound could give her a bad headache. Her hyper-sensitive hearing forced her to live as far from modern civilization as possible, but sometimes it just wasn't far enough. Today, a hellacious noise started up in Hemmings a few miles away and took her by surprise. Chainsaws. *Oh great. Just what I don't need.* By the time the whine of the saws reached her ears, it was too late to avoid a migraine. The screaming saws chewed on her sensitive eardrums with vicious teeth. Her neck clenched and her eyes watered. The migraine began to pulse under her right eye. Time to get back home.

She took off toward Pine Siskin House like a spooked rabbit, maneuvering around cacti with the growl of the saws snapping at her back. *Damn it!* She had just started to lose the shudders of another awful dream in the warmth of the sun. She had not intended to walk quite so far from home, so she had no phone with her. Now she faced several uncomfortable realities. The desert sun rising in the sky beat down on her, and here she was without a hat. Worst of all, her noise-cancelling headphones still lay on the patio table where she left them. *What was I thinking?*

Her sister, Audrey, had warned her that the forestry crew would start work this week, but it totally slipped her mind. Pine needles whistled through the air and tree limbs hit the ground like sledgehammers. Even at this distance, her unprotected ears heard the impact as if the trees were landing at her feet. Just then an earthquake jiggled the ground for several seconds. Her toe hit a snake hole, and she tripped. *Could this day get any worse?* No time to worry about torn pants or scraped knees. She scrambled to her feet and kept running.

When she finally reached the patio, she scooped the headphones off the table and clapped them over her ears with a sigh of relief, but the headache had already taken hold. She yanked the patio door open and bolted into the kitchen. First order of business - migraine meds. She grabbed the bottle out of the cabinet, tossed one of the white pills to the back of her throat and gulped it down without water. She pulled her phone out of the jacket draped over a kitchen chair and raced for the bedroom to her refuge of last resort – a sound-proofed, cedar-lined closet. If the deep quiet of the closet and the meds didn't ease the clobbering in her head, she might end up in the hospital with a tranquilizer drip in her arm before the end of the day. She dove into the closet, pulled the door closed behind her, and dropped to the floor. Hands shaking, she punched in her sister's number.

Audrey answered after three rings. "Will, what's up?" her sister's voice boomed in her ear.

Willet held the phone away from her head. "They're chopping trees for that condo development today. I went for a walk and had to run for my life. Then an earthquake tremor hit, and I almost fell on my face. Plus, I had that dream again. This whole morning has sucked."

"Where are you now?"

Willet tried to control the quiver in her voice. "In the closet, of course."

"Damn," said Audrey. "I asked the crew manager on that job to let me know exactly, time and date, when they'd start cutting. I guess he forgot."

"I love this house, Auddie, but it needs improvements. I'm twenty-four. I shouldn't be hiding in a closet like the boogey man is after me."

"Did you take one of your meds?"

"Yes. I almost took a second one. My head is hammering."

"Will," Audrey admonished. "We discussed that after the last episode. You promised."

"I said I just took one."

"This is why I don't like to leave the pills with you. You don't want to have your stomach pumped again, do you?"

"I get it," Willet replied through clenched teeth. "I took the recommended dose, okay?"

"Well, hang on. I'm still debugging, but almost done for today. I have a lead on an acoustic engineering company we might hire to add sound proofing to the house. It got very good reviews. I'll stop on the way home to check it out. It'll take me a while to get out of downtown at this hour."

"Come home right after that, please. I don't want to be alone right now."

"I'll be quick as I can, don't worry." Audrey clicked off.

Willet kept down pillows and a blanket under the shoe rack for situations like this. She pulled them out, spread the blanket on the floor and lay down, smashing the pillows against her ears. There was

9

something oddly comforting about the closet. The smell of fresh cedar and leather shoes and the muffled quiet calmed her. The pill started to kick in, and the tension between her eyes eased. She slipped into that musing state between sleeping and waking.

I'd love to visit Paris someday. I could practice my French, walk along the Seine, and sit in the little cafés. I'd explore Montmartre and see where Chopin lived. Notre Dame has spectacular stained glass. Auddie would go with me, I bet. We could visit Dad while we were there…

She had practiced a Chopin Ballade on the piano just that morning and visualized the sheet music. Her fingers played the notes in the air. Her shoulders relaxed, then her knees. She dozed and drifted into a dream in which she stood on the banks of the river Seine. The bells of Notre Dame rang the hour. Water slapped against the concrete banks and a ferry boat puttered past. A man in a black frock coat and white frilled shirt with worn cuffs stood beside her, his frame thin, his brown eyes sunken. Chestnut hair curled over his shirt collar. She knew him immediately – Frederic Chopin.

"Monsieur Chopin!" she said, choked with awe. "Enchanté! You're my idol."

He turned, nodded, and smiled a sad smile. His long, thin hands lay on the handrail in front of them. He played air piano too, but she could hear the tune he played, the Ballade she had practiced just that morning. She listened hungrily to every note, absorbed by his mastery.

"Red Souls come," he said to her. His voice chimed. "Ka-la-ma-na, ka-la-ma-na," he sang in a ringing tone like a silver bell. "Worlds collide." Chopin pointed a long slender finger upwards.

She followed his finger with her eyes. Red smoke swirled in the grey-blue sky, and then twirled into a ball and dove at her at great speed, aiming for her head. Voices chattered in the smoke, hysterical and angry. She swatted the smoke away from her eyes and nose, but it seemed determined to attack her. She ran along the Seine with smoke all around her. It slipped into her mouth and down her throat. She coughed, and then stumbled. She had the sensation of falling and dropped heavily into her sleeping body as if she had been pushed from a high place.

She sat up in the closet, choking, her heart pounding against her ribs. *Can't breathe. Can't breathe. My head is splitting.* She jumped up, threw the door open and ran for the kitchen. She grabbed the medicine vial and swallowed another migraine pill with no feeling of guilt. The chainsaws had stopped for the moment. She yanked the kitchen door open to walk out on the patio and get a breath of air. It was already midday. The hot sun soothed her, but she didn't quite trust it. She closed her eyes, breathed slowly and tried to gather her wits. When she opened her eyes, a big, black dog with a white patch on its forehead sat on its haunches on the patio, staring at her with large gold eyes.

She yelped. "You scared the hell out of me! What are you doing here?" she said, her voice trembling.

The dog raised its head, and replied with a long, mournful howl. Willet backed away and ran back into the house, slamming the door behind her. She peered out through the window. The dog turned and trotted away, around the corner of the house and out of sight. Willet opened the door again and crept to the back of the house to see where it had gone. Over the broad, flat desert, there was no dog in sight.

*****

From the height of Griffith Park overlooking downtown Los Angeles, Gem Hawkins scanned the skies over L.A. County from desert to ocean, looking for signs of a breach in the Astral Gate. Lately, the Gate had suffered more breaches than usual. As Guardian of the Gate, it was Gem's responsibility to protect L.A. from whatever Underworld demons and fiends snuck into the physical world through a hole in the Gate. So, it had been for one hundred and forty years. She felt an ache in her chest whenever the Gate was breached, and her chest was getting uncomfortably sore.

Northeast of downtown, a phantom hole hovered in the sky, and red glittering smoke poured out. Red Souls from the Underworld escaped through the hole in the clouds of smoke and poured into the city on the streets below. Their objective: to attack the minds and emotions of human beings and drive them to despair.

A veil of vibrations separates the physical world from the many other worlds that exist. Only someone who can see through the veil would notice the hole in the sky and what was coming out of it. Someone like Gem. "There it is, Dora," she said to the big black Labrador Retriever sitting at her feet. "The third break this week. Above Covina, I would say. Trouble will soon follow."

Dora blinked her golden eyes, and the white patch on her forehead furrowed. Dora's physical size and presence intimidated anyone who saw her. She was the Hound of Hell after all. No one who heard her thunderous growl or saw her three-inch canines extend out of slobbering jaws would dare threaten the Guardian when Dora was by her side.

Guardian and Hound headed for the Jeep parked nearby. A shortwave radio mounted on the dashboard picked up gritty static from the police band along with reports of a fight among neighbors at an apartment complex in West Covina. The situation had all the earmarks of a Red Souls attack – sudden fighting, weapons drawn, and young children in harm's way. Someone had a knife to the apartment manager's throat, all for no apparent reason in a usually quiet neighborhood.

When Red Souls entered the physical world, they attacked the minds of human beings and preyed on their passions, planting vivid images of anger, violence, lust or greed. Whatever weakness a person had, no matter how deeply buried, the Red Souls would exploit it. Every time a person acted out violently, Red Souls enjoyed the vicarious thrill.

Gem drove onto the freeway as traffic conveniently split in front of her. With her foot heavy on the gas, the Jeep practically flew. She reached the neighborhood in West Covina and slowed the Jeep to a roll. As she expected, red smoke churned and glittered in the air over the apartment.

She parked down the street. "This is it, my dear," she said. Dora lolled her long pink tongue and whined softly. Gem closed her eyes, took deep, steady breaths, and chanted under her breath, tuning herself to a higher vibration like a tuning fork. Huuuuuuu. Huuuuuu. Thoughts drifted through her mind, nagging for attention. She released them one by one and focused on the inner screen between her eyes, waiting for the familiar soft sound in her left ear and the pinpoint of white light piercing the darkness. Suddenly there it was, a light so small, but rushing toward her, growing larger.

Then the Light crashed through her. A cool wave rolled into the crown of her head, down her spine and tingled in the soles of her feet. Ocean surf whispered inside her, mingling with the rise and fall of her breath. Her astral form peeled away from her physical body and floated through the door of the Jeep enveloped in luminous pink light. Dora followed in her own pink astral form, tail wagging

13

happily. They moved in an undetectable blur of speed to the apartment building.

A bank of hedges hid the pool area in back of the apartment from street view but could not hide the angry voices. Gem moved through the hedges like mist, unhindered by leaves and branches. Dora floated at her side. They emerged into the pool area of the apartment complex where people in swimsuits and beachwear stood on each side of the pool, yelling and waving their fists at each other. The silver of weapons flashed in some hands. Children huddled underneath pool chairs covering themselves with towels.

At the head of the pool, a man pleaded for help and tried to wriggle away from a larger man who was choking him with one arm and waving a knife in the other.

The phantom hole in the Gate hovered ten feet above the pool, visible only to someone with astral sight. Sparkling red smoke poured out of the hole and slipped into people's noses and mouths. The more they yelled, the more they inhaled the smoke. They were lost to their own hostile emotions, and their astral bodies looked like black and white X-rays of human skeletons. They hissed when Gem and Dora appeared. Gem's light glowed bright, and Dora bristled with energy, even more fearsome than her physical form. The skeletons crouched low, covering their skulls with boney arms. This was the emotional reality of the scene, so close to the physical as to appear simultaneous but vibrating at a different rate.

Lights in the smoke sparked faster and glittered brighter. Red Souls were excited by the anger. They darted in all directions in the streams of smoke. Dora howled if they dared get too close to Gem. Children huddled under chairs glowed pink. Each one twinkled like a star. They detect Gem's astral presence through their innocent eyes. Their astral-pink bodies slipped out from under the chairs and floated toward her with arms open wide, seeking safety with her.

14

One skeleton tried to grab a pink star as it drifted past. Dora's growl of warning rumbled like distant thunder. The skeleton dropped its arms and sank to the ground.

"Easy, girl," murmured Gem. "We do not want to frighten the little ones."

As Guardian of the Gate, Gem possessed an unusual power to freeze negative emotions, and she used it now. She threw her head back and blew an exuberant spray of ice and sleet from her mouth, showering the skeletons around the pool with freezing rain. Her breath sizzled as it hit them. The skeletons wailed and cringed. Their boney appearance faded, and their bodies turned a faint pink. It left them blinking and confused in their physical bodies, as if they had awakened from a bad dream. Such was the effect of the Guardian's Freezing Breath.

The situation unfolding at the head of the pool was trickier. Ruby beads of blood oozed from the manager's throat as the larger man pressed the knife against the manager's skin and locked eyes with Gem. The knife man showed a full astral skeleton. His eyes were black with rage, caught in the downward pull of negativity from which he could not escape. Red Souls screamed their encouragement of his violence. He let the knife slice fully into the flesh of the manager's neck. The manager screamed in pain. Gem blew a freezing breath at the two men, but the man with the knife was lost to his own rage and did not let go.

Gem would have to put the knife man in a hard freeze. She seldom used that kind of restraint on anyone. It left a person traumatized, but at this point, it could not be helped. The front of the manager's shirt was now drenched with his own blood, and his life was at stake. Gem had to act before the knife cut his throat.

She pursed her lips, formed an arrow-headed projectile of ice on her tongue, and spit it at the knife man with the force of a bullet. It hit him between the eyes. His eyes glazed over, and his aura turned grey. Frozen solid emotionally, he tilted to the side and fell, pulling the manager down on top of him. He would live, but the physical and emotional pain could be considerable. The manager needed an ambulance.

There was one more problem to solve. The breach above the pool still festered like a swollen blister. Red smoke oozed through cracks at the edges. Gem gathered another Freezing Breath and exhaled it, icy and strong as a gale, and sent Red Souls scattering in the smoke. They screamed, trying to resist the force of it, regrouped and charged at Gem. Dora jumped in front of the Guardian, howling with a keening ferocity that made every astral being at the pool cover its ears. The red smoke swirled away from Dora's howl as if it was a sonic shield and tried to escape the Guardian's breath.

Gem blew another frigid blast and sent the red smoke spinning up through the hole in the Gate. When all smoke had disappeared into the hole, she layered sheets of ice on the inflamed surface of the breach. It healed as it cooled and became nothing more than a shimmer above the pool, like sunlight gilding the water. She closed her eyes and listened to the calm roll of ocean waves, the sound of the astral plane. She breathed in synchrony with the waves, and in the absolute silence between flow and ebb, she recharged her energy. Dora's wet nose nudged her neck and brought her back to physical consciousness. They were sitting in the Jeep.

"Some of the Red Souls escaped us, Dora," Gem observed. "Where will they turn up next?"

The ground shuddered underneath the tires of the Jeep. Earthquake tremors were common in LA, but she never took them lightly. Gem glanced in the mirror. Her chocolate skin glowed. Her tight, blonde-tinged brown curls remained in place, but her lipstick had faded. She pulled a tube of Ruby Rosa lipstick out of the glove compartment and applied a light coat to her lips. Better to be ready for anything. The mirror rattled as another tremor rolled beneath them.

The police band squawked about a street fight near Bell Gardens. Once again, tempers had flared, and people threatened each other with weapons. The Guardian did not believe in coincidences. Were the Red Souls that just evaded her causing trouble in a new place already? But what if this was a new contingent, a new breach? It was troubling that she couldn't be sure. *How are they getting through the Gate?*

*****

At late afternoon, a green Porsche exited the I15 freeway on two wheels and sped up Pine Siskin Road. *Almost home, Will,* Audrey thought. *Please don't take any more pills.* The Porsche came to a squealing halt in the circular drive in front of the big stone house with wood gables. Audrey burst out of the car, hurried up to the front door and barged in. Willet was sitting cross-legged in the hallway, rocking forward and back, her body shaking. Curtains of lank blonde hair covered her face.

Audrey knelt beside her. "What's wrong, hon?" she asked. "What happened?" She pulled her sister into a hug, which unlocked a flood of tears and words.

"I fell asleep in the closet and then I was in Paris, by the Seine. It was so real. Chopin played the Ballade on the rail and red smoke chased me. I know that sounds weird, but it got in my mouth. I couldn't breathe. I had to take another migraine pill, sorry, I know I promised. And then a big black dog with gold eyes walked onto the patio and stared at me. He howled and really freaked me out, but

17

then he disappeared into the desert. I mean, totally disappeared, Auddie, and *that* wasn't a dream. I think I'm losing it."

This sounded bad, even by Willet standards. Audrey chose to downplay it. "Slow down, now. You know how those pills affect you, especially two, and you took one just last night."

"I keep having that same dream about the guy in the white hoody stalking me. He gets closer every time. I'm afraid he's gonna grab me eventually."

"It was just a dream," Audrey said. "He can't touch you in a dream. They don't mean anything anyway."

The sisters rocked together, hugging. Willet rested her head on Audrey's shoulder and started to calm down. After a while Audrey pulled back and examined her face closely.

"How 'bout some dinner? You look tired and pale and a little wild-eyed. '"

Willet tried to smile. "Oh, thanks, that's the encouragement I need. The headache is still burning my brain and I'm afraid to go to sleep. Other than that, I feel gorgeous."

"I'm worried about you Will. The voices, the dreams, they seem to be getting worse."

Willet hung her head. Her defeated weariness touched Audrey's heart as it always did.

"Well, this might cheer you up," Audrey said. "I think I found someone to sound-proof the house. His name is Dean Simmons. He's an audio engineer, as well as a rock musician and drummer. He's coming Friday afternoon to give us an estimate."

"Did you explain our situation?"

"I just said we wanted acoustic upgrades, full house. I didn't go into details."

Willet shrugged and her eyelids drooped. Dark rings circled her eyes.

Audrey hugged her closer. "Will, I know sound proofing the house will help some, but it won't necessarily eliminate the voices, right? I don't want you to get your hopes up."

"When was the last time *I* had hopes?" Willet muttered. "I think it was the seventh grade." She shuddered. "People will be coming and going with hammers and drills and stuff."

"Maybe an apartment rental or temporary office could work," Audrey offered.

"Yeah, but I won't have my piano," Willet lamented. "Morning is my best practice time."

"We could rent a piano. And it won't take that long," Audrey reassured her. "It'll be worth it in the end. The house will be quieter, and you'll be more comfortable. You'll see."

Willet gave a weak smile. "You look happy," she observed. "What's up? Is it the upgrade, or did that Dean guy perk you up?"

Audrey allowed herself a fleeting memory of the man in question, and then sniffed. "What do you mean? It's not a guy. Can't I just be happy?"

"I know you, Auddie. You try not to notice guys, because of me. Is Dean good looking by any chance?"

"Good looking? I don't know," Audrey dismissed it with a hand wave. "I suppose you could say he's good looking."

"What did he look like?"

"He has dark curly hair, blue eyes, sort of tall, muscles. Must be all the drumming or maybe the construction work..." Audrey's voice trailed off and she avoided Willet's eyes.

Willet would not be put off. "Auddie, please don't make me feel worse than I already do. I'm not a child. I want you to have your life, and I don't mean just working on the business. After the house is sound proofed, you need to start going out more. I'll be okay."

"We've been through this before, Will. It never works."

"Well, we're going to try again. Maybe you can start with Dean."

"I'm already starting," Audrey admitted with a cough. "He asked me to come hear his band play on Friday night. I gave him a tentative 'yes'."

"Well, I'm going with you. I'll sit in the car and wait for you, make sure you get home safely."

Audrey threw up her hands in exasperation. "See? This is what I mean. What about me having a life of my own?"

"You don't know this guy. You may need backup."

"From you? You can't be anywhere near the club! The noise would destroy you."

Willet's eyes pleaded. "I'm afraid to be alone right now. The walls are closing in. If I could just be nearby, it would help. We'll keep in touch by phone. I won't bother you, I promise. It would work out."

The alarm bells that went off in Audrey's head were loud as police sirens. *Willet should be nowhere near a rock club in West Hollywood. What am I thinking?* But Willet had little life outside their house. Audrey didn't want to leave her alone in her current state, so she relented as she usually did and tried to reassure herself. *I'll be in the club for forty-five minutes max, and then I'll leave. She'll be fine. We'll be fine. What could go wrong?*

Chapter 2: Entanglements

Dean Simmons leaned back in his office chair at Audio Environments Inc. and mused about his latest customer when he should have been going through all the mail and bills on his desk. She was choice. Honey-blonde hair thrown over one shoulder, big amber sunglasses, a blue cotton dress, mid-calf sheepskin boots – that was his first sight of Audrey standing in his store. She had one ankle wrapped around the other and jiggled it like she was shaking a tambourine. She asked him about headphones and sound proofing, and wanted work done ASAP. He could barely listen to her he was staring so much. She smelled like honey and ginger. Despite a packed schedule, he found a way to fit her into a prompt appointment.

The bell at the front counter started ringing repeatedly, interrupting his reverie. *So annoying.* He got up and stalked out to the front of the store.

TJ Barlow, Esquire, his pain-in-the-ass best friend, wingman and business partner, stood at the counter, merchandise in hand, banging on the bell with malicious glee. He dropped cables and batteries on the glass countertop with a clatter and leaned against it with the easy grace of a tall, lean frame. "Hey dude, I want service," TJ grinned wide. "What's wrong with this establishment?"

TJ's sun-bleached brown hair flopped over his forehead. He wore board shorts, a sleeveless tee-shirt and sandy flip-flops. His gnarled, brown feet suggested many hours on a surfboard. Dean had the same feet.

Dean could barely remember a time TJ wasn't in his life. In third grade, they collided with each other at second base during a Little League game and had been friends ever since. After spending an adolescence full of sun, surf, and prodigious partying, Dean went to Cal Tech to study acoustic engineering. TJ studied law and business at Stanford. Despite time and distance, they were always in contact. Holidays and summer breaks were spent together. Even as grown men, some things never changed, like the snark and banter of their youth.

"So, what's the deal with the Hemmings job?" TJ asked.

"I went out yesterday and wrote an estimate. Two sisters live in the desert east of there. They have unusual noise reduction requirements, to put it mildly."

TJ scratched the blond stubble on his chin. "A big job?"

"I bid high because of the complications. The older sister didn't even blink."

"Nice. What about your club gigs?"

"Don't worry, counselor, your club will still be happening."

"My club's always happening. I don't need you for that."

"Jackass."

"Dipshit."

After graduation, Dean started Audio Environments to finance his rock band, Shock Value. TJ invested in real estate and owned the club in West Hollywood where Dean's band played almost every weekend. They started a music publishing company together with

Shock Value as the first client. Where music was concerned, they were passionate and ambitious.

"So, what's the problem?" TJ asked. "You should be jazzed."

"The job has complications, like I said."

"Like what?"

"Well, the younger sister, Willet, can't be in the house while the work is done. She needs a space with zero noise, or else she gets bad headaches. It's a physical condition, something to do with her brain."

"What are you going to do about the construction racket?"

"She needs to be off the premises during the day. I offered my guest room to her older sister."

TJ stood up straighter. "Dude. Seriously. At your house? You're getting in deep here."

"Apparently hotels are a problem. You know how sound-proofed my place is. It made sense in the heat of the moment."

"I smell entangling alliances. We have an older sister and a young damsel in distress. You're the white knight. Remember the last time you rode to the rescue? You worked for two weeks and didn't get paid."

"Willet plays the piano, despite her problems. I respect that. Besides, I don't want the deal to fall though, that's all."

"Sure ya don't. Were you attracted to the older one?"

"Audrey. She's a looker, definitely. The younger sister, Willet, seems fragile, blonde, pretty..."

TJ shook his head and smiled. "Ah, the 'two sister' scenario. You are so screwed, bro."

Dean raised palms in protest. "Hey, it's a business arrangement, mostly, although Audrey might come to the city this weekend and check out the band."

"She's hot, right?"

Dean shrugged and nodded. "Satisfied?"

"So, the saga begins. Audrey stakes the first claim."

"There's no staking, no claiming. It's not that way. It's a health and welfare issue."

"Do they work?"

"Who cares? As long as they pay my bill."

TJ raised blonde eyebrows and flashed his straight white teeth. "Maybe family money."

"You have that look," Dean remarked. "You're looking for angles. Don't look for angles."

"How strong were the vibes?"

"You're deranged, Barlow. There are no vibes."

"There's always vibes. Pick one girl and go with it or walk on the wild side and try for both," TJ said with a leer.

"Idiot."

"Wank. You know jealousies will arise. You're a rock god, after all."

Dean gave his friend a withering look. "You're deranged."

"I *am* deranged, but I know women. You're a magnet for the females. That's why your band headlines the club - that, and the awesome beats, of course. You're not going to be distracted, are you? There could be industry people in the audience."

Dean rolled his eyes and turned his back on TJ. "I know what I'm doing," he muttered. *Would Audrey come to see the band?* He wondered. *That would be pretty cool.*

*****

The crowd at TJ's West Hollywood had already reached its Friday night buzz. Dean sat at the broad wooden bar, sipping an orange beer and surveying the crowd. He was ready to play.

A raven-haired girl named Delos stopped to chat. She wore a tight red tube dress, cage heels, cat eye makeup and bright red lipstick. Silver hoops dangled from her ears. She rattled on about her new album and her career as a performance artiste. Delos was a nice girl, despite the rock chick cliché. She just came on a bit strong.

He nodded and smiled, trying not to stare at her very white teeth. They were sort of pointed. She tossed her dark curls and twisted on one high heel, preening under his gaze as she prattled on. When she was satisfied that she had his full attention, she floated off into the crowd to bedazzle someone else. Dean turned back to the bar and wondered again if Audrey would show. Could she leave Willet alone at home? He heard someone call his name.

TJ made his way through the crowd in his usual Friday night black tee and jeans. He flashed his big smile and shook the hands of the customers he passed. He pulled up a stool beside Dan and knocked his knuckles on the bar. "So, we all set? Where's the band?"

"They're around. We're ready."

"I know some ladies from the studios that want to meet up with us after the show. You in?"

"I don't know. Maybe."

"Where's the enthusiasm? Are you holding out for Ms. Audrey? You barely know her."

"I'd like to get to know her better, that's all."

"Do you really think she'll show?"

"No, probably not." Dean swept his eyes over the crowd again, searching. He'd have to get on stage soon.

"Well, then," TJ rubbed his hands together. "Let's plan to party. I have a feeling about tonight. The band is going to rock, and the ladies will be choice."

Dean walked to the front of the stage and felt a light tap on his shoulder. He turned, and there she stood in tight jeans and a black tank top, her hair a cascade of gold over her shoulders. He drew in a breath and tried not to gasp.

"Audrey. I didn't expect to see you. Where's Willet? You look nice by the way."

She blushed. "Will's outside in the car with her headphones, listening to music. She didn't want to stay at home by herself. I can't leave her there long, but I did want to hear your band. Maybe I can stay for just a set if that's okay."

"Sure, it's great you're here. I have to start the show, but maybe we can talk at the break and have a drink."

"That would be nice." Audrey gave him a shy smile.

Dean took her hand, squeezed it gently, and then jumped on stage. After a couple of minutes of tuning, he tapped his sticks against the side of his bass drum. The band launched into their first song with a buzz-saw guitar, a scream, and a crash of cymbals. The set took off. Audrey swayed to the beat, eyes closed, as if hypnotized. Dean watched her dance to his music. *Yeah baby.*

*****

Audrey opened her eyes and caught Dean watching her. Suddenly self-conscious, she stepped back from the stage, but couldn't stop dancing. The music turned her muscles to rubber and her bones to water. She breathed deep, releasing tensions she didn't know she held. The thrum of the bass guitar beat against her chest.

Dean hit the drums with relentless force, smashed the high-hat cymbals and stomped on the bass pedal. His eyes narrowed when he sang. The muscles in his neck bunched. The chrome rims and sapphire bodies of the drums sparkled under the stage lights, making his blue eyes pop.

She felt over-heated and dizzy and couldn't take her eyes off him. Situations like this didn't arise often in her life. She knew she'd have to walk away soon, but she wanted to keep dancing just a while longer.

Chapter 3: Burning Man

Willet settled into the soft leather seat of the sedan, tilted it back just a bit, and plugged in her iPod. Chopin's Ballade #1 in G Minor rolled through the surround speakers, pensive and dreamy. She had practiced the piece many times.

She stared through the windshield at the grey streets, exiled to the curb like an unwanted stepchild. Despite the sound-proof sedan, she could hear the crash of cymbals, the thump of the bass drum from the club. Oh, to be normal enough just to walk in, listen to the band, and dance around with Audrey like a crazy teenager. She turned up the CD, trying to drown out the noise, and let Chopin's glorious music beguile her into a reverie. Then she started to dream.

Chopin sat at his piano in a black frock coat, fingers moving over the keys. His back and shoulders swayed with barely contained emotion. Warm, golden waves of music floated through her head. Passionate chords built to thrilling arpeggios. She sighed with contentment.

Chopin stopped playing. He turned to her with large brown eyes full of sadness. He placed an index finger against his lips. "Red Souls come," he whispered, and pointed to the street.

Her gaze shifted there, and an overwhelming feeling of déjà vu swept over her. It was him, the guy in the dirty white hoodie and jeans standing on the sidewalk across the street, staring at her. He crept toward the sedan like a cat, one careful foot at a time, looking right and left as he came.

She huddled low and started to tremble. Wailing voices came out of nowhere. She pressed the headphones to her ears to block them out, but the voices surged inside her head. 'Burn', they said. 'Burn.' The echo bounced back and forth between her ears, and a headache exploded like fireworks between her eyes. The man stared at the car for a long moment, their eyes met through the window. He reached out a hand toward the car, and then he burst into flame.

The fire started at his feet and quickly devoured his torso and arms. A cloud of red smoke billowed around him. Flames licked his neck and head, a wild scream of pain exploded from his open mouth, but he never took his eyes from her. He came closer with arms stretched out, screaming. He reached for the car door with flaming hands. Terror grabbed her by the throat and squeezed.

She bolted upright in panic and turned to Chopin. He was gone. She looked out her window at the sidewalk. The burning man had disappeared. Not a spark, not an ash, nothing. *It's official. I've lost my mind.* Her headache reached migraine strength. She pulled out her phone and called Audrey. The phone rang several times and then went to voicemail. She sent a brief, desperate message, fumbled for the door handle and bolted from the car.

A deafening barrage of noise hit her hard. Sirens blared and alarms wailed. Helicopter propellers flapped somewhere overhead. People shouted over megaphones. She saw nothing on this street. *What is going on?* She ran down the sidewalk in the direction of the club, zigzagging like a drunk, pressing the headphones to her ears as she ran. A couple walking in the opposite direction turned to watch her erratic flight. At the door of Club TJ, the sound of music pounded even louder against her already throbbing ear drums. The pain

29

spread from her ears to her forehead and into her neck. She hunched over to clutch her lurching stomach.

The guy at the door stared at her headphones and her obvious discomfort. "Did you see the accident?" he asked.

"Accident? No, I – no," she stammered. "I need to speak to Audrey du Place. Can you make an announcement or something?"

"The band's playing. It's pretty loud in there."

"I need to speak to Audrey. Now, please, before I get sick. She's my sister." Sweat trickled down her temples. Her body swayed. She was about to faint.

The bouncer's eyes went wide with alarm. "I'll call the boss. Hold on a sec." He pulled out a phone and made the call. "Boss, there's a lady here, asking for an Audrey du Place. Can we make an announcement? She seems to be having some major trouble."

The bouncer listened to brief instructions and hung up. "The boss'll be right out."

"I don't know the boss. I need Audrey." Willet started to hyperventilate.

"Easy, lady! Boss says he'll hook you up with Audrey. Stay cool a minute."

*****

It took all of thirty seconds for TJ to appear at the front door of the club.

"Willet. You're Willet, right? I'm TJ Barlow, Dean's friend. What's wrong?"

"I'm going to faint. I need Audrey."

30

"Hey now, let me take you to my office. The door's around the corner. It's a little quieter there. Then we'll find Audrey."

Too shaky to make reasonable decisions, she allowed TJ to lead her away to parts unknown. She found herself in an office behind a thick padded door, a quieter space though the music still vibrated in the walls. The beat of the bass made her temples throb. Her headache banged in time with the drums. TJ led her to a couch in the corner and helped her lay down.

She put a hand over her eyes, and then sat up suddenly, gulping air. "I'm gonna hurl."

TJ jumped back several steps. "Whoa! Not here. Use the bathroom, please, through that door."

Willet made a dash into the room he pointed to and slammed the door after her. She went directly to the toilet and gave up her lunch. She ran water and flushed, preparing for the next heave. After several iterations, she had nothing left. She patted cold water on her face, gargled away the bad breath and stumbled out the door. She felt drained. Sweat dripped on her forehead. Her body felt like lead.

TJ watched her, offering an arm in case she fell over. "Do you want aspirin, water, or something?"

"No, just Audrey," she whispered.

TJ went to the door, threw it open and hurried into the hall. The booming noise hit her like a brick. She went to the door, swung it closed and fell back against it, pressing her hands against her temples. She staggered back to the couch and fell on it. In minutes, Audrey burst into the room with TJ.

"Will, what are you doing in here? This is so bad for you. What is going on?"

31

"I had that dream again and this time the guy caught fire! I didn't know what to do. The noise outside the car just about killed me. My head is exploding."

Audrey reached for the small purse on her shoulder and pulled out a bottle of yellow pills. The 'super pills,' Willet called them. Audrey extracted one and handed it to her sister. Willet sat up, swallowed the pill, and dropped back on the couch in exhaustion.

"It'll take a few minutes for the meds to work," Audrey explained softly. "She'll feel better soon."

TJ paced between his desk and the couch. "She saw the man on fire? We should tell the police."

"No, we shouldn't," Audrey said. "Give us a chance to deal with the headache, and then we can get the full story."

"What can I do?" he asked helplessly. "Can I get her something?"

"Water will help, when she comes to," Audrey replied.

TJ charged out the door again.

Audrey sat down beside her sister. "Will? Tell me what happened?"

Willet's hands covered her eyes, breath slow, waiting for the medicine to work its magic. She desperately wanted to sleep. "I thought about running my head into a door it hurt so much. I thought I dreamed it, but everything seemed so real."

"Just a dream," Audrey murmured, placing a hand on her sister's forehead.

"But the exact same dream, Auddie," she said breathlessly. "Chopin played the piano, and then the guy walked toward the car. I thought he would finally break in this time, but his feet caught on fire. Flames shot up his legs and covered him. He screamed, I screamed. There were voices. The Silver Voice I always hear came from

Chopin! I think. He said something about Red Souls," "What does it mean?"

"I don't know, hon. Dreams are funny that way."

"This was so *not* funny."

"Of course," Audrey soothed her. "I didn't mean humorous funny."

"I messed up your evening. I'm sorry."

"Never mind that. The band is on break, so it should be quiet for a while. Rest now, and then we'll leave. Are you okay alone for a minute? I'd like to tell Dean I'm leaving."

"Go ahead."

Audrey gently slid the headphones from Willet's head, and Willet released a long breath. Although the headphones were very light in weight, they still put pressure on her head. She didn't notice it until it was gone.

"The music sounded hot, Will. I wish you could have heard it. Dean and his band are so cool."

Willet smiled a dreamy smile and winked. "Cool and hot, quite a combination."

"Yeah, you're funny. You must be feeling better. I'll be right back." Audrey slipped out the big office door and pulled it shut behind her.

Willet lay on the couch with eyes closed, letting the meds take her over. The door rattled and opened again.

TJ walked in. "Here's some water," he said, handing her the bottle. "Feeling better I hope?"

She sat up slowly, twisted the cap off the bottle, slugged back a long swallow, and looked at him with heavy-lidded eyes while she slowly licked her lips. His eyebrows shot up.

33

"Thanks Mr. Barlow," she wheezed after she drained the bottle. "Sorry for the drama. My life is a mess sometimes. Unfortunately, it affects Audrey."

"Please call me TJ. Dean did mention some health issues. Does this happen often?"

"Things are always happening. Fortunately, there are good meds."

TJ gave a small smirk. "Anything interesting?" His eyes were the green of rolling seas, and his smile warmed her. He reminded her of the precious few summer days at the beach she'd had as a child. The tang of salt in the air, the sea breeze and warm sun on her skin, and the way the waves swooshed and dragged on the sand. It had been a long time since she'd been to a beach.

"I don't think these pills would have the same pleasant effect on you that they have on me. They're very specific for my condition. *You* may get a brain bleed."

"Ouch. No thanks then. So, from what I heard, a man is lying on the street near here in a pile of ash."

Willet got up from the couch with a wobble, rolled her head on her neck and stretched out her shoulders. Her eyes narrowed. "Are you trying to be funny?"

"No, certainly not. It's just... You said someone was burning. What's a guy to think?"

Willet peered at him as if trying to figure out what species of hominid he was. She tilted her head and turned her right ear toward him. They were standing close to each other, close enough that she extended her arm and placed her hand on his chest. He looked down at the small hand but didn't move away.

"You have an obstruction in the blood flow to your heart. It makes a glubbing sound right about there." She patted the spot on his chest lightly. "Think about that. You should see a cardiologist."

34

TJ's megawatt smile faded. He frowned and stepped back from her. "That's not funny either."

"I don't joke about health matters, Mr. Barlow," she said with level calm. "See a doctor."

"What the hell, woman? You're nuts!"

The office door opened again. Dean and Audrey rushed in and stopped short when they found Willet and TJ in a standoff.

"What's going on?" Dean asked, looking from TJ to Willet and back.

"She's trying to tell me I have a heart problem. That's ridiculous, and it's none of her damn business anyway!"

"Why did you say that, Will?" Audrey asked.

"One of the vessels leading to his heart is partially blocked. It makes that particular sound I've heard before, and I just wanted to warn him."

Audrey turned slowly to TJ and took a deep breath. "I know this may seem abrupt, even rude, and I apologize, but Willet can hear things like that. You should probably take her at her word."

"She hears things, alright. She's a mental patient. She needs to be sedated," TJ growled.

Dean cleared his throat and stepped between them. "I see everyone is on edge, so Audrey, why don't you take Willet to my house until the gig is over? She can check out the place before construction starts."

TJ snorted with irritation. "I don't need a damn babysitter. You can leave too."

"I have to go back on stage for the second set. Audrey? Willet? Okay to travel?"

Willet turned to TJ. "I do thank you for your help, Mr. Barlow. I just wanted to help you in return."

TJ watched the sisters walk out the door, and then kicked it shut with a bang.

"Those women will ruin your life," TJ said in a low, angry growl. "Rethink the job, my friend. It's not worth it, whatever they're paying."

Dean shook his head. "They have issues, sure, but Willet has amazing hearing, beyond the normal. She heard my truck driving to her house from miles away."

"I don't care. No one can hear what's going on in someone else's body, unless he's a doctor with a stethoscope."

"Still, it wouldn't hurt to check it out," Dean said. "When did you see a doctor last?"

"I'm not seeing a damn doctor, not on her say-so anyway."

"Forget that, Teej. Everyone needs a checkup once in a while. You could prove her wrong."

TJ lightened a little at that thought. "Yes. I could, couldn't I? Maybe I'll do that. It would serve her right, the smug little freak."

"Harsh words, dude. She's not that way. Anyway, I gotta get back and start the set."

TJ stood in his office deep in thought after Dean left. He stared at his hands, felt his neck, and put a hand on his chest where Willet had touched him. His heart beat steady under his palm. He grunted in satisfaction. *I'm only twenty-eight, eat well, I work out. I'm totally healthy. There's nothing wrong with me, nothing at all.*

*****

Gem and Dora walked through the commercial district of West Hollywood well after 3:00 a.m., past boarded up warehouses, engine repair shops and industrial supply businesses. Dora had her head down, snuffling like a steam engine at the damp pavement shimmering under streetlights. Gem looked for signs of an astral breach above the silent buildings.

The big dog stopped at an intersection, and then she turned hard right. They moved quickly down a side street, past a building with a painted sign that said, 'Club TJ West Hollywood.' Four blocks down, Dora took another hard right, led down the side street to a row of apartments. She stopped and looked at Gem expectantly. Orange cones circled a large patch of burnt asphalt in the middle of the street where something had caught fire and burned. Astral and physical energies had collided right there.

"But where is the breach, Dora? The Gate appears intact here. Could it have been the Souls that escaped from the apartment complex?" Gem centered herself. The words of her chant ran lightly through her mind. She let her astral senses scan the street, looking for residues of Red Soul energy. The street felt clean. The Red Souls that had wreaked havoc earlier in the evening were long gone. They now roamed elsewhere in LA, looking for other people to provoke. About to turn back to the main street, she noticed a woman walking toward them from the opposite direction. The woman waved.

Light brown hair pulled back in a tail and a green fatigue jacket with many pockets, her tall, lithe figure loped along with purposeful stride, graceful but strong. She was the Traveler. Her long stride ate up the distance until she stood at Gem's side. Maria Sonrisa Degas de Megaro had been the abbess of a convent in Avila, Spain in 1593. A daughter of Spanish nobility, she was spiritually gifted at an early age, able to leave her body at will. She became a nun instead of marrying the noble her family had chosen for her. When she told stories about soul journeys into other worlds, people thought she was possessed by a demon. One did not tell such stories in Catholic Spain in the sixteenth century. The king ordered her to be buried alive in the family crypt to contain the demon. She escaped in consciousness to the Third Plane where she met a teacher who taught her to fold space-time and move freely to any time or place. And so, she became a Traveler. "Guardian, que es esto?" Sonrisa asked as she bent to greet Dora with a rub on the head.

"Despair haunts this street," replied Gem. "Someone was driven to suicide. I wish I could have been here in time."

"You cannot blame yourself, chica. We all walk our own paths."

"I am who I am. Why are you here, Sonny?"

Sonrisa chuckled. "Augustus sent me, of course. You will need support for what follows from this."

"I always welcome support. Why is now any different?"

"Red Souls appear in the north in inexplicable numbers. There are no obvious breaches, and the Gate does not stop them."

Gem nodded wearily. "The presence of Red Souls has increased. Fights break out in the streets. People grow panicked and desperate. Some take their own lives."

"The Deceiver has found a willing accomplice."

"Who?"

"You know him, your favorite nemesis."

"Richard Theese? That is not a surprise," Gem murmured to herself. "The Deceiver has taken him in hand. He must be watched. Can you do it?"

"Of course, Guardian. I go now." Sonrisa made a slight movement, and space folded around her into smaller and smaller sections like origami. The glow of the streetlight became distorted.

Gem felt squeezed and couldn't see through the blur, as if she had cataracts on her eyes. After a few moments, her vision cleared again. Sonrisa had disappeared through the fold in space-time. "Abrupt as usual," she said to Dora. Such are the ways of the Traveler.

She glanced around to see if anyone could have seen the disappearing act. Fortunately, the streets were empty. Sonrisa's movements could only be detected with Third Plane sight. However, in rare instances, an observant person might notice that a woman who had been standing on the sidewalk was suddenly not there.

On the way back to the main thoroughfare, something pricked at Gem as they passed Club TJ, a flash on the screen between her eyebrows that came and went. A lingering energy vibrated around the building, erratic, yet somehow familiar. Was the club involved in last night's tragedy? Someone significant had been there someone Gem would have to know.

Chapter 4: Aftermath

Audrey kicked back in the big black recliner in Dean's living room and dozed until a key rattled the door. She heard the door swing open. Someone stepped into the hallway. Dean dropped a large backpack in the corner and shrugged out of his jacket.

"You ladies okay?" he asked.

"Will's out cold. The meds kicked in and relaxed her. And she likes the quiet here. I think this will work, if you're still willing. I know it's a lot to ask."

"If it works, I'm fine with it. Are you okay with all the driving back and forth?"

"I live to chauffer." Audrey said with a shrug. "Besides, I have clients in the city."

Dean headed to the kitchen and Audrey followed him.

"I heard some news on the radio as I drove home," he said as he boiled water for throat-coat tea. "Apparently, a guy shot his girlfriend in West Hollywood, and then set himself on fire in front of her apartment. It was four blocks from where you parked the car."

"Are you saying Willet could have seen this guy?"

"She couldn't have seen him if she stayed in the car. She said the man in flames stood right next her. Did she wander off, maybe take a walk?"

"Willet wouldn't leave the car, and I don't see her walking around West Hollywood at night by herself."

"Well, that's one hell of a coincidental dream, don't you think?"

Audrey shook her head. "There has to be an explanation. I'll talk to her about it after she wakes up.

"What about you, Audrey? You must be tired too."

"Yeah, pretty much." Audrey put her elbows on the table and held her forehead in her hands. She was beyond tired.

"So, what's the deal, really?" he asked gently. "Willet hears voices. Are they hallucinations?"

"We don't know what they are. She started talking about voices when she was five. Before that, she just cried all the time. Our parents took her to doctors. Will has 'unusual' auditory anatomy – more sensory hairs in her cochlea, more nerves running between her ears and her brain, and a larger auditory cortex than most people have."

"That's a lot of anatomy."

"Oh, there's more," Audrey went on. "The fluid in her cochlear canal is slightly less viscous than normal. It takes very little sound to move her tympanic membrane. So, she hears *really tiny* sounds."

"Wow."

"Yeah, wow. That explains the extraordinary hearing, but nobody could explain the voices."

41

"What kind of voices?"

"Some voices scream and scare the hell out of her. She shakes so hard she almost chokes. One voice she calls the Silver Voice. It says the same things over and over, about 'Red Souls'. She says it sounds urgent, as if it's trying to warn her about something."

"Could it be the meds?"

"She heard voices long before the meds. With the meds, at least she can sleep."

"How long have you taken care of her?"

"Since Mom and Dad broke up and Mom started drinking."

"Oh. I'm sorry."

"My mother couldn't cope after the divorce. She thought Will was mental and blamed her for the breakup. Mom could be really mean, so I had to step in. I was thirteen, Will was ten."

Dean reached across the table and took Audrey's hand in his. They looked at each other, appraising, questioning. He rubbed his thumb across the top of her hand. "That's a lot to carry alone. Where are your parents now?"

Audrey flinched slightly and pulled her hand away. "Mother lives in New York. Dad is an archeologist and goes on digs. I think he's somewhere around Istanbul right now. We don't see them much. I'm not alone, though. Willet and I support each other."

Dean studied her, nodded and stood up from the table. "You should stay here tonight. It's too late to drive all the way to Hemmings, and Willet is already knocked out. You can take my room. I have a roll-away in my office."

Too tired to argue, she followed him to the master bedroom. Her back ached, and her eyes felt like they were full of sand. She had to lie down before she fell down.

 He turned down the gold bedspread on the king-size bed and pointed at the sheets. "The sheets are clean. You should be comfortable. In there's the bathroom. It's private."

"Thank you, Dean," she whispered, suddenly overcome with emotions she didn't expect.

He walked around the bed to her and took both of her hands in his. "You're safe here, Audrey, you and Will. You can relax. I'll be down the hall if you need anything."

She looked up at his strong chin, the kindness in his eyes. He hesitated, then smiled and slid the back of his fingers lightly down her cheek. Every inch of her skin flushed.

"I've wanted to do that for a while," he said softly before he stepped back. "We'll talk in the morning."

Audrey watched him disappear through the doorway into the hall. She went to the bedroom door and closed it. The barrier between them suddenly seemed painful, so she opened it a crack. She felt better being in the flow of air that circulated between his room and hers. That seemed so funny and inexplicable. She barely knew him.

*****

After he closed down the Club, TJ finally got to bed around 3AM, tossed and turned, and punched at his pillow. He tried to find a position comfortable enough for him to forget that Willet woman and get some sleep. He finally succumbed to weariness of both mind and body. A deep gong rang in his head, and he fell into a cave half full of water.

43

The cave shook, and the water slapped against the rock walls. He paddled hard to keep his head above the surface. A loud rumble shook the dome above him, and rock debris crumbled onto his head. He swam to the side and pressed himself against the wet stone. Red smoke poured through cracks in the walls and filled the cave. He gagged. His eyes burned. He ducked below the surface of the water to flush out his eyes and nose. Bobbing to the surface he gargled and spit out a stream of water to clear his throat.

A long limb, scaled and black, slid into the cave across the surface of the water, the appendage of an enormous reptile. Long wriggling fingers tipped with black claws poked at the water and scraped the sides of the cave, feeling for something. TJ plastered himself to the cave wall, but a sharp claw found him and flicked him like a bug into the center of the water. Leathery fingers wrapped around his neck and chest and squeezed.

A deep voice echoed off the walls. "There it is. She won't have this one to use against us."

The fingers dunked him under water until he went limp. He slammed back into his physical body and sat straight up in bed, gasping for breath. Pain shot down his left arm. He rubbed the shoulder joint, flexed the muscles lightly. *It doesn't feel like a cramp.* A feeling of fullness swelled in his chest below his left pectoral muscle. He struggled to take a breath. The image of a young woman with corn silk hair and serious blue gray eyes flashed on the dark screen between his eyebrows. She was speaking excitedly, gesturing with her hands. He couldn't hear a word she said, but he could guess her message. He reached for the phone and called 911.

*****

Willet opened her eyes, not sure where she was. Shower water thundered on the other side of the wall. She heard tooth brushing and a toaster popping. These were not the sounds of Pine Siskin House. She and Audrey didn't own a pop-up toaster.

She roused herself from the deep cushions of the couch and stood up, stretching and running fingers through her bed head. *Oh yeah, I'm at Dean's place.* She found her headphones, clapped them on her ears, and walked down the hall. Cheerful daylight beamed into the kitchen. Dean was making eggs and bacon. The morning chatter of birds and the roar of a passing car made her glad her headphones were in place.

"Good morning. Where's Audrey?" she asked, looking around the kitchen.

"In the bathroom, washing up, I assume. Did you sleep okay?"

"Yeah, you have a comfortable couch."

"Good. I'm making breakfast if you want some." Dean continued with breakfast prep, pouring orange juice and hitting the start button on the coffee maker. "When Audrey comes out, we should all talk."

"About what?"

"About that man you saw yesterday, the one on fire."

"You think I imagined it."

"No, I wouldn't say that, but we do need to talk."

Dean spread a newspaper across the kitchen table and pointed at a headline. Willet sat down and started reading.

Audrey appeared in the doorway of the kitchen, her hair damp and combed, her skin, rosy. She wore an over-sized tee shirt. "Will, you're up. Good. We need to talk."

"So I heard. Is this what you want to talk about - the guy setting himself on fire near the club? Do you think this was the guy I saw?"

The possibility she had seen something real comforted her momentarily, but then Willet considered the implications of a man burning to death in the street. She'd rather have an hallucination.

Dean sat down at the small table across from Willet. "The guy set himself on fire four blocks from where you were parked. And he screamed when he did it. You would have heard that. No evidence of fire, no body, no nothing by the car where you parked. Did you get out of the car and go walking? Could you have stumbled on the scene while it happened? That would explain a lot."

"I never get out of the car in LA. The street noise kills me. I did drift off for a while, listening to music. That's when I saw the man. I thought I was dreaming. Is he okay?"

Dean checked the paper. "Passers-by wrapped him in their coats and rolled him on the ground to put out the flames. But no, he's not okay. He died at the scene."

Willet shuddered. "Oh no."

Audrey joined them at the table. "Honey, did you turn on the radio? Maybe you heard the news after it happened. Or maybe you heard screams. Four blocks away is really close for you."

"I did hear screaming. I listened to Chopin and dreamt about him. He said Red Souls were coming. Then he pointed at the man out the window. The man walked toward the car, he started burning, and the voices were screaming. Then I woke up." Willet blushed. "That sounds crazy, I know."

"Maybe we should talk to the doctor about your meds. Maybe the dosage doesn't agree with you anymore."

Willet's spine straightened, and her small, pointed chin jutted out. "So, you think I'm a drug-addled zombie stumbling around the city without knowing where I am? Is that what you're saying?"

"Will, please don't be offended. I don't know what the explanation is. I'm just trying to cover every base. For you to have some kind of vision of a man burning and then have that very thing happen close by is difficult to explain, don't you think? How would you explain it?"

"I don't know. Maybe I *am* losing my mind. It's been happening for years. Everyone has said so. Mom, Dad, the doctors, they all say I'm nuts. Now it's official."

"You're going to spend time in this nice, quiet place of Dean's while he works on our house. Try to use it as a time to relax. Forget the weird stuff for a while. There's nothing we can do for the man who died. It's not your fault in any way. And we *will* find an explanation."

Chapter 5: Making Waves

The doctors found a blockage in an artery entering TJ's heart. They said he was in danger of a heart attack and needed an angioplasty to blow the blockage out. TJ didn't argue. They blew the thing out, and he had to admit he felt better afterwards.

Two days after he left the hospital, he gathered the courage to confront Willet. It was incomprehensible that she could know something like that about him just by listening. She would be at Dean's house that day, alone. They'd have a little chat. He'd get some things straight about her 'diagnosis', find out what her trick was.

He set out from the Hollywood Hills in late morning and drove down toward Manhattan Beach. He squinted into the midday sun, adjusting his shades in the rear-view mirror. The air conditioner worked fine in his car, but he couldn't stop sweating. Over the entire trip, he debated with himself. The more he debated, the more uncertain he was.

It'll be annoying if she's smug.

Oh yeah, she'll be smug.

She saved my life. Probably.

It's embarrassing. She invaded my privacy.

I still can't believe she could hear something in my chest without a stethoscope.

What do I owe this woman? Simple thanks? A lifetime of devotion?

I need to even the scales. How can I do that?

He parked the car at the curb and walked up to the front door, as he had done many times over the years Dean had lived there. He rang the bell twice. After a minute, someone peered back at him through the fisheye. The deadbolt slid, the knob turned, and the door cracked open. Willet looked out through the crack.

"Mr. Barlow." She gave him a perfunctory nod. "Good morning. Dean's not home."

She seemed distracted. He decided to be direct. "I came to talk to you. And please call me TJ."

"Oh good, another talk. Just what I need. Come in."

He didn't understand her response but he stepped inside. She closed the door behind him. She turned her right ear slightly toward him and listened in that odd way.

"You had the blockage taken care of. I'm glad."

"Yeah, about that. I'm grateful, *very* grateful, but I'm finding it difficult to believe you could have heard it. I'm glad you heard it, don't get me wrong, but the idea someone could hear something like that with regular ears is hard to accept."

She shrugged. "The human heart is just a noisy pump. Blood sloshes and squelches around in there. When an artery is blocked, it sounds like a clogged drain. Not a big deal for me to hear the difference, and besides, I don't have regular ears."

"I see that now. I hope I haven't interrupted anything. You seem…upset."

"I'm concerned about the wind and ocean waves I keep hearing. It sounds like a storm in here. I don't know where it's coming from."

"We're two blocks from the Pacific Ocean," he said slowly. "Even I can hear it."

"You can't hear the waves in the house, can you?"

"Well, maybe not in here, this place is pretty sound-proofed. If we walk outside, I can hear the ocean clearly."

"Of course you can hear it *outside*," she replied with impatience. "The question is why do I hear it in *here*? These ocean sounds are coming from far away, and it's storming. We're not having a storm outside, are we? What does 'TJ' stand for, by the way?"

The abrupt change in the direction of conversation took him by surprise, but he went with it.

"Uh, well, it's Thomas Jefferson, my father's favorite president. My mother favored Abe Lincoln. I never felt like an 'Abe,' so I guess I lucked out."

She gave a small laugh. "Thomas Jefferson, huh? That's a lot to live up to. How do you measure up?"

"I'm not into politics, at least not yet, but I'm an entrepreneur, like he was."

"Well, Thomas Jefferson, I'm having an issue right now, so forgive me if I seem off. Sounds I can't account for always drives me nuts."

He watched her walk down the hallway and lean into each room, stopping a minute, and then moving on, until she got to the kitchen doorway. Then she turned around and walked back to where he stood.

"I thought maybe Dean had an ocean CD playing somewhere, but I can't find one. So that leaves sounds inside my head. I do not want new sounds inside my head. I have enough of those already."

"That happens to you quite often, from what I hear."

Her smile faded, and her jaw got visibly stiff. "Don't think you know or understand me from what someone else says. The source of a physical sound can be quite remote, and I still hear it. Sometimes it's difficult to judge near from far."

"I didn't mean to offend you. All I can say is I don't hear the ocean from inside this house."

"Of course you don't."

They glared at each other. TJ tried a softer approach.

"You could step outside for a minute and make sure you're not hearing the waves from the really big ocean down the street."

"In the middle of the day? I absolutely could not!"

"Maybe this place isn't soundproof enough for you. As you say, you're hearing is really sharp. Think of the peace of mind you'd have figuring out where it came from."

She harrumphed at him. "You're a good salesman."

"So I've been told, but I'm not trying to sell you, just trying to help."

"Well, if I did it quickly, *really* quickly, then maybe."

51

"Can you try it without the headphones?"

A look of terror flashed across her face, but she pulled the headphones off. He slid the dead bolt back. She walked up to the door resolutely and opened it, extended her neck just beyond the threshold, like a turtle. After just a moment, she backed away with a wincing expression on her face. He closed the door, and she rubbed her temples.

"Yes, I heard that ocean, along with a deafening hedge cutter and lots of traffic."

TJ studied her. "You have a hard time going outside, don't you? You're like a vampire burned by sunlight. That must be a very difficult way to live."

"You have no idea."

Her shoulders curled forward. The look of defeat touched him.

"I'm not here to cause you more stress," he said gently. "I guess I'm here to say thanks, for the heads up. You did me a great favor."

"You're welcome. Acute hearing occasionally has its upside."

"You've been this way all your life?"

"Yes."

"Can't doctors do anything for you?"

"It's the way I'm built. Difficult to change."

Silence fell between them. She seemed to shake off whatever occupied her thoughts. "Would you like tea, coffee, or something?"

"Coffee would be great."

She took the headphones from the coffee table and slipped them on. He followed her down the hall to the kitchen at the back of the house. A pleasant breeze fluttered the curtains in open windows. Sun glinted off the stainless-steel appliances. She opened the fridge and pulled out bottled water and a bag of coffee. He couldn't help but notice her small frame. She had to walk around the kitchen in headphones just to have a window open. *What a horrible way to live. She's a true damsel in distress. No wonder Dean got sucked in.*

She poured water for him, pulled out a bag of coffee from the cupboard and scooped it into a paper filter. Then, she stopped and listened. "There it is again. Crashing waves and the wind is howling."

He wasn't sure how to respond without offending her. "Uh, that doesn't make any sense."

"I've never heard wind and waves like this. It's not a bad sound, not like the wailing and the angry voices. I heard those sounds just before that man caught fire by your club."

"Yeah, about that..."

"I know. Dean showed me the story in the newspaper. The guy set himself on fire. It's awful. I wasn't anywhere near him."

Her hands shook as she poured water into the carafe, and then stood at the counter with her head down.

TJ cleared his throat. "Maybe you need to visit the real ocean. We could walk down there in five minutes. Take your headphones. At least you would know which ocean you're hearing when you're hearing it."

She blanched white. "Walk outside? What if there are lawnmowers? Or motorcycles? What about the hedge-cutter?"

53

"That's a risk, of course. But you have those headphones. How well do they work?"

He walked over to her and slid the headphones off her ears. She gasped when he removed them, clapped her palms to her ears.

"They were designed for astronauts on the space shuttle," she said. "They use a special algorithm to cancel noise. They eliminate those grating, whining, repetitive sounds I can't tolerate. It's the best set I've had."

She watched nervously as he handled the headphones. Her eyes began to water. He handed them back to her with a reassuring smile.

"Then you're well protected. You can take the walk. We won't be far from the house. If the noise is too much, we'll run right back. I'll carry you if necessary."

She slipped the phones over her ears and breathed a sigh of relief. She followed him down the hall to the front door. He opened the door and walked out in the sun, turned to her and held out his hand, inviting her into the light.

She straightened her shoulders and walked out the door, closing it behind her. He crooked his arm to her, and she slipped her arm through his. Her vulnerability at that moment rattled him. He had taken responsibility for her, in a way. Fortunately, the hedge-cutters had stopped.

They walked down the short sidewalk to the beach. At the end of the street, a set of weathered wooden stairs led down to the sand. He held her elbow to steady her as they descended. The ocean spread across the horizon before them, a heaving green presence. Waves rolled and shushed. She took a deep breath, slipped her sandals off and curled her toes in the warm sand.

"This is my favorite place," he confided to her. "I feel better at the ocean than anywhere."

"It's glorious. Thank you for suggesting it, for bringing me. I spend so much time indoors."

She curled her arm around his again. He patted it. "My pleasure. Can you walk a little closer to the water? How's the volume?"

"I'm doing okay. The waves are gentle today, not crashing. It's soothing. And they drown out some of the traffic noise."

Walking closer to the water, they splashed through the frilly white surf, and strolled along the sand. There were few other walkers. She inhaled the fresh, salt air, and exhaled strongly, as if expelling something old and stale. She rolled her neck. He gave her a sideways glance.

"Is your neck stiff? I could massage your shoulders. Sometimes it helps."

"Well, you don't have to do that…"

He stepped behind her anyway and began to knead the muscles running from her neck into her shoulders, pressing his thumbs into the back of her neck on either side of her spine. Her arms went limp and her shoulders dropped. After a few minutes, he stopped.

"How's that? Feel better?"

She opened her eyes and smiled. "That felt sooo good. Thanks."

"You look happier," he remarked. "You seemed a little beat down before."

She breathed deep again. "It's like waking up in a new world."

"You should come every day while you're at Dean's and take advantage of it."

"I think I will, though I do feel safer with company."

He smiled and tucked a strand of golden hair behind her ear. "I'll have to come by and make sure you get your exercise."

She flushed pink.

They studied each other, looking for clues, and then smiled at the same time. The ocean glinted green and gold, the white surf shushed and rolled. They chatted as they walked. TJ pointed out swells farther out in the ocean that would make for a good ride on a small surfboard.

He wrapped an arm around her shoulders. She snuggled slightly under his arm and beamed.

After a while, the pressure on her ears began to make her headache. They climbed the wooden stairs and walked back to Dean's house. Once inside, with door closed, she stopped and listened.

"It's definitely a different ocean in here," she said. "The wind is still blowing too. Who knows where it's coming from? I'm not going to worry about it."

He turned toward her and pulled her a little closer. She didn't resist. He tipped her chin up and softly kissed her lips. They were velvet, and she tasted like apples. Her eyes were closed when he pulled back and looked at her. So, he kissed her again, firmer this time, his lips lingering on hers. Then he stepped back. She opened her eyes, her gaze steady and direct.

"What now, Thomas Jefferson?" she said in her low voice. "Is this where you make your getaway?"

He pulled back in surprise.

"I don't want to get away. It feels nice right here. But I do have to go. Business calls."

He kissed her again, lightly on the forehead. She searched his face, as if memorizing it. He turned and walked out. The door clicked softly behind him. He strolled down the front steps jangling the keys on his index finger. When he got to the car, he turned back for a last look at the front door.

I wonder if she's watching me through the fisheye. He waved. An unexpected flicker of guilt flared in him, followed by embarrassment.

I'm helping her, not trying to play her. She's a strange girl for sure. Funny and very pretty, but strange. Nice lips too. I wouldn't mind kissing her again.

He cast another quick backward look before getting in his car. *What am I going to do with you, Ms. Willet? This is already more complicated than I expected.*

Chapter 6: Sound Prints

Construction was well underway at Pine Siskin House. On Monday morning, Dean drove out to assess progress on the sound proofing project. The Audio Environments crew covered and taped every wall and floor and draped the furniture in tarps. The smell of drilled wood and sawdust soon filled the air. Dean's crew chief, Alex, set up a small radio to listen to talk shows while he worked. He liked to tune in to the Richard Theese Show. Alex said the guy made him laugh. Richard Theese rubbed Dean the wrong way. The guy was just a loud-mouthed gas bag.

Richard Theese called himself a 'Defender of the American Way' and conducted his broadcasts out of a house in Azusa. He had a bombastic voice and ranted all day about things he didn't approve of. Paranoia about the government and the military fueled his message. Foreign countries offended him, along with other races and religions, scientists, vegetarians, librarians, people without guns, and people with them. Apparently, a lot of people shared those views, because his listening audience spanned the country.

Today, he complained about women in the military. In his considered opinion, women should be at home where they belong, cooking and having babies, and not endangering the lives of real soldiers.

Dean's crew worked steadily through the day, and wrapped up around 3:00 p.m. They had to make the drive back to LA before rush hour. Audrey brought Willet home at 4:00 p.m. They shuffled in the front door with backpacks and bags, dropping everything in the hall. Audrey found Dean immediately.

"So, what do you think?" Audrey asked with excitement. "Is the house hush-able?"

"There's a lot we can do, but it won't be absolutely sound-proof. I can't guarantee that. How did it go at my house?"

Willet pulled off her headphones and listened for sounds before answering. "I liked your house, Dean, really quiet. And I went to the beach with TJ! Can you believe it?"

Dean really *couldn't* believe it. "TJ showed up at my house. Why?"

"He wanted to tell me about his heart. It wasn't easy for him, poor guy. He was so sweet about it, and then we walked down to the beach."

TJ knew how to be sweet with women. Willet had lapped up the charm like rum punch. Most women did. *I thought he didn't like her. What is he trying to do now?* Whatever it was, her voice bubbled with giddiness.

"Glad to hear the day went well," Dean said. "You went to the beach? Wasn't that kind of loud for you?"

"I couldn't believe it either," Audrey called from the kitchen.

Willet rolled her eyes. "Beach sounds aren't too bad if the waves aren't crashing. Today they were small and gentle. I got used to them and tuned them out."

Audrey walked out with two wine glasses in her hands. "Is anyone up for a glass of wine or beer? It's the official start of our renovations. Let's celebrate."

Dean thought a beer sounded good and followed Audrey to the kitchen the big, gourmet kitchen of blonde wood and granite counters flecked with gold and black, with a huge built-in refrigerator. A round maple table and four chairs sat under a brass light fixture. Murano glass globes shed a soft gold light over the table.

Audrey pulled a wine bottle out of a rack in the fridge along with a beer. Two glasses of white wine were poured, along with the beer for Dean. They clinked frosted glass and toasted. Willet sipped on her wine and giggled. Audrey smiled.

"I haven't seen you this happy in a while, Will. The beach trip did you good."

"I didn't get much of a headache." Willet's eyes turned dreamy. "TJ said it's his favorite place."

Audrey and Dean exchanged looks. Her forehead creased with uncertainty.

Dean shrugged and sipped his bear. *Who was he to judge?* He would definitely have a talk with TJ, however.

"I'm going to walk down to the beach every day I'm at your house, Dean. TJ said he would come with me to make sure I'm okay. Isn't that nice of him?"

"Yeah," said Dean. "TJ's a real giver."

TJ didn't usually make such commitments. He'd had nothing good to say about Willet and now he promised to escort her to the beach? Something didn't smell right.

"Fresh air and sunshine are good for you, sweetie," Audrey said. "Your cheeks are rosy."

Willet took another sip of her wine, stood up and walked toward the refrigerator. Then she stopped. She stood there for several moments, unmoving, before they noticed.

"Will, do you need something?" Audrey asked finally. "What are you doing?"

No answer from Willet. Slowly, she turned in their direction, and stared over their heads. Her eyes were glassy and her expression blank. Her arms hung limp at her sides. "You can't be too paranoid," she said in a flat voice. "Just because you're paranoid, doesn't mean someone isn't out to get you."

"What do you mean? Will, answer me please," Audrey asked again.

Willet gave no indication that she heard. "A woman's place is in the home. Those women in pants, who are they kidding? They're aberrations. They're trying to be men." Her tone of voice remained flat.

Audrey and Dean stared at her and then at each other.

Audrey went quickly to her sister's side and took hold of her hands. "Willet, you're scaring me." This seemed to bring Willet back to the here-and-now. She looked around in confusion.

A memory clicked in Dean's head. "Did you listen to Richard Theese today?" he asked.

"Who's Richard Theese?" Willet asked in a dull voice.

61

"He's that talk show guy on AM radio."

"I don't listen to the radio. The static makes me grind my teeth."

"Richard Theese said those exact things you just said. I heard it on the radio this morning."

"What things I said?" Willet said suspiciously.

"You don't remember talking about paranoia and women in pants?"

"Why would I say that?"

"Hon, sit down," Audrey said, pulling a chair out for her. "I could make you a cup of tea. You don't seem yourself."

"I'm myself, and I don't need tea. Stop patronizing me." Willet turned and stalked out of the kitchen. Audrey followed her.

As Dean thought about what just happened, an idea occurred to him that seemed incredible, but for Willet, who knew? When Audrey returned, he broached the subject.

"Alex played his radio here while he worked. Those exact things she said were said on the radio this morning. Does she listen to the radio?"

"No. Like she said, too much static."

"She repeated it word for word, Audrey. It's as if she can still hear the guy speaking. Maybe the sound waves are still in the air."

Audrey dropped down at the table and rubbed her temples.

"No, no way… I just don't know. I used to think I understood what we were dealing with. Now I'm not sure."

"Sound travels in waves of air pressure. Maybe traces of fluctuating pressure remains, enough for her to pick up those sounds. Like she's hearing sound prints."

"Sounds after they happen on top of what she hears in real time? How much more can she take before she snaps? The doctors will want to put her back in the hospital if we tell them."

Dean tried to think of something reassuring to say. "You could let it go and see if it happens again. Maybe someone in Hemmings is listening to a Richard Theese repeat right now. He's syndicated everywhere."

"I like that explanation better." Audrey searched his face for answers he didn't have. "What about that trance? She acted like a zombie. She's never done that before."

"I don't know, Audrey. I'm just guessing here."

They both rose from the table.

Dean walked around the table to her. He folded his arms around her and hugged her. He couldn't think of anything else to do at that moment.

Chapter 7: Meeting of the Minds

Gem parked the Jeep in a lot in Downy and sat back, sipping mint tea and munching a bagel. The Richard Theese Radio Show flooded the airwaves, and the voice of the man himself droned from the speakers. Theese was on a roll. Immigrants, both legal and illegal, were the subject of his rant. Some immigrants did not fit his profile for an American. They needed to be 'sorted out.' The fact that almost every citizen in America descended from immigrants did not enter into his logic.

Theese had devoted listeners. He communicated discretely with his 'people' through code words in his broadcasts that hid his real meaning from the FCC. Lately, certain phrases had caught her attention. 'We will take a stand,' 'let's show them the real America,' 'take back our country.' Gem listened to his show every day, hoping he'd let a detail slip that would tell her if and when he planned to take action. It sounded like Theese had been drinking. His words slurred with alcoholic bravado.

"The poison enters our beloved country every day," he railed. "We know where it comes from, though the government does nothing to stop it. They attack us and spy on us, corrupt our children, and everyone ignores it. But we know. My listeners know where it comes from. It must be stopped. Lions will fall. We won't tolerate blasphemers and murderers. We'll fight fire with fire. Stay tuned, friends."

Dora crouched down in the back seat and put her front paws over her ears. Gem closed her eyes and breathed steadily. As Theese's tone became a declamatory sneer, she felt the oppressive weight of negative energies assaulting her, trying to invade her consciousness. She refused to allow it. She blew a long breath at the black smoke swirling in her third eye. The smoke dissipated, and bright light filled the inner screen.

"'Lions' is a clue, Dorita," Gem said, "And fire will be involved. Is he going to burn a zoo?"

Gem searched the web on her tablet, mapping out possible targets, places associated with immigrant populations where there might be lions. She tapped fingernails on the screen, thinking. *Does he mean lions literally? And when? He never said when.*

Lions were common in Asian culture and décor, so maybe Chinatown. A Japanese garden in Van Nuys had no lions she knew of. Churches and centers for almost every religion in the world were represented in L.A, and so many restaurants with exotic foreign cuisine. Islam did not allow depiction of living things in their art, so that argued against the mosques. Attacking an embassy would draw attention from the federal government. He would not want that. A museum? Not a strong enough statement.

If he wanted a large, visible target, he might choose Chinatown. If he wanted a symbolic target, he would attack a church.

"He is too smart to interfere with commerce. Loss of profits would draw extra scrutiny. We will start with the churches."

Gem threw the Jeep into gear, tires squealing out of the parking lot.

Dean sat on a stool at the bar at Club TJ after midnight and reviewed his song list. Shock Value had just finished their first set, which included another new song by Dean. Meeting the du Place sisters and getting involved in their bizarre drama had inspired his songwriting. Words seemed to flow out of his head, and his fingers found their way to interesting chord progressions on the piano. He almost had enough new material for a full CD.

Out of the corner of his eye, he saw a mass of dark curly hair bouncing through the crowd in his direction. *Uh oh, it's Delos.* He really wasn't in the mood for her company.

She tottered up to him on booted stilettos and waved a home-printed invitation to her next performance art event under his nose. The scent of patchouli tickled his nose.

"Love the new tune, Dean" she gushed, flashing over-large white teeth and chomping on her gum. "It's so cool, and like, mystical. 'Red Souls,' yeah, I have a friend who talks about Red Souls. She says they come out of walls or something. She's, like, psychic, very tuned in. It's so funny you both know about that."

That got Dean's attention. He spun on his stool and turned the spotlight of his attention on her. She preened under the warmth of it. "Your friend sees Red Souls," he repeated, to be sure he understood her correctly.

"Yeah, her name's Gem," she chomped the gum and nodded. "She sees Souls from the other side. Says they look red."

"Souls from the other side, like, dead people?" he asked cautiously. He didn't know Delos that well. She might be out of her mind.

She sniffed and tossed her black curls. "Souls never die, Dean. Don't you know that?" She examined her fire engine red fingernails with casual boredom.

"Clearly, I need to know more. How did you meet Gem? Where can I find her?"

"You don't find Gem. Gem finds you. I met her when I was coming home late one night, and someone tried to jack my car right in front of my house. He had a gun and grabbed me around the neck. I gave him the keys and then he tried to push me into the car. I was, like, totally freaked." She clapped palms to the sides of her head as if to keep her brains from exploding.

"Wow, Delos," Dean said. "That's major."

"Yeah, I could have ended up a statistic, but all of a sudden, there she was, standing in front of the car with her big black dog. The dog lets out this wicked growl. Gem just points at the guy's head and says, 'Leave her.' She was stone-cold cool." Delos paused to catch her breath.

Dean nodded encouragement. "Go on."

"After that, it was so weird. The guy kind of giggles like a little girl and he let go of my neck."

"Why would he do that?"

Well, I don't know. I take the cue to slip in the car and slide out the other side. He's trying to aim his gun at her, but his hands were shaking so bad he couldn't hold it, so he drops my keys and backs up half a block, then takes off running. It was SO awesome."

Dean nodded again. "Awesome."

"Yeah, I offered to buy her dinner or something, but she said no. She came in the house and had some juice, we talked. I asked her why she walked around so late. She said she had to take care of some business and 'had a feeling' she needed to check out. I told her I was psychic like that too. We talked about souls and different planes and stuff." Delos ended her story with a flourish of her shoulders under her black leather jacket.

"I'd really be interested in talking to Gem," Dean said. "Could you arrange a meeting?"

"Yeah, she gave me a card with her phone number. If I want to get in touch, I just leave a message."

"When could it happen?"

"I could bring her over to a show. She might come, if the vibes are right. She's very sensitive."

Dean didn't want to seem too eager, but he thought Willet might want to talk to Gem. "The club is pretty loud. Could we meet somewhere quiet? I have, er, business clients that share her interests."

Her brows wrinkled in suspicion. "Like, who?"

"They're sisters. I'm doing construction on their house. They know about the Red Souls too."

"I guess," she said, pouting a bit.

"If you make it happen, I'd be really grateful, Delos. And I want to see you, of course."

That seemed to warm her up. "I'll see what I can do, handsome." She turned on a stiletto heel and sauntered away, hips swinging.

*****

Delos did make it happen. She arranged a meeting for Dean and the sisters to meet her friend, Gem. To accommodate everyone's schedules, they agreed to meet rather late Sunday night at a campground in the desert east of Hemmings. Willet wondered what she had gotten herself into.

Gem talks about Red Souls, but that might mean something completely different to her. They had met with clueless experts and psychic charlatans many times over the years. Every time, it had turned out to be a dead end.

Dean and the sisters piled into their sedan and drove into the desert night. Tiny stars pierced the sky, twinkling brilliantly. They drove down a dirt road and pulled into a parking area near a trailhead. A VW Bug occupied a space. Dean pulled a small flashlight from his jacket pocket and led them along a trail through sage and cactus until they reached a cluster of large boulders. A flat camping area lay behind the boulders. The smell of burning mesquite scented the air.

Delos sat cross-legged in front of a fire pit ringed with stones. A crackling fire burned before her, lighting up her face. She waved to Dean. The newcomers came to the fire, exchanged introductions, and dropped to the ground around the fire ring. Delos shared hot coffee from a metal pot sitting on a stone near the fire. They each wrapped their hands around warm cups of brew.

Dean cleared his throat. "We're here because Gem might have information that would help Willet. Is she coming?"

"Yeah, she said she would," Delos said. "Her schedule is kind of crazy. She works a lot at night."

Dean and the sisters relaxed in front of the fire, sipping coffee and staring into the flames. A half hour of small talk went by.

"Do you think your friend got held up?" Audrey asked. "Maybe we need to meet another time."

Delos uncurled her legs and stretched. "If she said she'll be here, she'll be here," she said with a toss of her black curls. "If you guys have somewhere else to be, by all means go."

"We can wait," Willet said. "I want to wait." Another half hour went by, and then Willet looked into the dark beyond the camp site. "I hear someone coming."

Minutes passed before a soft sound rustled the brush. A large dog with absolute black fur emerged from the darkness. A patch of white beamed from its forehead. The dog's gold eyes reflected fire light.

Willet gasped and rose to her knees. "That's the dog, at our house, on the patio!"

Another shadow appeared behind the dog. A woman stepped into the fire light. She had short, curly brown hair with blonde highlights and molasses skin, wore a denim jacket, long maroon skirt and short black boots. Bracelets on each wrist jangled and reflected light. Silver chandelier earrings swung from her ear lobes.

"This is Gem," Delos said, with a wave of her hand.

"Your dog came to our patio the other day," Willet said, pointing at the dog. "Why was it there?"

Gem approached the fire and sat down next to Delos. The black dog lay beside her. "Are you sure?" Gem asked.

"Yes, I'm sure."

"Dora comes and goes. She has her own reasons. Perhaps she wanted to meet you."

"Why would she want to meet *me*?"

Gem shrugged and nodded at the headphones hanging around Willet's neck. "Why do you have headphones?"

"They protect my ears from loud sounds," Willet replied.

"There are no loud sounds out here."

"Crickets are loud. Coyotes. Owls."

Gem sipped from the cup in her hand. "How good is your hearing?"

"Very good."

"Can you hear sounds from the other side?"

"The other side of what?"

"The astral plane beyond this physical world - can you hear it?" The question dropped in the midst of the group like a flaming soufflé, impossible to ignore.

"I'm not sure," Willet said, voice wavering. "Is that where Red Souls come from?"

"Yes." Gem pursed her lips. "Do Red Souls speak to you directly?"

"Sometimes. Do you hear them too?"

"I see them. What do you hear?"

Willet stared at the fire. "It's difficult to talk about. Nobody believes me when I do."

"*I* will believe you," Gem said firmly.

Willet shifted her shoulders and re-crossed her legs. "I hear a voice that talks about Red Souls. It says they're coming. I have a dream where I see a burning thing full of holes. Angry faces try to break through. They're screaming." She took a deep breath. "I wish it would stop."

Gem watched Willet with steady almond eyes. "The Spirit of All has called you to service."

"Why would it call me?"

"You have a gift."

"What kind of service? What am I supposed to do?"

"Red Souls are confined to the astral underworld for a time, to pay karmic debts, but they try to find ways back to this plane to indulge their appetites for physical excess. They penetrate human consciousness to feel and taste, see and hear the self-destructive things that humans do. It is dangerous for souls of this world."

Willet gulped. "How do you know all that?"

"It is my job to keep the worlds separate. I guard the Astral Gate."

"There's a gate?" Willet asked. "What kind of gate? Where is it?"

"The gate is an energy barrier between the worlds that normally cannot be crossed. However, under certain circumstances, it breaks down."

"What circumstances?" Dean asked.

Gem shifted in her seat and arranged her skirts. "It happens when negative emotions run out of control in the physical world. Physical energies synchronize with energies of the lower astral world. Rates of vibration become the same, so there is no barrier. Lower astral beings can move from their world into this one."

"Seems like that would be happening all the time," Dean mumbled.

72

"Outbreaks of violence in the city often have an astral component," Gem replied.

The campfire crackled and spit, everyone waiting in silence for another shoe to drop.

"This is what the silver voice has been talking about?" Willet finally asked.

"Essentially, yes."

"But why is the voice talking to me?"

"Because *you* are able to hear it."

Audrey threw up her hands. "This is ridiculous! You're a guardian of a gate to the astral plane, is that what you expect us to believe? How does this help Willet?"

Delos folded her arms and stared daggers at Audrey. Gem, however, did not seem to take offense. She continued quietly.

"Red Souls gain strength from dark passions of body and mind, like anger, vanity and gluttony. They especially enjoy violence, so they try to incite it. Violence creates more violence. Once the cycle starts, it is very difficult to stop. It requires someone like me."

Willet swallowed and whispered, "Why you?"

"I see astral energies. I know when they break through to this world. I can send them back to the other side."

Willet looked down at her hands folded in her lap. Her mind could barely digest it all.

Audrey was less restrained. "Will, you can't be buying this, can you? The woman is deluded. People have tried to scam us before."

The ground beneath the camp site shook lightly at that moment. In the next moment, it shook again, and then a third time. Another earthquake tremor.

Willet looked up at her sister. "You're concerned, Auddie, I get it, but this is the first person I've met with anything specific to tell me about Red Souls. I need to learn what she knows. Then I'll come to my own conclusions."

Gem tucked her skirt around her legs. "We have a problem in Los Angeles. Attacks from the astral Underworld grow stronger and more numerous. Red Souls have found a hidden channel between planes that I have not been able to see. I know they chatter about it. Your ability to hear them would be a great advantage." She rummaged in her pocket, and pulled out a plain white card, handing it to Willet. It bore a single name, 'Gem,' and a phone number. "Contact me if you are interested in knowing more. We can conduct a lookout together in the city." With that, she got up and walked out of the circle of light, the black dog following at her heels. The desert darkness swallowed them.

"What was your dog doing at my house?" Willet called after her. She got no response.

"Well, she's rude, that's for sure," Audrey said. "I hope you're not considering her offer."

"Actually, I am," Willet replied. "How else can I figure anything out?"

"Willet, this is crazy. You're really going to go into LA with this woman? How could that possibly work? It would be dangerous, and the noise would incapacitate you."

"Auddie, you've taken care of me almost my whole life. I love you, but I'm not a baby. I need to make this decision for myself."

Audrey backed pedaled. "Of course, it's your decision. Maybe you could sleep on it, and we can talk tomorrow. It's been a long evening, lots to think about."

"Yes, lots *for me* to think about," Willet said.

Silence fell on the circle again.

"Well, thanks, Delos, for setting this up," Dean said by way of closing the meeting. "Very informative. Please give Gem our thanks for talking with us."

Delos scowled and jabbed at the fire with a stick.

Dean rose and headed back toward the parking lot. Willet and Audrey gathered themselves and followed.

Willet's mind spun. Could it be a ruse? What would Gem have to gain by that? And could Willet stand it. Even in a sound-proofed sedan, she needed sedation almost everywhere she went. She wouldn't be much help in that condition.

On the other hand, cringing in a closet was no life, waiting for pain or recovering from it, dealing with phantom voices and suspicious looks from other people. Gem seemed to see value in her ability. Maybe they really could help each other.

Willet joined Dean and Audrey next to the car. She racked her brain for a way to sway her sister but couldn't think of anything. So, for once, it had to be her decision alone.

Chapter 8: The Temple

Gem and Dora walked along the winding roads of the Hollywood Hills at a steady pace. They reached an overlook point and climbed up to search the sky for signs of astral disruption. Her Gate seemed intact, but Red Souls swirled through the clouds and in the streets. She had to find their path into the physical world and close it down or she would lose the ability to protect L.A.

In the last two days, she had interrupted a robbery in Torrance, prevented a police shooting in Compton, and cooled a jealous husband about to strangle his wife in Pasadena, but she had not yet identified the target Theese hinted to his followers. She suffered through segment after ten-minute segment of his broadcast, full of bluster, alternately cagey and glib, implying much but revealing nothing.

"Something will burn, and lions are involved. It is not enough to go on, Dora," she said in frustration. "I wonder why it has not happened already."

Gem and Dora looked out toward the Pacific Ocean from the overlook. Sunset shades of red, gold and orange spread across the horizon in watercolor brush strokes. The city seemed to hold its breath before the sun slipped under the water. The sky slowly turned a deeper blue. Scattered stars glittered like diamond chips on velvet.

Gem enjoyed this time of day. At the moment between day and night, time balanced on the head of a pin. LA spread out a carpet of flickering lights and welcomed the evening. The night glittered with possibilities.

The phone in the pocket of her long maroon skirt began to buzz. She pulled it out and saw a number she didn't recognize. When she answered, she heard a small, hesitant voice.

"Is this Gem?"

"Of course."

"Uh, this is Willet du Place. We met in the desert the other night."

"I remember you."

"I have something to tell you. Maybe you'll understand it."

"Tell me."

"The Silver Voice I talked about spoke to me again, in the shower."

"What did it say?"

"It said 'Red Souls burn.' It never said anything like that before."

"Did you hear anything else?"

"I heard angry voices, so angry. They were buzzing like bees."

"Could you tell what direction they were coming from?"

"Direction? You mean like north, south?"

"Yes."

"No," Willet replied slowly, "but there were other voices I'd never heard before, humming really low, almost growling. It sounded like bears in a cave."

Gem closed her eyes, trying to visualize. "Could you be more specific? To my knowledge, bears don't hum."

"They sang a low note, almost musical, but deep in the throat. Like they were snoring, or gargling."

"Can you hear it now?"

"No, not now. I do remember a kind of ringing sound in the background too, like the echo of a bell."

"Was it perhaps the bells of your silver voice?"

"No, this was a deeper ring. Really deep."

"A church bell?"

"Yes, maybe…"

"This is important," Gem advised her firmly. "Listen for the sounds. You might hear them again. Write down everything you hear."

Willet protested weakly. "Is that all I'm supposed to do? What about the hidden channel?"

"You must first learn to control your attention. Focus. I will help you to do that through contemplation exercises. But now I must go. We will speak at length later."

Gem clicked off abruptly and led Dora to the Jeep. Sitting behind the wheel, she tapped the steering wheel nervously with both hands and stared out the window. Dora leaned over from the back seat and rested her head on Gem's shoulder with a "harrumph." Gem put her arm around Dora's smooth black head and patted her.

"Thank you, Dora dear."

Dora sighed. They sat together, letting confusion roll away like retreating storm clouds, until only a clear, steady light in the space between her eyebrows remained. Gem gazed at it for many minutes before rousing herself to action.

"Let's go out in the world and see where Spirit leads us."

She put the Jeep in gear and took off down the hill, not sure of her destination. She switched on the radio. Theese babbled on. She cruised through downtown, over to Wilshire Boulevard, then up into northeast LA, scanning the skies as she drove. In the deepening dusk, a small astral break might not be visible until it turned into a large one. She had all but tuned out Theese's voice when he said something that caught her ear.

"Come on down to the rancho, folks. We're having a barbeque for all my friends. Party starts at eight."

Gem sat straight up. That was a definite appointment. She glanced at the dashboard clock: - "7:00." Whatever the plan was, it would start in an hour.

Bears in caves, humming. The echo of a bell, a deep bell, like a cowbell, a heavy chime, or a church steeple bell. What kind of church? It has to be a place of worship, but which one – there are hundreds. Who rings a deep bell besides the big cathedrals?

Gem's eyes popped open. The Buddhists monks –they sang their chant words in a low growl at the back of their throats. And they hit a gong to signal the start and end.

Puzzle pieces fell into place. The Buddhist Temple in Rancho Park would be a high-profile target with low political and economic sensitivity. It just so happened that stone lions flanked the front entry.

Now 7:15, she turned the Jeep around and headed east, hoping to miss the worst of the rush hour traffic. She had forty-five minutes to get to the temple before the fireworks started.

Miles flew by as the Jeep powered down the Pomona Freeway, dodging other cars, and taking a few shoulders to save time. She exited at Azusa Avenue and headed south at well over the speed limit. At 7:40 a full moon rose above the horizon. Her astral sight detected a fiery crack in the sky above the temple. What looked like molten lava churned behind the crack, and thick smoke tumbled into the air.

"Why does Theese bother these people?" she remarked to Dora. "Buddhists are peaceful."

She and Dora parked on a nearby street, jumped from Jeep and hurried on foot to the temple grounds. A broad paved courtyard lined with trees opened before wide temple steps leading up to the front doors. A red roof with fluted corners and dentate carvings around the edges topped the building. The moon flooded the courtyard with iridescent white light and cast shadows across the stone lions perched on pedestals at each corner.

Gem and Dora walked to the steps and sat down, facing out to the courtyard. She took slow, even breaths and sang her chant until her astral body rose. The sounds of ocean waves rushed over her. Dora remained crouched beside her, guarding her physical body.

Theese's people lurked behind trees around the courtyard. Dirty brown auras surrounded their astral bodies, betraying their hateful intentions as they waited for the signal to hurl whatever incendiary devices they had brought for this "barbeque." But another

80

consciousness occupied the courtyard with them. A soft saffron-gold light emanated from the temple, pulsing slowly like a beating heart. The energy of the monks surrounded the temple with imperturbable serenity.

"Of course, they would be aware of all this," murmured Gem.

The stone lions glowed pure white, and their eyes opened as Gem moved to the center of the courtyard.

"You there behind the trees," she called out in a ringing tone. "Leave this place. Your aims will not be met tonight. Your fire will be turned to ice."

The lurkers hissed and one stepped out from behind a tree, revealing an astral skeleton. His jawbone flapped up and down under his mouth as he spoke.

"Who are you to stop us? The people here are spies and corrupters. They must be made an example."

"I am the Guardian of the Astral Gate. You have been deceived. There are no spies or corrupters here. Go home."

The skeleton bared its teeth at Gem, raised its arm, and threw something grasped in its bony fingers.

Dora's deadly growl rumbled out of her throat like an underground earthquake. The projectile, a tin can, flew toward Gem's physical body on the steps. The can burst into flame in the air. Dora jumped at it, turning her body to block the can, and knocked it off course. Then she leapt at the thrower, digging her long white fangs all the way to the bone of his shoulder as she dragged him to the ground.

Gem sent a gale of icy breath at the can, turning it into a block of ice before it hit the ground. It fell to the pavement with a dull thud. She turned and aimed her glacial breath at those hiding in the trees. When the cold hit them, they screamed, and their bodies smoked.

The four stone lions awakened at the sound and roared. Their eyes glittered like red jewels. They turned massive heads toward the screams, rose to their feet and jumped off their pedestals, stalking toward the skeletons. The skeletons ran for the street under cover of the trees. The lions bounded after them and chased them to the end of the temple grounds, watching them go with low growls. After the intruders had left the courtyard, the lions jumped up to their pedestals and resumed their stone vigil.

Gem looked at the burning crack in the sky. It still gaped like an angry red mouth. With a long exhale of her breath, she iced it until it withered, swallowing its own smoke as it closed. Then she turned toward the temple. She bowed low to the golden light pulsing from it.

"The Gate is closed. Our work is done," she called out to the souls who guarded the place. "Thank you for your assistance."

The golden light pulsed once more and then faded slowly until the moon shed the only light left in the courtyard. Gem's astral body dropped back into her physical body on the steps. She took a few deep breaths to reorient herself. She and Dora slipped away into the shadows. As they walked, Gem kept her hand on the holstered gun in the pocket of her long skirt. Theese's people might be waiting for them on the streets.

"They will watch for us now, my dear. It will be more difficult to surprise them in the future."

Chapter 9: Alliances

Gem and Dora were driving back to the city when another call came in from Willet. Gem answered this time and heard Willet's exasperated voice.

"Why didn't you answer my calls?"

"There was much to do."

"Well, what happened last night? Did you find out what the bears were?"

"Yes. All is well for now."

"I helped, right? I deserve to know what happened."

"It is safer for you if you do not know, baby girl."

"I'm not a 'baby girl'. If I'm going to be part of the mission, I need to know what's going on."

Gem considered this. "Yes, that is true. You *are* the Listener."

"The Listener? What's that?"

"You hear across great distances. You connect worlds. Your gift is essential to our mission."

"Wow. I have a title?" Willet said. "If you let me know what you're doing, I could help more."

"The bear sounds you heard were the chanting of Buddhist monks. They were in danger, and we helped them, Dora and you, and me."

"Dora helped you?"

"Yes, she did."

"How did she help?"

"She protected my physical body while I was in astral consciousness."

Silence from Willet.

Gem changed the subject. "Have you been able to bring your thoughts under control?"

"I'm not doing it right."

"Chant and focus. Huuuu. Huuuu. Repeat it."

"Huuuu. Huuuu."

"Find the light within. Let it become your single, pure focus."

"Everything looks dark when I do that. I keep going to sleep."

"Listen for the sounds of Spirit. I know you hear them."

"I hear so many sounds. I'm not sure which ones are the right sounds to listen to."

"We will meet and practice."

"When can I join your mission?"

"We will try a lookout run when you are able to focus more effectively. Then we will determine what is possible for you."

"When can we practice together?"

"This evening, I will come to you. For now, I must go."

*****

Gem hung up on her, again, but at least they had a firm appointment. Willet needed to get Audrey to agree with her plans, or at least give in. Gem could be as ingratiating as a prickly pear cactus, and Audrey had no patience for what she considered foolishness. A meeting could end up in spontaneous combustion. Willet had to figure out a way to avoid fireworks and learn how to control her own thoughts at the same time. She wasn't sure which challenge was bigger.

Since she had the morning alone at Dean's house, she decided to practice focusing her thoughts. Gem had given her so little to go on. Chant, focus, look and listen. She certainly knew how to listen. "Chant" she could do. "Focus" was harder.

She sat in the hushed silence of Dean's office in his big leather chair. Gem had suggested she concentrate on a word that was positive for her until she could find the light. She visualized the word "music," sang it until musical notes floated before her eyes, and then she dozed off. When she awoke with a start, she went to the kitchen for water, returned to the office and tried again. Her mind wanted to think about all kinds of things at the same time.

She got up and stretched, sat back down. *Let's try this again.* She thought about Gem and breathed slowly. Gem's brown eyes were clear and steady, stern in a way, but kind. Gem had smiled at her when they met by the campfire. Willet pictured that smile and felt warmth in her heart. It rippled through her whole body. Her ears

85

pulsed with the sound of quiet, the sound of the void. The present moment absorbed her.

"Baby girl," Gem's voice said. "Stand up."

Willet felt someone take her hand very gently and try to pull her up from the chair. Her body felt so very heavy, she couldn't rise. She tried again and the hand pulled harder. She felt herself roll forward and land lightly on legs that weren't really there.

The light around her glowed radiantly. A soft wind whistled. "Lissssten," it said. Far off ocean waves rushed to shore. She looked back at the chair and saw herself sitting in it. Her body seemed deflated, like an empty suit of clothes. The eyes stared, vacant

She realized. *I am not my body.*

She fell backwards into the chair like a bag of rocks, and her eyes popped open.

Chapter 10: The First Lookout

Dean maneuvered through an obstacle course of ladders, scaffolding, scattered tools and stacks of acoustic tiles to recheck the latest installations in the living room of Pine Siskin House. When the front door opened and the sisters walked in, the atmosphere turned frosty.

"Hey ladies, take a look." Dean pointed at the ceiling and walls. "We've got most of the tiles hung. What do you think?"

Willet continued on to the hallway as Dean watched her go. A minute later, he heard a door slam, shaking the whole house.

Audrey winced at the sound. "She slams the door when she's really mad, even though she'll get a terrible headache for it."

"She doesn't like the living room?" he asked, half-joking.

"I'm sorry, Dean," Audrey replied. "It's not the living room. Our arguments about Gem have escalated to the point of name-calling. I can't reach her anymore."

"Maybe you need to give her some space," he said. "Let her make her decision and learn from the experience. If all goes well, then no harm done. If it goes badly, lesson learned."

"I wish it were that simple. You've seen how badly things can go with Willet. Gem is coming by tonight, supposedly to talk to both of us. Could you stay for dinner? I could use backup."

Dean really didn't want to be in the middle of the "talk" between Gem and the sisters. "Willet's an adult. You can't always protect her."

"She wants to be a vigilante, Dean. It's insane. Why doesn't she see that?"

"Maybe she thinks it's worth the risk, living her own life and all. You could live your own life too."

"I've looked after her for so long," Audrey said. Her shoulders sagged. "It's a difficult habit to break."

Dean searched for something helpful to say but drew a blank and said what he really thought. "You're not her mother, you know."

This brought out a defensive tone in Audrey's voice. "I'm as much of a mother as she's had."

He raised his hands in surrender. "And it is totally not my place to comment, which is why I shouldn't be here when you talk to Gem. I don't know what help I'd be."

"You'd be a neutral observer, so it's not just me versus both of them. I feel outnumbered."

"I think you're holding on too hard. Not sure if that's being neutral."

"I figured she would want more independence eventually," Audrey said weakly. "I never dreamed it would happen under circumstances like these."

*****

The doorbell clicked inside Pine Siskin House. Willet ran to it and swept it open.

"Gem, come in, quickly," she said in a whisper. "I have something important to tell you before Audrey comes in here."

Gem walked in and put a small, embroidered bag down on the floor. "Tell me."

"I had a dream or experience or something. I heard your voice, and I felt someone pulling on my arm, but I didn't see anyone. I saw a bright light, and I heard the ocean."

"I see," Gem said.

"I think I got out of my body. Did you pull on my arm?"

"Why do you think that?"

"I heard your voice, telling me to stand up."

"Are you sure?"

"It sounded like you."

"Did you see me?"

"No. I felt you somehow. Now I'm not sure…"

"You must decide the truth of your own experiences. Otherwise, it is not your truth."

Audrey and Dean emerged from the kitchen, the scent of toast wafting around them. Audrey gave a cool nod to Gem and turned to Willet. "What's going on, Will?"

Willet pointed to the living room and said, "Could we all sit down, please?"

Audrey pulled tarps from a couple of sofas and sat down. Dean sat next to her. Willet sat on the other couch next to Gem.

Willet cleared her throat. "I'm going to go out on a lookout with Gem. She needs to figure out where all the Red Souls are coming from. I hear them, so I want to help."

"You want my sister to go with you on this lookout?" Audrey asked, staring at Gem.

"Her ability to hear astral voices could give me early warning when Red Souls are about to strike. We might prevent the chaos and despair they cause."

"LA is a violent city. What kind of strikes are you're talking about?"

"I try to prevent situations where there might be direct bodily harm, murders or assaults, as well as mental and emotional damage that is difficult to reverse."

"You stop murders? Do you step between people holding guns and ask them nicely to stop shooting?"

"I cool emotions before they burn out of control. The people involved may not know I am even there."

"How do you accomplish that?"

"By the power of Freezing Breath."

"You breathe on them. Is that what you're telling me?"

"Yes."

"And what will my sister do while you're "cooling emotions?"

"Red Souls are bypassing my Gate by an unknown route. I need to find it. They do a lot of chattering, and she may hear something that helps me."

Willet sat up straighter in her seat. "I already told her things that helped stop something bad happening to Buddhist monks. Maybe it's my mission too. Auddie, I want to help. I need to try at least. Please understand."

Audrey's hands were shaking. She pressed them against her thighs. "Monks, really?" her voice almost squeaked. "I'm trying to understand, Will. It's your decision, but I picture two women driving around LA alone, with no protection except her ability to breathe on people. What am I missing?"

"They should bring a bodyguard," Dean said.

Audrey's eyes opened wide, and she turned eagerly to Dean. "That would be great if you went with them! Would you mind? It would give me a little peace, at least."

Dean backpedaled like a circus clown on a bicycle. "*ME*? Well, that's not what I…I mean, I'm not really …I'm not a…"

"As long as you don't interfere with the run," Gem said slowly. "It would be all right. Willet, is this acceptable to you?"

"As long as everyone agrees, I'm fine with it."

Audrey stood and faced them. Her eyes looked red enough to burn. She avoided eye contact. "It's settled then," she said in a curt tone. "Thank you, Dean. I appreciate this."

She turned and walked resolutely out of the room, disappearing down the hallway. They heard a door slam somewhere in the back of the house. It was Willet's turn to wince.

"Audrey's upset, I know" Willet sighed, rubbing her temples to ease the stab of pain. "I'm glad you're coming, Dean. You'll be able to tell her everything's okay."

Dean shook his head, seemingly dazed at the swift turn of events. "I hope I *can* tell her everything's okay," he mumbled.

*****

Gem preferred to work alone with Dora who understood her implicitly. Now she had a team to manage. The benefits of Willet's assistance were obvious, but Dean was a wildcard. She depended on her inner guidance to show her what to do.

How will they react when worlds collide? Help me to keep them safe.

They already had questions. Willet wanted to know what to expect. Dean wanted to know where they were going and why. She had to make them understand the importance of the task without revealing what they were fighting. They would see that soon enough.

Thursday morning Gem picked Willet up at Pine Siskin House. She had spotted a wavering in the Astral Gate over central Downey from the 710 Freeway. It had not cracked yet, but she wanted to check on it. This would be a good opportunity to see how the partnership could work. Willet carried aspirin, water and meds in a backpack, and wore her trusty headphones. Dean would meet them at the

Downey Landing mall. The morning rush hour had already passed. It seemed an unlikely time for an astral flare up, but that didn't mean it couldn't happen. Gem had learned to be skeptical of apparent calm.

Dean stood in the parking lot of the Landing when they arrived. He climbed in the passenger seat and adjusted it back to accommodate his long legs. His foot hit something hard. He looked down and saw the muzzle of Gem's Magnum sticking out from under the seat. His eyebrows flew up into his hair.

"What the hell! You carry a gun?" he exclaimed. "You didn't mention anything about a gun."

Gem picked up the Magnum, checked the safety, and casually stowed it under her own seat. "There is a Colt in the glove box too, if you need it. You didn't think I drove around LA at all hours with no protection, did you?"

"You have a license for that thing?"

"Of course."

"Do you know how to use it?"

"I am a trained marks-woman. What good would it do me if I did not know how to use it?"

Dean looked to the back seat. Willet sat next to the enormous black dog with the patch of white fur on her forehead. Dora flashed Dean a glimpse of her sharp teeth.

"Is she one of the hounds of hell? What is her name again?"

"Dora is my partner and my friend. She would never hurt anyone who did not hurt me."

Dora stared steadily at Dean and broke into a pant.

"Dora seems okay," Willet said. Her skin had turned a pale green. Perspiration beaded on her forehead.

Dean's eyes narrowed at her. "Are you feeling alright, Will? You don't look well."

"There's more noise in the Jeep than I'm used to. My head hurts a little." Willet swallowed hard and forced a wan smile.

"Are you going to be able to do this?"

"I'll try," she said.

"Well then, where are we going?" he asked as he buckled his seat belt. "And what do we do when we get there?"

"We will not go anywhere until we are focused. Listen to the word I chant, and then sing it with me. Center your thoughts"

"We're going to sing first?" Dean asked, incredulous.

"The astral forces we fight are very strong," replied Gem. "Our connection with the All-in-All must be just as strong."

"How is singing going to help?"

"Red Souls will try to overwhelm us with negative emotions. We sing the charged words to deflect them."

Dean stared at her for a moment, and then shook his head. "Go ahead, then. Do what you do."

Gem closed her eyes and breathed deeply. A low, musical sound formed in the back of her throat. She blew it out, soft and sibilant like a whisper. She sang it in one long, slow exhale of breath, repeating it twice. "Huuuu. Huuuu." When she opened her eyes, she looked at them.

"That is a sound from the high planes. It can raise your consciousness. Negative emotions will not defeat you."

Dean frowned. "We're fighting negative emotions. I thought we're fighting Red Souls."

"Indeed." Gem closed her eyes again.

"OK. Whatever."

Dean closed his eyes when Gem did and listened to the chant vibrate inside the Jeep. Minutes passed. Gem ended with a "thank you" to the Spirit of All. Dean squinted at her, and then looked away.

Willet bent forward with eyes closed and took deep breaths. "Silver Voice says 'Red Souls break.' It's never said that before. And there are other voices."

"What do they say?" Gem asked.

"Curses and groans. The voices are coming from behind us."

"How about you, Dean? Did you hear or see anything out of the ordinary?"

Dean scratched his nose, then his ear. "Heard a car go by. Nothing else, sorry."

"Give it time," Gem reassured him. "It takes practice, along with the right attitude and intention."

Dean chuckled. "If you say so."

"If the Gate isn't broken, what are we supposed to do?" Willet asked.

"Red Souls wait for a catalyst on this side to help them break through. If there is an emotional flare up of any kind, it increases their strength. We need to move nearer to that part of the Gate and watch for disturbances that might trigger a break."

Dean chuckled again. "What are we going to do, consult a Ouija board?"

Gem glared at him. "We can reduce pressure on the Gate if we balance the negativity. Your sarcasm works against us."

"Uh, sorry," Dean said with a sheepish grin.

They drove north through commercial and industrial areas along Bellflower Boulevard. Eventually, Gem slowed to the curb near a squat stucco building, which turned out to be a dialysis clinic, a plain, single-story structure with a glass door and a small sign over the door in green letters.

She pointed at the sky above the building. "The Gate is still unbroken."

Willet and Dean looked up, squinting at the empty sky where she pointed.

Gem turned to Willet. "What do you hear now?"

"Lots of grumbling, definitely louder. My stomach feels really queasy."

"We have arrived in time. That is good."

Dean stared out the window, saying nothing.

"Let us see what we can see or hear."

Everyone got out of the Jeep. Gem hooked a lead on Dora's collar, and the big dog jumped to the sidewalk.

Gem took Dean's elbow and pointed him toward the sky over the clinic. "Red Souls may break through in this area. What is the likely catalyst in a neighborhood like this? Maybe it is the dialysis clinic itself. People are very ill when they go there. Red Souls are drawn to the misery of the people inside."

"That makes sense," said Willet.

Dean nodded. "Yeah, the clinic makes sense."

At that moment, a group of boys appeared around the corner two blocks away, laughing and running down the street past the clinic. One of the boys, the biggest in the group, held a large rock in his hand. The rest of the boys followed him. Gem and Dora began to walk toward them. Dora growled low in her throat, and then barked her thunderous bark. The rest of the boys turned and looked at Dora, but the big boy pulled his arm back and threw the rock at the glass door of the clinic with his whole strength.

The glass shattered, spraying shards of glass over the sidewalk. A gaping hole remained where the door had been. The boys ran to the corner and out of sight down a side street, still laughing.

"That should be the catalyst." Gem said softly.

A woman in a business suit and heels stepped out of the smashed clinic door followed by a young man in green scrubs. They exclaimed over the damage as two more people from inside came out to see what had happened.

A crack opened in the Astral Gate above the clinic like a giant maw, exposing jagged teeth. Red smoke poured from the breach, down to the street. Willet pressed her headphones to her ears and groaned. She bent over to be sick, emptying her stomach at the curb. She hung from the waist, panting, saliva hanging from her bottom lip.

"Red Souls are screaming," she said between huffed breaths. "'Smash glass.' I think that's what they're saying. It's too loud to say for sure."

Buildings all around them had glass windows - warehouses, industrial buildings, the clinic itself. A three-story office building fronted entirely in green glass sat on the corner of a side street. The sign at the top of the building read "G.H. Jefferson Controls Inc." Red smoke drifted toward it in thick clouds and swirled up against the windows.

"There is the target," Gem said, pointing at the building. "Red Souls are already pressing the glass. If anyone is inside, glass will shatter on them like shrapnel. We have to warn whoever is in there."

Willet retched violently. Gem bent over her to hold her hair and prevent her from falling forward. She looked up at Dean with a stern expression.

"Go into that building and pull the fire alarm. Make the people come outside."

He looked at Gem in shock. "You mean me? I could be arrested for that!" he hissed a panicked whisper, looking around for anyone who might be listening.

"It will rain glass very soon. We have little time."

"This is nuts!"

"People will be hurt if you do not, Dean. Go now!"

Conflict twisted Dean's face. He looked at the building and back at Gem. Willet heaved again and groaned. He turned and ran across the street, yanked the lobby door open and rushed inside. Moments later he bolted out the front door of the building, wide-eyed and panicked. An alarm blared inside the building.

Dean crossed the street at a dead run and slid to a halt beside the two women. "Let's get out of here," he panted.

Dean and Gem each took one of Willet's arms and lifted her off the ground. They carried her back to the corner of a nearby building and stopped in a patch of shade. Dora brought up the rear, dragging her lead behind her. Willet dropped heavily to the ground, hanging her head between her knees. Sounds of sirens far away headed in their direction.

Dean crouched down, breathing heavily. "Someone might have seen me."

"Dean, pull yourself together now," Gem said. "What you did had to be done." She peeked out from the shade to watch the red smoke press on the green glass building. The windows of the building bowed inward, straining. Red smoke collected in the bowls of glass. The front doors of the building opened, and people walked casually out to the sidewalks laughing and talking as if it were a training drill. Gem feared the building would not empty quickly enough.

The first fire truck reached the building and pulled up to the curb. A second truck made the turn onto the street. Fire crews jumped from the trucks and looked up at the building with puzzled stares. A strange silence fell on both the fire fighters and the people gathered outside.

The glass finally cracked. Every window imploded into the office behind it. Jagged shards slid down the sides of the building and shattered on the sidewalks. Onlookers screamed and scattered out of the way with arms over their heads as glass splinters rained on them. Red blossoms bloomed on bare skin. Fire fighters quickly donned their suits and directed people away from the building. An ambulance pulled up at the curb, lights flashing.

Willet crouched on her knees, dry heaves shaking her shoulders. Dean and Gem put their hands under her elbows, lifted her again, and draped her arms over their shoulders. Gem gave a grim glance back at the building. "We have done what we can to avert a catastrophe," she said. "Now we must be gone."

They hauled Willet to the Jeep and lifted her into the front seat climbing in after her.

Dean mumbled to himself. "What just happened? The windows smashed. It's not possible."

"Imagine what will happen if we allow Red Souls to flood the earth. They can exert a catastrophic physical effect if the energy barrier between the physical and astral planes breaks down," Gem said. "The results we see here are just a shadow of what they can do. We must find their entry point and close it."

The Gate still needed to be sealed. Gem chanted silently and rose into astral consciousness, her astral body floated above the Jeep, and she aimed her breath at the break. A blast of icy cold hit the hole, and it began to shrink.

A patrol car drove slowly by on the cross street. The Jeep would surely be scrutinized parked so near the scene of an unexplained explosion. They needed to be gone before the patrol made another pass. She didn't have much time to finish the job.

The gaping hole had shriveled into something resembling a lopsided smile. Streamers of red smoke still escaped and drifted aimlessly in the air. Gem blasted the break with sleet. The Gate swallowed the remaining smoke and sealed shut.

She dropped back into her physical body, started the Jeep, and headed in the opposite direction of the patrol car. Willet had closed her eyes in exhaustion and leaned her head against the back seat. Dora stayed close to Willet, laying a paw in her lap.

Dean sat in the back on the other side of Dora with slack jaw and glazed eyes staring straight ahead. Stray wisps of red smoke slipped in through the open window next to him and flowed into his nose, ears and mouth. The smoke glittered as he inhaled it.

Chapter 11: Explanations

Dean owed Audrey a report. He also wanted her to know how he felt about the lookout, but he felt so many different ways that he wasn't sure what to say.

"Audrey, your sister hears dead people."

"Gem pulled Willet into the deep end."

"Willet and Gem are astral policewomen."

He rehearsed alternative speeches as he drove east toward Hemmings. He'd feel better if he could get the whole thing off his chest. If she wasn't home, he'd wait for her. He wanted to talk to her alone, preferably when Willet wasn't home. What he had to say would not sit well. She'd need time to digest it before speaking to her sister.

104

A caretaker in a golf cart dropped him off in front of Pine Siskin House. The Porsche was already parked in the circular drive. *Good, Audrey's home.* He wanted to get it over with. The crew had packed up and left for the day. An odor of paint and cut wood permeated the air inside the house. All the windows were open to let the room air out. Willet wouldn't like that, but it had to be done.

No need to worry, that's what he could say. He just wasn't sure he could say it with conviction. Gem carried a gun. Willet puked her guts out on an LA street, and he saw the windows of a building shatter into a rainfall of glass, just like Gem said they would. They were so in over their heads. And yet, they had helped people, probably saved lives. Could anyone else in LA have done what they did at that moment? Dean didn't know the answer, but he now knew what he would say to Audrey. What they did was necessary. She needed to understand that.

Dean found Audrey in her office at the back of the house, sitting at a large mahogany desk. Behind her, a long picture window opened on a peaceful view of rolling hills. Audrey typed on a laptop, absorbed in her work. Dean hesitated to interrupt her, but she heard him and looked up. Her expression turned to alarm, and she stood.

"Dean, what happened? You look upset. Willet wouldn't tell me anything when she got home yesterday. She went straight to bed and didn't come out of her room all night. Today she said she didn't want to talk. I'm worried."

So much for breaking it gently. "Audrey, I want to tell you what happened yesterday, but it's difficult to explain. I'm not sure how to say it. So just let me get the whole story out. Then you can ask questions. Okay?"

Audrey sat down again and gave a short nod, her face white.

"Willet heard voices that helped Gem prevent people from being hurt or killed. That's the short version."

"I want the long version."

Dean stopped to take a breath. He glanced at Audrey's stone face. As he gave her the details, her complexion paled from white to deathly white, and her eyes narrowed. She swallowed hard.

"Could this be some kind of illusion?" she asked in a small, strained voice. "Or hypnosis?"

"Every window in the building blew apart. People on the ground were hit by flying glass. It wasn't an illusion. The fire fighters saw it."

Audrey stood up again and began pacing in front of the window, head down, shaking.

"I knew Gem was trouble. I knew it."

"Gem needed your sister. Otherwise, she wouldn't have figured out what to do."

Audrey's strained composure broke, and she whirled suddenly on Dean. "You can't possibly expect me to believe that Willet should be involved in this insanity. I have to conclude you were all either drinking or doing drugs. Shattering glass? The fire department was involved? Who drove – you? Gem? Your judgment can not be trusted, and Gem is out of her mind. I should have stuck to my instincts."

Dean sagged against the doorway. His head felt like a pricked balloon. Now that the story was out, his remaining energy drained away. He just wanted to lie down and sleep.

"I can say, for what it's worth, that Gem and Will did a heroic thing. They should continue to do it, if they can." Dean turned from the doorway.

Audrey whispered. "Dean, I'm sorry. I'm upset. I'm not thinking clearly."

When Dean turned back, her eyes were desperate. He gave her a weary shrug. "No worries. It's a lot to take in."

She hung her head. Her shoulders curled forward. "We've wondered about Will's voices for years. I can't believe this is really the explanation."

"I don't know if it's an explanation. But it's part of it."

"What should I do?"

Dean shifted uncomfortably, foot to foot, and turned toward the door."It's not for me to say or for you either," he said over his shoulder. "It's Willet's life. You can't decide for her."

*****

Audrey waited a while before going to her sister's bedroom. She wasn't sure what to say. When she did look in, she found Willet lying on her bed with headphones on and a wet cloth across her forehead. Her eyes were closed, and her hands folded over her belly. She breathed soft and steady. A pile of clothes lay at the foot of the bed where they had been dropped the night before. Audrey tried to slip away noiselessly. Of course, that was impossible with Willet.

"Auddie, what's up?" Willet said, opening one eye to look at her. "You and Dean had quite a conversation. Now you don't have to ask me all those questions."

"I just wanted to make sure you were okay. You looked beat when you came home."

"Yeah, still am. But I'm getting better."

"Dean said you and Gem did some brave things, saved people."

Willet snorted. "I heard my usual voices, threw up everything in my stomach plus pieces of my esophagus, and then I could barely walk. Gem and Dean had to pick me up and carry me. My role on the team is 'Chief Vomiter', apparently. It was so embarrassing." She closed her eyes again and sighed.

"I should let you sleep then," Audrey said uncertainly.

"No. I'm just thinking about things," Willet replied. "I've decided I don't want to take the meds anymore, or at least take them less often."

"Why?"

"I want to be sure of what's real and what isn't. I don't want them interfering."

"Okay. Do you mind some company?"

Willet opened both her eyes and patted the bed beside her.

Audrey went to the bed and lay down next to her sister. They stared at the ceiling in companionable silence as they used to do when they were children. "Will, your experience yesterday. I don't understand it. I'd like to know what happened, from your point of view."

"I don't understand it either. Everything happened so fast. The Red Souls were screaming in my head. 'Smash glass, smash glass,' and then glass smashed for no apparent reason. Gem said red smoke pressed against the windows of that building until the glass cracked. I didn't see a thing, but I do know if Dean hadn't run into the building and pulled the fire alarm, people inside would have been hurt or killed. "

"He didn't mention anything about pulling a fire alarm."

Willet chortled. "He didn't want to do it, that's for sure."

"I'm really grateful he went with you. But now you see how dangerous it is, going out with Gem. You're not doing it again, are you?"

"I never expected anything like this," Willet said. "I don't know what I expected, really. I see what Gem does and it's frightening. I was so scared and so nauseous, I had to lie down on the sidewalk. But I could hear what the Red Souls said, and it helped Gem figure out what they were going to do. I made a difference. I don't think I can stop now."

Afternoon turned into early evening, and shadows began to play on the walls. Audrey cleared her throat.

"If that's your decision, then I want to come with you. I want to see what you and Gem do. Maybe I can help. Dean has a life. He can't be with you on every run."

Willet rolled on her side toward Audrey and propped her head on her hand. She stared hard at her sister.

"Why would you want to come? Not just to babysit. I don't need that."

"No, not for that," Audrey said. "I want to know more. The story's incredible. I want to see for myself how such a thing could happen."

Willet continued to stare. "You don't believe me? Does what I tell you matter?"

"Of course, it matters. It's what matters most in all of this. But you're the only one who can hear the voices, Will. I don't pretend to understand that either. Maybe if I saw *how* you and Gem work together, combine your abilities, it would help me appreciate what you're doing."

Willet relaxed her shoulders and laid her head on her outstretched arm with a tired sigh.

"I have to admit you were right all along, Auddie. What Gem does *is* seriously dangerous. I can't let you risk being a part of it."

"If you can risk it, I can too. I'm more worried than ever now that I know what's involved. I'm also very curious. If you've been hearing Souls from the astral plane all this time, and I can't believe I'm saying this, think about the implications. On the other hand, if Gem is a fake, then we could figure it out together. We'd both be sure either way."

"This is quite a change. You're being so… reasonable."

"What else can I do, Will? Dean tells me to let you live your life. I know he's right, but I can't just sit back and wait until you get hurt. You're my sister. I love you."

Willet studied her sister's profile as she spoke. She knew Audrey's face so well and yet it seemed she saw her again after a long separation. Life had already changed. She struggled to find the right words. "The du Place sisters together again," she said softly. "It would be easier for me if you were on board. No more tension between us."

"Let's talk to Gem. I promise I'll keep an open mind and I won't interfere."

Willet lay back again with a measure of peace she had not felt in a while. The sisters rested together, hands clasped, and chatted about small things until they both fell asleep like they did when they were children.

*****

Dean went home to shower, eat and rest before the Friday night show, but he felt jumpy. He went into the practice room and climbed behind the drums. He picked up the sticks and started bashing cymbals, beating skins, and kicking the base drum as hard as he could.

His blood flowed and his muscles burned. He played until sweat dripped off him into puddles on the floor. The fire of exertion spread through his body, replacing tension with oxygen. It felt good. After a half hour of non-stop drumming, he finally relaxed enough to sleep.

He went to the master bedroom, pulled off his soaked shirt and used it to wipe the sweat off his face and chest. Then he fell on his back on the bed and closed his eyes. He began to doze almost immediately, but his mind still buzzed. In the fuzzy space between sleep and dreaming, flickering images appeared and disappeared.

A building with empty windows floated on the screen of his inner vision. A large flock of black birds flew in and out of the windows. The building slowly changed shape and became a skull. Bird wings flapped and scuttled as the flock entered one eye socket and exited from the other. He drifted forward to inhabit the skull. It became his head. He frantically tried to brush the birds away from his eyes.

Someone called his name, and he turned to see Delos standing beside him. She wore a laced-up corset, thong panties, and thigh-high stockings, all in black silk. She balanced on black patent stilettos. Her raven curls were piled high, and her lips were lacquered fire engine red. She smiled at him, displaying her white, pointed teeth. She touched her tongue delicately to the point of one canine.

"Dean, don't you know? Souls never die," she said with mocking laugh. She turned and bent over. She wiggled her ass at him and looked back over her shoulder, still smiling. "Take the ride, handsome," she coaxed. "But look before you leap."

Every artery and vein in his body pounded with blood. He grabbed her around the waist and pulled her against him. Delos laughed and rubbed her backside against his groin. He snarled with lust. His inner vision turned scarlet red, and flashes of fiery light burned his eyes. No question in his mind that he would take her right then, but the scene had already begun to fade. She turned to grey mist in his hands and disappeared.

He sat up on his bed, confused and agitated, heart pounding. He stared around the room and barely recognized it. The details of the dream were so vivid, and he still felt that grip of desire. He went into the bathroom, turned the shower on cold, and soaked himself until he shivered. The stinging cold water hit his skin like needles.

"What the hell, Dean," he muttered. "You haven't had that kind of dream since high school."

His head cleared, but his body remained on high alert. All this tension would fuel the evening show. He would bang the hell out of the drums tonight. And then he was going after Delos.

Chapter 12: The Listener

"Heat lightning," Gem grumbled to Dora. "I've never seen so much heat lightning. Someone is trying to block my sight." Dora offered a sympathetic whine and bumped Gem's leg with her rump.

Gem and Dora stood on a rocky promontory at the top of Oat Mountain, with a view over the San Fernando Valley and the Santa Susana Mountains. Thick clumps of grey cloud hung low over LA as dusk overcame day. The warm, humid air sizzled and flashed gold above the cloud cover, arcing from horizon to horizon like a strobe light. At this hour on a Sunday night, they were alone at the mountain top.

"We must seek the breach in the Astral."

Gem sat with Dora beside her on a flat slab of rock. She hummed and then sang her song out loud. Air currents synchronized with her. Lightning in the sky flashed faster.

Both Gem and Dora separated from their physical bodies and rose into astral consciousness. The sudden bright light of the astral sun blinded Gem for a moment before her sight sharpened.

In a moment, she and Dora were walking in a desert of orange-gold sand dunes under a sapphire blue sky. Not a figure, not a plant or structure broke the outline of the rolling sands. The light pulsed, and a wind whistled lightly. Gem watched and listened, humming along with the wind. Dora hummed too, low in her throat, almost a growl but not quite.

In the distance, a cloud of red smoke moved erratically over the sand. As it got closer, the cloud sprouted a pair of legs and feet. The feet were running. Hands emerged from the cloud and tried to bat away the smoke. The cloud whimpered, and a head of blonde hair emerged.

The Listener is here. What is she doing here?

Gem blew a flurry of snowflakes at the red smoke swirling around the frantic girl. The smoke complained as it scattered. Willet ran faster. When she eluded the cloud, Gem hit the smoke with a blast of ice breath and froze it.

Willet collapsed at Gem's feet, sobbing and gasping for breath. She rolled on her back. Her labored breathing turned into a hacking cough.

Gem knelt beside her and turned her onto her side. She pounded firmly between the shoulder blades with the heel of her hand. Willet coughed from deep in her lungs. Red smoke belched out of her mouth like a dust cloud. Gem blew the cloud away.

"The smoke tried to suffocate me," Willet panted between deep, labored breaths. "It followed me wherever I ran."

Slowly, Willet caught her breath, and the heaving of her shoulders eased. She noticed Dora and looked up at Gem, squinting into the sun.

"What are *you* doing here? What is this place?" she asked.

Gem sat down on the sand. "This is Behove, the astral desert. How did *you* get here?"

"I don't know. I went to sleep, in my bedroom. The red smoke covered my face. Voices screamed at me, the usual. I got out of bed and jumped out the window, but the smoke followed me. Red Souls were trying to kill me again."

"You had the dream before?"

"Yes." Willet pulled herself up to a sitting posture. "The smoke attacks me, tries to get in my head. I hate this dream."

"So, change it."

Willet frowned. "How do I do that?"

"Chant the words I taught you. Visualize another outcome."

Willet picked up a handful of orange sand and watched it pour through her fingers. "It can't be that easy."

"It requires practice."

"Am I dreaming now?"

"Yes."

"So, this isn't real."

"It is a real place on the Astral Plane. You came here in the dream state, in your astral body."

"Are you dreaming too?"

Gem slowly shook her head. "No. I am not."

Willet stared out at the open desert. Gem crooked a finger under her chin and turned her head to look in her eyes. "What did you hear when Red Souls screamed at you?"

Willet pulled her chin away, her eyes dull. "I don't want to talk about it. I'm tired."

"What did you hear, Baby Girl?" Gem persisted gently. "I need to know."

Willet lifted her shoulders and let them fall. "They said, 'Kill the Listener.' They say that a lot."

Gem exhaled a long breath through pursed lips. "So that is how it is. You are not safe here."

"What's that pounding sound? It's coming from under the ground."

"It is the sound of Souls in torment beating on the door of the Underworld."

Willet yawned and closed her eyes. "I feel so tired, but I'm afraid to sleep."

The wind picked up, scattering sand. Gem stood and spread her skirt to shelter Willet from the flying grit. "Chant with me," she said. "Surround yourself with light." She hummed in a light, pure tone. "Huuuu. Huuuu."

Willet chanted with her. Threads of red smoke escaped her mouth as she sang. She lay down on her side, pillowing her head on her hands. "I'll just rest a minute…" The light around Willet briefly glowed pink, then faded. Her astral body disappeared with a twinkle.

Gem rose and turned to Dora. "Very well, my dear, time to dig him up. We need to have a little chat."

Dora sniffed the sand, nudging into it with her nose. She ran from spot to spot, then stopped and started digging. Her front paws spun through the sand like high-speed land movers, digging deeper and deeper. She stopped, staring down into the pit she had dug.

"Jat the Deceiver," Gem called out. "You are summoned."

The ground rumbled, and a geyser of black smoke erupted from the pit. A plume of flame followed the smoke. Gem and Dora jumped

119

back to avoid the scorching air. A wavering face within the flame opened a grotesquely wide mouth and began to speak.

"Do I have your attention, Guardian?"

"You inflame the souls of the underworld with your own dark thoughts. You foment a frenzy that cannot be allowed to reach the physical world."

"The earth will feel the heat of my breath, the heel of my foot. Those of my kind will escape the hell to which you have condemned us."

Gem sniffed. "I condemn no one. Your hell is of your own making."

"We will return to the world from which we came! We will tear the Gate to shreds. Surely you have seen the evidence of my power."

"If you mean the heat lightning, it did not impress me."

The wide mouth grinned with malice. "Liar. It obscured your sight. You will never see us coming, where we break through the Gate, or when. Your city will be reduced to ash and dust. This I vow."

Gem shook her head. "Why do we repeat this same conversation? I always find you."

The flame rose twenty feet high and curled toward Gem's face, looking at her eye to eye. "Do not attempt to lecture me, pup! "I am older than your city. I create my own light. Remember my fire. It will consume you and all you protect."

"You deceive yourself," she replied calmly. "Your light is but a shadow of the light of Spirit."

Gem's mouth filled with ice balls. She huffed them into the towering flame. The flame sizzled, quickly curling backwards to a safer distance.

"That is your pathetic response?" Jat laughed. "The High One loses power over the earth. The Gate that keeps us out is already riddled with desperate emotion. It will inevitably fall."

"The Gate between worlds must stand. Such is the will of the All-in-All." Gem gathered her breath again, tasting the freeze in her mouth. Ice filled her throat. She showered a frozen rain at the flame that steamed as it hit. The flame sparked wildly and shrunk back into the pit, leaving black smoke drifting in the air.

The voice echoed from deep underground. "You and your hellhound will not stop us. We will destroy your Listener, your Traveler, and your Ring Thrower. You, most of all, will suffer, Guardian. This I vow."

"Your bluster is pointless," Gem replied firmly. "You will not block the Guardian's sight. And you will not harm the Listener. This *I* vow." She threw her head back, inhaled deeply, and drew all the escaping smoke and steam into a dense cloud in the sky over head. She blew hail into the cloud, seeding it with moisture. It grew dark and heavy. Rain began to fall into the open pit, starting as a downpour and increasing to a flood. The sand saturated and puddled. Rainwater collected in the pit and kept falling as anguished voices below ground wailed, their fires doused.

Dora howled at the sky and danced circles in the rain. She turned her rump to the pit and used her hind legs to kick heavy wet sand into it, refilling the pit as quickly as she had dug it. She stepped all over it to pat it down firmly.

"The sand will bake dry under the desert heat, their fires will start again, and the attacks will resume. Let us see what damage has been done to the Gate."

Gem and Dora stood together and returned to their bodies on the mountain. The heat lightening had eased, giving them a clear view of the sky. The Astral Gate looked as if it had been chewed by wild animals, punctured and shredded. "It will take much breath to repair it, Dora. No time for sleep."

Dora dropped her head on Gem's knee. They would work through it together, as they always did.

*****

Willet floated between worlds surrounded by a halo of golden light. Red smoke swirled around her and tried unsuccessfully to pierce the halo. Screams of frustration emanated from the smoke. She smiled blissfully and ignored them until she fell into her sleeping body with a thud that woke her. Her protective bubble popped. Suddenly, every cell of her body was on fire. She sat up and put her hands over her eyes. Her eyeballs felt hot, and her throat burned.

She bolted to the bathroom and switched on the light. Standing over the sink, she coughed into it, and pulled her eyelids wide open to check her eyes in the mirror. An oily red film swam over the surfaces. She fumbled for eye drops in the cabinet and squeezed the bottle into her upturned eyes. Drops of liquid cooled the surfaces for a moment. It penetrated into the vitreous fluid of her eyes, but the burning returned. The pupils only seemed to glow redder.

"What is going on?" she whispered to herself. Her hands were shaking, and her legs felt like rubber. She wobbled into the bedroom and sat on the bed. The clock showed "6:30", almost time for her daily ride to Dean's house. But the Red Souls wouldn't leave her alone. Their voices screamed in her ears.

She recalled the desert dreamscape. Gem told her something important. Chant and change the dream, that's what Gem had said. Willet sat straight, planted her feet on the floor and folded her hands in her lap. She closed her eyes and chanted the word Gem had taught her. Breathe in, breathe out and chant. The urge to cough challenged her concentration. She cleared her throat numerous times. Panic set in, but finally she let it go with each exhale, and visualized a curtain of golden light wrapped around her like a cloak.

Red Souls battled for her attention. They squealed, a sound high-pitched and sharp as a knife. She flinched and her light cloak fell away. They buzzed like wasps, so close to her eardrums that she worried they would sting. She focused her attention, exhaled panic and raised the curtain again. The angry sounds had begun to recede. For a few precious minutes she enjoyed quiet, but not for long.

Audrey knocked sharply on her bedroom door. "Will, I've got that client meeting at ten thirty. Need to get going. I hope you're up."

"Yes, I'm up." Willet shook herself "Be there in a sec."

They met in the driveway. Audrey stowed her laptop and briefcase in the trunk of the sedan with brisk efficiency. Willet caught her casting a wistful eye at the Porsche parked near the sedan and knew Audrey would love to be driving that car instead.

Audrey squinted at her. "What's with the shades? It's a little early in the day, isn't it?"

"I had a headache this morning," Willet replied defensively. "I'm trying to fight it without meds."

"Okay, just wondering. No need to snap."

"I didn't snap, and I can decide when to wear what, thank you." The heat rose in Willet's voice. She pressed her headphones tighter to her ears.

Audrey raised both hands in surrender. "Sure, okay, no problem. Let's go."

The ride to the coast calmed Willet. Eyes closed behind big sunglasses, she crossed arms over her stomach, breathing steadily. She sensed Audrey's glance at her from time to time but said nothing. She needed to concentrate on the curtain of light around her, muffling the persistent voices.

When they reached Manhattan Beach, Audrey gave her a hard stare. "Are you going to be okay at Dean's today? You don't seem yourself."

"I'm perfectly myself."

"Is something wrong?"

"Nothing is wrong."

Audrey stopped the sedan in front of Dean's house, the motor idling. "Call me if you need anything."

"I'll be fine."

Willet felt guilty for the way she spoke to Audrey, but she didn't need coddling, thank you very much. She got out of the car, swung the door shut behind her and walked to the house without looking back.

*****

As soon as Willet walked into Dean's house, she dropped her glasses and bags on the floor, closed the door, went into the bathroom and peered at her eyes in the mirror. They were still flaming red. She repeated her chant silently the entire ride from Hemmings, keeping herself wrapped in light as best she could. It seemed to help.

She walked back to the hallway and gathered her things, not sure what to do with herself. Usually, she would head for the piano, but not today. She headed for the kitchen and checked the refrigerator – nothing appealed to her. In the freezer, she found a container of chocolate ice cream, already open. Ice cream for breakfast sounded just fine. She scooped some into a bowl and found a spoon, and then stared out the window without seeing anything and swallowed spoonful after spoonful. The icy sweetness soothed her throat. After a minute, she looked down at the empty bowl and frowned. "What am I doing? Ice cream upsets my stomach."

Her phone buzzed. She hoped Audrey wasn't checking up on her. She pulled the phone from her bag and looked at the number. TJ. Suddenly, every nerve in her body sparked. When she clicked on, his voice sounded mellow as honey.

"Hey girl, I'm in Manhattan Beach. Are you up for a walk?"

"A walk, God yes, I'd love a walk. The walls are closing in on me."

"Really. Well, the ocean beckons. I'll be there in a few minutes."

The few minutes felt like an eternity to Willet. She returned to the bathroom to brush teeth and comb hair, apply a little mascara. She stood in the hallway, tapped her foot and jogged in place. When he finally knocked, she had to restrain herself from running to answer it. Gathering her poise, she approached the door with measured steps and opened it sedately. There he stood.

"Hey, babe. You ready?" He flashed his wide grin.

She melted under the warmth of it and tried not to gawk. His surfer physique filled a white T-shirt and cut-off jeans with long, lean muscles. His blonde hair looked wind-blown. His eyes were the color of the Pacific Ocean, like a god of sun and sea. Blood flooded her cheeks and proceeded to other parts of her body. She swallowed hard and asked in a breathy voice, "Did you go surfing this morning?"

"Yeah, the waves were choice at Lunada Bay." He peered at her and frowned. "Why are your eyes so red?"

She had forgotten about her eyes. "They were sore when I woke up," she mumbled, embarrassed. "I tried eye drops."

"If I didn't know better, I'd say you've been smoking pot."

She snickered in spite of herself. "I don't do drugs. I've got enough problems as it is."

"So, let's get some fresh air."

She continued to stand and stare, not moving.

He took her shoulders and shook them gently. "What's wrong?"

She stepped closer to him, put her arms around his neck, and pressed her lips to his. She pressed her chest against his chest, pressed the length of her body against him. She closed her eyes and let the strong feel of him soak into her like steam heat. His arms slid around her waist, pulling her even closer. He returned a deeper kiss before he pulled back from her and smiled.

"Does this mean we're not walking?"

"We'll walk, eventually. Right now, there are other things we could do…" She stepped back, took his hands in hers and walked backward, pulling him until they reached a doorway. She led him inside the room and wrapped her arms around him again. "Does this room have a bed in it?" she whispered between kisses. "I couldn't see."

"This is Dean's bedroom."

"Would he mind if we borrowed it?"

TJ disentangled himself from her arms and stepped away, removing his lips from hers after snatching a few more quick kisses. "As interesting as it would be to explain this to Dean, I don't think he'd appreciate it. Let's reconsider."

He grabbed her by the waist and almost carried her out of the bedroom to the hall. He pinned her against the wall and rubbed his lips lightly on her cheek and neck. She groaned softly. He looked directly in her eyes. "I don't know what's gotten into you, and your eyes are kind of freaky. I like this vibe, but I'd want you at my place, so I can entertain you properly."

She giggled. "Can we get there in five seconds?"

"No, we'd have to plan ahead."

"Like a date?"

"Yes, a date."

"I bet you'd be a good date."

"I'm pretty good at it, so I've been told."

They stood smiling at each other. She basked in the warmth of his smile. The thought of losing that warmth suddenly made her sad. "I've never felt this way before, Thomas," she said softly. "I don't know what I'm doing, but I know I want you. I feel like I'm gonna jump out of my skin."

He kissed her forehead gently and winked. "My animal magnetism finally got to you, eh? It happens."

"There are extenuating circumstances. It's difficult to explain."

His smile turned quizzical. "Try."

"I've been having the same dream over and over. I had it last night. I dream that Red Souls are trying to suffocate me. Their smoke gets in my face. I think my eyes are red this morning because I breathed so much of it. Gem says they stir up emotions when they get inside people. Whatever I feel is more intense than normal."

"Ah, yes, Gem. I should have known she's behind this. You and Dean are drinking the same Kool-Aid."

"Gem helps me fight the smoke. She helped me last night, in the astral desert."

TJ stared at her, smile fading and held her at arm's length. "Smoke in the astral desert? You're scaring me, Will."

The chasm that opened between them twisted her stomach into an anxious knot and sucked breath from her lungs. She clutched her hands together, resisting the urge to pull him back to her.

"I know it sounds nuts, but it's true. I fight them, and they attack me even harder."

"Why would anyone want to suffocate you?"

"Because I hear what they're saying, what they're planning. We can stop them from doing bad things, Gem and me, because I hear them." She was desperate to make him understand.

"So, you want me because smoke is in your head."

"I want you just because you're you. But now, I'm practically frantic with wanting you. I can't tell if it's a natural reaction or if I'm influenced by *them*. I'm sorry. I know that sounds lame."

"It sounds like you're saying the devil made you do it."

"It's not the devil. I don't think. Gem never calls them 'the devil.'"

TJ snorted in disgust and walked to the front door. "Will. You're an intelligent woman. You can't really believe this stuff."

"I don't believe. I've experienced it. I know."

He opened the door and glanced back at her. "I'm going to the beach. Are you coming?"

She found her headphones and keys and followed him to the door. When they walked into the sun, she reached for his hand. He gave her a side glance, and took the hand she offered, shaking his head. The knot in her stomach eased.

Chapter 13: About Gem

Dean had a show at Club TJ on Thursday night, so Audrey volunteered to help out on the next lookout run. She drove Willet into the city in their sedan.

"How'd you manage to ride in that Jeep last time?" Audrey asked.

"I turned the white noise up on my headphones, did my contemplation exercises. Then I got sick."

"We can avoid *that*, at least. I brought anti-nausea meds."

"Thanks, Mom."

"The sarcasm is getting old, Will. Gem's a bad influence."

"That's so not true! Why do people keep saying that about her?"

"What people?"

"You. TJ."

"Ah. TJ sees it too."

"Not everything about me has to do with Gem. I've got my own concerns."

"Yeah, I think I'm aware of that."

Willet bristled. "I told you. Red Souls have been attacking me. They're trying to kill me in my sleep."

"No wonder you've been grumpy. Did you eat something weird before you went to bed?"

"It's not indigestion!" Willet's voice rose. "I couldn't breathe. They tried to *smother* me with *smoke*. Do you get that?"

"Okay, I'm sorry. But dreams can't kill you for real."

"Gasping for air felt pretty real. My throat was sore when I woke up."

Audrey stared out the windshield. "These lookouts are dangerous. Whatever you're hearing is affecting your mental and physical health."

"That's what I've been telling you."

"No need to snap."

"I didn't snap."

The sisters reached the city center meeting spot, a parking lot on Alameda Boulevard, and found Gem's Jeep. Gem's long skirt of black, purple and white swirled out of the front seat. Willet had told her Audrey would ride along, but her eyebrows still rose. She appraised Audrey.

"You could hinder us if you're not positive. I need to know we have your support."

Audrey restrained a hot response. "I'm concerned about my sister. I don't want anything to happen to her, or to anyone else, for that matter. That's the extent of my commitment."

"The forces we deal with are very unpredictable. I make no guarantees."

"I don't expect them, and I don't want to interfere with your...work. I just want to make sure Willet is protected."

"And who will protect you?"

"I can take care of myself."

"You do not understand the nature of the challenges we face."

Before the conversation deteriorated into a tit for tat, Audrey reined in her emotions and attempted a detente. "Gem, I don't want to fight with you. I'm actually curious about what you do and how you do it. Will's welfare is my concern, of course, but I'm not here to hinder you in any way. If I can help, I will."

Gem eyed her, and then nodded. "Very well, we drive through East LA tonight. Your sister heard chatter suggesting the Souls have an entry to the physical plane in that area. We must find it and close it."

133

Since Dora always travelled with Gem, they had to take the Jeep. Willet got in the passenger seat, and Gem sat in back with Dora. Audrey took the wheel.

"Why are we doing this at night?" Audrey asked. "Isn't it more dangerous?"

"Sometimes it is necessary. We have the cover of darkness if we need to take action. Two blonde gringas in East LA might attract unwanted attention."

They headed east on Rosa Parks Freeway, speeding through a blur of headlights and road lights. Gem looked out the window and scanned the skies. Willet sat silently, eyes shut, listening for voices. It wasn't long before she asked for the anti-nausea meds.

Audrey pulled off the freeway and drove west on Cesar Chavez Avenue, while Gem and Willet discussed what they saw and heard. Angry voices rose from down the street. Gem directed Audrey to turn left toward Obregon Park. The closer they got to it, the louder the voices became. Audrey pulled up to the curb. The park was decorated for a party, with colored lanterns and streamers hung and tables laden with food but clearly, something had gone horribly wrong. People yelled at each other, and punches were thrown. Gem quickly climbed out of the Jeep.

Audrey rolled down her window. "Where are you going?" she exclaimed. "You'll get us killed!"

The red smoke swirling through the park could not be ignored, even though Audrey and Willet couldn't see it. Gem let a freezing breath loose in one long, sweeping gust. The red smoke blew to the far side of the park, swirled upwards and disappeared. It left behind a field of weary, battered fighters, wondering what had just happened.

Audrey watched as Gem expelled breath through pursed lips. "What are you doing?" she asked.

Gem swept another long, frigid blast across the fighters. Those still moving stopped in their tracks. Some dropped to the ground and passed out.

She searched the skies for signs of a breach in the Astral Gate. After a thorough scan, she returned to the Jeep. "The Gate is intact. Red Souls came from somewhere else. That is troubling."

"What are you talking about? What gate?"

"I am talking about the Gate which separates our world from the Astral Underworld. I believe we have discussed this before. The Souls' point of entry is somewhere else. We must find it."

"That's it?" Willet asked incredulously. "We're not doing anything? People are bleeding. We need to call an ambulance!"

"Sirens indicate the authorities have been notified," Gem replied. "Our work here is done."

Audrey grumbled about *gates* and *souls* and *insanity,* put the Jeep in gear and headed back toward the freeway. She decided to get a few questions answered. "You talk a lot about the astral plane? Is that where, uh, departed people go?"

"Not all. Some souls linger here, not ready to give up their physical existence, and some go to other planes."

The direct answer surprised Audrey. "I could, maybe, accept life after death, in principle, but I have no evidence."

Gem nodded. "You are right to be skeptical. Blind believers can be led like sheep. Seek your own experiences of Spirit. It is the only way to know truth."

The LA night whizzed by outside as they entered the freeway. Willet had her own questions. "How did you learn to do what you do?" she asked. "Did you have a teacher?"

"I did go to the University, so I have had many teachers, but Augustus has been my spiritual teacher since I was a child. Those of his Circle learn to travel the higher worlds in full consciousness."

"Does Augustus teach somewhere in LA?"

"Augustus is very old. He is no longer corporeal."

Audrey could not restrain a short laugh. "So... he's a ghost."

"Not a ghost, no," Gem said simply. "He resides on the astral plane now."

"You say that like he retired to Florida."

"Augustus guarded the Astral Gate in Imperial Rome. Brutality and passion of the Romans tore the Astral Wall apart, and he watched the city fall to invaders. Since then, he has trained students to guard the cities of earth, so civilizations can be protected from their own worst impulses."

"There are other Guardians?"

"Yes, most large cities have one, and some smaller places."

"I'd like to study with a teacher like Augustus," Willet said.

Gem stroked Dora's smooth head for a moment, looking into her brown eyes. "Augustus meets with his students on the astral plane. Anyone who wishes to study with him must be able to travel there."

Audrey bristled with exasperation. "See, this is too much. You expect us to believe a guy from the Roman Empire is still around, teaching school? That's absurd."

136

Gem shrugged. "It is true, nonetheless."

"How long have you studied with him?" Willet interrupted. "Maybe I could too."

Gem turned toward the window. "Augustus chooses his students, not vice versa."

"Sorry," Willet said gently. "I don't mean to pry. I'd just like to know more about your life."

"These questions do not help with our task," Gem said, but relented with a sigh.

"At a young age, I could travel out of my body, but only during sleep. When I turned twelve, a man walked through the wall of my bedroom. He glowed like a star. He took my hand and pulled me out of my physical body into full astral consciousness. We floated through my window into a beautiful garden full of palm trees and tropical flowers, such as I had never seen before. I still recall the sweet ginger scent of it. A group of people stood waiting. Augustus introduced me to the Circle. I have been a part of it ever since."

Audrey shook her head, eyes rolling. "I can't believe I'm listening to this."

Gem withdrew from the conversation, turning to watch the skies outside her window. "No more questions now."

Silence fell again, and then suddenly Willet sat straight up in her seat. "I hear voices."

"You hear voices all the time," Audrey said. "What's new?"

"Red Soul voices are different. They vibrate and kind of buzz above the other voices. Sometimes they grumble, sometimes they whisper, and then they scream."

137

"What are they saying?" Gem demanded.

"Sounds like 'Burn it down'."

"What does that mean?" Audrey looked at Gem in the rearview mirror.

Willet rocked slightly with eyes closed. "I hear another voice talking. It's familiar. It's…Dean. She opened her eyes and looked at Audrey. "What the hell. He's saying either 'Get it' or 'Get her'. What is he talking about?"

"I'm sure he doesn't mean that literally," Audrey said.

"Where is he?" Gem demanded.

"Club TJ. He'd never hurt anyone at the club."

"We must go," Gem said.

"We're going to West Hollywood now, seriously?" Audrey's voice rose.

A 'hurumpf' was all that came from Gem in the back seat.

*****

Audrey stepped on it, and they sped in the direction of the Club. The Jeep handled like a dream, moving through traffic and riding the drafts as if it had a gear that other cars didn't have.

A suspicion nagged at Audrey, wondering if Gem could have something to do with it. She looked into the rearview. "This Jeep is amazing," she remarked, "like it has a mind of its own." She got no reaction from Gem.

When they reached TJ's, Audrey screeched to a halt at the curb a block away. She and Gem jumped out, leaving Willet in the car with Dora, and hurried toward the music.

Inside the space in front of the stage undulated with heated bodies, arms waving and fists pumping the air. Shock Value had started its first set. The crowd moved in sync with Dean's relentless drumming.

Audrey and Gem climbed the stairs to the balcony overlooking the stage. It was packed up there. They elbowed their way to the railing to get a better look. The band members were thrashing their instruments into sonic frenzy. At the foot of the stage, a girl with curly raven hair shook and shimmied, waving her arms above her head. Delos.

Sweat dripped from Dean's temples and chin. Drops flew from his arms and drumsticks as he pounded the drums. Dean and Delos seemed to be laser-locked in eye contact. Audrey felt an unexpected sting at the attention he paid her.

Gem drew in a sharp breath and whispered in Audrey's ear. "Red Souls circle him like a funnel cloud. He is definitely in trouble."

"You mean he's possessed by demons??" Audrey whispered. "Does he need an exorcism?"

"Possessed by strong emotions that are not strictly his own. He needs to be reminded that he still chooses his own thoughts before he does something he'll regret."

Audrey snorted. "Delos would be happy to help him along, from what I see."

"Delos simply responds to the energy he exudes. She doesn't know it isn't really his. You might be able to help him get in touch with himself again. He has feelings for you."

Audrey wondered what it would be like to have the fire of his gaze turned on her, so direct and hungry. She shivered, imagining how it would feel to meet it head on.

Gem whispered again. "Astral smoke is swirling through the room and up to the rafters. That is not a good sign."

Audrey stared at the ceiling. "I can't see anything. What do we do?"

"This crowd must leave the club before anyone gets hurt."

The band wrapped up the first set with a final flurry of drums and screeching guitar. Dean climbed down from his drum set and received a high-five from Foster, the lead guitarist, who shook his head and said, "What the hell, man. What's got into you tonight?" Dean just smirked. He headed for the exit at the back of the stage. Delos wiggled out of her position at front stage and tried to follow him. Club bouncers blocked her, so she weaved through the crowd to the exit.

"Delos followed him. We must reach him first," said Gem. She headed for the stairs.

Audrey didn't know what they were supposed to do, or what Gem expected to happen, but she trailed her down the stairs. They found Delos with the band in the area behind the club where band members went to relax between sets. Snead and Alfonso, the base and rhythm guitarists, were having a smoke. Dean already had Delos in a lip-lock, his arm wrapped tight around her shoulders. He looked up when Audrey and Gem approached, and his eyes shot open. He broke away from Delos and looked from Audrey to Gem to Delos and back to Audrey, in confusion.

"Uh, hi Audrey, Gem, what are you doing here?"

Delos whirled around. Her eyes narrowed to slits when she saw Audrey. "Yeah, what are you doing here?"

"We need to speak to you, Dean. Please. It will just take a moment," Audrey said, trying to ignore Delos.

"This isn't the best time," he mumbled. "Got the gig and all. Could we talk later?"

Gem stepped up to him. "Dean, it is important we speak to you now. Is there somewhere private we could go?"

Delos went to Dean's side, sliding her arms around his waist and pressing herself against him. "Me and Dean are busy now. Right, baby?"

Dean looked down at her, plunged his right hand into the mass of her curls, pulled her head back and kissed her hard on the mouth. "Yeah, busy," he growled.

Delos arched her back and purred deep in her throat.

Gem stepped closer to him, tapped his left arm. "Dean. This is not you. Red Souls have taken you."

Dean stood straighter, pulled his arm back and stared at Gem. "What do you mean? I know who I am. What's your problem?"

"That day at the office building, you were not fully protected. Come with us now, and I will show you how to free yourself of negative influence."

Delos laughed derisively. "Dean's not under any influence but mine."

Dean looked down at Delos again, then at Audrey, confusion in his eyes. "I don't know what you're saying," he said.

"Please, Dean," Audrey said. "Come with us. We want to help you." She walked to him and gently took his left hand in hers. He dropped his hold on Delos.

"He's not yours," snarled Delos, slapping at Audrey's hand.

Dean pushed Delos away. "I'm not yours, either."

141

Gem spoke carefully to Delos. "You are not safe with him, Delos. Dean is under compulsion. Let us help him, and then he can make his own decisions where you are concerned. The forces that attack him can attack you too."

Delos backed off from Dean, rubbing the arm he had pushed away. She glowered. "Whatever. But that wench has no claim," she pouted, pointing at Audrey.

"I have things to do, Delos," Gem said. "These other issues are your own."

Dean pulled his hand from Audrey's grasp. "The second set is about to start. I can't go anywhere right now. Whatever this is will have to wait 'til after the show."

He waved to Snead and Alfonso, who were watching from a distance with puzzled expressions. Dean headed back to the club, and they followed.

Delos wrapped one of her curls around her index finger and smiled a sour smile at Audrey. "You can't stop it, ya know. He's so hot for me, he can't see straight."

"He does not see you at all," Gem said. "Red Souls have blinded him."

"I want Dean. I've always wanted him. Now he wants me too. Deal with it." Delos turned and stalked out of the back yard, disappeared down the dark street.

Gem watched her go. "If she finds him first, it may be difficult to divert his attention again."

Gem and Audrey walked back to the Jeep to check on Willet who was sitting in the front seat with her lips moving and her eyes closed.

142

Dora sat behind her on the back seat, watching the rocking movements with rapt attention.

Gem opened the driver door. "Tell me."

Willet shook herself. "'Red Souls burn," she whispered. "And hiss."

Gem turned quickly and looked back at Club TJ. "The Gate here is wavering, on the verge of breaking. We will not have much warning if it does. Audrey, you know the club owner. Alert him to the possibility of a fire. Tell him to clear the club. I will watch Dean." Gem headed for the front door of the club.

"Auddie, I don't want to stay here by myself," Willet pleaded. "This neighborhood gives me the creeps."

Audrey recognized the breathiness in her sister's voice. Her sickly pale complexion said full-on migraine. "You know TJ better than I do. Come with me. I don't think I can tell him to clear his club with a straight face."

"I've got a migraine."

Audrey pulled out the pillbox and placed a white tablet in her sister's hand.

Willet swallowed it and got out of the Jeep with headphones pressed to her ears. "Thomas already thinks I'm crazy," she grumbled. "This will confirm it."

Chapter 14: Warnings

TJ stood in the doorway of his office listening to the club action. The wood paneled walls vibrated visibly as the bass guitar and drums pounded. The band sure cooked tonight and the crowd loved them. Soon, everyone would be thirsty, lining up at the bar during the break. It warmed his capitalist heart.

He wanted to open a new club in a more prominent neighborhood with Shock Value as the house band. The property on Santa Monica Boulevard would be perfect, great exposure for the band, and he'd get a building in a prime location that would pay for itself. The current owner bargained like an amateur, but TJ had an experienced negotiator on his side. He turned to look at the man sitting in an office chair in front of his desk, real estate attorney extraordinaire, Matt Gregg.

TJ knew Matt from law school. They invested in real estate together - malls, condos, offices – and put together an enviable portfolio. Despite the faded jeans, Shock Value T-shirt, and longish brown hair, Matt made deals like a shark. He was well-connected in LA real estate and somehow knew about hot properties before they came on the market. If anyone could pry the Santa Monica property out of the owner's hands, Matt could.

"So, what kind of pressure can we exert on Mr. Alessio?" TJ asked.

Matt tilted back in his chair, hands behind his head.

"He says he has two competing offers, but I don't believe him. He's got one tentative from Kalvin Co. Not sure how committed they are to the purchase. Alessio's secretary told me they're meeting at the end of the week to discuss a bid. I'd like to be a fly on the wall at that meeting. We'd know what kind of terms they're proposing."

144

"Alessio needs to unload the place," TJ replied. "He can't afford the property taxes on an empty building. If we knew the bid, we could slide in with a better offer while the property is still in pre-market limbo. Once it goes on the open market, someone will outbid us for sure."

A sharp rap on the outside door interrupted their meeting. TJ got up and opened it, found Audrey and Willet standing in the doorway. He started in surprise.

"Thomas, we have something important to tell you," Willet said in a fluttering breath.

TJ stepped back and waved them in, turning to his attorney. "Matt, these are the du Place sisters, Audrey and Willet. They wouldn't be here if it wasn't VERY important," he glared at them. "Ladies, this is Matt Gregg, my attorney."

Matt appraised them. "The sisters du Place. TJ has mentioned you. Glad to finally meet you."

Audrey gave a brief nod and quickly turned to TJ. "Willet has something to tell you," she announced, and then stepped back with a wave of her hand at her sister.

Willet dropped onto the couch and pressed fingers against her temples, taking long breaths until she composed herself. "There's a possibility of fire in the club. You should evacuate the building immediately."

TJ laughed. "Evacuate the club? You're joking! The place is packed. We'd have to refund everyone's money!"

"I'm not joking," she muttered. She laid elbows on her knees, and let her head hang toward the floor.

TJ gave her an uncertain look. "Is this one of your – do you *hear* a fire starting somewhere?"

Willet sat up and shrugged weary shoulders. "Thomas, you need to trust me here. It's difficult to explain. You may not have a lot of time."

"It *may* start? I'm supposed to evacuate 300 paying customers for something that *may* happen? When will you know if it *will* happen?"

"It depends on Dean. Like I said, it's hard to explain. We're going with Gem's guidance on this."

Matt stood up from behind the desk and cleared his throat. "Are you saying Dean Simmons is planning to commit arson? I'm an officer of the court. I'd be duty-bound to report that if it comes to pass."

"Of course not," Audrey snapped at him. "Dean's not going to set a fire." She turned to TJ. "Willet heard something indicating fire. You know how she is. It's best not to ignore it."

"Yeah, I know her." TJ groaned, running his fingers through his hair in frustration. "But this is business."

"The band is on break now," Audrey said. "It's a good time to clear the club. That includes staff. Tell the audience there's a problem with the sound or something, that you have to check the sound system."

"It might be prudent to clear the club, just in case," Matt offered quietly. "A fire would be costly and could damage the club's reputation, not to mention the insurance issues."

TJ hissed a string of expletives through his teeth. As preposterous as it all sounded, he couldn't ignore this kind of warning from Willet. He made a quick decision and went out the door to the club floor.

Audrey and the attorney were left eyeing each other. In the club an announcement blared through the speakers, followed by the sound of feet shuffling off the dance floor. Willet went back to holding her head with eyes closed.

"Don't worry," Matt smiled reassuringly. "No one can hear us. That's why TJ and I meet here. It's virtually impossible to be overheard with all the club noise. So, what's really going on?"

Willet rocked back and forth and started reciting as if from a script. "What kind of pressure can we exert on Mr. Alessio to pry that building out of his hands?" she said in a flat voice. "He says he has two competing offers, but I don't believe him."

Color drained from Matt Gregg's face.

Willet droned on. "I picked up from Alessio's secretary that they're meeting at Alessio's office at the end of the week to discuss a firm bid. I'd like to be a fly on the wall at that meeting."

Matt swallowed hard and cleared his throat again. "Is there a recorder in this room?"

Audrey sat down next to her sister and put an arm around her shoulders. "Will, this is not the time for sound prints."

TJ charged through the office door at that moment, like a bull in front of a red cape. "The club is emptying out. Now what?"

Another knuckle rap hit the back door. TJ pulled it open to find Gem standing there. She looked around him to speak to Audrey and Willet. "Everyone is leaving. Let us find Dean."

"This is your doing," TJ said. "If it turns out to be a hoax, I'll sue you for loss of profits."

Gem eyed him coolly. "Your club is in danger, Mr. Barlow, along with everyone in it. I am sorry to tell you this. I already sense smoke at very low levels."

TJ bristled. "I have smoke detectors installed throughout the club. If there's smoke in the club, an alarm would go off."

"Your detectors will not detect this type of smoke until it is too late. There is smoke in this room right now as a matter of fact. It is circling your head."

Everyone in the room stared at her. Matt squinted at TJ, trying to see the smoke.

"The temperature in the club is rising," she continued. "An electric spark or a gas burner could set off an explosion. I recommend you do not allow people back inside tonight. And everyone in this room should evacuate now."

TJ remembered another unwelcome warning he'd received from a strange woman in his office. He hadn't wanted to believe that warning either, but it saved his life. He couldn't take any chances. "Audrey, please take your sister out to a safe place."

He turned on Gem. "You're a menace. Stay off my property. If I see you here again, I'll have you arrested."

Audrey took Willet's elbow and led her out the door after Gem. TJ and Matt exchanged a glance and started haphazardly collecting papers from the desk and stuffing them into a briefcase. They'd lost control of the insane asylum. In minutes they exited the office.

Chapter 15: Misguided

Despite TJ's warning, Gem confronted him again in front of the club. "People are too close. You must move them away from the building."

The evacuated patrons milled around on the sidewalk near the front door. A few cigarettes were lit. TJ looked like he might object but decided against it. He directed the crowd farther away from the club.

Gem pulled Willet and Audrey across the street. "Listener what do you hear?"

Willet shrugged. "I hear arguing. It's Dean and Delos, in the parking lot. Not difficult to pick that up."

"We need to find them before they start swinging at each other."

Willet pointed down the street. The arguing got louder as they tracked the sound.

Gem advised Audrey and Willet as they walked. "We must not add negativity to the situation. Remain neutral, no matter what happens."

Dean and Delos stood in a circle of yellow-grey light cast from a light pole. Gem motioned to the sisters to stay behind her in the shadows about six feet from the fighting couple.

"I don't have time for you right now, Delos," Dean said loudly. "TJ gave me some BS about a fire, and my second set may not happen. I need to find out what's really going on."

"Baby, we've got time," Delos pleaded, pulling on his arm. "Let's do what we want to do."

Dean clenched and unclenched his fists, and then stepped close to Delos, wrapping his fingers around her neck. "You talk too much, Delos," he snarled. "You're really buggin' me." His fingers tightened.

Delos' eyes got wide. "Dean, baby, you don't mean that." She grabbed his wrists and tried to pull his hands off her neck.

"Oh, but I do. I really, really do," he said as he squeezed.

Gem stepped out of the shadows into the circle of light. "Dean, remember who you are," Gem said quietly.

Dean's head whipped around. "I know who I am," he snapped, but he let his hands drop. "Why do you keep saying that? This is your fault. You stopped my show."

Delos snorted. "Yeah, you interfering pain in the ass. Go away and leave us alone."

"There is smoke in the club. Willet heard voices that lead us to believe a fire is likely. Remember what happened to that office building. Do you want the club to burn down?"

Dean's rigid shoulders dropped from his ears. His eyes darted back to the club.

Audrey and Willet stepped out of the shadows and stood next to Gem.

"Oh, great!" Delos raised her voice and stamped her foot. "Of course they'd be here. Dean, tell them to get lost."

"Don't tell me what to do," he growled at her.

From the circle of light, Audrey stepped closer and extended a hand to Dean. She stood with her hand out, saying nothing. Dean looked at her, at her hand, then walked toward her and took hold of it. She smiled at him, still silent.

"Remember what's important to you," Gem said. "Think of your music and your friends."

Dean's breathing slowed. He looked at Audrey's hand in his. She gently squeezed his hand, and he looked at her. "I want you." He closed his eyes and shook his head. "I don't know why I said that."

"Dean," Audrey answered calmly. "Let's go somewhere to talk."

He opened his eyes and spoke in a low voice. "I need to find TJ."

"Yes," she encouraged him. "Yes, you do. Let's find him now. I know where he is."

She pointed toward the street. He followed her out of the parking lot. Willet went with them, leaving Gem to deal with Delos.

"I'll never forgive you for this," Delos snarled.

"Delos, listen to me. You're surrounded by Red Souls. It clouds your judgment. Let me help you."

Delos looked at her with contempt. "I'm tired of all the Red Souls talk. You're supposed to be my friend, but you didn't take my side. You sided with those women."

"I do not take sides. Let me help you, before it is too late."

Delos pulled a key from her pocket, unlocked the car door next to her, and slid in. Gem watched a haze of red smoke swoop into the car with her. She drove out of the parking lot with squealing tires and flying gravel.

Gem sighed and looked at the Astral Gate over Club TJ. The surface bubbled like a hot stew. It did not bode well. She hoped Audrey could talk Dean down from the emotional cliff he hung on. And now an emotional cyclone spun loose in the world. Delos would have to be found before she got herself into trouble.

*****

Audrey led Dean back to the front of the club. As soon as Dean saw TJ, he went to him and pulled him aside. Their voices rose, hands waved, interruptions flew back and forth. Finally, they shook hands.

After twenty minutes, no fire had started. People stood around, not knowing what to do next. They started to drift away toward the parking lot.

TJ announced that the band would resume their set in ten minutes, now that they had "checked the sound system wiring." He offered a round of beers on the house to everyone returning for the show. A cheer went up, and people rushed back to the front door, the evacuation forgotten.

"What do we do?" Willet asked Gem. "They're going back in the club."

Audrey could not disguise her irritation. "Yeah, what do we do, now that we've wasted our time and everyone else's over a fire that didn't start."

"That's rude!" Willet protested.

"Well, I feel ridiculous. Don't you? We talked your man into emptying his club for no good reason."

"I know what I heard, Audrey. 'Red Souls burn'. The voices mean something."

Gem cleared her throat. The eyes of both sisters flew in her direction. "You two can argue later. The Gate is still unstable. It must be frozen before we leave."

Audrey glared at her. "What does that even mean?"

"The barrier between the astral and physical worlds is failing here. If it breaks, this area will be flooded with negative energy. More than the club will be at risk. Negative emotions must be frozen."

"Well, you do whatever," Audrey said. "I need to get back to my car. I'm going home."

"We will return to the parking lot when our task is done," Gem said. "That is the commitment *you* made." Gem turned toward the Jeep and walked away. Willet followed behind, with Audrey trudging sullenly at the rear.

In the Jeep, Willet settled herself in the back seat took some long breaths. She chanted softly with eyes closed. Audrey looked at Willet and then at Gem. Both of them seemed absorbed by something within. Gem began to chant in a clear voice, "Huuuu. Huuuu," breath slow and measured. Willet joined her.

Audrey wasn't sure what to do with herself, so she closed her eyes and put her head back against the head rest, relaxing her shoulders. Maybe she could grab a quick nap. The sounds of chant were soothing. Her own breath slowed, falling into synchrony with Gem and Willet. She listened to the soft and steady beat of her own breath. *What did Will say about the blank screen between the eyes?*

Audrey looked for it and stared with disinterest. Nothing there except for a sheen on the surface that swirled like oil on water. Maybe some very faint pinks and blues in the oil slick. And a tiny pinprick of light – *where did that come from?*

The light grew bigger, very slowly at first, then faster. The light seemed to move toward her at an accelerating rate of speed. Her heartbeat faster as it flew toward her on a collision course impossible to avoid. Suddenly the light exploded in her field of vision. She opened her eyes, sat up with a gasp and looked around. It was quiet except for Willet's light snoring.

Gem glanced at Audrey and nodded. "Almost there," she said.

Audrey frowned. "What?"

"The tunnel. You were almost through it."

"What tunnel? I wasn't in a tunnel."

"Were you not? The light you saw. Did you think it was it an oncoming train?"

"How'd you know what I saw?"

Gem chuckled. "Just a guess."

Audrey's eyes narrowed in suspicion. "Were you doing something to me? Some kind of mind control?"

"I never interfere with anyone's state of consciousness. That is against spiritual law."

Audrey stared out the window, biting her lip, replaying the experience in her mind. She was sure she hadn't been asleep, but how could it be anything but a dream?

Willet stirred in the back seat. "What's going on?" she asked, groggy with sleep.

Gem started the Jeep and backed out of the parking space. "The Gate is sealed. I will take Audrey back to her car. Your sister wants to leave us."

"You're leaving?" Willet protested. "We're not done!"

"I can't take any more of this," Audrey said. "You should come home with me."

"I'm staying with Gem."

"How will you get home?"

"I'm an adult. I can find a way home."

The sisters turned away from each other and maintained stony silence for the rest of the drive. The Jeep sped toward downtown LA. Audrey studied Gem's profile, swept by lights and shadows. She wondered, not for the first time, if Gem was dangerous. Gem glanced at her at that moment and gave her an odd smile. *Did she know what I was thinking?*

*****

Gem dropped Audrey off at her car, and then she and Willet went off to find Delos. Gem knew where Delos lived. They drove by, but the house was dark. Dora needed a walk, so they headed for Poinsettia Park.

They parked on the street and walked onto a wide expanse of grass in front of a stand of trees. Sleepy birds chirped as they settled down for the night and small animals skittered in the brush. A cool breeze rustled the leaves and rushed through the scrub oaks and purple-flowered jacarandas. The air was fragrant with the moist breath of green plants.

Willet felt comfortable enough to take her headphones off and let nature's quiet soothe her. She rolled her neck and shoulders, took some long breaths and turned to Gem. "Are the Red Souls, like, a cold or flu? Will they just go away after a while?"

Gem chuckled. "They do not leave willingly. Anger is an intoxicating emotion, especially when combined with lust. It is easy to incite violence in a human being who has those inclinations. Once it begins, the Souls have established a hold on consciousness and are very difficult to remove."

"It's like a disease, then."

"It is always a matter of choice."

"If it's a choice, then what can you do about it?"

"I freeze negative emotions. It gives a person a moment to make a different choice."

"What about free will?"

"I do not interfere in the free will of Souls. That also is against spiritual law."

"Have you ever frozen my emotions?"

"No."

"That's good. I don't want to be the pathetic head case you'd rather be rid of either."

"You are the Listener, an important member of my Circle. And you are not a 'head case'." Gem hesitated and then smiled a small smile. "Besides, I enjoy your company."

Such a personal expression of regard from Gem warmed Willet and also confused her. "I thought maybe you didn't need anyone…"

"I appreciate companionship as much as anyone else," Gem replied, rubbing the top of Dora's head.

"Wow, I never thought…" Willet suddenly slammed her hands against her ears. "What the hell is that?"

A phantom cloud of red smoke came rushing through the trees into clearing where they stood. Shrill, chattering voices in the smoke rose to an ear-shattering scream before the cloud hit them full in the face. Willet's eyes rolled up. She doubled over, wrapped her arms around her head and collapsed. Gem dusted her with snow and blew the smoke away. The cloud of Red Souls shrieked and took off with the speed of a cyclone.

Gem turned Willet on her back and lifted her eyelids. Her reddened eyes flicked side to side. She babbled deliriously. Gem sprayed her with iced rain until the Red Souls let go of her and sped off following the main cloud.

"*Now* you have been frozen," Gem said. "My apologies, Listener. Sometimes it is best." Willet began to calm. Gem grabbed her elbows and pulled her upright. "We must follow them. Wherever they are going, there will be a fire. Time to move."

Chapter 16: Something in the Air

Despite what she had told Gem and Willet, Audrey didn't want to go home. Why should Gem's silly false alarm interfere with this rare opportunity to venture out alone and have some fun? The thought of Dean drew her back to Club TJ. The crowd had thinned out a bit since the evacuation, but the floor was still crowded. She angled into the throng trying to find a spot closer to the stage. The smell of sweat and beer was intense. A space opened up in front of her and she quickly stepped into it.

Bass guitar thrums and drumbeats hit her in the chest, almost painful. She closed her eyes and let the onslaught of sound crash into her. When she heard Dean's voice, she opened her eyes. He sang Muddy Waters 'Please Don't Go' with a guttural roar. The crowd roared back. The bass and drums shook her and shattered the stiffness in her bones. She danced in place, swaying and shuffling her feet.

A mass of curly raven hair bobbed right past her headed toward the stage. Delos had a tall, beefy blonde guy by the hand, pulling him along behind her. They reached the stage and stopped in front of

Dean, whose eyes narrowed when he saw them. Delos waved her arms in the air, undulating like a snake, and wrapped them around the blonde guy. She pulled the guy's head down to her mouth and kissed him hard. Dean's mouth curled into an ugly snarl. He banged the drums so hard the skins could split.

Having made her point, whatever it was Delos towed her beefy friend away to the back of the crowd and disappeared. Just as well. Audrey didn't want to see her again. Audrey looked back at Dean. He just about beat his drums to death, driving the band into a string of frenzied riffs. She forgot about Delos and surrendered to the music, watching Dean through half-closed eyes. And then she sneezed. A gritty, pungent smell filled her nostrils.

Smoke.

*****

Gem headed toward West Hollywood with Willet shaking in the passenger seat. Her eyes closed and she mumbled.

Gem looked from the road to Willet and back. "What do you hear, Listener?"

"I hear music. They're going to the club."

Gem hit the accelerator.

Willet rocked harder, digging fingers into her scalp. "It's already burning."

Gem rounded the last corner on two tires. The Jeep came to a halt across the street from the club. Gem jumped out and stared at the sky. Long slashes ripped through the sky over the club like the claws of a tiger. A bubbling black substance oozed from the slashes and dripped on the roof of the club.

"I froze that breach two hours ago," Gem said with exasperation. "Something happened here after we left." She pulled her phone out of the glove compartment and called the LA Fire Department from speed dial.

Willet shuddered in the passenger seat and sucked in deep breaths. Her head hung to her knees. "I can't be here when the fire trucks arrive," she whispered. "The sirens'll kill me. And I need someplace to throw up."

Gem gave a curt nod and handed the phone to Willet. "Before you vomit, call your man. He may not see the flames until it is too late."

*****

Everyone in the club seemed to notice the smoke at the same time. Beside the smell, a dark haze hung in the air. Patrons started coughing. A crush of panicked people pressed Audrey from all sides. She glanced back at the band. Band members were rapidly handing their equipment off stage piece by piece in a bucket brigade through the backstage curtain.

The fire sprinklers burst on, and the crowd shouted. The shoving got rougher. Audrey concentrated on not falling over. Her feet barely touched the floor. The tide of panic carried her toward the exits. The smoke got thicker, and it became difficult to breathe. She pressed a hand over her nose and mouth to block the hot, gritty air. Her throat felt scalded.

She finally got close enough to the exit to escape, but an eddy swirled in the sea of humanity and threw her toward a wall. She struggled against the tide. It pushed her backward, further away from the exit. An elbow jabbed into her arm hard enough to bruise, a big boot crushed her foot, and a knee hit the side of her thigh repeatedly. The crush grew tighter. She elbowed her way into the wake of a big guy pushing through the crowd. When she started to lose him, she wrapped her arms around his hips and hung on. The guy turned and looked down at her, frowning, but then nodded. He grasped her forearms and towed her behind him.

That's when the lights went out. The place erupted in screams. Serious shoving almost tore her away from her male life preserver. The big guy tightened his grasp on her left arm and pulled her to his side, wrapping his arm around her shoulders. She clutched his belt with one hand and wrapped the other arm tight around his waist. Exit doorways loomed on each side of the ticket counter, and emergency lights glowed like welcome beacons. She could see the street outside. They both leaned forward, trying to stay upright in the packed queue of bodies pressing toward the doors.

They finally reached the exit and he pulled her through to the sidewalk like a cork from a wine bottle. People streamed in all directions. The streetlights seemed blinding. They staggered down two blocks and across the street to get clear of the smoke and the crowds. Wailing sirens approached from the main street.

Audrey bent over with hands on her knees, shaking and coughing the smoke from her lungs. He pounded her firmly between the shoulder blades. She gagged out the last foul breaths and gulped fresh air.

"You okay?" he asked in a rough, wheezy voice.

"Yes, thank you, so much. You're a prince. I wasn't sure I'd make it out."

"Yeah, it got dicey in there."

"Are you okay?" Audrey asked.

161

"I'll live. The fresh air feels great," he said between long inhales.

"What's your name?"

"Bart. My first time at the club. Some luck, huh?"

"Lucky for me. I'm Audrey. You're my hero."

"No big deal. I had to do something. You would have been trampled."

Audrey stood straighter and looked up at Bart. His breathing still sounded a bit labored. He had smudges of soot all over his face and arms. She could only imagine how she looked. "I thought I might die in there," she said.

Bart's hair and eyes were brown. He had an open, honest face above big shoulders and muscular arms in a faded grey T-shirt. He stood tall in jeans and looked solid as a tree trunk.

She rose on tiptoes and kissed his cheek twice. "You saved me, Bart. I'll never forget it."

Bart shuffled and turned slightly pink. "Happy to help, miss," he said with a courtly bow.

Audrey closed her eyes for a few moments, grateful to be free from the crush of bodies. When she opened her eyes, Bart smiled at her. She smiled back. "I'd like to cook dinner for you. To say thanks. Would that be okay?"

"Well, that's kind of you. You really don't have to…"
"I want to. Do you have a business card or something?"

Bart fished a wallet out of his back pocket and found a business card in it. "Bart Johnson, Geologist, California Department of Conservation," he said as he handed her the card.

"A geologist? What do you do?"

"I study earthquakes."

"I'd like to hear more about that."

He laughed. "I'll try not to bore you."

"I'll call you, then. We can set something up for next week if that works for you."

"Sure, sure, sounds good…"

Audrey looked back over her shoulder. Seeing the club engulfed in smoke twisted her stomach. She thought about Dean. "I need to find out if a friend made it out. He's in the band."

"No worries," Bart said sheepishly. "I'll see you later, then."

"I will definitely call you. Thanks again, Bart." Audrey watched him go as he turned and walked off down the street. She couldn't help putting a hand over her heart in salute. And then a familiar voice called her name.

Dean rushed up to her and grasped her shoulders. "I got worried. How did you get out of the club?"

"A nice man helped me. Otherwise, I would have passed out from the smoke."

Shadows of grey, green and purple flickered over Dean's face, and a red film swirled across his eyes. Audrey wondered if it was a trick of the lights.

"A nice man, huh?" he said in a low voice. "That's interesting, I should have been here."

Audrey didn't know why it should be so interesting and felt too tired to ask. "I need to go home," she said.

Chapter 17: Cold Shoulders

Three fire trucks blocked off the street in front of the club. Red and white lights flashed, and firefighters in full gear carried equipment around the building. Long streamers of water from fire hoses hit the roof and sizzled into steam. TJ watched in numb disbelief. He felt detached from the scene like news on TV, but his business brain already traversed the web of financial decisions he would have to make.

The fire chief in charge approached him. "Mr. Barlow, the fire is just about under control. The investigators will come in after us to determine the cause. A full report will take a few days."

"Thanks, Chief. Any clue how the fire started?"

"Seems it started on the roof, but we can't be sure until the investigation is done. The floor of the building is still intact, though there's a lot of smoke and water damage. The investigators will be able to tell you more."

TJ signed the papers the fire chief presented to him. Out of the corner of his eye, he saw Dean and Audrey walking toward him. The tension in his chest eased. He would not have to look at the smoking corpse of his club alone.

Dean reached him first. "TJ, man, I can't believe this." They clasped hands and embraced.

"Everybody in the band okay?" TJ asked.

"Yeah."

Audrey walked up to him, put her arms around him and gave him a hug. "TJ, I'm so sorry. This is awful."

Her sympathy surprised him. He hadn't taken her warning seriously and let people back in the club too soon. He didn't know Audrey well but appreciated the absence of "I told you so" in her attitude. "This has been a crap night. I'm glad you guys are here. I'm waiting to hear about injuries."

A fog of smoke and water vapor filled the air. Most of the roof had caved in by this time. The fire had eaten the walls down to a square of jagged teeth. Club TJ would not reopen anytime soon.

"You're insured, right?" asked Dean.

"Of course. At this point, it's not high on my list of my concerns."

Paramedics laid the last few victims on stretchers. Smoke inhalation, burns, sprained ankles and a broken foot. Those were just the injuries TJ knew about. Patrons and members of his own staff had been hurt. The weight of responsibility sat on his chest, heavy as stone. It hurt to breathe. "Willet called to warn me about the fire. I didn't even know it had started until I went and looked at the roof. Not sure how she knew it. Where is she, anyway?"

"She's off with Gem, looking for trouble," Audrey replied. "I'm sure they'll find some."

"Maybe I owe Gem an apology."

She sighed. "Yeah, maybe we all do."

TJ walked over to the paramedic trucks to offer any assistance he could. He felt helpless, but he spoke to one of his waitresses as a paramedic helped her onto a gurney. He held her hand as she lay with an oxygen mask over her mouth, taking deep lungs-full of air. When they lifted her into the back of the truck and closed the double doors, he stepped back and watched it pull away.

At that moment, Willet appeared at his side and slipped her hand into his. He squeezed her fingers and leaned down to kiss her cheek. She put her arms around his neck and hugged him for a long moment.

"Where have you been?" he whispered, relieved to have her there.

"Gem let me off at the corner just now. When we saw the fire earlier, she called the fire department and I called you. I couldn't be here until the sirens died down."

"I'm glad you're here now."

"How can I help?" she asked.

"Just stay with me, babe. That's all." He hugged her, his cheek against her hair, and didn't let go.

*****

Angry words flew between the sisters like hardened spit balls. Each one left a mark. They accused each other of abandonment and dredged up slights from years gone by. Audrey turned her back with arms crossed. Willet left with TJ without saying goodbye.

Due to the lateness of the hour, Dean drove Audrey in her sedan to his house in Manhattan Beach. Little conversation passed between them. Off and on, Audrey dozed in the passenger seat. She felt exhausted, sad and wired at the same time. Her mind blurred.

Dean roused himself from his reverie. "Delos is a witch," he said through his teeth. "She's a black widow spider, sitting in a web waiting to bite my head off. I'll step on her the next time I see her."

The violence of this image jolted Audrey, but she didn't say anything. Dean retreated into his own thoughts until they reached the coast and pulled off onto his street. Instead of parking in front of his house, he drove the two short blocks to the end of the street and parked next to the wooden steps leading to the beach. She lowered her window and laid her head back against the seat. The sound of ocean waves rushed in. The night air tasted fresh and cool.

She closed her eyes and let the long, disturbing evening drain away from her with the receding waves. She might have dozed for a minute, but she awoke to the feeling of Dean's fingers brushing the hair off her neck.

Leather seats squeaked as he leaned toward her and pressed his lips softly to her throat. She opened her eyes. He put a hand around the back of her neck and pulled her to him. His kiss on her lips almost burned. She closed her eyes and let it happen. When Dean broke from her and sat back, she shivered at the sudden coolness on her face.

"I want you in my bed," he said, his voice rough, hungry. His eyes bore into hers. He had never looked like that before. Despite her fatigue, every inch of her skin flushed warm.

"I'm not Delos," she whispered. "You need to be clear about that."

With a snarl, he opened the car door and got out, stalked around to her door and swung it open. He grabbed her arm and pulled her out, onto her feet, and pushed her against the side of the car. The length of his body pressed against hers. Sudden cold hand slipped under her jacket and brushed over her breasts. She gasped.

"Audrey," he murmured in her ear. I know who you are. I've wanted you since the day you came into my store. You're beautiful, like sunshine, and you smell like honey. You make me crazy."

He buried his hands in her hair and crushed her lips to his for a bruising kiss. She wrapped her arms around his waist, clung to him. His hands left her hair and searched her body, burrowing under her shirt and between her legs. She moaned. Her knees started to wobble. He grabbed her elbows and pulled her to standing.

"Let's go to the house," he commanded. He grabbed her wrist. She let him pull her down the street, stumbling after him like a child. When they reached his front lawn, she stopped short and pulled back. He turned to her with lightning in his eyes, grabbed her by both arms and tried to drag her toward the porch.

She wrenched her arms away and back-peddled several feet. "Dean, stop it!" she hissed into the quiet night. "You're scaring me."

He looked confused again, like he just woke from a dream and didn't know where he was. His arms dropped to his sides. "I didn't mean to scare you. I thought we were in sync."

"We were, I thought. Things are moving too fast. You're pulling me. I don't like to be pulled."

"Oh. Well, sorry. Are you coming in?"

"I don't think so. I'm not comfortable."

Dean's eyebrows crossed. "Why?"

"You're not yourself, Dean."

Dean laughed harshly. "Not myself, really? You think you know me so well?"

"Something's different. I don't know what it is. Something to do with the lookouts, the fire, all the weirdness... Maybe it's Gem."

"You're letting Gem get into *your* head. Otherwise, we'd be in bed by now."

"You need to get it together first."

Lightening sparked in Dean's eyes again. "Now you're giving me an ultimatum. *I* don't like ultimatums."

"You said yourself you didn't understand why you were so attracted to Delos. Maybe there's a reason, something you need to understand first."

Dean turned to his front door and pulled out his keys. "I'm going in. You can find your way home I assume." He stepped inside and closed the door. The porch light clicked off.

Audrey dropped down on the bottom porch step, head in hands. The day had wrung her out. She didn't know what to think about her own behavior or anyone else's. She had been ready to do just about anything with Dean. He turned her on so much. But he became cold, self-absorbed. He wanted what he wanted, no matter what. She thought of Bart's kind face, the way he had taken care of her in the smoke-filled club. It was a stark contrast. Tears started to flow onto her palms.

A few minutes later, the porch light turned on again. Dean opened the front door and stepped out. "I'm glad you're still here," he said quietly. "Audrey, I'm a jerk, I don't know what got into me."

She stood up, sniffling and brushing away tears with the backs of her hands. "I'm leaving."

"Please don't go. It's late, you're tired. I'm tired. The fire…"

"I'll be fine."

"I'm sorry, Audrey, really. You're right to be mad. Words came out of my mouth like they were from somebody else's brain. Please. I'll sleep in the office like last time. I swear I won't bother you. I'm sorry."

She looked up, into his eyes. They seemed clearer and calmer, more like the Dean she thought she knew. Encouraging, but not sufficient. "You really scared me, Dean. You were like a stranger."

"I would never try to force a woman to do something she didn't want to do. My mother would disown me."

"I don't know." She stood up and teetered on weary legs.

"Please. You could go in the bedroom and lock the door. Or I'll pay for a cab. It would be a long trip to Hemmings, but if that would make you feel safer…"

Home seemed so far away. "I can sleep in my car."

"I can't let you sleep in a car outside my house. How big an asshole do you think I am?"

"A pretty big one, at this point."

"Okay, that's fair. Just let me make it up to you. Give me another chance."

A wave of fatigue rushed up and hit her in the face. *If I don't lie down soon, I'm going to collapse.* Dean jumped down the stairs and put an arm around her waist. He took her arm and walked her carefully up to the front door, pushed it open and helped her inside. The door closed behind them.

A Dream of Darkness

Dean smelled sweat and canvas and heard cheering. Hot klieg lights beat on his bare shoulders. His hands and feet were heavy, as if they had weights tied to them. He stood in a boxing ring surrounded by people in stands yelling and waving their arms. Their mouths were open, but he couldn't understand anything they said. He looked down at his hands. They were encased in boxing gloves. Who was he fighting?

A deep voice announced "round three" over a loudspeaker and a bell rang. A smallish fighter with black curly hair rose from the opposite corner of the ring and came toward him with gloves raised. *It's Delos!* She immediately closed in on him and tried to throw a punch. He stepped back in shock and ducked it. She followed him, protecting her face, and tried to back him into his corner. He evaded her, but she landed a hard punch on his right arm. The arm ached and it made him mad. He rose up on his toes and jabbed in her direction. She backed away. A look of surprise flickered across her face. Apparently, she didn't expect him to fight back.

She leered and danced around the ring just out of reach. Then she moved in and tried to punch his left arm. He bristled. *The bitch!* He jabbed back at her. She threw a lightning quick punch at his nose with her right. He stepped back and she caught him under the chin with a left hook. The crowd howled. Delos smiled as she danced out of range.

His nose began to swell, and something turned poisonous inside him. He moved toward her steadily with his arms up until he closed within striking distance. She threw a flurry of punches which he easily deflected. Then he landed a punch to her left eye, one to her mouth, and a sequence of punches to her stomach. She doubled over and sank to her knees. Her left eye closed and streamed fluid. Her lower lip swelled to a reddish-purple bruise. She fell sideways to the canvas and did not get up. Dean stood over her sweating and panting, looking down on her crumpled frame with grim satisfaction.

He raised his fists in victory to the cheers of the crowd, and then confusion and panic rose inside him. He had punched her hard in the stomach and knocked her to the ground. *What if she's dead?* He knelt down to check her breathing. A light flutter of air brushed his fingers under her nose.

Everyone in the stands went crazy. Their enthusiasm for his violence made him angry. *What are they so happy about?* He looked up at the crowd. Despite their ordinary clothes and human appearance, they emanated a reddish heat. Their eyes glittered with a lust for blood and jagged teeth filled their roaring mouths. *I know who they are – these are Red Souls.*

A dark form loomed out of the front row, larger than the others. Aura of black, eyes boiling red, and more reptile than human, the shape swelled in size. A long neck grew out of the center of the blackness, carrying its head toward him, closer and closer, until they were nose to nose. Its eyes burned deep into his core. He had no defenses. The thing knew everything about him.

"Go ahead, finish her off," the deep voice insinuated into his mind, smooth as honey. "You know you want to."

He did want to. He wanted to punch her until he could punch no more. At the same time the idea horrified him. He froze, and then a calm, cool voice said, "You have a choice, Dean."

He looked down again at Delos' lifeless body on the canvas floor, her pale white face so bruised from his blows. His stomach turned.

"No," he said. "I won't do it.

"You lie," the black thing said. A torrent of boos erupted from the crowd. The black form opened an enormous mouth with dripping teeth. The mouth dropped over Dean's head. Its teeth bit into his neck.

Dean woke up shrieking. He sat up and swung his legs over the side of the bed, heart racing, looking frantically around the room. The stink of fetid breath still filled his nostrils. He rubbed at the piercing feel of teeth on his neck. He'd do almost anything to avoid that mouth. *I wouldn't kill Delos. Would I?*

A Dream of Light

Audrey stood at the edge of a forest of oaks and maples. The leaves were a green so pure she could practically taste the chlorophyll. Shafts of sunlight penetrated the canopy of leaves above her, throwing patterns on the ground around her feet. In a clearing just beyond the forest, a granite cliff rose, black and grey rock shot through with veins of silver, with a grotto carved into it. A waterfall tumbled into the grotto from the cliffs above, bubbling like a child's laughter. The water pooled in a large pond of splashing crystal water.

Gem stood on a large rock in the pond. She waved at Audrey, beckoning her to come closer. "See," she said, pointing to the water. "The Water of Life quenches all thirst. It is pure Spirit. There is nothing to fear." She knelt down to the pool and scooped up the water with her hands. She put her hands to her lips and drank. The water sparkled like liquid light.

174

Audrey watched, yearning for a taste of the water. Her throat felt so parched and dry, every inch of her skin ached for moisture. She walked to the pool and knelt at the edge. She did as Gem had, scooping up water with her hands and drinking until the glorious liquid ran down her chin, cool and refreshing. She splashed it on her face and pressed cool palms to her eyes and temples. The water relieved her deepest thirst, the fever of her brain. She sat on a boulder next to the pond and dipped her feet into the water, and then let the water rise to her knees. The coolness tingled on her skin. She rejoiced to the depths of her being.

"This water is full of sound and light," Gem told her. "No evil can stand against it. It will sustain you when you enter the Circle."

Gem drank again and laughed. Then she stood and threw her head back, lifting her arms into the air. A pure white light encircled her. She floated into the air toward the source of the light. Ecstatic joy beamed from her face as she rose higher and higher. Audrey watched Gem rise until the yellow-pink soles of her feet faded from view.

Chapter 18: Refuge

TJ maneuvered his SUV through the traffic on the Hollywood Freeway. Even late at night, cars still whizzed by on either side. When he finally pulled off onto Mulholland Drive and followed the winding streets up into the Hollywood Hills, traffic died down.

A sigh escaped Willet's lips. She tilted her head back and closed her eyes. "That's a little better," she sighed.

"How you holdin' up?"

"Borderline migraine. You?"

TJ heaved a sigh. "I've been better. It's quieter in the Hills. We'll be above all the noise. Does that help?"

"Yes. I've been blocking background noise constantly. I heard twenty-six car crashes around the city and had to stop at a park to throw up in the bathroom. My meds will help me sleep, thank God. I apologize in advance for the impending coma."

"Wish I could take one. I could use a good coma."

Willet reached out to rub his arm. "I wish I could help more. I'm so sorry about the club."

He looked earnestly into her eyes. "If you hadn't called me, there would have been casualties."

"At least I could do that, between all the barfing and fainting."

He smiled a rueful smile. "We've been through the ringer tonight, haven't we?" he said.

"Like wet laundry."

"I'm not used to feeling this blind-sided." His laugh had a grim edge.

"What will you do? About the club and all."

"I'll think about that tomorrow. My brain's kind of numb."

"You don't have to make any decisions tonight."

"What I'd really like is to find out why the club burned."

"Thomas," she said in a gentle voice. "Please listen to me. There are things in this world that cannot be explained by normal logic. I don't pretend to understand it all myself, but Gem does. Surely you see that now."

TJ's voice rose. "But *how* did she know? How do I know it wasn't her that set the fire? If I find out she had something to do with it…" He kept his eyes on the road. His fingers clutched the steering wheel so hard the bones of his knuckles looked about to split the skin.

Willet watched his profile in the shifting shadows, his eyes in slits and his jaw tight. Tension emanated from him like radioactivity. She withdrew her hand from his arm and faced forward. "Gem's a good person. She fights for people, protects them. She'd never put anyone in danger that way. Besides, we were together all night, nowhere near the club when the fire started."

"I'm sorry, I don't mean to blame her, and she did warn me. I'm just grasping at straws here."

She returned her hand to his arm and looked at him. "Like I said, there may not be anything logical to grasp."

The SUV turned into a narrow asphalt driveway, climbed and passed a small stand of palm trees, banana trees and birds of paradise. The dark windows of a single-story house peeked through the foliage. Security lights flooded the property as they pulled up to it.

"This is it," he said. "Let me turn on some lights before you come in." He got out of the car and walked up a path lined with canna lilies. In a couple of minutes, a small porch light beamed, and lights flickered on in the house.

Willet made her way to the front door, sampling ambient sounds as she went. The noise of the city still reached her, but softer, distant, floating somewhere below her, not gone, but easier to ignore.

She walked through a small hall into a living area on the left that flowed into a large kitchen on the right. The floors and walls were all hardwood – oak floors, maple walls, exposed teak beams in the white-painted ceiling, in deep, warm browns. The wood gleamed under the lamplight. A wide sliding-glass door opened onto a patio that looked out over the city. A hallway led off to the right to other doorways. She walked into the large chef's kitchen with high-end appliances, wide granite counters, and a central butcher block island. Spices and coffee scented the air.

"Well, this is home," said TJ when he emerged from the hallway.

"This is a cook's dream. Do you like to cook?" she asked.

"I do, actually, when I have time. I'm pretty good."

"No doubt."

He walked to her and slid the headphones off her head, gently rubbed her scalp, pressing his thumbs into her temples. "How can you stand wearing those things all day?" he asked. "Don't they drive you crazy?"

She groaned with relief. "They're pretty light weight. Not having them is worse. So, I deal with it."

He moved his fingers to her shoulders and kneaded the muscles in her neck. Tension melted out of her like warm butter. "Would you like to go out on the patio?" he asked as he worked her muscles. "The view is nice."

"Okay, but I'll give you 30 minutes to stop doing that."

He took her by the hand and led her through the sliding door onto the brick patio with a hundred-and-eighty-degree panorama of LA's sparkling night lights below them. The ocean brooded darkly on the horizon.

"Wow," she whispered. "It's awesome."

"Yeah, I like coming home. This is always here, waiting, no matter what happens during the day."

He stood behind her and rubbed her neck and shoulders as they both took in the view. LA was as quiet as LA could be.

"Thomas?"

"Hmm?"

"I'm sorry."

"For what?"

"I didn't try hard enough to make you understand about the fire. I should have convinced you to keep the club empty and no one would have been in danger."

TJ turned her around by the shoulders to face him. "I'm a money-grubbing block head. I doubt you could have changed my mind, and the fire was not your fault."

"My sister could have burned or suffocated." Her voice quivered. "I might have lost her. After the way we parted, I feel like scum."

"You're not scum."

"I should have respected her point of view. I should have listened better, done more, something. Gem did all she could."

TJ cleared his throat. "What did Gem do, exactly, besides call the fire department?"

"She froze the break in the Gate and sealed it shut so Red Souls couldn't escape. Something must have happened to crack it open again after we left."

He looked into her eyes for a long moment. "I can see you believe that. I just can't accept it right now."

She put her arms around his waist and leaned her cheek against his chest, sighed. "You're a stubborn man."

They stood in silence, breathing together. A cool breeze off the Pacific swirled lightly around them. She finally looked up at him. "The migraine is knocking on the inside of my skull. I need to take the magic pill, much as I would like not to. Besides being scum, I'm also a pill head."

He chuckled and wrapped his arms around her shoulders. "You're kind of nuts, Ms. du Place. But in an entertaining way."

"You used to think I was deranged and dangerous."

"You're definitely dangerous." He kissed her softly. "These are dangerous lips."

He kissed her again, long and slow. His hands slid over her shoulders and wandered down to her waist, lightly brushing her breasts, and continued down, grasping her hips to pull her firmly against him. He looked into her eyes to gauge her response.

She felt him harden and shivered at his touch. Her eyelids fluttered. "I *really* wish I didn't have a headache," she murmured.

He took her by the hand and led her back to the kitchen, filled a glass of water as she pulled the pillbox from her pocket. He took the box, opened it and picked out one pill. "This is it, eh?" he said, examining it more closely.

"My personal crutch, a cure for all ills."

"Open your mouth."

Her eyes locked with his and she opened her mouth. He placed the pill delicately on the tip of her tongue. She swallowed it and followed with a sip of water.

"You're ready for dreamland now," he said. He kissed her again, took her hand and led her down the hallway. They stopped in front of an open doorway. "You can have the guest room, if that makes you comfortable."

"It's too far away from you."

"You'll be out like a light, won't you?"

"Yes, but I'll know you're there."

In the master bedroom, he helped her shed the clothes she'd been wearing through the very long day. He pulled his own shirt off over his head, dropped his shoes and belt on the floor. She lay back on the large bed and heaved an exhausted sigh.

"I have to make a call," he told her. "Be right back."

He went out to the kitchen to find his phone, sent a text to the building contractor he used for his businesses, requesting a crew at the club first thing in the morning. By the time he came back to the bedroom, climbed on the bed and knelt over her, kissing her on the forehead, lips and chin, she was snoring lightly. He curled up next to her and hugged her to his chest.

Chapter 19: Choices

Gem parked the Jeep across the street from Delos' apartment, a two-story clapboard house with shutters, no lights on inside. Her VW parked haphazardly in front was covered by a cloud of red smoke. Gem ran to the car and blew the cloud away with a swift, cold breath. She tried the door, found it unlocked and pulled it open. Red smoke filled the interior. She opened the door on the opposite side and blew the smoke out the passenger doors.

A body was curled up on the back seat with arms folded to pillow a head of disheveled black, curly hair. The body didn't move.

"Delos, wake up," Gem urged.

She shook Delos' foot, got no response. She climbed into the back seat and rolled Delos over onto her back. The inert woman had an ugly green-black bruise around her left eye and a badly swollen lip. She barely breathed.

Gem noticed an empty pint of Jack Daniels on the floor and an orange medicine bottle curled in Delos' limp fingers. She grabbed the bottle – sleeping pills. It was empty. She immediately called 911 and prepared to administer CPR

Delos stirred and her eyelids opened a crack. "Le' me alone," she slurred. "Wanna sleep."

"Delos, you must not sleep. Tell me what happened?"

"I ran into an old boyfriend." Her voice cracked a hollow chuckle.

"You took pills. What were you thinking?"

"Guys treat me like dirt. So tired of it." Delos sighed and tried to turn onto her side.

Gem stopped her. "Look at me, Delos, stay with me. I am your friend." Gem removed the girl's shoes and rubbed her feet vigorously.

"I don't have friends," Delos murmured.

"Nonsense. I am your friend since the day we met in that bookstore."

Delos managed a weak smile. "You told me to buy the book on spirit sounds. I wanted the one on Tarot Cards."

"Yes, even then you did not listen. Listen to me now. You must try to hold on to your life."

"I went back, you know," Delos whispered, "for the book about sounds. You were right. It was better." Her eyes closed, and her mouth went slack. Her spirit rose and hovered above her physical body.

"Do not do this," Gem pleaded, searching the eyes of the dull pink specter before her. "It is not too late if you return this instant."

Delos reached for her lifeless body, but her spirit drifted farther away. "I can't get back." Her eyes filled with confusion. "I'm lost."

"We are never lost, dear one, we just forget," Gem said softly. "Light is there for you, Delos. It is always there. Reach for it."

The specter receded slowly and then disappeared into shadow. The body on the car seat lay white and still.

Gem dropped her head into her hands. Dora came to her, licked her fingers and put her head in the Guardian's lap. Gem wrapped her arms over the warm, solid scruff of Dora's neck, laid her cheek on top of the smooth head and wept.

*****

Sonrisa Degas stepped out of a fold in the darkness and stood right beside the car in a fraction of a second.

Gem raised her tear-stained face. "Do not startle me, Sonny. Please announce your presence."

"Amiga mia, que paso? You are in distress."

Gem sighed. It was not her place to reveal the choice Delos had made. "I have lost someone in my care. I arrived too late to help her, and now she must face the uncertain darkness of the lower Astral until she can find her way back to Light. My heart is heavy with it."

Sonrisa knelt before Gem and took the tear-drenched hands into her own. "Lo siento, chica. I would take this pain from you, but my message is urgent. A pestilence of negativity floods the city. Red Souls attack people at every turn. Violence increases. Surely you are aware of this."

A siren sound approached from the distance. Gem, stepped out of the car, wobbled a bit, and headed toward the Jeep with Dora beside her. Sonrisa supported her elbow on the other side. "I am aware," Gem said. "It has been a long and troubling night."

"How do Red Souls reach this plane in such numbers, Guardian? Surely you have found their entry point."

"No, I have not. The Gate appears intact. They have found another way. I suspect Theese is involved."

"Theese left his house in Azusa and moved to a large compound in the mountains north of the city. He appears to be engaged in a mining operation."

Gem stopped short. "Mining what? Where?"

"In Mount Wilson. His men dig extensive tunnels through the foothills. They extract some kind of black rock."

"Why would they do that?"

"I do not know the nature of the rock, but it is unusual."

"What about his radio station?"

"His studio also moved to the new location. His broadcasts continue."

Gem chewed on this information. She wiped the salty moisture from her face with the backs of her hands and pulled herself together. Dora looked expectantly between Gem and the Traveler.

"The compound attracts dark energy," Sonrisa said in a quiet voice. "It has become a center of instability. The Deceiver gathers his strength there. You have your Listener and a potential Ring Force, and Warriors to support them. The Circle must close. The Deceiver has Theese in hand to do his bidding. Only the power of a Circle can restrain him."

186

Gem gave a weary nod. "I know, Sonny, I know. We have lost too much already, but the Circle is not ready. For now, I will go to the mountains to see what Theese is doing. Join me there."

Sonrisa turned on her heel and disappeared into a seam of space-time between one moment and the next. The paramedics were on their way to take charge of Delos' body. Gem and Dora would not be there when they arrived.

Chapter 20: Morning After

In the morning, Audrey laid in bed thinking about the dream she had of Gem. She still felt that spring water in her mouth, the first cool drops rolling down her throat. No liquid had ever tasted that refreshing. She got up and walked to the window of the guest room. Dawn light had begun to cut through the cool grey haze.

She felt joyous, like she could float in the air.

She dressed hurriedly and walked to the kitchen. Dean sat at the kitchen table, staring straight ahead with hands in his lap. Memories of the previous night slowed her, and she approached cautiously.

"G'morning. Feeling any better?" she asked.

Dean turned his head to her and looked up. His eyes were ringed with blueish shadows, bleary and dull. "I would never hit a woman. You know that right?" he said in a husky voice.

She walked to the table and sat down across from him, her light mood sagging. "Um, no, I wouldn't think so. Why do you say that?"

"I hit Delos in a dream. I hit her hard enough to kill her. Maybe I did kill her." He shook his head and looked down at his hands.

"You dreamed this last night?"

"I punched her in the stomach on purpose. I wanted to do it. It felt good. And it didn't feel like a dream."

The violence in his words, especially after the previous night's experience, shocked her. She tried to think of something neutral to say, to steer him to a less dangerous topic.

"You two fought last night, for real. Strong emotion can affect dreams."

"Is that something Gem told you?"

"Gem makes sense sometimes. And I can't argue with her predictions."

Dean snorted. "My life is a mess since I got involved with Gem. I can hardly sleep, and I don't know what I'm doing half the time. Look at last night."

"Last night was strange, that's for sure. You scared me, Dean. I feared for my safety."

"That's exactly what I'm saying. I've never had a woman react to me like that. It's not who I am."

"What does Gem have to do with this? She wasn't even there."

"I don't know, but she's got something to do with it. She's a menace."

"You can't blame her for everything. We choose our own actions, don't we?"

Dean shook his head and looked away. "I never chose this."

Audrey didn't know what to say, so she looked around the kitchen. "Is there coffee?"

Dean nodded toward a cupboard.

Audrey pulled out a bag of ground coffee and a paper filter and made use of Mr. Coffee sitting on the counter. Water sputtered in the carafe, and the scent of brewed coffee soon filled the air. "Last night was awful, with the club burning, people getting hurt. No wonder you had bad dreams."

"Not just a nightmare, Audrey. It happened. I was there."

Audrey felt the same way about her own dream but did not want to discuss it with Dean. "Where will your band play now?" she asked, just to change the subject.

Dean stood up and stretched his neck and shoulders. "We'll find some place," he said, sounding unconcerned. "TJ has the bigger problems right now."

"Of course. Are you going to call him?"

Right now, I need to get in the ocean. Clear my head."

He accepted a mug of black coffee and headed down the hall. After a few minutes, Audrey heard the front door open and close. She sat and sipped her coffee, replaying her own dream in her mind. Maybe she should talk to Gem. They had parted on less than friendly terms, and she blamed herself for that. She felt a restless urge to do something, find something. There were unanswered questions she couldn't quite put her finger on. Somehow it involved Gem.

She went back to the bedroom, gathered up her belongings, and walked out the front door, closing it behind her. The fresh salt air greeted her as she stepped outside. She enjoyed a deep breath and walked the two short blocks to the sedan next to the beach stairs. When she reached the car, she stowed her purse under the passenger seat and got in.

At that moment Dean emerged from the surf, dripping wet in black trunks, with black swim fins clutched in his hands. He shook drops of water from his hair as he walked across the sand in her direction, tan skin glistening, drummer's muscles flexing across his chest. She crouched behind the steering wheel and watched him.

Audrey, get a grip. She felt her mouth hanging open, and snapped it shut.

A tall girl with long brown hair walking along the beach intercepted him. They stopped to talk. The girl wore a coral bikini top and short cutoff jeans. They smiled, chatted, laughed. The girl reached up to brush a dark wet curl from Dean's forehead. A sudden ache stabbed Audrey in the chest. *Jealousy? No way.* She rejected that emotion immediately.

They know each other, obviously. Better than he and I do, I'm sure. What he does is his business. I have my own things going on...

She felt foolish and wanted to be gone. She started the sedan and backed away from the beach as unobtrusively as she could. She didn't care if Dean noticed her leaving, but she hoped he hadn't.

*****

TJ got out of bed as quietly as he could to let Willet sleep. He slipped out to the kitchen with clothes in hand and dressed in the living room. He brewed herb tea and took his cup out on the patio to watch the city wake. Lights left on from the night before winked out here and there. The grey haze of dawn slowly burned away. Almost like any other morning, except for the dull ache in the back of his brain that wouldn't go away. His club, burned. He'd have to deal with that today.

A strange dream about fireflies lingered in his mind. Odd, he hardly ever remembered dreams, and when he did, they were very fuzzy.

191

This one left an impression. Fireflies had swarmed through the dark around him. Their small lights converged into fast-moving ribbons of bright light that sizzled, leaving trails. The images still burned on his retinas. He could still see them when he closed his eyes. Why would he dream that? Nothing about last night made sense.

On pad and paper, he wrote a note and left it on the kitchen counter.

Good Morning, Sleeping Beauty, Going down to the club to pick up a few things. Help yourself to coffee, tea, anything in the kitchen. Relax, enjoy. I'll be back soon to drive you home. T

TJ put on steel-toed work boots and drove down to West Hollywood. Light traffic at this hour of the morning. He got to the club quickly and walked the perimeter of the property, looking for frayed electrical lines, exposed gas lines, anything that could produce a spark or flame. He stepped under the yellow tape, unlocked the front door and tromped in.

A strong smell of wood smoke, melted plastic and burnt rubber assaulted his nose. Piles of trash and roof debris sat in dirty puddles on the floor, the stage, the bar. Every wooden surface had been charred. The mirrored wall behind the bar was blackened, the shelves of liquor covered in ash and soot. The wood walls had been water damaged. They looked chewed at the top where the roof used to be. In the kitchen, black water pooled in the burners of the stove. Soot covered the stainless-steel appliances. The food in the big refrigerators already smelled bad.

Frustrated anger surged in him, and a stream of epithets spit through his teeth. This was his first business, his baby. He didn't know who or what to blame for the fire, but he wanted to identify someone.

A sparkle of light on the floor caught the corner of his eye. He bent to pick up a small piece of what turned out to be hard, shiny rock. As he looked at the rock, a thin thread of light sparked across the surface. TJ shut his eyes and opened them. After a few seconds, the sparkling current ran across the rock again. He looked up to the sun through the gaping roof, thinking it might be a trick of the light. Sun shone steady under thin cloud cover. He looked down at the floor again and saw the same little currents of light running here and there across the floor.

 He gathered up as many odd bits of rock as he could find and held them in one palm while he shaded them with his other hand. Currents sparked across all the rocks, so fast he would have missed it if he weren't watching. *What are these things?* He slipped the rocks into the pocket of his jacket, determined to find out.

He walked to his office, let himself in with his key, and found the room soaked but intact. A firewall between the club and the office protected his lair from precisely this situation. *Good call on the firewall, Thomas Jefferson.* Water from the fire hoses had leaked through the partially burned roof to puddle on the floor. The rug squelched under his feet. The computer equipment might be a total loss. *Damn, when did I do a backup?*

He pulled files and disks out of the thankfully water-proof file cabinet, tucked them under his arm and walked out, locking the door behind him.

At the front of the club, a crew was already working. TJ had hired the crew chief for jobs on several of his properties. They shook hands. "Sorry about the fire, Mr. Barlow."

"Thanks for coming, Bill. I appreciate the help. The place needs a temporary roof and any other repairs that will keep thieves or weather out. Make sure there are no exposed wires or utilities. Check all the locks. We'll need a chain link barrier around the place. You know what to do."

193

"Sure thing, Mr. B. We'll take care of it."

Satisfied, TJ got in his SUV and headed back to the Hills. He looked forward to seeing Willet at his house. The thought of her there, maybe still in bed, made his blood heat. Her clear blue eyes and sweetly curved body were vivid in his mind, and a whiff of her perfume lingered on his skin. He accelerated into traffic, braying the horn at any car that dared slow him down.

Chapter 21: Crossed Signals

Willet woke and stretched, felt beside her for TJ, but he wasn't there. She dimly remembered him leaving early. The pills always made her head so groggy. She needed a shower to revive herself. She swung her feet down onto the hardwood, put on TJ's tee shirt, and looked around the room.

Bedspread and curtains in cream, gold and red draped the king bed and framed a long picture window. Brass lamps sat on teak tables beside the bed. *Nice taste, Mr. Barlow. How's the bathroom?*

The bathroom had a marble walk-in shower and lots of fluffy towels. She turned the water on hot and lathered with a soap that smelled like honey and almond. *Heaven.* By the time she finished the shower, shook out her clothes and put them on, she felt more like herself.

In the kitchen she found his note. She took his advice, heated some water and steeped a bag of ginger tea, taking her mug to the living room. A champagne-colored sectional couch faced the sliding glass doors in an open square. She took a seat, leaned back into a plump brown throw pillow and sipped her tea, letting her mind drift.

Is there a party going on next door? She heard glasses clinking and people talking, laughing. Music played. Too early in the day for a cocktail party - where are the sounds coming from? A man's boisterous laugh echoed along with several female voices.

Willet put her mug down on the table and walked through the house, trying to find the source of the voices. She walked from room to room looking for a TV or radio left on, a window open. She found nothing, yet the sounds of light revelry continued in the kitchen and living room, dying away down the hall.

In the master bedroom, the sounds changed as she listened. Heavy breathing, skin slapping softly against skin, moist sucking noises, then a deep groan, a soft sigh – the sounds of lovemaking were unmistakable. Willet put her hands over her ears, took them away. The sounds were still there. Her cheeks burned with embarrassment. *Are these sound prints?* If so, it had to be TJ and another woman.

She turned and fled the bedroom, ran down the hall. Of course, he had a life, other women, but she had no desire to hear it or know about it. The sounds of laughter mocked her, a party from his other world, full of beautiful, interesting people that did not include her. What had she been thinking? She couldn't face him now.

She found her phone and called her sister. When Audrey answered, she couldn't help tearing up. "Auddie, I'm so glad you're okay."

"Why wouldn't I be okay? What's the matter with you?"

"I'm at TJ's. Could you pick me up? I really need to get out of here."

195

"Did he do something to hurt you?"

"No, it's nothing like that. He's got enough to deal with right now. I don't want to bother him. Are you at home?"

"I just left Dean's place."

"Could you come up to the Hills and pick me up?"

"Yeah, I guess I could do that. It's good you caught me before I headed too far east."

"I was mean to you last night, and thoughtless. I don't know what I was thinking."

"Don't dwell on it. Sit tight, I'll call when I get close."

"Thanks Auddie. You're the best."

Willet gave her sister the address, praying Audrey would get there soon. She put on her headphones, went out on the patio and slid the glass door closed behind her. What to do now? She paced back and forth, tried sitting down, got up and paced some more. Audrey was on her way. Some of the tightness eased in her chest. What would TJ think when he got back and found her gone? How could she explain it to him? Her chest got tight again. The anxiety was almost painful.

I need to relax, contemplate. That's what Gem would say.

She sat down, closed her eyes, and took deep breaths, gulping for air at first. Her breath slowed. She settled into a steady rhythm and began to chant.

*****

Traffic came to a dead stop on the Hollywood Freeway with mid-morning constipation. TJ gritted his teeth, squirmed in the leather driver's seat. He wanted to climb out the window and stand on the roof of the car.

Let's go. Let's go already! What the hell is the holdup?

He had Willet in mind - soft, sweet Willet in bed, on the patio, in the shower, on the floor. He imagined her on top of him, long gold hair draped on her shoulders, eyes closed, head thrown back, pumping like a bareback rider. He imagined her pinned beneath him, looking into his eyes. He tasted her lips, felt her breasts in his hands, heard her moan, calling his name, begging...

Oh yeah, Will, you're so beautiful, your soft skin, mmm those lips, those lush...

He looked up to see the traffic still not moving, and cursed at the top of his lungs, banging the steering wheel with both fists.

Damn fuckity-fuck! Get out of the way!

He called her cell, but it went to voice mail. He left a message. They deserved some quality time together, didn't they, after all they'd been through? He imagined her flushed and ready for him.

Oh, baby, I bet you taste sweeter than cream puffs, mmm...

The pressure in his groin grew intense and he had to take a piss. He couldn't stop thinking of her standing naked in his kitchen while he licked orange marmalade off her most sensitive parts. He could hear her purring in his ear while he did it, but a traffic report on the radio kept interrupting his reverie. A three-car pile-up lay ahead with possible fatalities. His curses turned low and dark, threatening violence to everyone in his way.

I'm going to strangle this guy in the Mustang. He's blocking me on purpose. And that woman in the Buick is too old to be driving.

Ten minutes later traffic started to trickle and then picked up speed. Traffic control personnel waved him around a cone area surrounding fire trucks, an ambulance and an overturned pickup truck. He didn't bother to slow down to look when traffic opened up in front of him, but instead angled over to the far-left lane and pushed the pedal down, picking up speed, veering around slower cars with barely a look. He made it to his house in fifteen minutes. The trip normally took twenty-five.

Practically frantic when he finally pulled into his own driveway, he took deep breaths to steady himself.

Don't want to scare her. She'll think I'm demented.

He jumped out of the SUV and hurried to his front door, fumbling for keys with shaking hands. When he pushed through the door, he growled out her name.

*****

Center, relax, breathe, and focus.

Willet's attention kept straying to thoughts of TJ with another woman, but she kept pulling it back to the spot of light between her eyebrows. The sound of her own chant vibrated in her ears. Ocean waves whispered to her. These waves sounded closer than the Pacific Ocean, as if they were inside her head. *Not the phantom ocean waves again!* As soon as that thought took her attention, the waves went silent, and the spot of light disappeared. She groaned inwardly and started over. *Center, relax, breathe, focus.*

All her attention focused on that point of light that seemed so far away. She could sit forever, just breathing. The point of light expanded, rose like the morning sun over the distant horizon and illuminated a vast ocean. She stood on the shore, watching the dawn come. Waves rippled on the surface of the shimmering blue-green water breaking at her feet. The waves echoed her chant. She knew peace, felt a cooling joy.

A familiar voice called her name. She didn't want to leave this shore. No. But the sun receded from her view. She fell backward through darkness and slid into her body.

Chapter 22: Rocks

TJ called Willet's name again. No answer. *Did she leave?* He walked down the hall to the master bedroom. His bed had been made. There were telltale scents of a shower in the bathroom. He returned to the kitchen and walked into the living room. When he glanced out the glass slider, he found her standing on the patio, looking toward the ocean. He went to the door and slid it open.

"Will, there you are. Did you hear me calling you?"

She turned slowly in his direction. "Hello, Thomas," she said, her voice low and calm.

"What are you doing out here?"

"A contemplation. I needed to relax."

"Well, good, I'm glad. Did you enjoy the morning?"

"Yes."

She did not approach him, simply looked in his direction with a dreamy, distant gaze.

"Is something wrong?" he asked.

"No."

He went to her and bent to look into her eyes. She seemed to notice him all of a sudden. Something made him hesitate to get any closer. After thinking all morning about touching her, now he couldn't bring himself to do it.

"I'm sorry. My mind was on other things." Her voice trailed off.

"Like what?"

"I saw the other ocean. The one I told you about, remember? It's a real place. I stood on the shore and listened to the waves. I watched the sun rise."

He studied her. "That's nice. Something's different about you."

She didn't seem to hear him.

"Do you hear the air humming? The light is almost white. Does it seem that way to you?"

"No. Maybe you need to sit down."

"I'm fine. I feel like I'm...floating."

"It sounds like you're light-headed. Why don't you come inside? I thought we could spend the day together."

"Audrey is coming to pick me up. I didn't want you to have to drive all the way to Hemmings."

The disappointment stung him. "I wouldn't mind driving you home. Or you could stay."

"I can't. There are memories in this house that make me uncomfortable."

"How could that be? You've never been here before."

"Not my memories, Thomas. Yours."

He stared, trying to understand what she said, and then he guessed. "You mean those sound print things? What did you hear?"

"Things that are none of my business. Personal things. I shouldn't have heard them."

He couldn't remember anything unusual that happened in the house, playing back recent events in his mind. Mostly he was here alone. A small party a few weekends ago, Barb had come over. *Oh. Uh oh.*

"God, Will, I don't know what to say. I'm sorry."

"You have *nothing* to apologize for. This is your home. I'm the intruder."

"You're not an intruder. I want you to be comfortable at my house."

Willet looked down, closed her eyes, and took a long breath. "You might be better off without me complicating your life."

He pulled her into his arms. "I want you in my life. I've been thinking about you all morning. We can make our own memories and drown out everything that came before."

She leaned against his chest and sighed. "I'd like to believe that."

"You were here for me last night, Will. It would have been rough without you."

She drew back and gave him a small smile. "I was happy to help."

"That's one of many reasons why I want you with me."

He planted a soft kiss on her cheek, took her by the hand and led her to the couch, settling her among the pillows. "I went to the club this morning. It was a mess, but I found these." He fished in his pocket, scooped up the rocks and laid them out in his palm. She studied them uncertainly.

"Uh, they're rocks. Black."

"Just wait."

They watched the rocks on his palm until a current of light darted across one rock, then another. Willet blanched and sat straight up. The rocks flickered wildly.

"These were in your club?

"Yeah. Weird, huh?"

Willet held them to her ear. "They're whispering. I know those voices. Gem should see these."

TJ chuckled, shook his head. "Gem, again. Here, take these. Maybe she can figure them out." He dropped three rocks into Willet's hand.

She held them gingerly between her fingers. They felt warm. Then her phone chimed. "That's Audrey on her way. You've probably got work to do anyway, and we need to get back home, take care of the business. Seems like we've been away a month."

"Can you come back this weekend? I'll cook dinner, with candles, like a real dinner date. We can make new memories here, Will. You'll see."

She smiled and gave him a shy nod. "That sounds nice."

*****

Willet left TJ at his front door with a lingering kiss and walked out to the waiting sedan. The sisters drove out of the Hollywood Hills in silence until they reached the freeway.

"What's going on?" Audrey asked. "Looks like you and TJ are still on kissing terms. Why am I picking you up?"

Willet shifted in her seat, and shifted again, adjusting her sunglasses against the glare of the sun. "I got confused."

"About what?"

"About things I heard at his house, sort of embarrassing things. I wanted to get away, and then he came home, and I didn't know what to do…"

"What did you hear?"

"Sound prints, the intimate kind. When I realized what they were, I got so embarrassed that wanted to leave immediately."

Audrey considered this a moment. "Now that you've tuned in to this little trick, you seem to pick up prints more easily. You could get work as a spy."

"I feel like a snoop. I hate it."

"So, TJ has other women in his life. Does that surprise you?"

"It doesn't surprise me at all, but it's another thing having to hear it."

Audrey nodded. "I suppose it would be. What are you going to do?"

"We have a dinner date next weekend at his house. He's cooking."

203

"Oh," said Audrey with mild surprise. "You're choosing to overlook it. That's reasonable."

"I'm not sure I *will* be able to overlook it. We'll see."

They settled into silence and drove a short distance before Audrey began to sniff the air.

"What's that smell?"

Willet sniffed. "It smells like smoke."

Audrey turned on air conditioning and closed the outside vents.

Willet looked around for any fires that might be burning next to the freeway. The smell of smoke grew stronger. "Is it coming from the engine?"

Audrey slowed the car, pulled off to a narrow shoulder and peered through the windshield. Smoke surrounded the car. She grasped the handle of her door to get out, and then pulled her hand away with a wince. "What the...? The handle's hot! We have to get out!"

The inside of the car slowly filled with smoke. Willet tried the passenger door handle. It burnt her fingers. She used the pocket of her jacket to grasp the handle, jerk the passenger door open and jump out to the shoulder as the traffic screamed by. She pressed her headphones to her ears and groaned.

Audrey followed her out the door. They retreated as far from the smoking car as they could, then stopped and looked back at it. The smoke had already started to dissipate. "It looks like the worst is over," Audrey said. "Let's get in and see if we can make it home."

They got back in the car and opened the windows to let out the rest of the smoke. Within a minute, smoke began to fill the interior, and the air became unbreathable. They got out again and retreated up to a wider part of the freeway shoulder. When they looked back at the car, the smoke had stopped.

Audrey waved her hands at the car and yelled, "What is going on? Is the car allergic to us? This is too weird." She pulled out her phone and called TRIPLE-A.

Willet sank to a crouch next to the concrete barrier beside the shoulder and wrapped her arms over head, shuddering and gasping. She couldn't catch her breath.

Audrey bent next to her. "Will, we need to call someone to help us. Do you think TJ is still at home? We're not far from his house."

"Call Gem," Willet growled at her. She pulled out her phone and thrust it toward her sister without looking up.

Audrey called Gem and ended up in voicemail. She left a message.

"Gem doesn't answer. I'll try Dean."

Audrey tapped in Dean's number which went straight to voicemail. She didn't leave a message. "This is silly. I'm calling TJ, he's close. If he's not there, we'll have to rely on TRIPLE-A to take us home." She found TJ's number in Willet's phone and clicked it. In a minute, he answered.

"Will, what's up?"

"TJ, this is Audrey. We're stranded on the 101 near Moorpark. Something in my car is smoking, and it's strange. Could you possibly help us, pick us up and take us somewhere off the freeway? Willet is hyperventilating with all the highway noise."

"I can be there in, like, fifteen minutes. Can you wait in the car?"

205

"That's the problem. Every time we get in the car, it starts smoking, and the door handles get hot. The smoke stops when we get out of the car. I told you, it's strange."

Silence on the other end, then a long exhale. "I guess I shouldn't be surprised. Can you hang on 'til I get there?"

"We'll be the two pathetic females huddled on the shoulder, trying not to get hit by a truck."

TJ clicked off, and Audrey went to crouch down beside her sister. "TJ's coming."

Willet groaned. "I feel like an idiot. He wanted to drive me home and I told him no. Now I'm dragging him out here to rescue me. My skull is about to crack open."

"It might be a good time to take a med."

"Yes. A med would be good, where are they?"

They both searched pockets until they found the pill box. Audrey helped her fish out a pill and Willet swallowed it. "What if I pass out right here? Can we get arrested for that?"

"It would be the least of our worries at this point."

"When is he coming?"

"Fifteen minutes, Will. Just hold on for fifteen minutes."

TJ's SUV finally arrived. It pulled over to the shoulder behind the TRIPLE-A tow truck that was already there. A mechanic had hooked the sedan to the tow line and was reeling it up an incline. Audrey and TJ grabbed Willet under each arm, lifted her to her feet, and helped her into the back seat of the SUV. She lay down immediately and closed her eyes.

Audrey finished paperwork with the tow truck driver before climbing in the SUV. TJ took advantage of a miniscule break in traffic, punched the gas and sent the SUV hurtling onto the freeway like a cannonball.

"What the hell is going on, Audrey?" TJ demanded.

Audrey sat upright in her seat. Her hands were shaking. "My car is almost brand new, serviced regularly. It's never done anything like this before."

"You said the car only smoked when you were in it. That's nuts, excuse me for saying so."

"I know," she sighed. "Maybe it doesn't like my perfume."

Willet snored lightly as she slept in the back seat. When TJ took the freeway exit to Hemmings, she stirred in the back seat and sat up, bleary, looking out the windows. "Are we home?"

"Very soon, Will," TJ reassured her. "How's the head?"

"The head feels like a bowling ball on my shoulders. And what are those voices? Someone's whispering my name."

TJ checked the sound system. "Everything's off. There are no voices."

Willet sat still and listened intently, even lifting her headphones off her ears. Her eyes got wide. "They're talking about me. 'Burn the Listener'. They keep saying that."

TJ looked at Willet in the rear view, then at Audrey. "Do you hear voices?"

"No, but that doesn't mean anything."

Audrey turned in her seat and stared at her sister. "Gem calls you the Listener, right? Who would want to burn you?"

Willet started patting the pockets of her jacket. "Ouch! That's hot!" She pulled the jacket off, turning it inside out. "I think my jacket's burning!"

Audrey snatched the jacket out of Willet's hands and felt the pockets. She turned the pocket inside out, and three black rocks fell in her lap. Threads of light ran across their surface, sparking wildly. She brushed them onto the floorboard.

TJ looked down. "Those are the rocks I gave you. You're telling me they get hot?"

TJ had already turned onto Pine Siskin Road, passing the little parking area, and continued to the circular drive in front of the house. When he stopped the car, everyone scrambled out.

TJ ran around to the passenger side and scooped the rocks off the floorboard. "They're hot alright," he said, tossing them from hand to hand.

Willet stood by him, peering into his hands and trembling. "They're cursing at me."

"I don't want a fire to start here," Audrey said with panic in her voice. "Bury them in wet dirt. Maybe that'll cool 'em off."

TJ knelt at a plot of succulents by the side of the driveway, dug a hole in the dirt with his hands, and dropped the rocks into it, hastily covering them and patting the dirt down. He stood up, brushed dirt off his fingers and surveyed the bed. "Now would be a good time to water these plants."

Audrey ran for a hose while TJ turned to Willet. "Okay, Will, if you know what's going on with the rocks, tell me."

"Well, they have some kind of consciousness inside them, and they may have something to do with the fire at your club. Other than that, I have no clue. When Gem sees them, she'll know what they are, I'm sure of it."

"It's always back to Gem," TJ grumbled.

"My thoughts exactly," Audrey replied, as she soaked the ground with water.

Willet threaded her arm through TJ's. "I'm sorry to keep dragging you in to this, Thomas. Why don't you come in for a while? Let me fix you lunch." She hugged closer to him. "And thank you for getting us off the highway. I would have been embarrassed to throw up right on the 101."

"I'll come in for a bit, sure. But I have another ten of those rocks at home. Now I'm worried about *my* house burning down."

"All the more reason to talk to Gem," Willet said. "I left her a message. I hope she calls me right back."

*****

Richard Theese pulled an old polyester work jacket over his crisp, white-collared shirt and navy-blue vest, pulled the vest down over his broad belly, and grabbed his hardhat from a hook on the back of the office door. "Andy, if this isn't a real emergency, you're fired. I go on the air in thirty minutes. I don't have time to referee fights between nincompoops in the mine. That's your job."

Andy Tate had to trot to keep up with Theese's long strides as they hurried out the front door of the office building. "Boss, it's a freak show down there!" Andy huffed with exertion. "Lights are flashin' and guys are yellin' and hittin' each other. Red and me don't know what to do with 'em. It's like they don't hear us yellin' at 'em. Somebody's gonna do somethin' stupid."

They climbed into a black pickup parked in the large gravel lot in front of the office at Theese's compound in the Mount Wilson foothills. Theese threw the truck into gear and kicked up dust as he circled past smaller offices and utility sheds and exited the parking lot onto the main road. The truck soon veered off to bump along a narrow dirt road winding up the mountain. In five minutes, they reached a small cave next to the road, the entrance to the excavation project.

Three years ago, right after he bought the Mount Wilson property, he took a hike and explored this length of the old Toll Road. It had been a stroke of luck that the entrance to the old mine was still accessible. He found the opening in the grey granite, walked in with a flashlight, and discovered the first small patch of dark crystalline rock. It had been warm to his touch. Veins of light sparked through it. When he bent closer to examine it, it whispered, giving him a gift from the angels, payback for all he had suffered and lost.

He was sure the crystal would be valuable, and he had a mission. With enough money, he could change things in America, steer the country on the path of righteousness, away from undesirables and those who didn't pull their own weight. The crystal would make that possible.

When they reached the mine and jumped out of the truck, Theese pulled a ring of keys from his coat pocket and found the one for the heavy grate door that barred the entrance. Andy swung the door open with a grinding squeal. Shouts and curses drifted up from the depths of the mine. "Damn it all," Theese muttered with exasperation.

He led the way along a corridor lit by utility lamps to a stairway next to an open elevator shaft. They hurried down three flights of metal stairs and turned a corner into a full-scale brawl. Men twisted and strained in a scrum of sweat-stained denim, sun-browned arms and clenched fists. Light streamed like neon through the crystal, throwing shadows on the ceiling. Yells and curses echoed off the walls.

Red Starley, the mine foreman, stood on a cart, banging a bucket with a hammer and calling for order. No one paid any attention to him.

Andy raised his voice. "Stop! Stop fighting!" The men were lost to the heat of battle.

Theese strode forward, separating the men and throwing them back against the walls with all the force of his six-foot-three, 240-pound bulk. "Stop the fighting, now, or I won't pay any of you a damned nickel!" he bellowed.

The shouting of angry voices slowly died away. Men shuffled back from their fights like punch-drunk boxers, shaking their heads. Bruises bloomed on many faces and cuts ran with blood. Some men bent over, panting, hands on knees.

"We have work to do," Theese yelled. "There's money to be made, and I won't allow anyone to slow the project down. Get back to it, all of you, or you're through here."

Dark grumbling filled the tunnel. "This crystal stuff is growin' in the walls. It's ain't normal," snarled a tall, burly man with sweat-matted hair and tattoos on his neck. "The mine is cursed."

"The mine is not cursed, Mr. Sledge, it is blessed, with a special crystal that will make us all rich. We've been blessed to find this treasure, and we'll provide it to the world at cost plus 50 percent."

"Judd's right, Mr. T," whined a thin, young guy in baggy overalls. "The rock ain't natural. It's messin' with our heads. I don't wanna bring no curse home to my kids."

Theese tried a more cajoling tone. "Your kids will get new bicycles and you'll send them all to the best colleges. Isn't that what you want, Ray? I guarantee the crystal will not hurt you."

"And what are we gonna do with this stuff after we mine it?" Andy murmured to Red.

Theese walked up to the tunnel wall and laid his palm on a thick crystalline vein. The crystal tingled under his fingertips like a live wire. What Andy said was true – the strange crystal had spread through the rock wall, branching into new veins in every direction. He didn't want to think too deeply about how that happened. It was the work of the divine. Who was he to question it?

With head bowed, he closed his eyes and thought of Jimmy, his dear boy, his son. Anguish over the loss of his son gnawed constantly in his gut. Jimmy had died in service to his country, an army soldier and hero in the Mid-East wars. The country should be worthy of that sacrifice. His father would make sure of it. He would use his coming wealth to become a political force strong enough to influence politicians and change laws.

Large-wheeled platforms with barrels on them stood at either end of the tunnel. Men drilled and dug crystal out of the wall and shoveled it into the barrels. When the barrels could hold no more, the men pushed the platforms down a narrow track in the floor toward the elevator.

Shaking himself, Theese picked a piece of the sparking rock from a barrel as it passed by and hefted it in his hand with a nod. "For you, Jimmy," he said softly. "I swear I'll make you proud."

"But Boss, rock don't grow. It's gotta be the work of the devil."

"We have righteousness on our side, Andrew," Theese told him with a stern look. "Remember that."

"If you say so, Mr. Theese. It still gives me the creeps."

Chapter 23: Hidden Gifts

Sonrisa Degas hiked through the flat, colorless wasteland of the Astral Underworld, crunching flint-dry rock under her boots. The air, gritty with smoke and stinking of sulphur, burned the eyes and nose. In a field of broken boulders, emaciated bodies collapsed to their knees on the ground, wringing thin hands and shaking their heads at the desolation around them. She sang her words of Spirit to keep her consciousness light. *Huuu, Huuuu.* Loss of hope could easily seduce anyone in this place.

Red Souls flew out of smoking craters and grabbed at her, long talons scratching against her leather jacket and leggings. They cackled in her face. She brushed them away with windmill strokes of her arms.

"We will inhabit the earth world again," they chattered. "The Guardian will not find us this time."

"Of course she will find you, deluded ones."

"The Great Jat promised us a return to the earth."

"And you believe the Deceiver? When will you learn that he lies?"

"He would not lie to us. We are his."

"Where is he? Tell me now."

The Souls practically squealed with glee. "He is in the Temblas, with his claws are buried in the guts of the earth. He is making doorways for us."

Sonrisa headed toward the Tembla Mountains towering in the distance. The silhouette of jagged black peaks cut across the plain like a serrated knife. She covered the distance to the mountains in long, rapid strides over the rocky plain and found the path leading up. She squared her shoulders and started the climb to a wide plateau. When she reached it, a stone staircase rose at the far end. She hiked to the stairs and mounted them two at a time. Shadowed caves in the breast of the mountain opened at the top.

Whenever she hiked in the Temblas, she encountered new abominations. Inside pitch-black caves, savage eyes burned, and voices screamed in misery. A piteous wind wailed continuously.

At the base of what the local denizens called Thief's Peak, she listened for the Deceiver. His breath wheezed and blew like a bellows. The rumble of an explosion shook the rock underneath her feet. She followed the sounds to a massive cavern swirling with red smoke. Rock debris lay everywhere around the entrance. Inside, the dark form of Jat the Deceiver wavered like a mirage.

"Maria Sonrisa Degas Megaro," he purred. "How nice of you to visit my humble abode. Won't you come in?"

"I think not. I am here on the Guardian's business. You have involved a Richard Theese in your schemes. What does he do for you?"

"Theese?" Jat sniffed. "I do not recognize the name. You will have to excuse me, Traveler. I am up to my elbows in a new venture. No time for questions."

215

Sonrisa moved closer to the cavern entrance and peered inside. The Deceiver hovered over a large hole in the ground ringed with broken rock. Red Souls swarmed around him and dove into the hole with piercing screams. "If you have trespassed in the earth world again, the Guardian will slam the Gate shut in your face," she warned him.

"The earth world vibrates in harmony with my domain, so close I can almost touch it," Jat snapped, exhaling fire. "The energy difference between us grows weak. When I am done, there will be no Gate. The Guardian will not stop me this time."

The Deceiver rose slightly and then plunged both arms into the hole. The mountains shook, and Sonrisa stepped back to avoid shards of flying rock. When he pulled his arms out, he held a large chunk of dirt-covered crystal in each clawed hand. Red smoke swirled inside the crystals.

"You are witness to my brilliance, Traveler. Veins of this crystal run from here to the earth. My creatures travel through the crystal into the physical plane right under the nose of the Guardian, bypassing her pathetic Gate. The Souls shelter within it until the crystal is cracked open by those digging for treasure. Then they are set free to roam the earth. Are you not impressed?"

"Why would Theese dig the crystal for you? What did you promise him?"

"The man believes the wondrous properties of the crystal will make him rich. He also believes he has been wronged, and his petulance serves my purpose. Besides, he invited my power," Jat said innocently. "In exchange, I indulge his petty fantasies, at least for a while. That is fair, is it not?"

"You do your job too well, Deceiver."

The edges of an empty mouth curled into a sneer. "Eternities of practice, Traveler."

"Nevertheless, Red Souls have not earned their way out of the Underworld. You know the law of the High One."

"I do what I must, and the High One will do the same. You know this too. Now, I have a pressing engagement."

The Deceiver's form dispersed into mist and disappeared, leaving Sonrisa shaking her head. The Guardian would not be pleased, but at least now they knew what Theese was digging in the mountains. She found a crease in space-time that led to Gem, and stepped in.

*****

Gem drew her arms to her sides and pointed her toes as she flew, blissfully free from gravity. She glided left and right, skimming a breeze that whispered in her ears, floating over the rolling hills of the astral countryside. Stands of trees brushed feathers of green and grey leaves against the blue sky. Pink and purple lilacs burst like fireworks from patches of foliage. In the distance, pure colored lights swirled out of the Mountain of Light in the heart of the Lotus City, her destination.

She could have projected there directly but preferred to take the scenic route. She swooped down to a large rose garden near the Temple, her feet touching lightly on a wide, white, stone walk. Rose scents wafted up to her, mixed with the woody scents of fir and pine. Bushes bursting with buds offered delicate blooms of every hue. On the other side of the walkway, dahlias big as dinner plates stood in cultivated beds, their heavy heads nodding. The songs of birds mingled with the languid strum of a harp.

217

The round Temple building glittered in white and gold stone, with high windows all around the base of the dome. The stone walk circled the Temple in a broad boulevard. A walkway led to the front doors. She followed the walkway and stood before the doors, waiting for them to acknowledge her. They soon opened and she stepped inside.

The large space vaulted into the high dome. Clear light streamed from the ring of windows. People gathered here and there, standing in conversation or sitting on benches in small classes. At the far side of the interior, a piercing bright light filled an alcove. The sound of ocean waves rushed toward her from that direction. She stood a moment to absorb the light and sound before she went to find Augustus in his usual teaching studio. A high window flooded his room with golden light.

Augustus sat at a small wooden writing desk in the middle of the room. He glanced up when she entered. His white hair brushed his shoulders and glinted silver in the light. He wore an ankle-length white robe, with a gold lariat cinched around his waist. His eyebrows matched his hair and warm light glowed in his skin. "Dear one, the sight of you makes these old eyes glad." He beamed at her and rose from his carved wood chair.

She quickly closed the distance to him, walking into his open arms with a sigh of relief. "Augustus, I have missed you."

Love radiated from him. She basked in it before drawing back to meet his gaze. The light of joy in his blue eyes pierced her heart. She had so much to ask him. She pulled up a nearby chair and sat.

"How are you, my dear?" Augustus asked. "And where is the darling Dora? Usually she is with you."

"Dora guards the Jeep, and my physical body. We are parked at the beach. She likes to watch the people."

"Pat her noble head for me. She is in my heart, as you are. To what do I owe the pleasure of your visit?"

Gem fidgeted in her chair. "Can I not simply enjoy your company?"

"You seem troubled."

Augustus was too astute to evade, so Gem got to the point. "I have lost a friend. She has gone to the Underworld. I could not save her."

"I am so sad to hear this. How can I help?"

"I do not want to lose anyone else before the Circle is formed, and certain members remain unconvinced. How can I demonstrate the urgency of our mission?"

"Truth cannot be forced on anyone. It must be accepted freely, as you well know. It is best to release your hold on the situation and let each Soul find his or her way."

Gem knew that would be his answer, but she still had to ask. "Would a journey out of the body be appropriate?"

"That is your decision, Guardian. You know them better than I. Are they stable enough in mind and heart to handle it?"

"I think they are very strong. They do not yet realize their own strength. When they do, they will be a formidable Circle."

"There. You have your answer."

She sighed and took a luxurious stretch. "It is wonderful to be free of the mortal shell. Between my body and the Jeep, I feel that I drag a ton of cement around with me wherever I go on earth."

"The dross of that world is heavy, indeed. How long have you been in that body?"

"One hundred sixty-six earth years."

"Are you ready to drop it?"

"I have people who depend on this form for now, so, no."

"Then what else is on your mind, hmmm? I sense something more."

She shifted in her seat, a bit uncomfortably. "I seek your counsel."

"Ah, it is a matter of import. I see concern in your eyes."

"Troubled souls from the lower astral have entered my city by unknown means and cause havoc everywhere. They evade my sight and my breath. A deluded man who does the bidding of The Deceiver is helping them. I worry I will be unable to stop a full-scale attack."

Augustus leaned toward her and took her hands in his. He looked deep into her eyes. "Never doubt your own power to create, dear one.

"I need guidance, Augustus. Help me."

He smiled at her kindly. "Build on the foundation you have established. You will find the strength and the means to direct the troubled Souls back to their rightful place."

"The Circle isn't ready."

"Are you sure?"

"The people of this age are distracted. It is more difficult than ever for them to discover the inner worlds."

"That is not an answer to the question I asked," he chided.

Gem drew a deep breath. "I can show them what is possible, if they will pay attention. They want to look everywhere but within."

"Reveal what must be revealed. They might surprise you with their readiness. A Circle cannot form without trust."

Augustus rose, walked to the wall under the high window and waved his hand at it. The stone melted into water drops and fell away, revealing a view of the circular drive at Pine Siskin House. An SUV was parked in the driveway near a green Porsche.

"It seems the sisters are at home entertaining a guest," he murmured. "Who do you suppose it is?"

The view moved through the front door into the living room. Audrey, Willet and TJ sat around a low table, talking over glasses of green liquid and a plate of cheese and crackers.

"There are three of your members in one place now. A happy coincidence." He gave a sly glance in her direction and smiled.

Gem stared at the tableau before her. "My physical body is far away at the ocean. "

"A temporary form could bring you directly to them."

"I could materialize another body, that's true. But the fifth member of the Circle is not there."

"Trust in Spirit, dear one. And do the best you can."

The view through the window moved back to the front of Pine Siskin House. Gem walked to the window, stepped through it onto the circular driveway and into a body that looked exactly like her own.

She wore her usual white peasant blouse and an azure blue knee-length skirt. Leather sandals wound around her feet.

The ground trembled for several seconds. She looked back over her shoulder to see the window to the Astral Plane close and wink out of sight. She walked up to the front door and rang the bell.

*****

Willet gawked when she opened the front door and found Gem standing there.

Gem nodded. "I apologize for arriving unannounced," she said, with a small smile.

"Gem, it's you! I didn't hear your Jeep. How did you get here?" Willet said as she peered around to the driveway.

"I parked down the road at the little parking spot and walked up."

"You could have taken the cart. Where's Dora?"

"Um, I left her sleeping, in the Jeep."

Willet opened the door and waved Gem inside. "I left a message on your phone. Did you get it?"

"No time for messages. I must speak to you and Audrey, TJ and Dean, too, if possible. It is a matter of great importance."

"TJ's here. Dean's not. We had an emergency this morning, and we need to talk to *you* about *that*."

Gem followed Willet to the living room. "Dean must hear what I have to say. Time is of the essence."

In the living room, Audrey and TJ looked up with the same surprised expressions. "Dean is on his way over, as a matter of fact," Audrey said. "We're settling the final bill on our renovations. Why do you need to talk to us?"

Willet sat next to TJ, and Gem settled herself in a chair across the coffee table. She leaned forward and rested arms on her knees. "There is a problem to solve," Gem said, choosing her words carefully, "and you are in a unique position to help me solve it, so I am asking for that help. And I need you to keep an open mind."

TJ fell back against the couch and groaned. "Is it another phantom fire?"

"The fire at your club was not 'phantom,' Mr. Barlow. Surely you see that now."

"What I see is trouble whenever you're around. I don't need any more trouble. I'm going to be sued by at least twelve people, and I'll need tens of thousands of dollars to rebuild my club. You warned me, sure, but I still don't get how you knew it would happen. Until I figure that out, I don't trust you. And how did those rocks end up in my club?"

Gem's eyes narrowed. "What rocks?"

"That's the emergency we had this morning," Willet interrupted with a small cough. "Thomas found some rocks in his club after the fire. They have weird lights in them, they get hot, and they whisper. Our car engine started smoking when I tried to bring three of them home in my pocket. Auddie and I were stranded on the freeway for almost two hours."

"The rocks whisper? What did they say?"

"They said, 'Burn the Listener.'" Willet gave a small shudder.

Gem rose to her feet. "Where are they now?"

"We buried them in the yard and watered them," Audrey said.

"Show me, please."

Audrey and Gem headed for the front door, Willet and TJ behind them. They went out to the spot in the flower bed where TJ buried the rocks. He dug in the wet dirt and turned his palm up to Gem.

"Here they are," he said, brushing off loose dirt.

Gem took the rocks into her own hand. Lights sparked inside them. She held one up. Dark but not opaque like obsidian or dense like granite, it glittered against the sun. Definitely not coal. It had facets like a crystal. She knelt and dropped the rocks on the pavement. Grabbing a smooth, solid rock from the decorative border around the flower bed, she smashed one of the rocks to pieces, and then to powder. As it disintegrated, red smoke only she could see whiffed into the air and blew away.

Willet covered her ears. "They're screaming. Could you cover them up again?"

Gem recalled Sonrisa's report about Theese's mining activities. "These are not the only such rocks in Los Angeles. There are many more. This is why I am here."

"You want us to smash rocks?" Audrey asked.

"I wish it were that simple. When does Dean arrive?"

Audrey pulled out her phone and checked messages. "He'll be here in half an hour or so."

"Good. We have time. Now, what kind of green beverage were you all drinking? It looked very refreshing."

"Fresh lemon-limeade," Willet told her. "Would you like a glass?"

"Yes. Then we will discuss states of consciousness."

TJ grumbled. "I have business to take care of…"

"Your participation is needed, Mr. Barlow. Please bear with me."

"Stop with the 'Mr. Barlow' already. Call me TJ. I'm probably older than you, anyway."

"TJ," she repeated with a small frown. "And believe me, you are not older."

Willet took his arm. "Please stay awhile, Thomas," she cajoled. "It wouldn't hurt to hear what she has to say. You still have those rocks at home. It would be good for you to understand what to do with them. Besides, Dean will be here soon, you'd like to see him, wouldn't you?"

"I'm not a child, Will," TJ warned her. "And I don't like being managed. Besides, I'd like to know in advance what she's going to say," he said, shifting his attention back to Gem, "so I can decide if I want to stick around."

"What I have to say may change your point of view on many things."

"I like the point of view I have. It's not insane."

Willet led a reluctant TJ back to the house while Audrey and Gem stood on the driveway looking down at the remaining rocks.

"What are they, really?" Audrey asked.

"It is a form of crystal. Red Souls can hide inside them."

Audrey stared at Gem. "Souls hide in the rocks. That's your explanation?"

"Do you prefer that I coat it with sugar for you? When you see for yourself, it will be clearer."

"You can show me Red Souls?"

"Yes. The question is what will you do when you see them? Once seen, they cannot be unseen."

"Why do I have to see them at all?"

"You need to know what we are fighting, Audrey, because it *is* a fight, and I need your help most of all. You have an ability that you will soon realize, and it will tip the balance of strength in our favor."

Audrey rubbed her temples with eyes squeezed shut. "Gem, I think you're a well-meaning person. I even like you, sometimes. But this makes no sense."

"I will show you what I see, and Willet will share what she hears. Then decide for yourself." Gem patted her shoulder awkwardly. "And try to remain calm."

Chapter 24: Circle of Trust

Dean drove east to Hemmings for a final walk-through of the renovations at Pine Siskin House as sunlight thinned at the end of the afternoon. He would present the bill. Amazing how the weeks of work had flown by, and what a big part of his life the sisters had become. Would Audrey want to see him again after today? He sensed she didn't trust him. She had left his house the morning after the fire without saying goodbye, and he hadn't talked to her since. Given his atrocious behavior the night before, he couldn't blame her.

He pulled off the freeway and headed for the house, parked the truck in the lot and took the usual ride to the front door in the caretaker's cart. Audrey opened the door. He shuffled in, holding a white envelope in one hand and a clipboard full of papers in the other, mumbled a hello, and then noticed Willet and TJ sitting in the living room.

"What are you doing here, TJ?"

TJ shrugged. "I got kidnapped."

"We're waiting for you," Audrey said. "I've been worried about you. Have you been able to sleep?"

"Not really... What's going on?" He knew he looked like hell after little rest and many bad dreams. He wished now he had changed out of his work clothes before he came.

"Gem wants to talk to all of us," Audrey said, peering at him. "You look really tired. Your eyes are bloodshot."

"Yeah, thanks, I know that."

"Gem might be able to help you."

Dean snorted. "Maybe she can explain the nightmares. I've never had so many before."

"It so happens she's here. Can you sit down?"

"I'll do the walk-through first. If she's still here when I'm done, we'll see."

He made notes on his clipboard as he walked through the house while Audrey followed a step behind. He listened for air sounds at windows, examined acoustic tiles, and checked the ceiling modifications in each room. He used a tone emitter and a meter to measure sound amplitudes. By the time they returned to the living room, he felt better than when he arrived. Work took his mind off the guilt and confusion tearing him apart. He cleared his throat. "Do you find the improvements satisfactory?" he asked formally, pen poised over the clipboard.

Audrey smiled. "Yes, they're satisfactory. Thank you, for everything." She walked closer to him and looked up into his eyes. "You've been so kind to Willet and to me. You let her stay at your house all those weeks, took good care of us. You made our home quieter and more livable for Will. You shared your music with us. We owe you more than money." She rose on her toes, wound her

228

arms around his neck and planted a gentle, lingering kiss on his cheek before stepping back.

Dean couldn't help a small smile. "Uh, thanks, Audrey." He flushed and looked down as he put the white envelope in her hand.

"Dean, could you stay for dinner? I know Willet and TJ would like that. I would too. We've all been through a lot together."

"Well, maybe, that sounds okay..."

Gem emerged from the kitchen at that moment with a tall glass of green liquid in her hand. She stopped short and looked Dean up and down. "Red smoke surrounds you like a shroud," she announced. "It will suffocate you. "

The sudden accusation startled him, and then it pissed him off. "Haven't you caused me enough problems?" he growled. "You and Delos. That woman will not get out of my head."

Gem's eyes narrowed. "I must inform you that Delos has passed away. If she is 'in your head', it is for reasons of your own."

Willet gasped. "Oh no! That's awful!"

Dean felt his stomach drop. "When? How did it happen?"

"The night of the club fire, after you two argued. The details are personal."

He closed his eyes, picturing his dream. "I dreamed I punched her. Hard. I wanted to keep punching her. Could I have had anything to do with it?"

"Red Souls drove your emotions, both of you. What low astral interactions you two may have had, I cannot say.

Audrey put a hand on his back. "This is terrible news. Please, come in and sit down."

He followed her into the living room, to the square of cushioned chairs and sofas around the coffee table. She helped him slip off his jacket. He dropped onto a chair and put his head in his hands, wishing he could just lie down and sleep. He heard a soft scuffling noise. When he looked up, Gem sat across from him on the couch, watching him intently. They were alone in the room.

*****

"I think I've been cursed," Dean began as a deep weariness settled on his shoulders. "And now the news about Delos – I feel responsible."

Gem folded her hands in her lap. "Red Souls have gained a foothold in your emotional body, as they did in Delos. They play upon your tendencies to anger, lust and guilt. You can remedy this condition if you choose."

"How do you know what my tendencies are?" he asked sharply. "You don't really know me."

"Do you deny it?"

It seemed pointless to argue, and he was too tired anyway. "So, you're the expert. What am I supposed to do?"

"First, see what I see."

Gem got up and walked to him. She knelt on one knee in front of him and placed her index finger gently on the spot between his eyebrows. He twitched in surprise but didn't resist.

"Close your eyes and chant with me now," Gem said. "Look at the screen under my finger." She began to sing Huuuuu, Huuuuu, quietly and with full breaths.

Dean closed his eyes, cleared his throat and echoed her in a soft mumble. His breath slowed to a steady rhythm, and his eyes turned toward the spot where he felt the warmth of her fingertip. The dark space between his eyebrows glowed and grew brighter until it blossomed into a flame with a white heart. Then he heard a small pop. He stood apart in a separate body that shed a dull light.

Bright light suffused the atmosphere around him. The light itself hummed. He felt it vibrate up and down his spine. His familiar physical form stood next to him. He studied his own face and body. The eyes were empty, the hands clenched, the mouth frozen in a grimace. He felt so oddly detached from it.

Hysterical voices shrieked. "Failure! You don't deserve to live." The voices came from inside him. His rage rose like mercury. He reviled his own weakness and cursed his physical form. "This is your fault," he hissed at himself. "I hate you."

The voices laughed. Thick red smoke swirled in and out of his mouth and nose. He swatted at the smoke, tried to blow it away, but it swarmed him furiously. He started to choke, and his eyes watered with helpless tears. "Gem, help me!"

His physical body gave him a blank stare. This infuriated Dean even more. He moved toward the body with raised hands, wrapped fingers around his own neck and squeezed. His physical eyes bulged, and the body slumped. Its skin turned pale grey. He felt the link with his physical being fade. He tried to loosen his grip, but he could only squeeze harder.

"Stop!" a voice shouted behind him. "It is not time to give up your earthly life." The voice echoed as if it came from far away.

He turned his head, startled. Like surf at the ocean, the sound of an oncoming wave rushed toward him. Light shimmered and expanded, took shape, and suddenly Gem floated in front of him in a body spangled with stars. An aurora borealis of lights swirled in her eyes and a brisk wind whipped around her. The humming sound he heard came from her.

"I don't want to kill myself," he gasped.

"Do not listen to the voices, Dean. They lie."

"What do I do?"

"Remember the word I gave you. It is the key," her voice echoed.

The red smoke gathered around him for another strike. He tried desperately to remember the chant word she'd given him but couldn't recall it.

Gem blew a long, chill breath into his face through purple lips, and then blasted him with ice crystals. He rubbed away the burn in his eyes with chilled hands and looked down at the body he wore. It glowed brightly.

He could no longer see Gem, though he still heard the hum of her presence. Unseen hands grasped his shoulders and pushed him back into his physical body. His eyes popped open. He felt disoriented, split in two. After a couple of minutes, he recovered his sense of physical unity.

Gem sat across from him on the couch, watching.

232

"What happened?" he asked in a rough voice.

"You tell me."

"I saw my body, like a separate thing. I tried to strangle myself."

"Your physical body is not you."

He looked down at his hands, legs and feet. Their solid connection to him was hard to deny. "I'm me. This is me, my body"

"Your physical body is a suit of clothes you wear. What else did you see?"

"That red smoke you always talk about. It choked me. Was it a hallucination?"

"The effects were real enough, were they not? What will you do about it?"

"Maybe I need to see a doctor."

"You can do that, of course."

"I felt hands on my shoulders. Someone pushed me back into this body. Did you do that?"

"Yes."

He hesitated to speak his mind. It sounded insane, but he had to ask the question.

"What are you, exactly?"

Gem's eyebrows lifted. "I am a person, a Soul being, like you."

"You blow ice out of your mouth. You sparkle. You're not what I thought you were."

"What did you think I was?"

"I thought you were one of those delusional hippies who dabble in bullshit magic and burn a lot of incense."

She sniffed. "Nonsense. I do not care for incense."

"That's not the point. What *do* you do?"

"I serve the Spirit of All."

Dean sat back against the couch cushions and closed his eyes. His muscles ached.

"What does that mean?"

"It means I do not serve myself."

He wasn't sure if that was good or bad. "I've dreamed so much about red smoke. It's always in my nightmares. Is it the same red smoke?"

"Yes."

"How can I make it go away?"

Her demeanor softened. "I can show you how to dispel the smoke," she said gently. "But Red Souls will return if you give them an opening in your consciousness. You must learn to protect yourself against their influence."

He stared at the ceiling. "You said something about words, but I couldn't remember them."

"Practice the chants I teach you until you can hear them in the air around you," she said. "Replace fear with trust."

"Who am I supposed to trust, you?" he said with a hard look.

"Trust yourself and the light inside you."

His gaze returned to the ceiling. "I can't really trust myself right now."

"You have more control over your dreams than you realize. If you focus attention on the light within, your control over them will grow stronger."

"Maybe you hypnotized me."

She brushed that off with a wave of her hand. "That is for you to decide."

"I don't know what to believe." His voice sounded as dull and leaden as his body felt.

She leaned toward him. "Dean, you must pull yourself together now. I need your help to prevent an imminent catastrophe."

His chest tightened as he remembered the lookout. "You mean like the glass exploding in that building?"

"That was a minor event in comparison. I mean a catastrophe. Many people will be lost. All of Los Angeles will suffer. You are a warrior, and we don't have much time left to stop it."

"You think *I'm* a warrior? You're kidding!"

"Indeed not."

"What do you expect *me* to do?"

"A Circle of Trust can generate sufficient positive energy to fight the onslaught of negative energy that is coming. You, me, the sisters, Mr. Barlow, we can create such a Circle."

"TJ won't go along with the chanting and happy thoughts. I'll tell you that right now."

"Mr. Barlow will find his own path like everyone else."

"Then what can I do for you? What can any of us do?"

"Use your awareness. You have experienced the Red Souls. You know what harm they do. Use your inner strength. Our Circle will have skills that surprise you."

He paused and considered his options. "If I help you, will it keep the smoke away?"

She shook her head. "There is no bargaining with Spirit, Dean. Service must be freely given."

The tension between his eyes pounded. He massaged the bridge of his nose with two fingers and thought. It seemed dangerous to be drawn into Gem's schemes. He had almost convinced himself the whole exploding window thing never happened. Now he pictured Gem in that swirl of white stars, emerging from a snowstorm, emanating a frightening power. She blew away the red smoke with a torrent of ice and cooled his fever. It was inexplicable. She terrified him.

Maybe it had been a dream. Deep down he knew it was something different. What Gem called Red Souls had somehow caused his nightmares, and she had driven them away. He had misgivings, but it was a debt that had to be paid.

"My mother taught me to help when people are in trouble," he said with a resigned shrug.

Gem nodded. "Your mother is wise."

*****

Lamp light sparked to life in the living room after sunset. A warm glow spread over the oak coffee table and the faces of everyone seated around it. Willet looked flushed. Audrey stared at Gem. Dean stared off into space.

TJ's eyes narrowed. "What is this, a séance?"

"No," Gem assured them. "We are going to take a trip together."

"Are pharmaceuticals involved?" he said with a snicker. "Or do we use broomsticks?"

She ignored the sarcasm. "We will use a very efficient method of travel."

"Are we going to sing one of your chants?"

"Of course," said Gem.

TJ gave a derisive snort. Willet took his hand and put an arm around his shoulders. "Where are we going?" she asked Gem. "How do we get there?"

Gem sat up straight and looked into the eyes of each person as she spoke. "Briefly, we are going to take what some call a 'soul journey' to investigate a disturbance in the mountains north of Los Angeles. Astral forces have opened a door into the physical plane that should not be there."

TJ shook his head, chuckling. "You've got to be kidding."

"That's what I said," Dean mumbled.

"It is your conscious self that will travel. I will assist you in separating you from your physical body, because you do not yet know how to do it yourselves."

"Isn't that like dying?" TJ's voice rose. "I don't want to die!"

"Your body will be fine," replied Gem quietly. "It will be here, waiting for you, when you get back."

"Back from *where*?"

"From the mountains, as I said."

TJ scanned all the faces around the table. "Why are we listening to this? Dean?"

Dean glanced at him and shrugged. "I have my own reasons for playing."

"Why us, Gem?" asked Audrey. "What do you need all of us for?"

"In different ways you have all experienced the negative astral forces I speak of, seen or heard them or have been touched by them. You will understand me when I say they are dangerous. There are bonds of love among you, a growing trust. I need that positive energy to fight the influx of negative energies in the mountains. I need to form a Circle."

Everyone around the table looked at her, at each other, back at her.

"A circle?" TJ demanded. "What for?"

"The rocks you found are a kind of crystal that carries Red Souls through the subtle veil of energies separating astral and physical planes. Veins of crystal run in the mountains north of Los Angeles, and a man named Richard Theese is digging it out. When he does this, the Souls escape into this world. We must stop him."

"Souls," TJ repeated, squinting at Gem. "In the rocks."

Dean looked to the others in confusion. "What rocks?"

"Mr. Theese does not yet know that Los Angeles is riddled with veins of crystal. It has spread because of his digging. A massive earthquake will crack the crystal and release the Souls on a large scale. No one will be safe from psychic attacks. However, a committed circle of people with sufficient positive energy can prevent this. I will create such a circle with your help."

TJ glanced briefly at Willet. "Seriously?"

"You can prevent destruction and chaos in your city," Gem said. "And I will help you experience your true nature as Soul, apart from the physical body. I do not offer this assistance often."

"You're trying to scare us," TJ said, "or make us feel guilty."

"It is simply the reality we face," Gem replied calmly. "So, I ask you all - will you accept this mission?"

"I will. I want the experience," said Willet. "And I want to help."

"You know I'm in," Dean said, avoiding TJ's eyes. "But I want to know more about the rocks."

"Audrey? What about you?" Gem asked.

"I'll help if I can," Audrey replied slowly. "I'm reserving judgement about the whole Soul journey thing, though."

TJ exploded. "Are you all nuts? You're rational, educated people. I can't believe you're buying this baloney." He got up and walked rapid laps around the square of couches. Then he dropped back on the couch next to Willet and glared at everyone.

Gem shrugged. "It is up to you, of course. I cannot force you."

Willet took both his hands in hers. "Thomas. We need you. Take a leap of faith."

"Faith in what, Will? What about this could I possibly have faith in?"

Her eyes held his. "You saw what happened to your club. Deep down, you know why. What if we can prevent something bad from happening to people? Isn't it worth doing?"

"Aw, now, don't look at me like that. I'm not a circle group kind of guy. You know that."

Willet looked to Gem. "Please explain what we have to do, *exactly*."

"I will chant a word. You will close your eyes and chant the same word with me. That's it."

"See?" Willet turned back to him. "It's simple. The worst that can happen is you fall asleep."

TJ groaned. "Willet, you're killing me. This is ridiculous."

"I'd feel better if you were there with me."

He sighed, shaking his head. "I could use a nap, I guess, but I can't promise anything more than that."

"The Circle is complete," Gem stood. "Let's see what we can do."

*****

"We will meet in the World between Worlds," Gem began.

That got a reaction. "Where's that?" "What do you mean?" "Never heard of it…"

"It is a region between the physical and astral planes where the rate of vibration transitions. Some call it the Lightning Zone."

"Lightning?" Willet fidgeted in her seat. "Lightning gives me a headache. Maybe I can't be in the circle."

"You will not hear it with your physical ears, so it should not be painful."

TJ grumbled under his breath about junk physics. Willet glared at him.

Gem waited for more questions. When no more came, she continued the instructions.

"Sit up straight, close your eyes and relax. Follow my voice. Take slow, steady breaths. Center yourself and look for the light in the dark space between your eyebrows. Then we will chant."

Gem closed her eyes, sat up in her chair with straight spine, and began a series of lung-deep inhales and long slow exhales. Willet began breathing with her. She heard distinctive breathing around the room. TJ sat next to her, his breath tentative and shallow. Audrey's breath whistled softly through her nose. Dean's breath sounded more like a light snore.

After several minutes of breathing, Gem chanted the syllables, drawing out each one on a long note. "Huuuuu. Huuuuu."

Willet repeated the words, listening to the rhythmic interplay of voice and breath. One by one, other voices joined hers, low and tentative at first, but then stronger. They seemed to breathe as one. She relaxed into the sound. Her heartbeat slowed and her breath whispered. A soft buzz vibrated in her left ear.

On the dark screen between her eyebrows, a point of light came closer and closer until it engulfed her. Pressure increased in her chest. She had the sensation of being pulled forward rapidly, head-first, until she popped through a distant opening and floated into dark space, drifting like an untethered balloon.

Chapter 25: The Wheel

Starlight pierced the vast darkness. Milky galaxies swept across the distant firmament. A small comet flew by with a hiss, dragging a sparkling tail. The enormity of the scene overwhelmed her. *So beautiful! I feel so free!* A spike of white lightning split the dark and boomed like a cannon shot just to the right. Instinctively, Willet tried to protect her ears, but here was no danger. The sound vibrated through her without hurting. Lightning cracked behind her, so close it sent her spinning. She let herself roll with the motion, surprisingly unconcerned.

A spinning light appeared suddenly in the distance and exerted a gravitational pull on her heart center. She sped forward and collided with it, ending up on the rim of a glowing wheel with a hub of silver light at the center. The rest of the Circle was there, wide-eyed and staring. TJ hovered on one side of her, Audrey on the other, and Dean across the circumference next to a brown-haired woman she didn't recognize. A beam of silver light attached each of them to the silver hub. They rotated slowly with the wheel. *Where is Gem?*

"Welcome to the Circle of Augustus." Gem's voice echoed, coming from everywhere at once. "Your consciousness has detached from your physical bodies, but do not fear. You are safe on this journey.

No harm will come to these light bodies or to the physical bodies you have left behind. Audrey, throw those rings, please."

Everyone looked at Audrey, and Audrey looked at her hands. She appeared shocked to find rings of gold light twirling around her fingers. After a few seconds of staring, she shook them off like drops of water from wet hands. The rings went spinning away into the darkness.

"Now then, Gem continued. "We are here to see and understand the crystal and what it contains. Chant. Focus."

The wheel descended in slow rotation and came to a stop above a mountain range draped in clouds. Mount Wilson. A narrow tower of metal scaffolding stood on one peak, studded with blinking lights – the solar observatory. On another peak, a white-domed astronomical observatory looked like an alien mother ship with its slit eye pointed at the stars. The wheel continued its descent. It touched the shoulders of the mountain and dropped through the rock. The massive mountain swallowed them.

Their descent ended in a tunnel lit by electric lamps, and the wheel they rode disappeared. Men in dusty overalls hacked at the walls of the tunnel with picks and shoveled loose rock into barrels. The rock walls were riddled with veins of crystal with fiery red lights streaming through them. If the miners saw the lights, they didn't react, nor did they look up from their work when the Circle arrived.

A wave of emotion hit Willet in the chest. She looked at Audrey, and Audrey stared back. Willet saw her own shock and elation mirrored in her sister's eyes. She turned to TJ and searched his face. His eyes darted in every direction, taking everything in. Dean looked dazed.

Gem and the unknown woman spoke silently to each other, and then Gem inclined her head toward the mine wall. "Observe the veins of crystal contained in the rock. Red Souls travel inside those channels. That is how they pass from the astral to the physical plane."

In one synchronized motion everyone's light bodies moved forward into the middle of a web of crystal channels in the wall. Fiery trails flew by them on all sides.

*****

We're inside a rock wall, TJ thought. *How is that possible?* He chanted feverishly to calm the panic. If he stopped, he began to lose his focus and his nerve.

"Focus," Gem's voice ordered. *Damn that woman.*

Streams of red light flowed through the crystal at furious speeds, ricocheted back and forth between facets in the crystal like an incendiary pinball game before careening out of sight. TJ got dizzy trying to track them. He wasn't sure what he was supposed to do.

He looked at Willet for a clue. She was watching the streams intently, and her lips moved as she chanted. He squinted into a stream. Wild red eyes and open mouths in amorphous bodies swirled in the fire. They chattered like magpies. He put out a hand t to feel the crystal, and his hand began to sting. He withdrew it quickly.

The heat inside the rock pressured him. He felt like he had a brick on his chest. He struggled against that weight and became despondent. Memories of loss flowed through his head. Resentment built, anger and depression followed in wave after debilitating wave. He questioned why he was alive, what was the point. He thought about death and what a relief it could be. He found himself at the edge of despair, looking into an abyss. He couldn't look away.

"Stand back, please, while I cool these veins," Gem's voice echoed in his head and jarred him out of his fixation.

245

A stream of ice as thin as a laser hissed through the veins of crystal. It hit the flying fire and turned it to steam. The Red Souls' hot chatter fell to muffled quiet, and the weight on his chest eased.

Gem's blowing ice out of her mouth. That is so... messed up. He reached out to touch a vein. It had cooled almost to freezing. He looked up to see how the others were reacting and noticed the brown-haired woman with the tail of brown hair over her shoulder was chanting with eyes closed.

Who is that? As soon as the thought came to him, the woman in question opened her eyes and smiled at him, her luminous eyes penetrating his head. She said something he couldn't hear, but somehow, he understood it.

"Warrior, you are free."

I'm free, he repeated. *I'm free.* A tingling energy rolled through him. Startled, he fell backward into darkness.

*****

Willet dropped into her physical body with a thud and her eyes popped open. A mechanical buzzing sound in the room was so loud she thought a small plane might be landing on the roof. The buzz died away until it was just a tickle in her left ear. She sat up and looked for Gem in the living room. Gem wasn't there. A hand-written note lay on the coffee table in front of her.

"Please forgive my sudden departure. Dora needs a walk, and I must speak with Mr. Theese. Write down anything you remember about our journey. I will see you again soon." -Gem

Willet went to the front door and stuck her head out to listen for the Jeep but didn't hear it. How could Gem have gotten away so fast?

They were in the mine just a few seconds ago. She returned to the living room to show Gem's note to everyone.

Audrey scribbled fast in a notebook. Dean was flat-out asleep, head thrown back on the couch, mouth slack. TJ sat with his head in his hands. Willet went to him and put an arm around his shoulders.

"Thomas, look at me. Are you okay?"

TJ looked up at her, his eyes bleary. "I don't know. Did you see what I saw?"

"We traveled to the mountain and watched Red Souls run through the crystal. Gem froze them with ice."

"Yeah, that's it. I could have had a heart attack if someone hadn't told me to get my arteries checked."

Willet kissed him on the cheek. "You're welcome. Can you remember anything else? Would you like some paper to write on?"

"I'd like to forget the whole thing. No, wait, I'd like to remember what that brown-haired woman said to me. It's on the tip of my tongue, but I can't pull it out. Who is she?"

"I have no idea."

Audrey snapped her notebook shut and stood up briskly. "I'm going to make pizza. Willet, do you want to help?"

"Sure, okay. Don't you want to talk about… you know, what just happened?"

"Not right now. I need to move around, get my blood circulating, before I lose my mind." Audrey disappeared down the hall to the kitchen.

*****

TJ watched Dean snore. He seemed so relaxed, TJ didn't want to disturb him, but he needed to talk to his friend, find out what he saw, what he thought. Maybe Dean had an explanation. The snoring sawed on. He nudged Dean's knee with his foot. Dean snorted, sputtered and sat up, looking around through slit eyes.

"What's goin' on? Where are the ladies?"

"In the kitchen," TJ said. "What's goin' on with you?"

Dean stretched, rolling his neck and pulling on his shoulders, and sat up straighter. "I think I had a really intense dream."

"You think?"

"A crazy dream. I was covered in red smoke again. Gem honked a mouthful of wet snow in my face and the smoke blew away. Then I floated around in the stars. We went into a tunnel, you Audrey, Will. We were supposed to do something…"

"Do you remember the red fire flying around?"

Dean stared at him, nodding. "Yeah, you saw that?"

"Yeah."

"It seems – incredible." Dean shook his head as if trying to clear cobwebs from his brain. "What can I compare it to? Peyote in the desert, acid in the jungle, even Foster's special home grown. Nothing comes close. Did Gem slip something in the limeade?"

"We saw the same things, Dean. Drugs don't work like that. Remember when you were tripping about monkeys in the palm trees in Mexico while I saw exploding orchids? That's drugs. We haven't done any drugs. How do you explain it?"

Dean sat back and extended his arms along the back of the couch with a dawning smile. "All I can say is I felt great, so in the moment, like when I surf storm waves or ski some really good powder. I'd do it again in a minute."

TJ sagged back in his chair. "I was so depressed that I wanted to kill myself. I never want to feel that way again."

"That's what Red Souls do to you. They make you desperate. Trust me, I've been there. Do you still feel that way?"

"I felt better after Gem iced that fire."

"Yep, definitely Red Souls."

"But that makes no sense, Dean! She worked us somehow. What does she want?"

Dean scratched his chin. "It's the Red Souls thing. They make people crazy, and she drives 'em away. It's what she does. I've seen it, felt it. Now you've seen it too. We have what they call 'independent corroboration.'" He chuckled.

TJ shook his head. "You're nuts. Having an hallucination doesn't corroborate anything. What about that woman holding your hand?"

"Yeah, that was weird. I could feel her hand on mine, but every time I tried to look at her, she turned kind of transparent. I couldn't make out her face."

"She said something to me. I can't remember the words, but I it made me feel better."

"See? Not an hallucination. We wouldn't both see her if it was."

Audrey's voice called everyone to the kitchen.

TJ glared at Dean. "I told you these women would be trouble," he said under his breath.

"Yeah, you told me," Dean replied with a shrug. "Too late now."

* * * * *

Willet led TJ out to the back patio to see the stars come out in the darkening desert sky. Audrey arranged slices of cheese and tomato on a circle of white dough with deft precision. She dotted the circle with mushrooms and pineapple chunks, slid the pan into the oven with a bang and closed the door. When she turned around, Dean was leaning against a counter, watching her.

He looked into her eyes and smiled. "I'm hungry after the *big trip*," he said with emphasis.

Her forehead creased in a slight frown. "What are you implying?"

"Implying? Nothing, I just mean, what a trip, right? Out of the body and all…"

"It seems incredible, but it happened, just like Gem said. I can't dismiss it. I just hope she's one of the good guys," Audrey murmured as she turned the light on in the oven and checked the pizza.

"Audrey," he began, but then stopped. "Maybe this isn't the time, but…"

"What?" she asked.

"I hope we can start over, you and me. The morning after the fire, you left my place without saying goodbye. I was a jerk, absolutely. Are you still mad at me?"

"I wasn't mad, Dean, just uncomfortable. It looked like you wanted to talk to that girl on the beach. I felt in the way."

"I wanted to talk to *you*. She was the one in the way."

"Oh," she said, suddenly flustered. She looked down to hide the blood flushing to her cheeks.

He walked up close to her, wrapped a curl of blonde hair behind her ear, and then lifted her chin with the crook of his finger. "How about we go out? Do you have any evenings free?"

His hopeful, almost shy smile touched her. She cleared her throat and tried for a casual response. "I can check my calendar, but I'm sure we could arrange something. You don't have to play with the band or anything?"

"The band hasn't been playing as much since the club burned. My evenings are open if we're not practicing." He smiled again. The full force of his blue eyes and handsome face hit her hard. "I'll call you in the next couple of days."

Audrey felt her lips go numb. "Yes, call me. Good," she mumbled.

Willet and TJ came in from the patio looking for pizza. Audrey's heart was beating so hard, she thought Dean might be able to hear it. That would not be cool.

*****

With everyone in the kitchen, Audrey decided to initiate a discussion of recent events. "Can we talk about what happened to see if we all saw the same things?"

General mumbling rose around the kitchen table.

"What do you remember, Dean?"

"We were floating in the sky in a circle. You threw some rings. We fell into the mountain, stood in a tunnel and watched the fire flying around until Gem shot it with something cold."

"Is that what you guys remember?" she asked, looking at Willet and TJ.

Willet said "Check." TJ just shrugged.

"Then we're agreed on the basics. Will heard voices too."

TJ turned to Willet. "What voices?"

"Red Souls were saying 'Take the city,'" Willet murmured. "Also, 'Get them', whatever that meant."

"You're talking about those red faces in the crystal?"

"Yes, those are Red Souls."

"Could they take the city?" asked Audrey.

"If there are enough of them."

The electric oven hummed, pumping out the toasty scent of browning crust and melting cheese. Willet pulled a pair of headphones from a nearby drawer and set them on her ears. Everyone stared at Audrey.

"Will experienced something the rest of us didn't," she said. "Was she the only one? We need details."

"Gem blew the red smoke off me before she pulled me onto the wheel," Dean said.

"The woman with the brown ponytail woman said something to me," TJ said. "I can't remember it."

"She always looked blurry," Dean added. "I never got a good look at her face."

"I saw her eyes," TJ said. "And heard her voice, sort of. I think she called me a warrior."

"This might be why Gem needs a Circle," said Audrey thoughtfully. "We all noticed different things."

TJ scoffed. "Gem doesn't need us. She iced that fire. Why does she need us?"

"Gem might be drawing on our energy to pump up her own power," Audrey said. "And then there were the rings."

"Yeah, the rings. How did that happen?" Willet asked.

"I heard Gem's voice when we flew over the mountains, like she was inside my head. She told me to 'throw the rings.' I didn't know what she meant, but then there were three gold rings spinning on my fingers. They got so hot I had to shake them off."

"We both have jobs now," Willet said.

"Where is Gem anyway?" Dean asked.

"The real question is whether we are on the same page," Audrey asked, ignoring him. "About the Circle, that is."

"What page *is* that, Audrey?" TJ asked with mild sarcasm. "A page out of *The Four Musketeers*? Or maybe *Lord of the Rings*."

Audrey returned his stare. "I'm talking about the page on which we decide to be members of the Circle of Augustus and fight those red things if they get into the physical world."

253

"I'm not convinced about that whole 'astral plane, physical plane' thing. It sounds bogus," he muttered. "And I didn't ask to be in any circle."

"None of us did. That's beside the point."

"Do you really expect me to believe we took a 'soul journey' with Gem? It's ridiculous. I still think we could have been drugged, or hypnotized."

Audrey stared at him. "So, that's your explanation? You're willing to pretend it didn't happen?"

"I don't know what happened. What, you're the boss now?"

"I'm not anyone's boss, and I don't pretend to understand any of this. I do know Will and I were almost asphyxiated in our car because of rocks that came from *your* club, which by the way, almost burned to the ground for no apparent reason. Is any of this ringing a bell? You were there."

"Yeah, so what, it doesn't mean the world is about to end."

Audrey bristled. "We all saw what happened, felt it too. I can say for myself that *I* wasn't drugged or hypnotized. *I* was definitely conscious. Can anyone say different?"

Silence.

"To me, that means we're dealing with a reality of some sort," Audrey continued. "Those rocks with the fire inside, call them 'Red Souls' or whatever. Are you okay with those things exploding out of the ground? I'm not. People I care about live in LA. Gem said we could prevent a catastrophe. I used to think of her as a self-righteous phony, but you know what? I can't dismiss her that easily now. If I just ignore what she showed us, and people get hurt I couldn't live with myself."

Audrey sputtered, slightly out of breath when she finished. Dean extended his right arm, palm down, to the center of the kitchen table. "I offer my sword, milady," he said solemnly, "for whatever good it will do."

Audrey gave him a wan smile. "Thanks, Dean. I hope we don't need swords." She placed her hand over his, and Willet put her hand on Audrey's.

TJ stared at the stack of hands in front of him. "You've got to be kidding. Okay, I can't deny we had some kind of bizarre experience," he griped, appealing to them. "But we don't really know why. What does Gem expect *us* to do about it anyway?"

"We're the Circle, dude," Dean said. "Warriors. We're supposed to fight."

"We'll do what we can," Willet added.

They all looked at TJ, waiting.

"Gaah! You people are nuts," he said as he covered Willet's hand with his palm. "And I'm the biggest idiot for going along with it."

Chapter 26: Face-Off

Gem hurried down the long drive leading away from Pine Siskin House. Out of sight of the house, her temporary physical form dissolved into the ether. A detour through the astral plane brought her quickly to the beach where Dora guarded the Jeep and her body inside it. She slipped into her sleeping form, sat up, and opened the door for Dora to jump out and relieve herself on a nearby patch of grass. The dog peed for almost two minutes, casting reproachful glances at Gem with big brown eyes. With business done, they were on their way to pay a visit to Theese's hideaway at Mount Wilson.

When Gem arrived, she parked high on the crest of a hill from which she could watch the activity in the compound through high-powered binoculars. Men unloaded wooden crates from the back of a truck onto dollies and rolled them into a long, low warehouse at the far-left side of the central parking lot. Other men wheeled empty crates out of the warehouse and hefted them onto the empty trucks. It all seemed innocuous, but Gem's second sight told a different story. The compound was full of astral energies.

A glittering cloud of Red Souls circled the warehouse in rapid spirals and slipped through cracks and doors. The warehouse was probably full of them, but that was a minor problem compared to the funnel of black energy twenty feet high that swirled over the center of the compound. Plumes of dense mist darted in and out of it. Three rings of gold light surrounded the funnel, holding it in check. The funnel seemed to strain against the rings, trying to break their hold. "Remember the Ring Thrower's rings, Dora?" Gem murmured. "She threw them from the Lightning World, and they found their mark here. A worthy first effort."

Physical manifestations also appeared. Electric sparks climbed a tall scaffold on the roof of one of the outbuildings and fountained from the top. The scaffold enclosed a broadcast tower. "The circuits in

Theese's radio studio have overloaded," Gem said. "I suspect he has some burnt electronics. We'd best take shelter until the Traveler arrives." Dora snuffed delicately and her pink tongue lolled out of her mouth. Gem and Dora climbed back into the Jeep.

Moments later, Sonrisa Degas dropped into the passenger seat next to Gem as if she slid out of an invisible tube. "Red Souls use the crystal to travel between worlds. That is how they get past the Gate. If the crystal breaks open, the Souls are released into the physical world."

Gem put down the binoculars and raised an eyebrow at the Traveler's sudden appearance. "Hello, Sonny. Good to see you too. We have a bigger problem." She pointed at the funnel of black energy. "Jat has taken form in this place."

Sonrisa nodded at the Red Souls swarming the warehouse. "It will be difficult to dislodge him if his followers flood the air."

"What are they doing in the warehouse, Sonny? Can you investigate?"

"Of course, Guardian." Sonrisa disappeared suddenly, but her voice echoed from her empty seat. "Someone comes."

A scuffle of feet kicked up dust beside the Jeep. Two men with assault rifles peered into the window at Gem. "Where'd that other woman go?" said one man in an angry voice. "I saw two."

"Yer seein' things, Red," the other man replied. "There ain't but one woman in the car. And a big, ugly dog."

Dora peeled her lips back and showed the man her teeth.

"What you doin' in there?" the man snarled, taking a step back and raising the barrel of his gun.

Gem rolled the window down. "I came to see Mr. Theese," she said evenly. "I'm interested in his mining business."

The man chuckled and pointed his gun at Gem. "Interested in business, eh? He ain't tellin' you nothin', girlie. Yer welcome to come down, talk to the boss, though. Now get out of that Jeep or I put a bullet through the window."

Gem opened the driver side door and stepped carefully out of the Jeep. The Colt under the seat lay just out of reach, but it wouldn't have done much good against two assault rifles. Dora leaped into the front seat and jumped out after her. Gem flicked her wrist, and Dora took off up a narrow trail leading into the brush. The other man turned quickly and fired into the brush after her. Dora ran between the rocks and disappeared. "Very stupid, lady. We'll have to go kill that dog."

"You will have to catch her first," Gem replied calmly. "She is very resourceful, and she moves like the wind."

*****

Red and Andy ushered Gem into the compound's main office. Theese sat behind a mahogany desk in a black leather chair. He wore a blue suit coat over broad shoulders, and his belly peaked above the desk like a crescent moon. Silver-haired, his bushy salt-and-pepper eyebrows shot up over wire-rim glasses balanced on the bump of his nose as he peered at them.

Andy shuffled forward and cleared his throat. "Uh, we found her on the access road, boss. Watching this place. With binoculars."

"Who are you?" Theese barked.

"I am Guardian of the Astral Gate. Your mining activities are compromising that Gate."

"The intrepid Guardian I've heard so much about?" Theese asked with a smile of delighted malice. "How nice to finally meet you. I've been curious. What brings you to our little corner of the world today? And where *is* that dog of yours? He bit one of my associates. I'd certainly like to get my hands on it." He wagged a stubby finger at Gem as if she were a naughty child.

Gem got right to the point. "Why are you digging the crystal? The energy it contains is dangerous."

The middle of Theese's forehead creased into a frown. He stood up behind the desk. Over six feet tall, he made the large desk look suddenly small. "Trespassing on my property *and* sticking your nose into my affairs? Again? I really can't be forgiving about it this time."

He stalked around the desk with predatory slowness. "How did she get onto the private road without being stopped, Red?" he asked in an ominous tone. "Aren't there guards on duty at the guard house?"

Red shifted back and forth on his feet. "Should be. Don't know what happened. I'll check the security cameras."

"She is nosy and perplexingly resourceful," Theese mused. "How does she know so much about my business? I'd like to keep an eye on her, for a little while at least. We'll put her in basement storage for the time being. I can't have her slowing us down."

Andy squirmed. "It's cold down there, boss."

"What's your point?"

With a sudden movement, Theese backhanded Gem across the face with all the force of his bulk behind it. Her head snapped back, and her eyes shut at the force of the blow. As her equilibrium wavered, she saw a disk of bright, white light between her eyebrows. It shimmered and hummed. From the center of the disk, a pair of blue eyes looked back at her, kind and loving. She felt strength return even as a throbbing bruise rose around her left eye.

Theese turned to his lackeys. "Take her downstairs. She can stew all she wants there."

Gem recovered her balance and opened her eyes. She stared up at him without emotion. "You have struck a Guardian," she said, shaking her head, "a serious mistake." She actually felt sad for him.

Rage glimmered in his eyes, his cheeks turned red, and his hands shook. Anger made him sputter. "We'll see who made the mistake today, you interfering witch." He punched her in the abdomen with a closed fist. She doubled over, gorge rising. An upward blow to the chin rocked her backward. Stars exploded in her head, her knees buckled, and her eyes watered. Andy and Red gasped in wide-eyed shock. Andy grabbed one arm while Red grabbed the other and caught her before she hit the ground. They set her down gently.

Theese stood over her, rubbing the knuckles of his left hand with his right thumb. "That's for damaging my radio station. I suspect you are behind all the burnt circuitry in the equipment. Do you know how much broadcast towers and sound mixing consoles cost? I'll be off the air for months." He turned to his men and waved a hand. "Get her out of here before I really lose my temper."

The men dragged her across the carpet and out the door of the office.

Chapter 27: Lucexine

Take it easy, Tommy boy. You almost sideswiped that truck. Stop thinking about her for a minute, will ya?

TJ had gone home for a couple of days to get his head back together after the inexplicable episode with Gem. Now he sped back to Hemmings to pick Willet up on Wednesday afternoon. He drove the S-class Mercedes that he leased for business, hoping it would be quiet enough for her not to wear the headphones. He didn't want her to get a headache.

They were going to his cabin in Big Bear for a couple of days of mountain scenery and fresh air. Willet looked pale and tired after the Circle experience. She needed to relax, forget all the craziness. He did too.

Since restaurants were too noisy, he planned a gourmet meal at the cabin. He enlisted the aid of his favorite LA chef, in whose restaurant, Le Rossignol, he had invested capital. Chef Andre was bustling around the kitchen at the cabin at that moment, preparing his signature coq au vin, pine nut raviolis, and braised spring vegetables. There would be something flambé for dessert. TJ had selected the wines himself, white, as the lady preferred. He also had a selection of Chopin in the car as well as at his cabin. She loved Chopin.

He looked at himself in the rearview mirror. *You haven't been this way about a woman since Valerie. Remember how that turned out.*

It was unfair to put Valerie Stanfield in the same category as Willet. Valerie, a garden variety spoiled brat, toyed with his heart in high school. Willet, on the other hand, could be a creature from another planet. She had seemed so fragile when he met her, ethereally

261

beautiful, and kind of irritating. She turned out to be really smart, and so sweet. When they walked the beach together and talked, she started getting under his skin. It seemed very promising before all the insanity began. He barely recognized his own life anymore.

He shook himself out of reverie when he reached the road to Pine Siskin House and drove directly to the front door. The Mercedes barely purred, but Willet would still hear him coming. As soon as he pulled up, she opened the front door and stepped out on the porch. *Man, she sure looks fine.*

Willet had a long, cream-colored cashmere coat wrapped around her, and carried a small overnight bag. She carried a pair of headphones on her left arm. TJ got out and walked to the passenger side to open the door for her. When he took her bag and helped her into the car, he caught a waft of lavender and sage.

In the car, she let the coat drop off to reveal bare shoulders in a red silk tank top. Her long corn-silk hair draped over her shoulders and her eyes reflected the blue of the sky. He had to take a deep breath. She looked so beautiful.

"Hey, babe, you look hot," he nodded as he slid behind the wheel. His eyes slowly traced her slender neck and the swell of chest under red silk.

She blushed and smiled. "Thanks. I don't get to dress up much. And you look very GQ in your charcoal three-piece suit. I like the green stripe in the tie. It matches your eyes."

"This is my barrister suit. I had a meeting at court this morning."

"Nothing serious, I hope…"

"No, just fire 'victims' trying to sue me into bankruptcy."

"That sounds serious."

"Fortunately, there were no major injuries," he said as he put the car in gear and took off around the circular drive. "Smoke inhalation, some scrapes and burns. Fire investigators couldn't figure out what started the fire, and they didn't find any evidence of negligence on the part of the club, so that helps my case."

"It wasn't your fault! The rocks started the fire. They almost set Audrey's car on fire."

TJ gave a wry smile. "I can't tell a judge that evil rocks started the fire. I'd probably lose my license to practice law." He merged onto the freeway and stepped on the gas. The windows didn't whistle, and nothing rattled.

"This car is pretty quiet!" she said appreciatively. "So, we're going to your cabin for dinner? Are you cooking for me?"

"I thought about cooking, but I made other arrangements. Hope you like French."

"Mmm, French is my favorite."

"Excellent." He pressed Play on the CD, and the first of the Chopin Ballades began to play.

Willet looked at him with pleased surprise. She leaned over and pressed her lips to his cheek. TJ smiled to himself. *Good call on the music, Barlow.*

TJ navigated the streets of Big Bear to the gravel road leading to his cabin. He got out, opened Willet's door, and held out an arm to help her from the car. One slim leg stretched to the ground followed by the other. She took his arm. He nodded and grinned at her red croc stilettos.

"Thanks for the approval, Thomas Jefferson," she said. "You can stop ogling now."

"I'll be ogling all evening. It's on the menu."

She smiled and her cheeks flushed rose. She wrapped the coat around her and walked with him to the house. He unlocked the front door, waving her in with a flourish.

"Something smells delicious," she said as she sniffed the air and looked around. "Wow, this is a great place."

A table set for two filled a small dining area next to the kitchen. White linen, crystal glasses and silver glittered under lit candles. A bouquet of wildflowers graced the center of the table.

"Did you do all this?" she asked in wonder.

"I made menu selections. Chef Andre made it happen," he said as he shrugged his suit coat onto a chair and went into the kitchen. The chef's assistant had left wrapped dishes in the oven, staying warm. He poured two glasses of wine and returned to her.

"Sancerre," he said, handing her a glass. "It's a good vintage, hope you like it."

She studied the wine, turning the stem of the glass between her fingers. "The Loire Valley is my favorite part of France that I've never been to. That's where the castles are."

He grinned at her.

She blushed and murmured, "I'm not a wine snob, really."

"Glad to hear it. Otherwise, we'd have to do a blind taste test to see how good you really are. Do you want to unpack, freshen up?"

"No, I'd like to take a look at that wonderful view you have. Can I see the lake from here?"

He slipped his arm around her shoulders and led her out to the back deck. The rocky hills fell away from the deck, undulating in grey gorges that tumbled toward the lake. Stands of pines and aspen brushed the blue sky as far as the eye could see. Far below, sunlight flickered on the surface of Big Bear Lake. Snow-covered peaks rose around the lake. The air tasted as fresh and cool as it smelled.

They gazed at the view without speaking, and then he turned her in his arms and kissed her, soft and unhurried. He felt her shiver. "Are you cold? Want to go inside?"

"No, this is so lovely."

Her eyelids closed. She made a sound of quiet contentment. He leaned in to inhale the warm scent of her neck, pressed his lips to her ear and whispered. "You smell delicious, Red Riding Hood. I might have to take a bite."

Willet's eyes fluttered open to look at him.

He took her glass from her, placed it with his on a nearby table, and casually backed her against a wooden pillar of the porch. He wrapped a hand around her neck and pressed a deep kiss to her lips. She slipped her arms around his waist. He continued the kiss and slid his hands under her coat to grasp her torso. His thumbs brushed the sides of her breasts through the thin red silk. She drew a sharp breath and tried to move closer to him. He pulled back a little to look into her eyes.

"Are you hungry?" he murmured.

"You mean, for food?"

"We haven't even had the appetizers yet. Let's see what Chef Andre made for us." He took her hand, pulled her back into the cabin. She smiled a small smile and followed him to the dinner table. Beeswax candles filled the air with a light scent of honey. She slipped out of her coat and dropped it on a chair in front of the stone fireplace in the living room. A red silk skirt matching her silk tank top swirled around her legs as she turned to the table.

They ate chilled prawns with glasses of Sancerre. With the coq au vin, they drank an aged Sauvignon Blanc from Pessac Leognan, mellow with flavors of nuts and honey custard. Willet picked up a roll, broke it open and spread butter on one half with the butter knife. She savored the roll with closed eyes and a contented smile. Then she picked up the other half, slid the butter knife over it, and looked at TJ thoughtfully.

"I'm feeling as buttered as this roll," she said, matter-of-fact.

TJ cupped the glass in his palm, sipped the wine, and watched her over the rim. "Whatever do you mean?"

"Well, this is wonderful, of course. How many of your guests get the Chef Andre treatment?"

"It's not a 'treatment.' I've never done this for anyone else. I wanted you to relax and enjoy, that's all."

"I *am* enjoying myself, Thomas. After everything that's happened, it means a lot to me, being in this beautiful place with you. But now I know there are other stories going on behind what I see with my eyes. I'm questioning everything. Help me not to do that."

TJ sat back from the table and folded his arms. "Are you asking about other women coming here?"

"I guess I am, sort of, among other things…"

266

"There have seldom been women here, honestly. But now it will just be you."

Willet looked down at the table. "Are there sound prints in this room? Do I have to be careful?"

TJ chuckled. "You want to listen in, don't you? It's driving you crazy."

She looked up again. "No, I don't! The last time I listened in on your life, I didn't enjoy it."

"I've got nothing to hide. Go ahead and eavesdrop."

Willet took another bite of her roll, chewed slowly and looked at him, considering. "I think not," she said finally. "What I heard at your house really confused me, and I realized later I had no right. We haven't known each other that long. You've clearly had more of a life than I've had. That's not your fault."

There it is again, he thought, *good sense and self-assurance. I love that about her.* He put his glass down and leaned forward, making sure they were eye to eye.

"Despite what you may think, there haven't been that many women in my life. They've been around it, but not in it. I can count the actual relationships I've had on three fingers. I don't usually get serious." He paused, considering his words. "You've changed things, Will." As he said it, he realized how much.

"How have I changed things?" Her voice quivered.

"I trust you. That's rare for me. Besides, you're amazing."

She met his gaze. Thoughts and emotions flickered across her face.

"What's going on in that beautiful head of yours?"

"We haven't talked about the Circle, Thomas. What we saw and heard changes things too, changes life. Doesn't it, for you?"

He sat back with a sigh. "Ah yes, the Circle. I figured we'd get to that. Does it change life? I don't know. I've always felt like I had a pretty good grip on life, mine at least, and I tend to distrust things that don't make sense. What I saw that day made no sense, despite Gem's explanations. I didn't understand why I was chosen to see it."

"My friendship with Gem is important in my life. I'm a part of what she's doing now. The Circle is important to me." She paused, and her voice dropped almost to a whisper. "Is that a problem for us? Do you think I'm crazy? When we first met, you thought I was crazy."

"You look at things differently, that's for sure," he said. "You hear things the rest of us don't hear. I don't think you're crazy, no. You're – unique."

"What are you going to do about the Circle? Gem asked for our help. Will you help her?"

TJ paused before he spoke. "I've decided to suspend judgment for now. If I end up in that Circle again, flying through space, I won't be able to ignore it twice. I'll have to take it more seriously."

Willet smiled radiantly, got up and walked behind his chair, twined her arms around his neck and kissed him. "That works for now."

"Then we're agreed," he said solemnly. He pulled her into his lap. He raised her hands to his lips and kissed each one. "I'm in your hands."

*****

Since the night of the Circle's journey into the mountain, Audrey had trouble concentrating. Images of glowing rings and streams of fire dominated her thoughts, waking and sleeping. A low hum in her ears wouldn't go away. She caught glimpses of red shapes at the edges of her vision that weren't there when she looked directly at them. Are *Red Souls spying on me? Where the hell is Gem?* Audrey had so many questions and desperately needed to talk to her. Willet hadn't heard a word from her since the night of the 'soul journey.' However, Bart was coming to dinner, and she was determined to cook, so she had to pull it together.

At 7 PM, aromas of baked bread and sizzling steak already drifted through Pine Siskin House. Audrey arranged pink and cream Peruvian lilies in a crystal vase on the dining table. She had decided to wear a sleeveless, ice blue silk sheath dress and silver sandals, pretty but not too seductive. She wanted her appearance to say, 'I'm happy to see you' and not 'I want to drag you into bed' Her long blonde hair twisted back into silver combs behind her ears and flowed down her back. She kept her makeup light.

The doorbell rang promptly at 7:30 p.m. Bart stood in the halo of the porch lights in a brown leather jacket, dark, collared shirt, jeans and boots. His brown hair, a little longer than she remembered, curled around his ears and over his forehead. It matched his gentle brown eyes. *Had it really been only a week since the fire?* It seemed like a year ago.

He held a bunch of mauve-colored roses in one hand and a bottle of wine in the other. They stood for a moment smiling at each other. The cool night air raised goose bumps on her bare arms. She waved him in. "Please come in, Bart. I'm so glad you're here."

Bart filled the doorway as he walked in. He held the roses out to her. "Good to see you too, Audrey. You look really nice."

She couldn't help blushing, damn it, so she buried her nose in the soft petals and took a deep breath of their fragrance, soft and delicate as a French perfume. "They're lovely, thank you. Dinner's almost ready. Would you like a glass of wine, beer, or something?" she asked, nodding at the wine bottle in his hand. "We're having filet mignon."

"That sounds great. I think I brought the right wine. It's a Tempranillo, a red from Chile, hope you like it."

He shrugged off his jacket. Audrey brought it to the living room and laid it over a couch. They went on to the kitchen where two wine glasses waited on the counter. Audrey found a wine opener in a drawer.

Bart screwed the opener into the cork and pulled it out with a pop. "Do you have an aerator?" he asked.

"Yes!" She opened the drawer again and found an aerator, handing it to him. "You're a wine connoisseur."

He poured wine through the aerator into both glasses. "Not really. I have a few favorites and I stick with 'em. At least I know aeration improves the flavor. Points for me, right?"

"Points for you," she smiled. They swirled the glasses, raised them and clinked a toast.

"To survival," he said.

"Amen, and thanks. You are ever my hero." She looked into his eyes and smiled with all the sincerity she felt in her heart.

"A beautiful woman like you should always be protected."

She sipped the wine, holding a mouthful on her tongue to savor the complexities. Smooth, yet honest. *Wait, am I thinking about the wine or Bart?* She put the glass down and looked through the windows of the double oven. The filet bubbled in its juices in the top oven, and the rolls stayed warm in the bottom oven. She opened the bottom door and pulled the rolls out. The smell of baked bread filled the kitchen.

Bart inhaled with gusto. "Oh my god, those smell good."

Audrey turned to the stove top and checked the mashed potatoes, added a bit of cream and a square of butter. Asparagus steamed in a separate pot. Bart poured more wine and took the glasses to the dining room. Within minutes they were seated at the table over steaming plates. Candlelight flickered on the walls and table silver.

He cut a piece of the filet and put it in his mouth, chewing with eyes closed. "I'll have to rescue you more often. You're a great cook."

"Well, I hope never to need rescuing like that again, thank you very much. Maybe we can find another reason to have dinner."

"I'm sure we can think of something," he said, winking at her.

Hmm, he's not as shy as I remember. That wink is pretty cute. "We haven't talked since the fire," she said. "You didn't have after-effects, did you?"

"No, how about you?"

"Miraculously, no physical effects, thanks to you, but I can't say I escaped unscathed. When I close my eyes, I still picture it." Her voice fell to an almost whisper as she remembered. "The crowd pushed me so hard. I couldn't see, and the smoke burned my throat. I don't know how long I would have lasted before I got trampled." She looked down at her plate, shaking her head. Her stomach suddenly felt full of gravel.

"I'm glad I was there to help you," he said. He put his hand over hers on the table and held it tight.

271

The pressure of his hand felt warm and solid. It steadied her. She couldn't tell him that the club fire was not the only fire experience she'd had lately.

After dinner they refilled their glasses and took them into the living room. Bart started a fire in the stone fireplace with the oak logs and kindling stacked beside it. They knew so little about each other, besides the one crisis they shared. Audrey wanted to learn more. They talked and sipped wine and talked some more.

"Where did you grow up, Bart?"

"Emmett, Idaho, a small town north of Boise."

"You mentioned you're in geology, right? When did you become interested in that?"

"I got hooked on rocks when I was twelve, joined the spelunking club at school. I liked physics too, double-majored in geology and physics at Boise State. Did my masters and Ph.D. in geophysics at UCLA, got hired by the State of California. I've been with them ever since."

"Geophysics – wow. And now you study earthquakes."

"Earthquakes combine geology and physics. It was a natural for me."

"Do you still study rocks?"

"Absolutely. I have an extensive personal collection of rare finds, if I do say so myself."

She thought about the two sparking rocks hiding in the garden and wondered what a rock expert would say about them. Maybe he could explain what they were and how they ended up at the club. So, she made a decision. "If I showed you a rock, could you tell me what kind of rock it is?"

He shrugged. "I'm more a connoisseur of rock than wine. There's a good chance I'll be able to tell you something."

Audrey put her wine glass down and stood. "Wait here a minute. I have something to show you."

She went to the front door and walked out to the garden, plunged her fingers in the dirt, and fished around, pulling out the two rocks that Gem had buried. They seemed bigger than she remembered. As she held the rocks in her hand, she felt the phantom rings again, a warm current circling her fingers. Shivering against the cool night air, she brushed dirt off her hands and rubbed the rocks clean before running back inside.

Bart stared in astonishment as she placed a napkin on the table in front of him and dropped the rocks on it.

"Can you tell me what those are, geologically speaking?" she asked as she wiped her hands on another napkin.

He picked up a rock, scratched some surface dirt off with a fingernail and held it up to the fire. A thread of light flickered briefly in the rock. "What was that?" He fumbled in the pocket of his jacket, pulled out a small leather pouch from one pocket and a hard, round case from the other. The leather pouch contained small tools – picks, tweezers, a screwdriver and small scissors. He took out a pick tool and flipped a thick lens out of the round case. He used the pick to break one of the rocks into three pieces and held the lens over one piece.

"You come prepared," she observed.

"I'm a rock-hound. Never know when something interesting will turn up. This is definitely interesting." He studied the rock under the hand magnifier for a few minutes, turning it in all directions to trace its small currents, scratching at it with the pick. Then he stared at her. "Where did you get these?"

She didn't want to discuss the mother lode of crystal under the mountain. "Several pieces were found at the club after the fire, in the debris. Have you seen anything like that before?"

"It's a crystal, obviously, very unusual structure. The angles of the facets are unique. I'd have to take it back to the lab to be sure, but I'd say it looks like lucexine."

"What's that?"

"Lucexine is a crystal structure generated from an algorithm that was developed by a geophysicist at Stanford. It's designed to amplify kinetic energy. The structure keeps the energy flowing by bouncing it off the crystal facets, which are slanted at the perfect angles to accelerate the flow. A high, continuous voltage can be produced from a small amount of crystal."

"Like a battery?"

"Regular batteries store static, potential energy. Energy doesn't flow until the battery is hooked into something, like a flashlight or cell phone. In lucexine, the ions are already moving."

"So, these rocks could be lucexine."

"Lucexine is just a model for a mathematical theory. It isn't known to occur in nature."

Audrey reached for her wine glass and took a sip. The warmth trailing down her throat relaxed her.

"Maybe it does now," she suggested.

Bart shook his head slowly. "I don't think it's possible."

She pictured the streams of red energy flying through veins of the crystal in the mountain and watched the rock he held in his fingers. It certainly seemed possible to her.

"Why couldn't it occur in nature?"

"Lucexine is too perfect. Natural structures always have some random variation in them. Structures like snowflakes, crystals, honeycomb and shells are not identical. Nature doesn't work that way."

"Well, maybe it's not nature, exactly…"

Bart wasn't listening. He turned the rock over and over between his fingers, staring at it. He rubbed the bridge of his nose and peered through the lens again. "Wow, unbelievable. There's got to be another explanation." He shook his head. "Can I take these pieces to the lab? Are there any other pieces out there?"

She could say no more. "All I have is what's there. You can have them. I warn you they may cause problems. They almost set my car on fire."

Bart slipped the rocks into his jacket pocket and gave her a quizzical smile. "You're full of surprises, Audrey. Have to admit, I get jazzed by geologic mysteries. A smart, beautiful woman does that to me too."

He moved closer to her on the couch, splashed the last of the wine in their glasses, and placed his arm around her shoulders. Her skin warmed to his touch. Their glasses clinked together. She felt comforted and protected, allowed herself to lean into his embrace. He put his glass down and turned her chin gently toward him with a crooked finger. "Would you mind if I kissed you?" he asked softly. "As thanks for the wonderful dinner, of course."

Her head swam pleasantly. His scent reminded her of a forest after rain. She took a deep breath to say yes, but he didn't wait for her to answer.

"Great," he murmured, and his lips dropped firmly onto hers.

Chapter 28: The Deceiver's Bargain

Sonrisa stepped out of space-time into Theese's warehouse. In astral form, she vibrated at a different rate from the physical beings around her, so no one noticed. A particularly perceptive person might glance up, sensitive to the energy of her passing, before dismissing it as a fluke. Otherwise, she was invisible.

Computer desks lined the walls in a long white room with no windows. Someone sat in front of a laptop at almost every station. Sonrisa could not interpret anything she saw on the screens. Computers were not of her time. She was familiar with them, but she didn't bother about the details.

People in lab coats worked in assembly line fashion around a long table in the center of the room. Piles of crystal chips, small discs with black electrical cords attached to them, and squares of blue metal cluttered the table along with various tools. People handled the crystal chips with gloved hands, probably because the chips sparked wildly. The blue metal pieces were heated and folded into small boxes, about three inches square. A few chips were inserted carefully into each box and a disc was attached inside. The cord attached to the disc threaded through a hole in the side of the box. At the end of the line, someone soldered the edges of each box shut with a blow torch.

Sonrisa walked down the aisle of workstations. A blue metal box plugged into each laptop by its cord. There were no connections from the laptops to electrical outlets. She walked back up the aisle looking at the screens from different angles. Forms flashed in the background, hidden in the wavelengths of LED light. Crazed, furious faces stared with daggered eyes at the people sitting in front of the screens. Voices whined from inside, whispering words of anger and malice. The users seemed oblivious to the faces in the screen or the words, although they stared at the screen and wore earphones connected to the laptop. The subliminal impressions they received had to be affecting them.

Sonrisa put the pieces of the puzzle together. The crystal carried Red Souls. Each blue box contained crystal. The cable connection between box and laptop gave Red Souls a direct passage into the laptop. It was an astral Trojan Horse. Theese would surely get rich building a box that supplied power to the laptop without electricity. and the Deceiver had easy access to the subconscious of every person who used the laptop.

So, this is the Deceiver's bargain.

*****

Theese went down to the basement the next morning to check on his 'guest' and brought bottled water as a peace offering. He did not approve of hitting a woman under normal circumstances. What had gotten into him? A whisper in his head reminded him of the righteousness of his mission. He heard the voice deep inside himself, like an echo of his own thought. He trusted that voice. It had led him to the mine and the crystal. He concluded the whole unfortunate episode must somehow be her fault.

Why is this woman dogging me? I'm just a businessman, trying to run a legitimate business. She seems to know a lot about my operations. How does she know so much?

278

He had tried the iron fist. Maybe it was time for the velvet glove. He wanted her out of his hair, one way or the other. He unlocked the heavy metal door to the storage room and pulled it open, not sure what to expect. Pretty cold in there, just as Andy said, but more than cold air hit him as he walked in.

There was a low hum in the room, almost indistinguishable from silence. He took a deep breath and listened. Where did that sound come from? Electrical wiring and plumbing ran through the ceilings and floors upstairs. He didn't hear it anywhere else in the building. The only electrical wiring to this room ended in the single bulb hanging overhead.

He flicked a switch on the outside wall next to the door. The bulb cast a dim cone of light on a camp cot in the middle of the room. The woman laid unmoving, eyes closed, her jaw visibly swollen. A purple-red bruise ringed her left eye. He winced at the sight – could she be dead? He dragged a metal folding chair from the corner of the room, pulled it up beside the cot and sat down.

"Lady, what are you doing here?" He wrung his hands, beseeching her. "What do you want from me? This is some kind of mistake. I don't want to hurt you, but you give me no choice. You're sneaking around, spying on my business. I can't have that. Please understand."

The woman's breath sounded shallow. He poked her left arm gently with his index finger. No response, but the humming got louder. It seemed to be coming from the cot. He shook his head, stuck fingers in both ears and wiggled them to relieve the tickling vibration, and then bent closer to her and appealed to her in a conspiratorial whisper.

"I'm onto something big here, a real discovery. I'm talking about unlimited energy. Think about it – a source of energy that never runs

279

out! It'll change the world *and* earn me loads of cash. It's a sign from God! I'll deal you in if you'll just leave me alone."

Theese hung his head a moment, picturing his son, Jimmy's face the last time he came home, impressive in his Marine uniform. He missed the boy so much. A breath caught in his chest as tears overcame him. He squeezed his eyes shut, trying to hold them back, but they leaked out anyway.

"You need help, Mr. Theese," a voice murmured from the cot. "You are being led astray. This is not the way to honor your son."

Theese's head snapped up. He quickly wiped the wetness from his face with both palms. The woman stared at the ceiling through half-lidded eyes.

"You're alive," he said in a hoarse whisper. "Are you...well?"

She cleared her throat with a weak flutter. "I am bleeding internally, and my jaw is fractured. Otherwise, I feel wonderful."

He blanched at this assessment and unscrewed the top of the water bottle, unsure how to let her drink. It might be dangerous to move her. "I have water here," he said. "If you can sit up..."

She made no response. He screwed the top back on the bottle and placed it on the floor next to the cot.

"I regret hitting you," he offered. "I shouldn't have done that. You're a woman. But who do you think you are that you can just waltz in here and tell me what to do?"

"I am the Guardian of the Astral Gate in this city," she said. "I maintain the balance between this world and the next. You are destroying that balance."

He sat back, staring at her. "I thought you meant that as a joke. You really believe you're some kind of Guardian?"

"Belief has nothing to do with it. The crystal you dig contains destructive energy. It is a danger to this world, not a boon. Grief for your son clouds your judgment. You have been deceived by the Master of Deception."

Bitterness hardened Theese's muscles and his hands tightened into fists. He stood over the cot looking down on this woman who would not stop challenging him. His lip curled. "How do you know what I do? You know nothing about me, or my son."

"I have watched you, listened to your radio show, observed your followers. And I see more than that. The darkness of the Deceiver swirls above this compound now, ready to swallow it. He twists your avarice to his own ends."

Theese gave a short, broken laugh. "You mean the devil? Why would the devil want me? I'm a law-abiding citizen and a god-fearing man. I pay my taxes, go to church."

"Do you remember the Buddhists? They are peaceful people. You incited your followers to burn their temple, because they hold different beliefs than you do. This is the influence of the Deceiver."

Indignation burned in his throat. "They are not American. Their ways are not our ways." He waved a dismissive hand in the air. "The building was closed, late at night. I wanted to send a message to all the misfits that have infiltrated this city. Not my intention to hurt anyone directly."

"Monks live in that temple building. You might have killed them, not to mention the damage to property."

Theese fell silent at that. The hum pressed on him and made his head hurt. His teeth ground together. He rubbed the back of his neck, wondering why it suddenly ached He'd have to be more careful when planning an 'event.' Other than that, nothing had changed.

"You are on private property. I could have you arrested."

"How would you explain my injuries? Did I fall off a bicycle?"

He narrowed his eyes at her. "Better be careful, missy. You're on thin ice. There are many holes in the ground around here. I could easily make you disappear."

She drew a long, weary breath. "You cannot threaten me, Mr. Theese. I will do what I must to close the Gate."

A tight knot twisted in his stomach. "I don't know about any gate, or what you think you're going to do, but you better stay the hell out of my way when you do it."

"If you continue to mine crystal, our paths will cross again," she said and closed her eyes.

He folded the metal chair and stared at it a few moments before he hurled it against the concrete wall with a clattering bang that echoed around the room like a shotgun blast. No reaction from the cot. He walked out and slammed the door, locking it behind him.

*****

Space-time snapped open like a canvas sail, and Sonrisa stepped out to Theese's basement room. She found Gem's astral body floating in the air, cross-legged, eyes closed in contemplation. Gem's physical body lay on the camp cot, under a cone of blue-green light coming from the ceiling. Dora's astral body lay beside the bed. Dora turned

282

alert eyes and perked ears toward the Traveler. "Guardian, we have no time for this," the Traveler said. "You must leave this place with me now. Theese's purpose has become clear."

Gem opened her eyes and waved vaguely toward her body on the cot. "That thing is broken," she said and sniffed with displeasure. "It needs more healing before I can use it again. What did you find in Theese's warehouse?"

"Theese chops the crystal into small pieces and seals them in metal boxes. The boxes provide power to computers and release Red Souls into them. A user of such a device will not recognize their presence inside the box. The influence is insidious."

Gem harrumphed and lapsed into musing. "The Deceiver seduced him with visions of earthly riches. We know that what the Deceiver giveth, the Deceiver taketh away. The question is, when?"

"What is your plan?"

"We will summon the Circle, but first I must deal with Jat's presence here." Gem frowned again at her physical body. "I will leave it for now. Dora will protect it. Her physical form sleeps somewhere in the upper hills. She will come when we need her."

Sonrisa, Gem and Dora's astral forms slipped into a channel of space-time, leaving Gem's injured body on the cot.

Chapter 29: Knuckles

Willet and TJ were still holding hands over the dining table, eyes on each other, as the candlelight dimmed. They had finished a dessert of vanilla crème brulee with flamed cherries in port wine. Willet felt giddy, her cheeks flushed. TJ's sea-green eyes and hair the color of beach sand reminded her of their walks by the ocean. He smiled the sly smile she had come to know so well and dreamt about most nights. She wanted more of him.

"Tell me about your family," she said, as she speared a last cherry with her fork. "You've never told me about them."

"My parents own an organic farm outside Santa Cruz. They bought it after my father retired. He was a lawyer and businessman like me. They grow their own food, raise animals and stay close to nature. They're hippies, really."

"Any siblings?"

"Just my sister, Libby. She's a pediatrician in Oakland, the do-gooder in the family. I'm the capitalist."

"Are you two close?"

"Yeah, we're buds. Now that we both have lives in different cities, we don't see each other as much as we used to. We were really close growing up. What about you? Anything I should know that I don't already?"

"Well, you know Audrey and I are almost joined at the hip. We don't have other siblings and our parents live far away. Audrey went to Wellesley. I wanted to go to, but I couldn't. Just getting through high school was difficult enough. Tutors had to come to our house. I settled for online courses through New York University and managed to finish a couple of bachelor's degrees."

"Really? In what?"

"Math and music history. I didn't have to go to a classroom to study those. It worked for me."

TJ poured two shots of brandy and raised his glass to her. "You've lived a challenging life, yet you found a way to make it work. I respect that. Look at the beautiful, intelligent, accomplished woman you turned out to be."

Willet blushed and put her brandy down. "That is so sweet to say."

TJ rose, walked around the table and held his hand out to her. She put her hand in his. He pulled her to her feet and kissed her lightly on the lips.

"Come with me, please," he murmured.

He led her into the master bedroom. Lit candles threw a bronze glow into the room, reflecting off of copper-colored bedspread and curtains, brass lamps and warm wood. He walked up behind her, grasped her shoulders and lightly bit her ear lobe, brushed his lips along her neck. A shiver ran over her skin. His hands slid down to her legs and swept the red silk skirt up above her hips. He pulled her back against him, his growing hardness pressed at the small of her back.

She leaned into his chest and sighed. "Thomas. I'm not that experienced."

"Do you want to be?"

"Yes, if it's with you."

He pulled the red tank up over her head, unbuttoned the skirt and let it all drop to the floor. She stood in a black lace bra and bikini panties trimmed with red ribbons. He kissed each shoulder, unhooked her bra, and slid his hands softly over her breasts. Her knees started to buckle.

He turned her to face him, lifted her by the waist, and brought her to the foot of the bed, laying her down gently. His eyes swept over the length of her with a look of undisguised hunger more thrilling to her than any touch. He unbuttoned his shirt and pants, let his own clothes drop, never taking his eyes from her. She reached her arms out to him, asking for him. He climbed on the bed until he hovered over her. His fingers slid under the red-ribbon edge of her panties.

She gasped at his light touch and a moan escaped her. She closed her eyes and whispered, "Oh no."

He paused as he pushed her panties down to her ankles and leaned to whisper in her ear. "Oh no what?"

Her back arched and she giggled. He chuckled too, trailed kisses across her chest, shoulder to shoulder. She tried to wrap her arms around his neck, but he grasped her hands and entwined his fingers with hers, placing them beside her head. She twisted under him and sighed, relaxed and open, gasped when he pushed into her. Honeyed candlelight flickered on her eyelids. Wind sighing through the pines mingled with his soft breath. He felt like silk as he slowly filled her, the pressure growing unbearably sweet. Her moan dropped an octave.

They rocked together, breathing as one. She clenched him inside. When he bit her right nipple and gently sucked it, the shudder of her climax shook her whole body.

He rocked faster, pressed hard and deep, and released himself with a groan, then sunk down beside her with a ragged breath. They lay together side by side for a long time, fingers entwined, listening to sounds in the dark.

She rolled to face him, cupped a hand on his cheek, and kissed his lips. "Thomas."

"Hmm?"

"I love you. Maybe it's too soon, but I can't help it."

He wrapped his arms around her. "That's a good thing, isn't it? Loving someone?"

"I've never felt this way before. It scares me. Please don't make me love you if you can't love me back."

He stared at her, his expression unreadable, and touched his forehead to hers. "You worry too much," he said in a husky voice.

"What I mean to say is let me know how it is with us so I can deal with it now. I can handle things if I'm prepared. Later, it would be so much harder..."

He crushed her to his chest and rested his cheek on her hair. "Will, when I said I'm in your hands, I meant it. You have my heart in your hands. It's not given lightly."

She closed her eyes, let worry recede. They lay silent, dozing, their bodies pressed warm skin to warm skin, until sleep pulled them under.

*****

Gem followed Sonrisa onto the roof of Theese's warehouse with Dora beside her. They stood in their light bodies, watching astral energies churn through the foothills of Mount Wilson like unsettled winds. The funnel of black astral energy spinning over the compound had become a cyclone of towering height, almost as high as the mountain itself. Audrey's three gold rings still held the tail of the funnel in place but struggled against the force of it.

The balance of power is tipping.

The warehouse leaked Red Souls from all the broken crystal inside. When they recognized the presence of the Guardian, they shrieked and streaked away in all directions. Gem covered the warehouse in a thick igloo of ice and sealed it shut with a hissing shower of sleet to prevent any more escapes.

The face of Jat the Deceiver flickered above the cyclone, a glittering black mask in the turbulence. He tsk'ed with false concern. "How's the jaw, Guardian? Still feeling woozy? My puppet packs a punch, does he not?"

"It is time for your return to the fires, Dark One," she said. "You have lingered here too long."

The Deceiver's low chuckle rumbled. "Not this time. Things have changed. *You* have changed. Surely you realize this. Your pathetic little band of followers has tethered you to this plane with chains of emotion. You no longer act with detachment."

288

Dora moved closer to Gem and growled low. Gem reassured her with a light hand on her head and addressed Jat. "Sower of doubt, your tricks do not work on me. I am not distracted, nor am I deterred. You will leave this place."

"Too late, Guardian. I will take root in the bedrock of this world. My talons will not be removed. I will squeeze the earth until it chokes."

Gem twirled a long, cold breath around her finger and spun it into a whirlpool of icy air, balanced it on the tip of her finger and tossed it into the air where it twirled like a sparkling dancer. The whirlpool slammed against the cyclone, causing it to wobble and slow.

The Deceiver's curses echoed off the rocky foothills. The angry screams of Red Souls answered their master's voice. Dora howled like a banshee.

"What a racket!" Gem exclaimed. "If the Listener were here, she would have a monstrous headache."

"Oh, she will hear me soon enough, Guardian," the Deceiver swore. "Make no mistake about that."

Guardian and Deceiver thrust and parried, whirlpool against cyclone. The cyclone suddenly whirled like a giant drill and strained against the gold rings binding its tail until the rings shattered. Then the cyclone rose higher, swelling in size. "No rings can hold us," the Deceiver howled. "No power can stop us, not even yours."

The Astral Gate opened above the compound and presented a window, an opportunity to enter that world. Gem exhaled a blast of icy breath to spin her whirlpool faster. It dragged the Deceiver's cyclone up toward the open window. The cyclone pulled back and dragged the whirlpool down, trying to suck the whirlpool into its mouth. Each vortex tried to consume the other in a tug of war of centrifugal forces.

Gem blew another freezing blast. The whirlpool rose again toward the opening, dragging the cyclone with it. The cyclone snapped back, out of the whirlpool's grip. The whirlpool disappeared through the window in the Gate, pulling a swarm of Red Souls in with it. The window snapped shut and glazed over, leaving the cyclone spinning below.

Gem gathered a gale force breath and blasted the cyclone with ice, trying to tear it apart. The cyclone teetered, listed to one side, but then righted itself. It drilled straight down into Theese's office building and buried itself to half its height, leaving its open mouth swirling around the building. "In tight as the bite of a well-turned screw," Jat cackled with glee. "You have lost the battle, Gemimah Jane Hawkins. You cannot remove me. Now where are those lackeys of yours? It is time they were introduced to the new Lord of the City of Los Angeles."

Gem bent to Dora's ear. "Return to the Jeep and guide the Circle when they arrive, my dear. Time has run out."

Dora took a giant leap off the roof, hit the ground running, and disappeared into the hills like a ghost. Gem turned, sprang off the roof, and dove into the mouth of the cyclone head-first, spraying a torrent of hail as she descended. She had to retrieve her physical body from the basement before the Deceiver discovered it. She hoped he'd be too busy choking on ice to notice it.

*****

Shafts of early-morning sun pierced the windows of TJ's bedroom in Big Bear. Willet woke with remnants of a dream fluttering in her inner vision like ripped curtains at an open window. She had been underground, in a cave, surrounded by dirt, rocks and tree roots. The cave shrank around her. Roots in the cave walls squirmed like snakes. The suffocating closeness of the cave almost choked her, and Gem's chant rolled into her consciousness – Huuu. Huuu. Willet repeated the chant, hoping Gem would answer. What she heard instead was the thudding heartbeat of the earth and the hiss and murmur of many low voices. She knew those voices too well, didn't want to hear what they had to say, but they spoke directly to her. "Listener, we rise. We will crush you and everyone around you."

She sat up in bed, brushing away the ominous words like cobwebs. TJ snored softly beside her. Outside, the morning sparkled with light and birdsong, and trees rustled in the wind. Heartbeats - her own, TJ's - drummed steadily. There was another beat too, lower, slower, deeper, pounding like a distant sledgehammer. She recognized it. The beat of something deep underground – she had heard it in her dream, and it was getting stronger. The intrusive dream made her angry. *I will not allow nightmares to ruin this day. TJ and I are together. The day will be beautiful. Wait, I think the bed moved.*

The bed vibrated and then the cabin shook like a tambourine, rattling everything in it. TJ bolted upright from sleep, grabbed her arm, and pulled her off the bed to the doorway. They huddled underneath it, braced against the door jamb. "Must be an earthquake," he murmured.

Shakes came in short, violent bursts. The ceiling cracked. Glass broke in the bathroom. The cabin rode a swell of movement over an eternity of seconds.

She held her breath, cringing before the next shake. TJ held her tight, whispering reassurances and cursing under his breath at the same time. The earth shuddered. Seconds turned into minutes, then a silent pause. They looked at each other. Was it over? No.

The frame of the cabin groaned and cracked as the whole cabin rose off its foundation, tilted thirty degrees and then dropped hard. They were thrown from the doorway, across the narrow hall, and against the opposite wall. The cabin tilted another ten degrees. The wall they leaned against became the floor. Now they were lying on their backs with legs up against the old floor like discarded dolls. Shoes, books, candles and candle holders, a hairbrush, slid out of the bedroom and fell on top of them. An end table rolled into the bedroom doorway and lodged there.

TJ swore like a sailor. The cabin shook again. Things crashed in every room. Willet sobbed and jammed her hands against her ears to block the noise.

The cabin finally shuddered to a halt. They stayed where they had landed, not trusting the silence. Minutes went by before they tried to move.

"Are you okay, Will?" TJ said. "Talk to me."

She held a red stiletto shoe in her hand, and her body shook. "This shoe fell on me, and this book, and this… heavy thing…" She knocked a candlestick off her leg. "Lucky the candles weren't burning." She reached for the other shoe nearby and picked it up. "I have shoes," she mumbled. "I need my lip gloss if we're going out."

Willet was in shock. "We need to get out of here before the ceiling caves in," TJ said. "I need pants or something. You do too."

TJ climbed up to the doorway of the bedroom, pushed the end table to the side and used it to pull himself into the room. In a couple of minutes, he slid back down to the hall on his butt with jeans and a bath robe clutched under his arms and a phone in his left hand. "Here," he said handing her the robe. "Put this on. There's going to be broken glass. You can't crawl around naked."

She wrapped the oversize white terry cloth robe around her and slipped on the impractical red stilettos. He pulled on his jeans, and they began the crawl down the now V-shaped hallway, one knee on the wall and one knee on the floor. They avoided the minefield of glass in the kitchen and headed for the front door, which tilted toward the ground. All the furniture in the living room had slid to one side of the room. Broken glass, pottery, lamps and tables were banked against the door.

TJ found his flip flops and put them on. He pushed the accumulated debris aside and pulled the door open for Willet. She slid down the porch as gracefully as she could on her behind, grateful she had shoes when her feet hit the ground. TJ eased himself out after her.

She leaned against a tree, picking splinters of glass out of her left knee and her palms, not yet trusting her legs to hold her up. Fat droplets of red splashed on the snowy white robe. She stared at the sudden bursts of color, numb to the implications. A sudden blast of profanity jarred her out of her numb state.

"Look at my cabin! Shit! Fuck!" TJ yelled. He kicked at stones, jammed his fingers in his hair and pulled at it like he was about to rip it out. He stalked off toward the back of the property.

Willet got up and tottered after him on her high heels, not wanting to be alone. She rounded the back of the house and saw three long ridges of rock protruding out of the ground that weren't there the day before. The ridges ran up the hill from the lake to the cabin like the bones of long fingers. Boulder-sized knuckles on the fingers had pushed the back of the cabin up on its side.

TJ walked over to one of the ridges, kicked and scraped at it with his foot. Dirt and grass fell away, revealing a harder substance underneath. It was a ridge of rock streaked with crystal.

She heard the unmistakable hissing and frantic chatter of Red Souls in the crystal. She fell into a crouch, held her hands against her ears, and hung her head. "I'm sorry, Thomas. I'm so sorry."

"It's that stuff we saw in the mine, the crystal with the fire inside, isn't it?"

"Yes."

"How did it end up here?"

Her voice shook. "It's here because of me. The Souls want to crush me." She felt so guilty she could barely face him.

TJ lifted her by the shoulders and shook her lightly. "Look at me, Will. This didn't happen because of you."

Tears swam in her eyes. "This is bad, Thomas. I have to talk to Gem."

"Can you call her? Maybe she knows what's going on." He pulled the phone from his pocket and handed it to her.

She dialed Gem's number with trembling fingers, got voicemail. "Her mailbox is full, I can't even leave a message," she clicked off in despair. "I haven't been able to reach her in two days. She said she was going to talk to Theese. It's not like her to ignore messages this long."

"She went to that place at Mount Wilson?"

"I think so. We need to find her. This won't be the end of it." Willet wobbled off in the direction of the car.

"Hey, slow down there. I need to find keys, wallet, and a shirt. You're wearing a bath robe with high heels. You can't go anywhere that way."

Willet looked down, realizing she had nothing on under the robe. Her memory of recent events had clouded, which was even more distressing than the lack of clothes. "I need clothes," she said, her voice rising into hysteria. "I can't go without clothes."

"Yeah, babe, okay," he soothed her. "We'll find you some clothes and then we'll look for Gem."

He put an arm around her shoulders and guided her away from the crystal ridges, mumbling under his breath. "If that Theese guy has something to do with this, I'll rip his windpipe out through his teeth."

*****

Dean couldn't keep up with all the music flowing through him. Silvery bells jingled in his head like Christmas, and voices sang hypnotic melodies in a language he could almost understand but not quite. Lights flashed in the corners of his eyes. His skin tingled. The scent of jasmine drifted through his house, though there were no jasmine bushes nearby. Swinging between amazement and confusion, he brewed numerous pots of coffee, forgot about them and then poured them out when they got cold. He didn't leave the house except to walk the two blocks to the beach and stare at the water. The pounding of ocean waves had never sounded so thunderous to his ears.

Is this how Willet hears the world? How does she deal with it?

To control the onslaught of sensations, he sat at his electric piano every day, writing syllables on a pad and trying to capture the melodic lines he heard in his head. Usually, he struggled to write music. Now it poured through him like a dam had broken. He struggled to get it all down.

His dreams had changed too, but not in the dark, freakish way as before when Red Souls invaded his head. These dreams were luminous, streaked with pure colors, lit by an unseen sun. He looked forward to sleep at night, to experience that sense of bliss.

Today he noodled on the keyboard, letting his fingers wander. The words he sought eluded his conscious mind, and he made no progress. He relaxed and just let syllables roll off his tongue. *Huuuu Ka-la Ohh No-ba, Ma-na Huu Huu.* He didn't know if that was a real chant, but he wrote them down, closed his eyes and whispered them. A swirl of lights formed in the space between his eyebrows. He watched with detached calm.

A pair of familiar brown eyes appeared in that space, Gem's eyes. Her mouth moved, but he couldn't hear her speak. She drifted backwards until he saw her whole body.

Then she held out her hand, beckoning him, and spoke out loud. "I am here, Warrior. Come."

A gentle tug at the area around his belly button pulled him toward the swirl of light. He wanted to enter that light and feel it, but his phone rang and brought him crashing back into his physical body. Reluctantly he picked up the phone. "Audrey? What's up?"

Audrey sounded almost frantic. "Dean, there's been an earthquake in Big Bear. Will and TJ are up there. I felt the tremors all the way in Hemmings. My laptop almost walked right off my desk. Did you feel it?"

"I didn't feel a thing. Are they okay? Are *you* okay?"

"I'm fine. Willet called. TJ's cabin got knocked over on its side, if you can believe that. Crystal came out of the ground and upended it. She said a lot of other stuff that didn't make sense, but they're driving to Mount Wilson to find Gem. She thinks Gem is in some kind of trouble, and she wants me to meet her there. She asked for you too."

"Me? Why me?"

"It's the Circle, Dean. We need the Circle. The earthquake released the crystal. The stuff's punching its way out of the mountains. It's spreading everywhere."

"I just thought about Gem, sort of. It seemed like she was calling me."

"Well, are you coming?"

Dean hesitated. "Are you going?"

"Of course I am! Willet could be in trouble. Maybe this is the crisis Gem told us about, the reason she called the Circle."

"Where are you going exactly?"

"Theese has some sort of hideout in the Mount Wilson foothills. We're all meeting at Red Box Road off Crest Highway. His place is up the road from there.

"You're sure this isn't one of your sister's phantom voices saying something that doesn't make sense? Not that I should talk, at this point."

"She's shaken up, sure, who wouldn't be, which is why I have to see her, and excuse me? The voices are *not* phantom."

"I'm sorry, Audrey, I didn't mean it the way it sounded, but if there's nothing specific, maybe you should get in touch with Gem, find out how she is?"

"Gem doesn't answer her phone, and her mailbox is full. Those are not good signs."

"It's a long drive up there from here."

"Yeah, it's a long drive from here too. What's your point? Gem may need our help. Willet certainly does. We have to step on it."

Dean took a deep breath. It seemed like a hasty trip. Gem had shown she could take care of herself very well. On the other hand, maybe something *was* wrong. Audrey seemed so sure. "Okay, fine, I'll meet you at Mount Wilson," he said, resigning himself.

After he clicked off, he looked down at the familiar pattern of black and white keys on his keyboard and took a deep breath. He had lived a normal, fairly quiet life so far, but at that moment, it seemed to balance on the head of pin. By going north to look for Gem, he risked knocking the pin over and sending his life flying. He might never get that balance back, yet his intuition told him with deep certainty that he had to go. Everything that happened in the last two months, since he met the sisters, led to this point.

Suck it up, Dean. The quiet life is over, and common sense has left the building. The future is up to you.

Chapter 30: Crystal Rising

The Porsche revved, straining to break free and run through Friday traffic, but congestion choked the road. Everything Audrey heard on the radio about the earthquakes in Angeles National Forest made her want to push the gas harder. Tremors had been rocking North LA all morning. Roads buckled, and buildings shook. Ridges of rock pushed up and out of the ground from Highland west to La Canada–Flintridge. No one had ever seen anything like it.

She approached the west-bound merge to the 210 Freeway and slowed to a near stop. Police cars, their lights flashing, lined the on-ramp, and orange cones divided the ramp, keeping the right lanes empty. Officers in reflective vests waved oncoming cars onto the two far left lanes. When she finally merged, she could see why. The right lanes were covered with broken rock. The hillside north of the freeway looked like it had developed a bad case of varicose veins. Ridges of rock ran down the hill to the road, causing slabs of concrete to thrust upward from long cracks.

Several vehicles in the right lanes had crashed against the unexpected obstacles: a sedan with a buckled hood, a Prius tipped on its side. A woman with a bloody scarf pressed to her head crouched next to her SUV, which had flat tires and dangling bumper. A fire truck doused a flatbed truck engulfed in smoke. It was a wonder any traffic moved at all.

Audrey inched along with the packed traffic and detoured around the stranded cars, amazed at the devastation. Broken concrete littered the road. The situation had escalated, as Gem predicted. Cracks in the road revealed the crystal underneath, probably leaking Red Souls. Her phone rang through the car speakers. She hit the pick-up button on the steering wheel. "Who is it?"

"Uh, Audrey, it's Bart. I've been trying to reach you. Are you okay?"

"Yeah, I'm fine." Her tone sounded brusque, but she couldn't help it. News helicopters flapped above her making it difficult to hear him.

"Is this a bad time?"

"It is... I can hardly hear you."

"Sorry," he said in a louder voice. "I worried about you, with the tremors and all."

"Yeah, I'm on the 210. It's a mess."

"What are you doing out there? It's dangerous."

"I'm driving up to Mount Wilson, to meet Will."

"Mount Wilson?" Bart's voice rose to a near squeak. "You can't go up there. That's the epicenter of seismic activity."

"I have to go, for reasons too complicated to explain now."

"I guess this isn't a good time to ask about the crystal..."

"What about it?" Audrey shouted into the phone.

"Uh, is there more of it where you found the other samples?"

"Why would you want more?" Audrey said, unable to hide her irritation. "That stuff is evil!"

"It's miraculous, is what it is. It's amazing."

"You should see it from where I'm sitting."

Excitement rose in Bart's voice. "You see it? Where?"

"It's under the roads and in the hills. I'm about to go up the mountain now, I might lose you."

"I think we've figured out how it works," Bart said. "Here at the lab, I mean."

"How what works?"

"What the crystal does, how it does it."

"I'd like to hear all about that, but now is not the best time…"

Bart didn't hear her. "The crystal reacts chemically with whatever's in the air around it, literally metabolizes molecules out of the air. The pieces I have are already 1.5 ounces heavier than when you gave them to me. Can you believe it?"

Audrey's throat felt so tight, she could barely get the words out. "Do you mean it's eating?"

"I mean it's cleaning the air and growing. The bigger it grows the more electricity it produces. Think about that."

Audrey thought about it, and it made her sick. Bart's call dropped when she turned northeast onto the Angeles Crest Highway and started up the mountain. On her left, the cliff side took a steep drop into the valley. The mountain of grey rock rose on her right.

The Porsche wanted to leap into every turn, but the looping turns were tight. A large piece of rock in the road made her swerve left. Only a low metal guard rail stood between the car and the cliff drop-off. She threaded her way between the rail and the rock with almost no room to spare. She eased up on the gas, slowed into a particularly sharp turn in time to see a large boulder fall from the mountain, hit the road and bounce off the cliff into the valley. Loose debris rained down on the hood of the car and littered the road. The tires swerved. She slowed down even more and maneuvered another tight turn.

Suddenly the road buckled in front of her, raising a four foot tall triangle of concrete. She stomped on the brakes as the Porsche hit the concrete at twenty miles an hour. The front end folded up like an accordion and stalled. Air bags exploded from the steering wheel and side panels, engulfing her in diaphanous fabric. She sat staring at the fractured windshield, barely breathing.

Shock sent muscle spasms through her body. She slowly regained composure, switched off the ignition, grabbed her pack and got out. The stink of burnt rubber filled the air. White steam and smoke poured from under the hood, and liquids of various colors leaked from beneath the car. She fished in her bag for the phone. No signal.

She stepped off the road to the side of the mountain, leaned against it and closed her eyes, trying to steady her breathing. The Porsche gasped and shuddered as it cooled, giving up its last breath. *I could have been killed.* She shook like a leaf at the realization, and then focused on her demolished car. *My Porsche is toast!*

More precisely, the finely tuned machine that used to be her little green baby was a steaming mass of bent steel with its hood buckled against a concrete slab. She dropped her bag and walked over to inspect the damage. What she saw made her angry. After a moment's thought, she scrambled up one side of the triangle and grabbed hold of the top edge with both hands. She pulled herself up and looked down into the space between the slabs.

Long arteries of crystal ran through the rock inside the triangle. The crystal streamed with boiling red energy and pulsed stronger as she looked at it. She felt a strong dread. *It recognizes me. It's aware. It grows and spreads. I'm in trouble.*

The ground trembled and swelled underneath her. The slab lifted another foot off the ground and wobbled as she clung to it. If it tipped backwards, it would crush her. She really should slide back down to the ground and get clear, but her fingers froze. Fear paralyzed her. She couldn't let go.

Rings of stinging heat began to circle her fingers and made her unclench her fingers. She had the same instinct as before, to shake her hands and cast the hot rings away. Bracing her feet against the slab, she climbed to the top and shook a hand over the crystal, flinging the rings off her fingers into the space between the slabs. The crystal reacted with an angry hiss, streaming faster and brighter.

She shook her other hand over the crystal. The slab she clung to bucked like a bronco. She let go of it and slid down to the ground with a gasp, bruising her tail bone in landing. A pair of hands lifted her by the armpits and dragged her back ten feet. The slab fell over onto the very spot where she had just landed and cracked in half. The heaving motions of the ridge subsided. Wisps of grey smoke drifted up from the now-inert crystal as streams of energy inside it stilled

"Audrey," Dean growled. "Are you out of your mind?"

She hadn't heard his truck pull up. She registered his presence but didn't take her eyes off the ridge. "It knew who I was, Dean," she said. "It wanted to kill me."

"What were you doing up there?"

"I had to see it for myself. Now I know for sure. Gem is right, the crystal wants to destroy us."

Dean held out a hand to her. "Can you walk? TJ and Willet are waiting at the Red Box Road intersection."

Willet's name roused her. She took his hand.

"It will try to kill my sister too. None of us are safe on this mountain."

"Ya think?" He pulled her to her feet. "If Gem can't help us, it's possible we won't be safe anywhere. We have to keep going until we find her."

*****

Gem dropped into her physical body on the cot with a gentle thud and assessed her physical health - hypothermic, dehydrated, a bit hungry, stiff and sore. She had bathed her body in green healing light for forty-eight hours, long enough to ease the most intense pain in her abdomen. The internal bleeding had stopped. Her jaw was knitting. All in all, she was in better shape than before, but there was still a way to go before she reached full strength.

A wave of dizziness came over her when she sat up. She paused to balance and then swung her legs off the cot to the floor. The bottled water Theese had left behind was at her feet. She picked up the bottle, twisted the cap, and poured water down her throat, letting it spill over her chin and neck. Her dizziness faded. *First things first - stand up and move around.*

She spotted the metal folding chair in the corner where Theese had thrown it. Standing carefully, she made her way over to it. Her arms felt weak, but she managed to unfold the chair and set it on the floor.

305

She sat on it with a sigh, closed her eyes and relaxed. Long, slow breaths expanded her chest. Her blood bubbled with oxygen, refreshing her muscles. She focused on the space between the eyebrows, and her inner vision burst into light. Violins played an exquisite tune that brought a healing joy to her heart.

Gem ended her contemplation when she heard the scrape and groan of the basement door. She gazed calmly toward it as Theese walked in. His clothes looked disheveled, and dirt streaked his face. He waved a gun with a frantic, furious look in his eyes. "This is your fault, conniving witch," he snarled. "You did this."

"Did what, Mr. Theese?" she asked in a flat voice.

"You're destroying my business." His voice rose to a bellow. "The mines are collapsing! My buildings are falling into shambles!"

"I had nothing to do with that. You have been misled by the Master of Deception. Making you rich was never his objective."

He stepped closer, lowering the gun until it pointed at her head. "I warned you what would happen if you interfered in my affairs."

"Violence will only bring more destruction upon you."

"Maybe," he said softly, eyes narrowing, his finger curling around the trigger. "But it will feel so satisfying to fire this gun."

*****

No cars passed through the intersection of Crest Highway and Mount Wilson Red Box Road. TJ leaned against the parked Mercedes, waiting.

Dean's truck finally drove up. He rolled down the window. "Teej, where's Willet?" he called out.

TJ turned and pointed at the Mercedes. Inside, the dim outline of Willet's head and shoulders could be seen, rocking forward and back, headphones pressed against her ears.

Audrey got out of the truck, went to the Mercedes, and climbed into the back seat. "Will, talk to me," Audrey said. "What's going on?"

"Red Souls say the Guardian is defeated." Tears streaked her cheeks. "They're howling. What does that mean? Is she dead?"

Audrey fished in her pocket and pulled out a tissue, handing it to Willet. "I don't know what it means. I do know we have to move. The crystal is erupting everywhere."

"Yeah, I don't know how we made it here." Willet snuffled and wiped her nose. "The car almost bottomed out on one of those ridges. We had to get out and push it over."

"The crystal seemed to recognize me," Audrey told her, "Which is even scarier. I think it knows who's in the Circle." She coaxed Willet out of the Mercedes and led her by the hand to the truck.

"So, what's the verdict?" TJ asked, looking at Willet with concern.

"Can't stay here," Audrey said.

Willet nodded in agreement. "I have the mother of all headaches, and may throw up any minute, but if there's a chance to find Gem alive, I have to go."

"Try not to hurl in in the truck," Dean said. He climbed up to the driver's seat and everyone else got in. He drove slowly, maneuvering around and over large ridges of earth thrust up along the road. The ridges shuddered and arched higher as the truck approached. They

307

turned off to Theese Enterprises at a trailhead with a small dirt parking area. A green Jeep was parked there. Beside it, a big black dog sat in its shade, looking expectantly in their direction.

"That's Gem's Jeep, and Dora!" Willet said.

Dean pulled over. Dora stood up and approached them with tongue lolling. She nudged her head against TJ's knee, sniffed at Willet's hand, and came to a stop next to Audrey's leg, bumping with her hind end.

Willet knelt down, stroked Dora's head. "Where's Gem, huh girl?" Dora yipped softly.

Dean peered in the windows. No one in the Jeep, but it was unlocked. Dean pulled the driver door open. "No sign of struggle. Maybe she's hiking, or, uh, using the little girl's room."

"Dora goes everywhere with Gem," Audrey said. "If they're separated, it's a bad sign."

Dean reached under the driver seat and pulled out the Magnum. He leaned over to the passenger seat and checked the glove box. The Colt was in there. "She always takes at least one of these with her," he said.

"Always," Willet repeated. "She calls them her deterrents."

Dean handed the Colt to TJ and stuffed the Magnum into a side pocket of Audrey's pack, shouldering the pack himself.

TJ slid the Colt into the waistband at his back. "I'd say the Jeep is abandoned. What now?"

Dora snuffed excitedly around them, turned in circles, and then trotted off down the road, stopping every few feet to look back at them.

"I think she wants us to follow her," Willet said.

They got back in the truck and followed Dora's lead. At a turnoff, they found an olive drab guard shack knocked over on its side, with no one around. Dean detoured around it and followed Dora down the road. At the top of a rise, Dora stopped and sat down. They stopped the truck and looked over Theese's compound stretched out below.

The area looked like it had been attacked by giant gophers with bulldozers. The warehouse had broken into pieces, one half tipped over, the other collapsed. The office building tilted to the left side, crushing the wall and cracking the roof. Other out buildings were knocked off their foundations or reduced to rubble. Wherever the ground had ruptured, crystal glinted in the sun from an exposed ridge. No doubt what had caused the damage.

"Gem is down there," Willet pointed at the biggest building. "I hear her voice. She's talking to Theese. I also hear multiple breaths from there – pointing at the warehouse - and scratching from the debris over there. People are buried."

Audrey pulled out her phone and tried to call 911 but got no reception. "Anyone get a signal?" No one could make a call.

"Maybe there's a working landline in one of the buildings," Dean said. "If people are buried down there, they'll suffocate. We need to get help out here quick."

Dora ran down into the compound and stopped at the front door of the office. She turned towards the truck and stared, waiting for them to follow. Dean drove into the yard and parked in the dirt parking lot. The compound appeared deserted.

Willet closed her eyes, shuddering. "There are so many voices here, I can't keep track. It's overwhelming."

"Human voices?" Audrey asked. "Red Souls?"

"Yes, and yes. And one very nasty voice I've never heard before. It's whispering."

"What does it say?"

Willet swallowed hard. "It says, 'Go ahead, shoot her.'"

Chapter 31: The Snake

Dean pushed through the unlocked front door of Theese's office building, and Dora bolted in after him. She ran down a back hallway, darted around the corner and disappeared.

Plaster dust and debris covered the furniture in the deserted lobby. Holes in the ceiling exposed wood beams under the roof. A dusty landline phone sat on the desk. Dean picked up the receiver. "There's no dial tone," he said.

TJ checked out the ceiling. "This building is ready to collapse. We should get out."

"Gem is here, I hear her downstairs," Willet protested. "We can't just leave her."

"It's not safe, Will," said Audrey.

"I'm going to find her," Willet replied. "You do what you want."

Willet hurried after Dora's disappearing backside, and the rest of the Circle followed her to a metal stairway leading to the basement. It clanked under their feet as they pounded down the steps into a grey cement room, dusty, full of boxes, with a heavy metal door in one wall.

Voices came from behind the door, and then the crack of a gunshot. Dora barked at the door, growled and threw her body against it. The door swung open.

A big man in a rumpled blue suit stood inside the room holding his arms straight up in the air. He had a gun between his hands and seemed to be struggling to get control of it. Dora charged him and clamped her teeth around his right calf. The man shook his leg to get her off, yelping in pain, but Dora had her teeth firmly embedded in his flesh. Blood trickled onto the floor from inside his pants.

TJ grabbed the Colt from his waistband. Dean pulled the Magnum from the pack.

Gem sat on a chair in the middle of the room. Her eyes were shut, her feet flat on the floor, and her hands curled in her lap. Blood flowed down her white blouse from a wound in her left shoulder, but she breathed calmly. Willet and Audrey ran to her. Gem's eyes snapped open. "Chant with me now," she said in a low, urgent voice.

"He's got a gun," Dean said, pointing at the struggling man. "We need to take it and get you out of here."

"Leave him," Gem said. "Mr. Theese, stop fighting me."

Gem began to chant in a clear, strong voice. The sisters joined her. TJ and Dean contributed their own low mumbles, but never took their eyes off of Theese.

"See what I see," Gem's voice echoed. "A world existing at the same time and in the same place as ours, but at a different level of vibration."

A hum like the soft whir of a fan filled the room. The hum rose in pitch, and the walls of the room dissolved. They were in a different room. Aquatic green and blue lights washed over the walls, and the sound of waves rushed in and out of the room from some distant ocean. The man with the gun had become a skeleton suspended in mid-air by ropes of light looped around his neck, arms and legs. He struggled as he hung there.

Dora circled below the skeleton, a growl curdling in her throat. She looked bigger and blacker than usual. Jagged teeth lined her blood-red gums, and her breath steamed. The white spot on her forehead glowed.

Gem took a long, slow breath. A shower of iced rain poured from her mouth and hit the skeleton. He writhed like a fish on a line. She took another breath and blasted him again. His movements grew sluggish. Finally, he went limp. His skull dropped to his chest.

An amorphous black shape gathered like a storm cloud over the hanging skeleton. "What have you done to my puppet, Gemimah Jane Hawkins?" a deep voice said. "You have injured him."

"I heard that voice before," Dean's voice quivered. "It almost bit my head off."

"It is the Deceiver himself, Lord Jat, Ruler of the Underworld," said Gem softly. "Do not believe a word he says."

The black cloud billowed into the corners of the room and sprouted crooked appendages with long, clawed fingers. There was nowhere to escape it. The voice chuckled. "I will miss this little game of ours, Guardian, but surely you can see you've lost. My fingers are buried deep in the earth. They cannot be removed now."

"*Your* place is in the realm of fires," Gem said coldly, "So Spirit has ordained."

The cloud of darkness churned. "Spirit resides in eternity, out of sight, out of mind. My power prevails here, in the fullness of time, though it will seem like eternity to the people of your city."

"You delude yourself as always, Jat." Gem blasted the cloud with shards of ice. The cloud thinned to a shadow, reformed and billowed out again. She blew a hailstorm at it, tearing the dark cloud to shreds.

Tattered remnants of the cloud drifted, constricted rapidly into a single point of absolute blackness and then exploded into the long, black body of a snake with ebony eyes and a slit mouth. The snake twisted and coiled. Its thin lips peeled back from needle-sharp fangs. Its tongue flickered.

"Ring Thrower," Gem called out, "rings will bind the snake."

Gold rings appeared on Audrey's thumbs and forefingers, spinning fast. She threw the rings at the snake. They flew through the air and slipped over the snake's head, encircling its body.

The snake hissed and thrashed. Its head darted fast toward the Circle with open mouth, but instead of trying to sink a bite, it showered them with a black liquid the consistency of tar, hitting them full in the face, chest and arms. The tar sizzled on their skin as it splattered. It delivered a stinging burn, but that was just the beginning. As they tried to brush away the drops of bubbling tar, the burn spread everywhere they touched. The Circle wailed in shock and pain.

Dean dropped to his knees and rubbed his palms frantically on the floor to ease the burning sting. TJ wiped his fingers on his pants, and the tar burned right through the fabric to his legs. Audrey shrieked as the tar burned through to the bones in her arms. Willet covered her cheeks with her hands, but it only made matters worse. Her cheeks and hands smoked.

"The tar is the essence of despair," Gem said loudly, "Jat's most powerful weapon. You must resist it." But the members of her Circle were losing the struggle. Gem faced the snake, hissed sleet through her teeth, and the snake recoiled sharply. It would have been a good time for the Ring Thrower to bind him tighter with her rings, but Audrey was writhing in the agony of her own burns. Gem hit the snake again, this time with ice darts that flew like arrows.

The snake dodged with sinuous movements of its long body and hissed back. "You have lost your little band of amateurs, Guardian. Whatever will you do?"

Gem looked to the Circle. Their bodies had been reduced to skeletons. They stared blankly at her through hollow eye sockets. Despair had taken them over. The walls of the room dissolved again, and this time the vast, empty desolation of the Underworld spread out around them. The skeletons collapsed to their knees, and the snake began to wrap its long body around them, claiming them for his own.

Gem pointed at the snake and exclaimed, "You have not won their Souls! They did not choose you."

A blur of black fur jumped into the air, aiming straight at the snake. Dora's golden eyes flashed, and her battle growl boomed like thunder. The snake disappeared and then reappeared far above, its tongue flickering. Dora's leap turned into flight faster than sight could track. She reached the snake, drove her fangs into its neck and began throttling it like a rag doll. The snake wrapped its tail around Dora's neck and tried to pull away from her teeth. Dora howled, let go, and then sank her teeth into the snake's thrashing body. Dog and snake blurred into a furious swirl of snarls and hisses.

Gem blew a cold mist into her hands and spread it into a large disc of polished ice, reflective as a mirror. She held it up to the view of the Circle. "See your true selves. Remember who you are. You are made of Light. Do not be fooled by the Deceiver's mirages."

The skeletons rose clumsily to their feet and peered into the ice mirror. Astral light flickered around their forms, and their boney aspect faded in the glow, replaced by their normal appearance. They hugged each other with fierce joy, an emotion incompatible with the Underworld.

Gem raised her hand above her head. "Dora, time to go," she announced.

Dora shot like a cannonball out of her brawl with the Deceiver and landed at Gem's feet, wild-eyed and covered in smoking burns. The sound of ocean waves rushed over them, the light turned green-blue, and the Circle dropped through levels of astral vibration back to the physical plane.

The voice of the Deceiver followed them. "This game is not finished, Guardian. Your Circle will yet call me Lord. Mark my words."

The Circle found themselves in the basement. Theese himself lay motionless on the floor in a pile of blue gabardine.

Gem slumped sideways in her chair. A sheen of sweat glistened on her face and blood poured out of the bullet wound in her shoulder. Willet and Audrey caught her before she fell to the floor. Dean and TJ helped her to the cot to lie down. Her hands and feet felt cold as ice. Audrey found a weak pulse in her wrist and rubbed her hands vigorously. Dora sat at Gem's side, whimpering, licked the blood on her shoulder and nuzzled her forehead.

The sound of shuffling and gasping breath caused TJ, Audrey and Dean to spin around. They had forgotten Theese. There he was with Willet pulled against his chest. He had her in a stranglehold, a thick forearm wrapped around her neck and a small gun pressed to her temple. His eyes darted nervously around the room and his gun hand shook. "Who are you people? What are you doing in my building?"

"We're here for Gem," Dean said. "Why is she locked up in here?"

"Shoulda known you were with the witch. I'll see you in jail if I don't shoot you myself. I'm pissed off and my leg is killing me. I intend to take it out on this lady here." The arm around Willet's neck pulled tighter, and she struggled for breath. He dragged her backwards toward the door.

The shock in Willet's eyes mirrored their own. "Let go of my sister," Audrey spit out at him.

Theese snorted. "You're not in a bargaining position, sweetheart. Me and the little lady are leaving, but first I'm gonna shoot that god damn dog."

TJ swung the Colt up and aimed. Dean leveled the Magnum at Theese's head.

Theese bumped his gun against Willet's temple and cocked the hammer. "Hold on there, cowboys," he said with a sneer. "I'd think twice if I were you. If this trigger moves the least bit due to my finger twitchin', her brains will splatter all over this room. Is that what you want?"

TJ and Dean lowered their weapons. With his gun wedged under Willet's chin, Theese opened the door with his other hand and sidled out pulling Willet after him. The door slammed shut, and the click of engaging locks echoed in the silent room. Willet's headphones rocked on the floor where they had fallen.

TJ and Dean pushed and pulled the heavy metal door, heaved shoulders at it until sweat poured down their faces, but it did not budge. TJ kicked the door over and over. "I'll blow it open," TJ panted. He pulled the Colt out of his waistband and pointed it at the door lock with shaking hands.

"Whoa, are you nuts?" Dean said. "That door is solid metal. A bullet could bounce off and hit one of us."

"If we don't do something, he might hurt her!"

"Yeah, I get that dude, but we need to think it through," Dean replied, gently guiding TJ's gun hand down to his side.

"Who are you now, the leader?" TJ sneered, yanking his arm away.

"I just don't want to get shot, okay? Stop waving that gun around."

"So, you'd rather just sit here 'til you die…"

"No, I'd like us to calm the hell down and think."

TJ walked in an agitated circle, grumbling to himself. "I knew I shouldn't have gotten involved in this mess. And Willet, definitely not."

Audrey bent to pick up her sister's headphones. "That man could kill her," she said, cradling the phones between her hands. "I may never see her again."

"We'll find her," Dean said, sounding more confidence than he felt.

Audrey dropped cross-legged to the floor, dropped her head in her hands. "Gem's out of it. We need her. What are we going to do?"

"Stop whining, Audrey," TJ snarled.

Audrey's head snapped up. "If anything happens to my sister, it's your fault, you coward," she yelled. "*You* let that man take her."

"He had a gun to her head!" TJ bit back. "What was I supposed to do? Provoke him?"

"You should have done – something. Tackle him, distract him…"

"You're delusional, you know that?"

"You're both pathetic," Dean muttered.

They all stared at the locked door, mute and weary. Dean walked around the room, looking for any way out. A small air vent just below the ceiling was the only other opening in the room, too small for a human body to wiggle through. He shouted towards it, calling for help. After a few tries, he dropped cross-legged on the floor near Audrey. TJ sat and took off his shoe to see if his big toe was broken.

Audrey cleared her throat. "Are we going to talk about the snake?"

"What's to say?" TJ said as he felt the toe. "We'd still be in that dead zone if it wasn't for Gem, and now she's out of commission too. The dog kicked butt."

"We looked like skeletons," Audrey continued. "Why did we look like skeletons?"

"Do you remember your skin burning?" TJ replied with a sneer. "That might have something to do with it."

Audrey persisted. "Yeah, our skin burned. Gem's skin didn't burn. I saw the tar hit her. She never flinched."

"Gem's from a different species," TJ muttered, putting his shoe on.

The only sounds in the room were Gem's ragged breathing and Dora snoring softly beneath the cot.

"I think she told us what to do," Dean said slowly. "We have to remember who we."

"So, who are we?" Audrey asked. "What are we supposed to remember?"

"Remember our faces in the mirror?" Dean replied. "We looked like skeletons, but then we were glowing."

"I refuse to be a skeleton," TJ said gruffly. "All skeletons look alike."

"Exactly," Dean said. "If we fight the snake again, we have to refuse to be skeletons, no matter how much it hurts."

Time ticked away. An inexplicable urge to sleep swept over them. One by one they stretched out on the hard floor and closed their eyes.

*****

Gem hovered in consciousness over the cot and watched her Circle argue. Green light poured through the ceiling and bathed her injured body in a cone of healing warmth. *A new injury to heal. How much can this body take?* Her astral form folded into the cross-legged posture of contemplation. She hummed a soft chant and then blew a cooling breath over the bickering Circle to help them rest and heal. The Deceiver's poison still lingered in them. Until it was gone, they would struggle and fight among themselves. Without the Listener, they would be deaf to the presence of Red Souls around them.

Who will lead them in my absence? Mr. Simmons seems to draw the right conclusions. Maybe he will be the one.

She looked down at her physical body. The bullet popped out of the bloody hole in her shoulder and rolled onto the cot. The bullet hole sealed shut and disappeared.

Chapter 32: The Underground

A deep rumble on the other side of the wall woke everyone up. The whole room vibrated, and concrete dust fell from the ceiling. Dean and TJ jumped up and reached for their guns. Audrey ran to the cot and covered Gem's face with a shirt. They all lifted the cot and carried it to the far corner of the room, lowered Gem to the floor, and turned the cot on its side to shield her. Then they crouched behind it and covered their faces against the billowing dust.

Something hit the wall and crashed through it like a battering ram. The impact boomed like a thunderclap. Chunks of concrete and broken rebar flew. Minutes passed before they peeked over the edge of the cot. A large wedge of grey rock riddled with ribbons of crystal had gouged across the floor and come to a stop in the middle of the room where they had just been sleeping. The rocky wedge shook and then settled.

"Holy buffalo," Dean whispered. He stood up and carefully approached the rock. "It's full of crystal."

"Don't touch it, Dean," Audrey warned as he got closer. "That stuff is evil." She walked to the rock and stood beside him. The fire streaming through the crystal sparked brighter at her approach.

"Remember the crystal under the mountain?" she said. "It's aware and knows who we are. It didn't break in here by accident." She felt her hands tingle. Rings of heat spun around her fingers. When her hands were as hot as she could stand, she shook them over the ridge. The rings slipped off her fingers onto the crystal, and it sizzled. The fires in the crystal guttered out as if she had doused them with water.

"Those are the rings, right?" TJ said. "Why do I see them now when I didn't before?"

"Yeah, you did that to the snake too," Dean said. "How did you know what to do with them?"

"Gem told me to do it. I don't know how it works or why. I get this burning feeling around my fingers. If I shake my hands until the burning goes away, rings fly off. The crystal gets nuked."

"That's a handy trick." TJ said thoughtfully.

"Your approval thrills me," replied Audrey, feigning a yawn.

Audrey righted the cot and Dean and TJ lifted Gem onto it. Then they got to work looking for weak spots in the broken wall around the ridge of rock, poking and probing until pieces of concrete fell away. Through a big crack, they could see into the corridor outside. Rebar protruded in spikes from the broken edges.

"We might be able to make this hole bigger," Dean said. "If we had something to dig with…"

The only objects in the room strong enough to hack through concrete were the metal folding chair and their guns. Using the guns seemed unwise.

Dean unfolded the chair and TJ bent the legs until they snapped off by stomping on the joints repeatedly with both feet. The legs made serviceable picks. After a half hour of hacking, the picks were mangled, but they'd managed to bend the rebar back and open a space above the rock ridge about a foot high and two foot wide.

"Audrey, check it out. Is this space big enough for you to slide out?" Dean asked.

Audrey climbed onto the rock and slid one leg and then another through the opening without a problem. "What if I get caught in here? Those are some rough edges."

Dean broke off the sharp concrete edges around the hole with his pick. He pulled off the flannel shirt he wore over his tee shirt and handed it to Audrey. "Here, wrap this around your head, so you don't get scraped. If it feels too tight at any point, we'll pull you back." He helped her gather her hair into the shirt and buttoned it over her face.

She lay down and inched through the opening, letting her hips scrape against the sides. She folded her arms and shoulders in and eased her torso along up to her neck. "Does it look like my head will fit?" she asked.

Dean and TJ eyeballed the space around her head. "Doable," they concluded. Dean gathered the shirt around her hair and eased it along with her.

"Easy for you to say." Audrey inched further through the opening. The shirt around her ears caught on the edges of the concrete. "Ow-Ow, I'm stuck." She backed up.

TJ chipped gently at the edges with the remains of his chair leg. Audrey resumed her slow slide through the hole. In a few minutes she slid out the other side.

"Great." Dean said. "See if you can open the door."

Audrey rolled to her feet and walked around the corner. She jiggled the door handle, pushed and pulled on the dead bolt, clicked buttons on the keypad. "I can't open the door without the combination," she called out to them.

"If we pass a gun out to you, do you think you could blow it open?" TJ asked.

"Is that your answer for everything? Blow it up with a gun?" Dean grumbled.

"Do you have a better idea, genius?" TJ snarled.

Footsteps suddenly rattled the metal stairs leading to the basement. The voices of Theese's men followed. "Oh boy, these stairs are wobblin'," one voice said. "We got damage down here, Red, one of those rock monsters busted up. Hope the little lady is okay."

"I don't like the look of it," another voice said. "We have to get her out of here now, no matter what the boss says."

"Hey, who's this now?" the first man asked. "How'd *she* get here?" They pounded down the remaining stairs and ran to the door where Audrey stood. "What're ya doin' down here, woman?"

One man punched the combination into the keypad, slid the dead bolt, and pulled the door open. The other grabbed Audrey by the arm, pushed her into the room, and walked in after her.

"Woo-eee. It busted right through the wall, Andy. Looks like the lady's okay, still out like a light. The black dog's in here! How the hell did that get in?"

Dora crouched beneath the cot. She gave a long, low growl, preparing to spring.

"The dog's *gotta* be put down before it bites us, Red" Andy said. "Go ahead and shoot it in the head."

Dean stepped out from behind the door and jammed the Magnum into the back of Andy's head. TJ came up behind Red and pressed the Colt against the base of his skull as Red raised his rifle.

"Drop the gun," Dean snarled, "slowly, to the ground, or I'll blow *your* fucking head off."

TJ nudged his gun harder to press the point. Red lowered his rifle and let it slip gently from his hands to the floor. He raised his hands in the air. Andy did likewise.

"Where is she?" TJ asked Red.

"Where's who? Who ya' talkin' about?"

"The blonde girl Theese dragged out of here." TJ banged the barrel of the gun against Red's skull to punctuate each word. "Where? Is? She?"

"I don't know! We haven't seen the boss all day."

"Where would 'the boss' take someone if he wanted to hide them?" Dean asked.

"Usually down here else maybe he'd go to one of the mines."

"You could be arrested as accomplices to kidnapping and assault, do you realize that?" TJ asked. "You've held a wounded woman in a locked room without medical attention. Your boss just shot her, and she might die. When the police find her, we'll tell them you kept her locked up in here."

"We had nothin' to do with that," Red whined. "It was Mr. Theese. We were agin' it, but he runs things."

325

"Do you really think the 'I just work here' defense is going to work for you if she does die?" TJ jeered. "You failed to report a gun assault on a woman. That means major jail time. Now what mine would Theese go to first? Think hard. You have five seconds."

Red twitched and shuffled. "Maybe the number 12 or the Alford Mine? There's lots of mines, see? I don't know. Some of 'em caved in."

TJ tapped his foot. "Clock is ticking. Give me something I can use."

"Wait, I have a map!" Andy offered. "You can use that." He pulled a creased, grimy piece of paper out of his back pocket and open it. The paper bore a thick wavy line with numbers on it, some of them circled. "This here's a map of the mine road. The mines are numbered, circled ones are active digs."

"Are the mines locked?" TJ asked.

"They have padlocks on the gates. And the elevators need a code." Andy pointed to the bottom of the paper. "See, here it is, written right here."

Dean narrowed eyes at him. "That raises an interesting question. What happened to the men working in the mines? Are they still down there?"

"Oh no, no," Red raised his palms in protest. "When the mountain got to shakin', the guys were workin' in number nine. They wanted out, but Mr. Theese didn't want 'em to stop diggin'. Me and Andy took 'em up in the elevator and gave 'em all a lift to their cars in the flatbed."

Audrey, Dean and TJ exchanged looks. "That's kind of heroic," Audrey murmured.

"Mr. Theese ain't been thinkin' clear lately," Red said, shaking his head.

"There are people buried outside under collapsed buildings," Dean said. "They've been there for hours, might be dead by now."

Andy blanched. His eyes grew round, and he looked at his feet. "I thought everybody turned tail and ran. Things went to hell so quick," he said.

"Someone has to dig down and rescue them," TJ said. "We have a woman to rescue."

"We'll dig," Andy and Red said together.

What to do about Gem was the dilemma. "We can't leave her here. What if another one of those rock things crashes in here?" Audrey asked.

"We need an ambulance," Dean said.

"We need the police too," Audrey added. "We won't get either one without a phone."

"The longer we wait to find Will, the more likely something will happen to her," TJ said.

"Okay, at the risk of sounding like the *leader*," Dean glared at TJ, "I suggest we carry the cot upstairs. Hopefully nothing will fall on her up there. If these guys dig for survivors, I'll stay and keep an eye on Gem. You and Audrey take the map and look for Willet. We'll meet back here."

Everyone chewed on this in silence. It became the plan.

TJ shrugged. "Fine, fearless leader, carry on."

"Audrey and TJ, take the rifles with you," Dean said. "I'll keep a handgun. We might need it. Now let's get her out of here."

Dean and TJ pushed Andy and Red toward the cot. Each man took a handle, juggled it a bit, and then lifted. A round metal object rolled off the cot and clinked on the floor.

"What's that?" TJ asked.

"Looks like a bullet," Red said. "What would that be doin' here?" He looked at the bloody hole on Gem's shirt and blanched. "What the…"

Gem's breath was calm and steady. She had lost that grey, sweaty pallor, but still looked pale. Dean would be close by, and Dora would stay with her for protection. That was reassuring enough for Audrey. She picked up Willet's headphones. TJ picked up the rifles and slung them on his shoulders. They followed the cot out to the metal stairs, which teetered and swung from loose bolts as everyone climbed up.

*****

Theese pushed Willet head-first into the trunk of his car and drove up a long unpaved road. The grinding of wheels over gravel and roar of the engine shredded her eardrums. She wrapped her arms around her head and tried not to scream. After fifteen minutes of excruciating noise, the car stopped. Theese pulled her out of the trunk and dragged her by the arm toward the shadowed opening of a mine. He didn't look at her or speak, even when she pulled back and begged him to let her go. He seemed distracted, as if his mind were elsewhere.

He hustled her into an elevator cage inside the mine, released a manual locking lever and pressed buttons on a keypad. The elevator groaned and dropped several levels into darkness. At the bottom, he shoved her out of the cage to the ground. The elevator immediately shifted gear and began to rise.

Willet realized her only means of escape was leaving. Survival instincts kicked in. She rolled to her feet, ran toward the elevator and grabbed for a hold on the platform before it was out of reach. She felt a metal bracket attached to the side and wrapped her fingers around it. Soon she was lifted into the air, feet dangling.

Theese called down to her. "Young woman, if I let this elevator drop, you will be crushed underneath. I advise you to let go right now." Not waiting for her to make up her mind, Theese kicked at the fingers laced around the bracket. She winced in pain but held on. He jammed his heel onto her hand. She felt a bone crack, let go and dropped to the ground.

The elevator climbed to the top of the shaft without her. She heard the locking lever engage. Theese stepped off the platform and walked out of the mine. A metal gate dragged across the mine opening and clanked shut with finality. The door slammed, and the car drove away.

Willet cradled her throbbing fingers and studied her surroundings. The darkness of the mine seemed absolute. Dim light from the entrance far above did not penetrate to the mine floor. Slowly, her eyes adjusted. There was a tunnel in front of her. The tunnel glowed an all-too-familiar red, and angry voices murmured.

She got to her feet, walked to the entrance of the tunnel and peered in. Veins of crystal streaked the walls, ceiling and floor. Like the inside of a living organism, something fluid flowed through the veins. She took a few steps closer and brushed her hand against a vein of crystal. It felt warm. At her touch the crystal sparked, and every vein flushed blood red. Voices rose to frenzied chatter as Red

Souls recognized the presence of the Listener. The light heated to crimson, and the temperature in the tunnel spiked.

She turned and ran back toward the elevator with the shrill chatter grating her ears. She tripped on a rock and went flying forward, skidded on her hands and banged her forehead against the ground. Her palms shredded with dirt and rock shards. A scrape opened over her right eye. She sat up and dropped her head between her knees to muffle the voices. Her thoughts ran in a tight loop of confusion and pain.

No one knows I'm here. If there's an earthquake, the crystal will crack, and the cave will fill with Red Souls. Is anyone looking for me? No one knows I'm here.

As if answering her thoughts, the ground shook at that moment, tremors sharp enough to send spider cracks running through the walls. She heard the hiss of red smoke seeping out of the crystal in the tunnel, headed her way.

 Red Souls swarmed her, exultant voices screaming in her face. "Listener, nowhere to run. You are forgotten."

Their unrelenting screams turned her head into a massive throb of pain. Their smoke enveloped her, penetrated her ears, spread through her brain. She could no longer hear her own thoughts, only Red Souls. She crawled over to the rock wall and crouched against it. She was alone and would die here if she didn't do something to save herself. Then she thought of TJ and was not ready to give up.

She closed her eyes and began to chant loudly, over and over. *Huuuuuu-Huu*, letting the words ring until the air vibrated. Her ears took a beating, but there was no help for it. The chant surrounded her like a shield and gave her strength to resist the bombardment of voices. She felt a rush of air brush against her skin, then another. She wanted to open her eyes but was too scared. A velvet silence wrapped her. She relaxed into it, content to just be. And then she was floating.

On the black surface of her inner vision, colors bled together like swirling paints. The surface fragmented into a checkerboard of colored blocks which divided into small dark squares. The squares shrunk to pulsing dots and dissolved in warm gold light.

A gentle and peaceful voice sang, Gem's voice. The fear of the moment turned to joy. *Gem, I'm here!* The voice sang on, unperturbed. Huuuu. Huuu.

Willet didn't want the sound of that voice to fade, so she kept singing along. Her body felt like melting butter, and her sense of being *Willet* faded. What was she - a point of view, a consciousness free of flesh? She let her body go, lost track of time and soared into the gold light with no cares.

*****

Space-time unfolded like origami, and Gem and Sonrisa stepped out onto the floor of the mine. Willet was propped against the rock wall, eyes closed and mouth open. She seemed unconscious. Red Souls swarmed near her but kept their distance. The cave was full of chant.

Gem heard it and nodded. "The charged words surround her. The Listener has taken steps to protect herself."

Sonrisa heard it too. "Perhaps our assistance is not needed?"

Gem looked at the cave walls and inspected the tunnel. "There is too much crystal here for her to fight alone. Red Souls must be eliminated." She filled her lungs with chilled air and sprayed the Red Souls around Willet's body. They squealed and darted away. She followed their smoke down the tunnel, blasting cold breath at the

331

walls and floor as she walked. Red smoke turned grey and then white until all that was left of them was steam. She returned to Willet and patted her cheek gently, then looked at Sonrisa. "Please check on the Listener, see that she is comforted."

Sonrisa smiled. Yes, chica. You are kind-hearted as ever."

*****

Willet awoke in a grass field full of pink, blue and yellow wildflowers with that familiar buzz in her left ear. A warm sun shone in the bluest of blue skies. No matter how she got there, she was content to lay on her back and stare into the sky.

A tall woman stood above her, with a tail of brown hair hanging over her left shoulder. The light shimmered around her. The woman regarded her with a calm gaze.

Willet blinked rapidly to focus her eyes. "Who are you?"

The woman gave a small nod. "I am Sonrisa Degas. I assist the Guardian. You may call me Sonny if you wish."

"Sonny. How did you get here?"

"I heard your chant. It was quite loud."

"I remember you from the Circle, when we were floating in that ring of stars."

"Yes, I was there."

"Where is Gem? Is she okay?"

"Yes. The Guardian lives. The Circle needs you now. We must hurry. Time grows short."

Willet rose up on her elbows. "Do I really have to go back? It's so beautiful here." She remembered her physical body but didn't feel it. "I don't know how to get out of the mine. Theese locked the elevator."

"These are temporary matters," Sonrisa said patiently.

"Can *you* get me out of the mine?"

"Your physical body is too weak for space-time travel. Its molecular structure may be scrambled."

"I'll go crazy in there."

"Do not despair. You saw how darkness fragments before the light. Nothing can resist it."

"I saw squares and dots. They got smaller and smaller. What does it mean?"

"Wherever you are, whatever may attack your mind, you can move through darkness to light. Darkness breaks down in the manner you observed. Your Third Eye is the doorway." The Traveler gave her a kind smile. "Meanwhile, you are safe here. I will assure the Guardian all is well."

She turned and stepped into a fold of space-time that opened next to her. It swallowed her and sealed shut as quickly as it had opened.

Willet gazed again into the blue sky, felt the soft grass underneath her and smiled. She felt fine right here. No need for haste.

Chapter 33: Guns

TJ drove the truck up the mining road while Audrey read Andy's map. They stopped at each mine. TJ blew the padlocks off the gates with his gun. Some mine entrances were blocked by rubble from cave-ins. If a mine appeared intact, they took stairs or elevator down the shaft to search the tunnel, walking deep into the dark with a flashlight, calling Willet's name. After searching seven mines in two hours, they had not found her.

On the map, Audrey checked off each mine they visited. There were thirty mines. They passed other cave openings that weren't even on it. Her mind and body felt heavy as lead. The possibility they would find her sister became more remote with every empty hole.

"Shall we continue?" TJ asked. He slouched in the driver seat with a hand over his eyes.

Audrey tried to hold back tears, but they leaked from her eyes.

"Oh, great, this really helps," he groused.

Tears started to roll down her face, and then she couldn't hold them back anymore.

He sat up, pleading. "Now, don't do that. Crying won't help." He took her hand. "Look, Audrey, I'm sorry. I was a jerk before. I know this is tough for you. It's driving me crazy, and I feel like crap. I never feel like crap unless I've been partying all night."

"That snake poisoned us, TJ. Gem said we'd be weak. We are. I'm a mess."

"Yeah, Gem. It always comes back to Gem. Everything she tells us comes true somehow. It's really annoying."

"This is what the poison does, apparently. I feel hopeless."

TJ patted her hand. "If the snake did poison us, and I can't believe I'm even acknowledging that, then we have to shake it off, remember ourselves like Dean said. Willet's still missing."

Audrey shook the paper in her hand in frustration. "All we have to go on is this map of holes in the ground. It's nothing. Theese could have taken her to Nevada by now."

TJ stared out the windshield. "And we should be dead by now."

"What? Why do you say that?"

"Think about it," he said. "When that pile of rock crashed into the basement, it aimed for us. Somehow it knew we were there. We got out of the way just in time."

"You're looking on the bright side now?"

"Walking away from certain death is no small thing."

Audrey brushed tears away with the backs of her hands. "Yeah. Maybe the snake spit is getting to me."

TJ chuckled. "Since I met you two ladies, things have gone crazy in my life. I've seen impossible things, didn't believe any of it, but now… I have to say something bigger is going on."

She snuffled, reaching for a tissue. "That sounds like faith, Mr. Barlow. I thought that wasn't your style."

"I'm not sure it's faith, but maybe the realization there might be things going on behind the scenes I wasn't aware of. Consider recent experience. A giant snake sprayed us with poisonous tar. Gem sprayed ice out of her mouth, and then our skin burned off and we ended up in hell looking like skeletons. And that's just what happened so far today. Don't get me started on my club burned down by some freakin' rocks or my cabin in Big Bear that got pushed off its foundation by the same rock. It will cost major bucks to rebuild if I can fix it at all. Remember spinning around in space and plunging into a mountain? I thought it was just a dream, but these are events I can no longer ignore." His voice rose in pitch and his hands pounded the steering wheel.

Audrey couldn't think of anything to counter his observations. It was all too true. "I wish it didn't involve my sister," she said, wiping away tears. "She's been through so much in her life. And now she doesn't even have her headphones." She looked at the headphones on her lap. Her heart hurt at the sight of them.

TJ patted her arm awkwardly. "Yes, we love her, and this Circle thing doesn't work without her. So, sitting here won't help. Let's get going."

Audrey hiccupped. Her wet eyes blinked. "You love her?"

"Yeah, I do. Is that so hard to believe?"

"Uh, I always assumed you were kind of a player."

He chuckled. "I do give that impression. Your sister saw right through it, though."

"I would think that'd scare you."

"At first it pissed me off. I thought she was playing *me*. 'Cuz that's the kind of woman I'm used to. But it's not her. She's real. She's funny and kind. And smart. I never know what's going to happen when I'm around her."

Audrey felt her jaw drop slightly and snapped it shut. "I'm glad to hear you appreciate her that way. Maybe you'll be good for her after all."

TJ shrugged and turned to the steering wheel, starting the truck. "That sounds a little like faith, Miss du Place."

He threw it into gear. They rolled up the rocky path in search of the next hole in the ground.

*****

Gem opened her eyes slowly, blinking into the light of an open doorway, and sat up. Dora yelped under the cot and scrambled up to take a look at her. "Yes, my Dora, I am fine," Gem said.

Dora nuzzled Gem's hand and whimpered. Gem stroked her head, feeling the smooth warmth of it in her palm. She took inventory of her own physical injuries. Jaw tight, stomach sore. Left shoulder mostly healed, but still ached. At least the internal bleeding had stopped. For the second time that day, she got to her feet and attempted to walk. A bit dizzy – her physical body needed water and food. A shower would feel wonderful. But there was no time for that.

A gun lay next to her on the cot – her Colt. She picked it up, checked for bullets, and then stepped quietly across the lobby to the back, looking down the hallway and into side rooms. Dora followed, sniffing the ground and waving an alert tail.

Part of the hallway ceiling had collapsed. A long crack ran across the floor and up the back wall. They walked to the door of Theese's office. Gem held the gun at her side, nudged the door open and looked inside.

Theese sat behind his desk surrounded by dust and broken plaster. A partially detached light fixture hung precariously over his head. Red smoke flowed in and out of his nose. He glanced up at her, then back to the desk. A handgun lay in front of him within easy reach. "Perfect. It's the psycho witch and her ugly dog. Get the hell out."

Gem watched him, saying nothing. Red Souls preyed on his mind. That was all too clear from the lost expression in his eyes. Even worse, a mass of oily black smoke swirled at the corner of the room. The Deceiver watched and waited.

Gem pursed her lips and blew a long, cold breath around the room. The red smoke dispersed, but Jat would not give up his puppet. Theese had succumbed to the poison of deep despair. She spoke to him with quiet firmness. "Resist."

Theese snickered, not looking at her. "Resist what?"

"Do not do what you are contemplating. It will not help you."

"Are you a mind reader now too, on top of all your other tricks?"

"The voice that speaks to you, it lies. Do not listen to it."

"Or what? Are you going destroy my life all over again?"

"Your life is not destroyed, Mr. Theese. You still live."

338

A deep sigh lifted his shoulders and his chest caved forward. "Who cares what I do or don't do? Everything is finished." His hand moved toward the gun on the desk.

Gem raised her Colt with both hands and fired. His gun went flying off the desk to hit the back wall, discharging a bullet into the ceiling. The gun landed in the back corner behind the desk, spinning in a circle. Theese jumped to his feet, eyes wide.

"Lunatic!" he bellowed. His body shook. "You could have hit me!"

Gem lowered the gun. "If I intended that, you would be missing fingers now."

He convulsed with crimson rage and clenched fists. His lips twisted as if he were chewing gravel, and his throat gurgled like something was about to explode inside him. "You know nothing about me. Nothing! It's my life, I control what I do, no one else."

Gem regarded him with no emotion and nodded once. "Very well, Mr. Theese, I will not intervene again, but consider your next decision carefully. There will be no turning back."

"Get out!" he yelled, spit flying from his lips.

Gem turned and left the room with Dora at her heels.

"You think you got me figured out," he shouted after her. "You have no idea. You'll see."

*****

Dean heard the gunshot from outside in the parking lot, shouldered his rifle, and ran for the office building. When he got to the lobby, he found the cot empty. He stopped and listened, but he didn't have to wait long.

Gem walked out of the back hall with Dora right behind her. "We must go." She brushed past him on her way to the door.

"What happened? I heard gunshots." He hurried after her.

"Theese likes to play with his gun. I urged him to be careful."

"Where are we going?"

"I know where the Listener is."

"How do you know that?"

"The Traveler found her."
"Who's that?"

"Do you remember the woman in our Circle, the one you did not know?"

"Yeah. What's a Traveler?

Gem didn't stop to answer. Dean followed her through the wreckage of tipped cars and broken asphalt in the parking lot and continued up the road, past the toppled guard shack. The Jeep stood ready by the side of the road. Dora jumped in the back, and Gem stowed the Colt under the driver's seat. She climbed behind the wheel and checked for firearms in the glove box and under the seat. Dean got in the passenger seat.

"You took the Magnum?" Gem asked.

"Yeah, and TJ and I both have these rifles." Dean laid his rifle on the floorboard.
"Where is the rest of the Circle?"

"TJ and Audrey are out looking for Willet. They're checking all the mines. We got hold of a map."

"The Listener is in mine eleven," Gem said as she put the Jeep in gear.

"Did Theese tell you that?"

"I saw her there myself."

Dean stared through the windshield as the Jeep pulled onto the road. How to ask the right question was a challenge with Gem. "But you were here, so…"

"The Traveler took me to her."

"Oh. Okay."

"It will be easier to show you than explain it."

*****

Audrey and TJ arrived at the entrance to the eleventh mine after a fruitless search of three more empty mines. TJ aimed the rifle at the padlock on the metal gate and blew it into pieces. Together they dragged the gate aside and walked into the cave.

Audrey shook her hands. Rings of heat circled her fingers in the now familiar pattern. "My fingers are tingling," she said.

"What does that mean?"

"Usually, I feel a burn when rings are forming. Something's different about this mine."

"Why would this one be different?"

"Gem said the Deceiver is never truly gone. He could be down in the mine, waiting for us."

"He probably knows where Willet is."

"Are we going to just ask him where?"

"Why not? He seems very chatty."

"He's evil, TJ! He'll poison us or sic the Red Souls on us until we go crazy!"

"Seems like your fingers would be on fire if he were actually down there. Willet might be, so we have to check."

Audrey's throat constricted. It was an effort to swallow. "If she's down there, she's in trouble."

TJ beamed the flashlight around the cave and found a walkway leading to an elevator. The code that had unlocked all the other elevators worked again. They stepped in, pulled the lever to release the locking mechanism and pushed a red button. The cage rattled its way down through dark grey rock to the mine floor. TJ waved the flashlight through the darkness. "I see something."

Audrey choked, "Will!"

They reached the bottom, threw the gate open, and ran to the body lying against the wall several feet away.

"Will, speak to me," Audrey said, dropping to her knees beside her sister. "She's breathing. Look at the gash on her head. It's oozing."

"Can we move her?"

"I don't know." Audrey picked up Willet's hands to rub them. "Her hands are like ice. Oh my God, her palms are cut up and bleeding!"

"We need to get her out of here." TJ put a hand on Willet's forehead. "She doesn't seem feverish."

"What if her neck is broken? Theese might have thrown her down the shaft."

"If he did that, she'd probably be dead. I can't wait to get my hands on that guy's throat."

Audrey gave a small whimper of dread. While TJ held the flashlight, she carefully probed Willet's arms, legs and neck, checking for anything swollen or protruding.

"I don't feel anything unusual, but I'm no nurse."

"Lift her eyelids and check her pupils." TJ shined the flashlight on Willet's face as Audrey slid her eyelids up. The pupils constricted to pinpoints.

Audrey looked hopefully at TJ. "That's a good sign, right?"

"I don't think her neck is broken."

A tremor ran under the ground and the mountain shuddered. Rock dust rained on their heads. The elevator creaked back and forth in its frame.

"Will, please, wake up," Audrey pleaded and stroked her sister's cheeks. "If we move her, we might do serious damage if she's injured anywhere."

The mountain shook harder. Cracks ran through the rock walls.

"We need to go now," TJ said, "before this mine caves in. If I pick her up, you support her head and shoulders. Keep her as stable and level as you can. It's all we can do."

Without waiting for agreement, TJ slid his arms under Willet's knees and lower back. Audrey braced Willet's head between two hands. They lifted her and stepped carefully onto the elevator. Another shudder from the mountain swung the hoist drum above them like a bell clapper. The cage swayed.

"Audrey, push the button," TJ said quietly

Audrey used her elbow to push the red button, and the cage started to climb, rocking as it rose. Pebbled rock pelted the elevator, and something in the circuit board behind the control panel sizzled. Midway up the shaft, the mountain shook hard. The cage banged around inside the shaft frame, hitting all four sides. Audrey grasped Willet's head between her elbows and held on to her shoulders, laying her cheek on her sister's forehead to keep it steady. The cage swung wildly. The twisted metal lift cables scraped against each other, throwing off a shower of sparks. At the last fifty feet, something buckled in the frame, tilting the cage to one side. The hoist drum squealed in protest.

TJ slid and braced his feet. Audrey leaned against the frame to steady herself. "Audrey, how ya doin'?"

"I'm fine. The control panel circuit board could catch fire. It's almost toast."

"If we don't make it to the top, we're toast anyway."

Metal ground on metal before the cage finally stopped at the top. TJ steadied Willet's weight in his arms.

"I'm going to step off this thing. The cage will be moving. Can you move with me?"

Audrey nodded and readied herself, adjusting her hold on Willet's neck. Sweat dripped down her face and back. Her stomach was in knots. "Yes, ready…"

The cage swung forward, hit the side of the platform and swung away before they could step out.

"Too quick," TJ said. "Let's try again."

The cage swung forward and back, slower each time, finally slow enough for them to take a long step out of the elevator. They were just clear of the shaft when the mountain shook again. The rock dome above the elevator cracked into pieces, and the massive bolt assembly that anchored the hoist drum to the ceiling fell away. The cage dropped and hit the floor with the impact of a bomb strike. Dust belched up, filling the mine shaft. They hurried for the mine entrance as quickly as they dared.

Outside in the sun, they laid Willet carefully downwind from the mine and covered her face with a tissue to keep out the dust.

"I'm glad Will wasn't awake to hear that," Audrey said. "She'd be screaming bloody murder."

Chapter 34: The Malevolent Whisper

A sliver of late afternoon sun still warmed the air, but the sun was dropping behind the mountain, leaving some roads in shadow. Gem drove the Jeep up the road behind the compound, past mines with wide open gates and heavy chains lying in broken pieces on the ground.

"I see TJ finally found something he could shoot at," Dean said.

At the top of a steep rise, Gem slowed into a sharp turn and parked quickly. She and Dean jumped out with Dora at their heels. They headed further on foot until they found TJ and Audrey on the shoulder of the road. TJ stood watch over Willet lying on the ground. Audrey sat at her head, stroking her cheek.

Gem hurried over and knelt beside her with Dean hovering over her shoulder. She grasped a limp hand, and spoke into her ear, "Baby girl, hear my voice. Return to your body. You are safe now."

Willet remained inert. Her head lolled between Audrey's hands.

"What's wrong with her?" TJ asked, shaking with agitation. "It's like she's catatonic."

Gem covered Willet's cold hands with her own. "She has chosen to detach her consciousness from her physical body to escape the din of the Red Souls."

"What, she's choosing not to wake up?" Dean asked.

"Essentially, yes."

"What can we do? She can't stay like this." Audrey said.

"We can wait for her to return, or we seek her in the place where she hides."

Audrey's forehead wrinkled. "Where is she hiding?"

"She has retreated to the other side of the Gate, into the High Astral."

"She needs medical attention, is what she needs," TJ said. "We don't know what her injuries are."

"Her injuries are of the psyche as well as the body, so she seeks the healing only the higher worlds can provide. When she returns, she will need the love and stability of the Circle to heal physically."

Dean snorted. "Stability? From this group? I don't know, Gem…"

"That will come in time," Gem nodded. "For now, let us aim toward love and survival."

Dora paced back and forth, huffing and sniffing the air, then lay down next to Gem and put her head on her paws.

*****

"That harpy!. She can't ruin my life and then act like she's done me a favor." Theese paced in his office, mumbling and punching the air with tight fists. The gun Gem had shot off his desk still lay in the corner. He couldn't bring himself to pick it up, didn't want to give her even that much acknowledgement. "Damn it all. I'd like to strangle her with my bare hands," he snarled at the walls.

Voices mumbled and hissed. A voice answered him from inside his head. "Strangle her," it echoed in a bitter whisper.

Yeah.

"Kill the witch."

Kill the... His pacing slowed to a stop. *Wait a minute. What?*

"She wronged you," the voice said.

She screwed me royally, sure, but...

"You deserve justice."

I do deserve justice.

"You know what to do."

Do what? I can't do that. Can I?

If you don't do it, who will?

No one else has the guts to face her.

"You have the guts."

Damned right.

"It's your duty."

It's my duty. She's dangerous, a menace.

"She's a menace."
It's for the good of the city.

348

"For the good of the city."

He went to the corner and picked up the gun. Then he reached for the box of bullets in the side drawer of his desk. He loaded the gun, pulled out a nylon shoulder holster and tucked the gun into it, buckling the harness across his chest. The weight of the gun under his arm strengthened his resolve. "Now we'll see who calls the shots around here." He headed out front door into the waning daylight.

At the far side of the compound, Andy and Red were digging in the rubble of the laboratory.

What are those two idiots doing?

He didn't stop to find out, kept walking to the side of the building to his car. As he pulled out of the parking area, Andy and Red watched him go, waving their arms to get his attention. He had no time for them. The woman had a head start, but he knew where she would go. He hoped to catch her before she found that girl in mine eleven. He rolled up the mountain road in low gear, tires barely crunching, trying to stay as quiet as possible.

After the ninth mine, he parked and continued on foot, keeping to the shade of the mountain wall. He heard nothing until he came to the curve in the road just before the eleventh mine - voices, several of them. They had already brought the blonde up from the mine. *Damn.* Apparently, her condition wasn't good. The presence of other people complicated things but wouldn't stop him. He had a job to do.

He pulled the gun from his holster. The woman had a gun too and knew how to use it. The two men with her were probably still armed. They wouldn't hesitate to shoot him this time. Only the element of surprise would work for him.

He crept along in the shade of the mountain to an outcrop of rock and peered around it. The blonde girl was lying on the ground with everyone around her. *What happened there? She was alive when I left her.*

Only fifteen feet away, the woman had her back turned, leaning over the blonde while the others watched. Then the big black dog lifted its head and looked his way, growling low, blowing his cover. That damned dog got up and stalked toward him. It was now or never.

*****

His mind began to spin.

I can't do this. Can I?

"Sssssss," the voice whispered in his head. "Do your duty."

My duty. Yes.

"She insulted you, robbed you."

Yes, she did!

"Hey, psycho," he called to her. "I'm not done with you."

Gem turned, squared her shoulders, and studied him with narrowed eyes. "Darkness wraps you like a shroud, Mr. Theese," she said. "It is not too late to resist. He lies."

The hint of reprimand in her voice hardened his anger. His heart felt like a grenade ready to explode in his chest. "I know what lies are and I don't need your direction."

"Do you think your anger is just, that violence is your right? Is that what he tells you?"

Theese stared in shock. No person could know his thoughts. It had to be the work of the devil. "You're a witch," he said between clenched teeth. "I shall not suffer a witch to live." He raised the gun and fired at Gem's chest. Dora leaped at him from the side and butted his elbow with her head. The shot deflected to hit Gem in the temple. Dora threw her whole body against him, jarring his gun hand as he fired another shot. This time, he hit himself in the neck and sunk to the ground. Fluid gurgled in his throat and foamed on his lips. He managed to turn on his side to keep from choking on his own fluids. Blood and filmy white liquid drained from his mouth onto the dirt. He stared listlessly at the people crouched over the body of the woman. Maybe he hit his head when he fell. Maybe the bright light hurt his eyes, or he lost too much blood. He certainly felt dizzy, and his eyes teared with pain. But deep down, he knew what he saw. He watched her body. It changed in an impossible way. He would swear to it to his dying day.

*****

Blood flowed from the hole in Gem's head. Everyone erupted into motion. Dean turned Gem on her back, ripped off his t-shirt and pressed it against the wound. TJ crouched beside her, pulled her chin up and administered CPR.

Audrey knelt over her, pressing her rib cage to keep her breathing. "Gem. Gem! Please," she pleaded. "Don't die. Please!"

"Damn," Dean said. "She's losing a lot of blood."

After several minutes of CPR, TJ fell back on his heels and felt for the pulse in her neck.

Dean slid his hand under her head and tipped her head back to keep her throat clear. "Gem, talk to me. Stay with us. We'll get you to a hospital."

Gem's eyelids fluttered open. She barely breathed, but she gave him a faint smile. "See what I see, Warrior," she said. She put the palm of her hand against his cheek. "Close the Gate." Her eyes glazed. The rise and fall of her chest slowed to a stop, and the color of life drained from her skin.

TJ pumped on her breastbone, one palm over the other, until the bone cracked. Audrey and Dean sat by her side frozen, waiting for an intake of breath. It didn't come. Gem's lips turned blue. TJ dropped back, filled his lungs with air and resumed CPR. After five minutes he sat back again and shook his head.

Dora curled up beside Gem, sniffed her face and nuzzled her cheek. When Gem's eyes didn't open, the big dog lifted her head and howled a long, plaintive dirge. Audrey buried her head in her arms and sobbed. Dean held Gem's hand in his and stroked her forehead. TJ stared out over the cliff with heavy eyes and defeated shoulders.

It was over it seemed, but then the air around Gem's body seemed to thicken. The light of trillions of tiny explosions flared as the molecules comprising her physical being broke apart, releasing their bond energies in small fireworks. Everyone scuttled back on their butts to get away from the strange light of physiochemical reactions. When the lights dimmed and winked out, Gem's body had disintegrated, leaving a thin layer of pale dust on the ground. They all gaped at the empty space where she had been moments ago.

TJ stood and put his foot carefully into the space where Gem's body had laid. A puff of dust rose around his shoe. His lips trembled. "What the hell?" he muttered, face pale as the dust.

"Ashes to ashes, dust to dust." Dean said.

The mountain rumbled underneath them. Rock debris and dust belched from the mouth of the number eleven mine as it collapsed.

352

Sparkling smears of red smoke streamed out with the dust. The air flushed red. The presence of Red Souls was a certainty.

"We're in big trouble," Audrey said, and scrambled to her feet.

"Cover your mouth and nose," Dean said. "Your ears too. They'll get inside you that way."

"Let's get going," TJ urged.

"What about Theese? We can't just leave him," Audrey said. His body lay motionless where it had fallen, eyes staring in their direction.

The ground bucked underneath their feet, and the mine belched again, spraying sharp, stinging chunks of rock onto the road. They huddled over Willet and covered their heads with their arms until the air cleared.

TJ looked around at Theese with disgust. "I say leave the asshole. What about the dog?"

Dora sat at the spot where Gem disappeared and appraised them calmly.

"We can't leave Dora. She should come with us," Audrey said. "Come, Dora."

Dora didn't move.

"Dora, come on, we're leaving," Dean beckoned to her.

Dora looked at them with baleful eyes and gave a soft woof. She stood and loped away down the road west without a backward glance, disappearing around the bend.

"Where is she going?" Dean asked. "Back to the compound?"

"Dora *is* Gem's dog," Audrey said. "Maybe there's something she's supposed to do."

The mountain jolted, and the ground dipped. "We need to leave while we can still drive out of here," TJ said.

Dean helped TJ lift Willet into his arms, and then ran for his truck and jumped in. Audrey dashed to the Jeep, climbed in the back, and pulled the belt over her lap. TJ laid Willet in her lap and shut the door, ran to the driver's door and got in. He jammed the key in the ignition with shaking fingers.

An explosion twenty feet behind them rocked the Jeep. A massive ridge of rock and crystal had burst from the mountainside and ripped across the road, blocking return to the compound. Fractured rock and dirt rained down. The only escape now was to the east. The truck tore up the road, tires barely touching earth and the Jeep followed. They cleared a tight turn, and another fist of rock punched out of the mountainside right behind them. One second slower, the punch would have pulverized the side of the Jeep where Audrey and Willet sat.

TJ floored it into a squealing lurch. "Maybe Will is better off wherever she is."

*****

Dean could hardly see the road ahead for all the swirling red smoke and rock dust. He needed all his strength and concentration to control the steering wheel and keep an eye on the road while driving as fast as he could. Nevertheless, a part of his mind did stray to thoughts he could not avoid. *Gem is dead. Her body turned to dust right in front of us. What the hell...*

"The Guardian has departed the physical plane," said a soft voice beside him. "The Astral Gate is still open."

354

Dean's head spun like a corkscrew toward the passenger seat. A woman sat there. Long brown hair in a tail draped over her right shoulder. The mysterious woman from the Circle gazed steadily ahead of her.

"It's you!" his voice squeaked. "Who are you?"

"My name is Sonrisa. I am a Traveler. What will you do to close the Gate, Warrior?" she asked. She returned his stare with steady brown eyes.

He fell into the depths of her gaze, mesmerized for a moment, until the steering wheel jerked out of his hands. He gripped it, trying to regain control of the truck. His head swung back and forth between the road and his unexpected passenger. "How did you get in here?" his voice almost squeaked.

She blinked slowly. "All existence is here and now. I focus my attention on the place I want to be, and I am there. But this is not the time for whys and wherefores. With the Guardian no longer in a physical body, the Gate is unprotected. Forces of the lower astral will escape the crystal. They will cause destruction on a grand scale in the city. What will you do to stop it?"

"*Me*? What am *I* supposed to do? I just follow Gem!" The road rocked under the truck. Dean's eyes darted in every direction, looking for signs of any large rock coming his way.

"The Guardian gifted her Sight to the Circle before she left this plane," the Traveler said. "You will see what you did not see before."

"What do you mean?"

"Red Souls are all around you. Now you can see them."

355

He looked forward into the smoke. "Yeah, I see them. How does that help me? I can barely see the road."

"If you see them, you can fight them, but you will need the Circle to help you."

"Willet is down for the count. We don't know how to get her back."

"Use the skills the Guardian taught you."

"Right now, I'd just like to get off this mountain before I get pushed off."

She put a light hand on his shoulder. "That is a valid concern, Warrior. Be prepared. Time will stand still for you."

The mountain wall exploded, and a fist of rock slammed into the side of the truck, sending it airborne. He watched the sky spin lazily past the windshield, felt the truck tilt into freefall over the cliff, moving almost in slow motion. A strange calm settled on him. He looked at the passenger seat. It was empty. He thought about the people in the Jeep behind him and hoped TJ would be able to stop in time. Nothing he could do to save himself, so he closed his eyes and chanted Huuuu.

TJ hit the brakes hard, skidding sideways right up to the thrust of rock and crystal that sent Dean's truck flying into the air. The crystal streamed and hissed with energy, spitting like oil in a hot pan.

TJ watched the truck roll in the air, and then disappear over the cliff. His mind blanked and his body went numb. *Not Dean. NO. Not Dean. Please, God, don't do this to me.* A pain spiked in his chest. Suddenly, he couldn't breathe. He doubled over and his head hit the steering wheel. Images flickered before his eyes like an old newsreel, burnished gold in his memory. Memories of Dean – his best friend - all of life ahead of them. He couldn't bring himself to look up into the empty space where the truck had been, where Dean no longer existed. *This can't be happening.*

TJ heard Dean's truck hit the valley floor. The crash echoed all the way up the mountain with a finality so brutal he couldn't deny it. His blood froze in his veins. Audrey's anguished cries in the back seat sounded far away. He couldn't help her. An avalanche of emotions erupted from his throat in a long wail.

The air suddenly felt thick and gelatinous. He heard a snapping sound, and his ears popped. He gasped for breath but choked and coughed instead. An arm across his chest pushed him back from the steering wheel, and a hand pounded him on the back. The hand squeezed his shoulder.

Right next to him, a familiar voice rasped, "TJ, it's me, man. Look at me. It's okay."

TJ slowly turned his head to look. Muscles in his chest locked. Shock set in.

Dean sat in the passenger seat, shirtless, white-faced and trembling, sweat dripped down his forehead. He stared back at TJ with haunted eyes. "I'm here. Don't know how, but I'm here."

TJ gulped a lung full of air. He reached out a tentative hand and pressed fingertips to Dean's shoulder. The damp skin, the hard muscle underneath, the warmth of living flesh – impossible but true. Tears blurred his vision. He pulled Dean into a fierce embrace. "Damn, Simmons," he gasped over and over. "Damn."

TJ finally sat back and searched his friend's face for answers. When he saw none, he punched him so hard in the shoulder that Dean winced. "You colossal asshole! I watched you go over the cliff. I almost had a heart attack! Did I have a heart attack and die? Are we both dead?"

Dean wiped sweat from his forehead with shaking fingers. "I don't know, I don't know, man. I thought I was finished."

TJ's eyes burned with tears. His whole body trembled. "How?"

"It was the Traveler. She moved me somehow. That's all I can say."

"What Traveler?"

"That brown-haired woman in the Circle we wondered about. She was there."

"You mean she was in the truck with you?"

"Yes, that's what I mean."

"No way," TJ said. "It's impossible."

Screams from the back seat had died down to wheezing. Audrey threw her arms around Dean's neck and buried her face in his shoulder, her tears dripping down his chest.

He patted her arms and turned his head to kiss her cheek. "It's okay, babe. It's okay. I'm here."

The mountain shook again. Rocks rained down on the Jeep. A boulder hit the roof and bounced off, bending it down almost to their heads. "We gotta get out of here, T," Dean said. "No fooling around, we're in deep doo."

TJ just sat with limp hands in his lap, shaking his head. "Ya think?"

Dean shook his arm. "I don't have any explanations, dude. For now, we need to be gone, so snap out of it. Can you drive us off this mountain or not?"

TJ looked down at the steering wheel like he'd never seen one before and shook himself. "I can drive, but what about that?"

TJ pointed at the mass of rock now blocking the road. It glowed like neon in the gathering dusk.

Dean stared through the windshield and grimaced. "Yeah, there's that. Thoughts?"

"My brain is toast."

"Think we can drive over it?"

"The Jeep might flip over, or the crystal might burn us before we got to the other side."

Dean and TJ sat in silence, studying the rock and all the ribbons of energy running through it. They looked at each other. Dean turned to the back seat. "Audrey," he said. "Anything you can do here to help us out? Now would be the time."

*****

Willet walked out of the grassy field and stood at the side of a dirt road where a line of painted wagons on wooden wheels rolled past. A calliope tooted a carnival tune, and acrobats turning cartwheels flipped in the air and walked on their hands. Boys in striped pants and beanies pedaled high-wheel bicycles. Two men pumped briskly on the handles of a three-wheel handcart.

If this is supposed to be a circus parade, it's the weirdest circus I've ever seen.

People in old-fashioned costumes adorned with flowers sat on the wagons, waving and smiling, as if they were entertaining a large crowd. Willet looked up and down the road. She was the only one standing there. At the end of the procession, a man in a brown monk's robe belted with a rope pulled a two- seat rickshaw. He came to a stop in front of her.

"Can I have a ride?" she asked him.

"Another time perhaps," he said, pointing to the empty seats.

"Uh, sure." She wondered why she couldn't ride now.

The man picked up the handle shafts of the rickshaw and followed the parade down the road. She watched until the procession disappeared over the crest of a hill, blinking her eyes a few times to make sure it wasn't a mirage.

Across the road the land fell away into valleys undulating between green hills dotted with trees. A range of rugged mountains soared at the horizon, grey and snow-capped. The sky was blue, and the air, warm. A light breeze rustled her hair, pleasantly cool. She took a deep breath. The air smelled of roses, though she didn't see any flowers growing nearby.

It's so quiet here, a little wind, a bit of music, so peaceful. Maybe it's heaven. Wait, I hear a voice. I know that voice.

Up the road, two people walked toward her, arm in arm. One was a woman, and the other was – a large circle of light with a man inside. The woman inclined her head to him, listening intently to his words. Willet knew that curly hair with blonde highlights.

It's Gem! Who's that guy she's with?

The couple strolled over the last rise. Willet waved. "It's me, Gem," she called. "I'm here."

Gem waved back. When the couple reached her, Gem kissed her on the cheek. "Hello, Listener, I see you've found your way to Samhasa."

"Is that where we are?"

"Samhasa is the province of the Lotus City, capitol of the High Astral. Look there," Gem said and pointed.

Willet looked into the distance at an enormous structure tucked into a shoulder of the valley. It looked more like a diamond embedded in the hills than a city, reflecting sunlight from a million sparkling facets. How could she have missed that?

"Am I in heaven?"

"'Heaven' is a relative term, baby girl. The High Astral is very beautiful, of course, but there are many higher and finer planes than this one. They are more difficult to enter."

"Am I dreaming again?"

"You are hiding. Let me introduce you to Augustus." Gem turned to the luminous being beside her, and her face lit with joy. Willet had never seen Gem so happy.

The light glowed so intensely that Willet could barely make out the person inside the nimbus. She shaded her eyes with her hand. "Pleased to meet you, Augustus. Gem told me about you."

The light pulsed brighter and then paled. A white-haired man in a white toga stood before her. His blue eyes pierced deep into hers. He took both her hands in his. "Hello, my dear, I am pleased to meet you also. We have been waiting for you." His words chimed like little silver bells in a breeze, such light, pure tones they almost twinkled.

Willet gasped in recognition. "Are you the Silver Voice? I thought it was Chopin. He talked to me in that voice. Are you he?"

"Alas, no," Augustus said. "I cannot claim the musical prowess of our dear Frederic. He did agree to visit you and deliver our message, because of the connection you felt to him. We thought his visage would be less startling to you."

Willet felt her mouth hanging open. Embarrassed, she snapped it shut. "You asked Chopin to tell me about the Red Souls?"

"Yes."

"So, I'm not schizophrenic."

Augustus shook his head and smiled. "Not at all."

"Why did you want to speak to *me*?"

"To warn you of coming dangers and prepare you to meet the Guardian."

Fears and doubts long buried in her heart melted away under the warmth of his gaze. She released a breath she had been holding for years. A space opened in her chest, but something still bothered her.

"Gem, you said I was hiding, I'm not hiding."

"You withdrew your consciousness from your body to escape the Red Souls. You traveled through the plane of no-thing. Then your chant brought you here to us."

"What am I supposed to do now?"

"The Circle has rescued your physical body from the mine, so it is safe to return to it."

Memories of a dark hole in the ground, choking red smoke and shrill chatter came flooding back. "Do I have to go back?"

"Yes."

"That woman, Sonrisa, left me. I didn't know if she'd come back. I thought I'd die in the mine."

"The Traveler came to check on you and reassure you," Gem said. "Mr. Barlow and your sister searched every mine until they found your body. He carried you out. They protect your physical form."

"This is such a beautiful place," Willet said wistfully. "I don't want to leave."

"It is not your time to leave the physical plane behind, Listener," Gem said. "The Circle needs you."

363

Augustus nodded. "Your world is under attack, and time is running out. The crystal will soon erupt from the mountains. An earthquake will crack the crystal and release a plague of Red Souls. The people of your city will be driven to violence and destruction The city will collapses into chaos."

"But what can I do about it?"

"You must be the ears of the Circle," Augustus said. "Listen to the chatter of the Red Souls. Their voices will betray their plans."

She felt totally unprepared for the task. "I may hear them, but I might not understand what they mean. Gem knows. She always shows us what to do."

Augustus raised his thick white eyebrows and glanced at Gem before turning to Willet again. "You must learn to use your own abilities to their fullest, you and your fellows. The Spirit of All will supply the rest."

"Do you hear your sister calling?" Gem asked gently. "She needs you now."

Willet listened. Someone was crying out, very far away, a woman's voice. "That's Audrey! What's happening to her?"

"Your sister is broken-hearted," Augustus said.

"I have to help her! And I hear Thomas – is he crying?"

Augustus' voice thinned to soft silver bells. "Go now and do what must be done."

The brilliant astral light dimmed, and she couldn't see him anymore. Gem stood at the far end of a long, narrow tunnel, waving at her from a circle of light. Willet tumbled backwards into the darkness of the tunnel. The light receded into the distance, shrinking to nothing more than a pinprick. She landed on her back, and her lungs inflated with a sudden gulp of air. Someone was crying. Her eyes popped open.

*****

Audrey didn't notice her at first. She was too busy hugging Dean. Then she looked down. "Will!" she exclaimed. "TJ, I think she's waking up, her eyes are open. Will!" Audrey shook her sister's shoulders and patted her cheeks.

Willet tried to clear her throat and speak. "Auddie," she murmured. "Why are you hitting me?"

Audrey grasped her hands. "Can you sit up? Are you okay?"

Willet sat up, and leaned weakly against Audrey, who wrapped her in a hug.

TJ swiveled to face the back seat. "Will," he said. "You're back!"

"I'm back," she said. With effort, she leaned toward the front seat, put a hand on his shoulders and whispered in his ear. "I was worried about you."

TJ pressed his forehead to hers. "We were worried about *you*, and then I thought we had lost Dean."

She kissed his lips gently and leaned back to look at him. "Why did you think Dean was gone? He's right here."

TJ cleared his throat with a small cough. "We've had some, er, issues while you were…away. There were accidents. I'll explain later. Right now, this mountain is shaking like it's about to lose its mind. A big earthquake's coming, and we have to leave."

365

"Gem and Augustus told me about that."

"You spoke to Gem?" Audrey asked her sister carefully. "When was this?"

"Just now."

"You spoke to Gem," Audrey repeated. "Just now."

"Well, she was with Augustus in Samhasa, where I was. I met her on a road after a circus passed by, but, you know, it's the astral plane. Things are strange there."

Audrey nodded slowly. "On the astral plane. I see."

"Where *is* Gem? Why isn't she with us? And why is everyone staring?"

"We'll talk about that, hon," Audrey said in a quiet voice, "when we're somewhere safe and you've had time to rest."

The mountain mocked that idea with a tooth-rattling tremor that sent boulders rolling down from the peaks. A large rock hit the back of the Jeep, cracking the rear window. Another rock landed on the front hood and skidded off. A giant boulder flew over them and hit the ground on the far side, knocking a big chunk out of the road before rolling off the cliff. The wedge of crystal-infested rock still blocked the road.

"Audrey," Dean repeated. "Focus, here. Can you do *anything* about the crystal like you did before? I don't know if we can drive over it with all those sparks. The gas tank might blow. Not to mention the red smoke…"

"*You* can see the smoke too?" Audrey asked. "I thought I was imagining it."

"Yeah, I can see it," Dean said. "Gem told me to see what she saw. Apparently, she meant it literally."

"Gem had astral sight," Audrey said. "Now we do too."

"I don't want to see it," said Willet. "But I do."

"Even I can see it," TJ said.

Audrey swung the door open. "Well, let's see what the rings can do. Watch out for boulders."

Everyone got out of the Jeep with her and approached the giant ridge of rock lying across the road. The crystal in it streamed and sparked. Red smoke seeped out of cracks in the crystal and swarmed them immediately. A fall of loose, jagged rocks pelted them. Dean's chest and back were scratched and bleeding from the rock fall. TJ brushed rock dust out of his eyes. A gash cut across his right cheekbone. Willet had a cut on her chin and tried to clean it with the edges of her shirt. The ground shook violently, knocking them off their feet like bowling pins and another boulder flew over their heads.

Audrey got to her feet, and TJ and Dean stood on each side of her. She shook her hands. Gold rings formed around her fingers. She spun the rings into wide circles. The rings were visible to everyone now.

"No way!" TJ said. "That's what you've been doing with your hands?"

"Yeah, these are the rings. Neat, huh." She flung them like horseshoes onto the crystal. The crystal sputtered in protest.

Scalding heat wafted off the rock, sending them back on their heels. "Son of a bitch!" Dean said, looking down at the red blisters rising on his arms and chest. "That burns."

367

"You need a shirt," TJ said. He peeled off his flannel shirt, leaving just a T-shirt, and tossed the flannel to Dean, who pulled it on with a sigh of relief.

"Red Souls are saying 'surround them,'" Willet said, swatting at the smoke-filled air around her.

"Really?" Audrey replied. "Let's see how they deal with this bling."

She spun up ring after ring, balancing them on the tips of her fingers, and threw them at the rock. Each time a ring hit, flames flared and then died. After a series of hits, the light in the crystal slowly faded. Large patches of crystal began to burn out. After a few minutes work, the rock looked charred and brittle, like burnt charcoal. Red smoke dissipated.

Audrey stepped back and stretched, rolled her neck and rubbed her lower back. She massaged her knuckles. "I haven't felt that much energy before," she said, "It's like lightning. I think you all gave me a boost."

TJ pressed his thumb gingerly into the side of the blackened rock. It crumbled to dust. "This stuff is really soft now. It would break down under a heavy weight."

Willet wiped blood from her forehead. "We just need a heavy weight."

Everyone turned to look at the Jeep.

TJ put the Jeep in gear and rolled it forward. He nudged the front bumper against the edge of the rock, accelerated slightly, and then rolled back. The bumper left a deep gash in the softened rock. The next roll forward caused the gash to crumble and cave in.

Forward and back, forward and back. The bumper crushed more of the rock with each push, and the tires pulverized it. The Jeep rolled a foot up onto the pile of pulverized dust, then two feet, then three, flattening a longer and wider path. After many patient advances and retreats, the Jeep rolled over what was left of the crystal ridge and onto the road on the other side.

Dean, Audrey and Willet scrambled over the rock and jumped in the Jeep with TJ.

"Good job, everybody," Dean said. "Let's get the hell out of here before we get hit again."

A minute later, TJ had the Jeep flying down the road, careening around curves on two tires, daring the mountain to hit them. The mountain obliged. Its massive shoulders shifted with an audible crack and sent an onslaught of boulders crashing down from the peaks. Rocks hit the road like cannonballs all around them. The Jeep dodged and weaved, bouncing through broken craters in the ground. The roof caved on the passenger side and all the windows cracked. Something underneath the Jeep dragged on the ground, trailing sparks.

"What the hell is that?" TJ growled. "Tailpipe? Catalytic converter? Part of the brakes?"

"Whatever it is, we can't stop now," Dean replied.

Willet started chanting and Audrey and Dean joined in. TJ followed in a low baritone while his eyes frantically tracked the road. The rhythmic wave of their voices flowed out. Chant calmed their hearts and cleared their minds.

The Jeep's headlights beat bravely against the growing darkness, but visibility was poor. They heard a boulder hit the ground beside the Jeep, and then another. Close, so close. They kept one step ahead and asked for guidance. From the far reaches of the universe, the answer returned in an echo. *Sound will guide you. Light will show you the way.*

Chapter 36: Freeway Jam

They navigated by the link between Sound and Light. Willet listened for the creak of a boulder breaking free from a high peak, the crunch of a boulder rolling over loose rock or the displacement of air as heavy rock dropped into freefall. She gave TJ a small window of time to maneuver the Jeep out of each boulder's direct path. She closed her eyes, concentrated, and barked commands.

"Incoming left. Ease right. Not too much!" TJ jerked the wheel and just missed a boulder landing to the left of the front bumper. The boulder rolled off the side of the cliff into the valley.

"Speed up speed up!" TJ steeped on it, and another boulder landed just a few feet behind them with a thunderous crack. "Slow down now, incoming ahead. Stop, stop!" she shouted.

A smaller boulder crashed in front of them and shattered into pieces. The Jeep rolled through the rubble and kept going. It banged and bumped over potholes, gears grinding and brakes squealing. Rock scree pelted and scraped at the Jeep with angry teeth, trying to chew through metal.

TJ gripped the steering wheel, jaw clenched, knuckles practically popping through the skin of his fingers, and laser-focused on the road while listening to Willet's directions. Audrey and Dean scanned the windows for heavy objects coming at them from the sides. Together they maneuvered through the gauntlet of the mountain's siege for two exhausting hours of hyper vigilance before reaching the bottom of the road leading out of the mountain.

By the time they drove out of the foothills and reached the 15 Freeway South, the side mirrors were gone, the front tires were losing air, and the front bumper had dropped off. Whatever had been hanging off the bottom of the Jeep – they figured it to be the tailpipe - was long gone. The tires could not be ignored. Fortunately, the Jeep had a spare. Dean and TJ stopped to replace the left tire. The right tire was losing air more slowly. They'd have to live with it until they could get to a service station.

Hemmings was still miles away, but at least they were off the mountain. At the 15/215 split, they took the 215 Freeway, veering southeast, in the direction of Pine Siskin House. They hit exceptionally heavy traffic for so late at night. It got heavier the farther south they went. The flat, arid land to the east beamed with lights – car headlights, campfires, even klieg lights big enough for an outdoor music festival. They slowed to a complete stop just north of Perris, and a crush of cars lined up at the exit off the eastbound off ramp.

"What is everyone doing out there?" Willet asked. "Is there a concert tonight?"

"People are camping," Audrey said. "Look at all the tents."

As traffic moved south out of the mountains, they got a better look at LA to the west. The crystal had already torn through in the city. Overturned cars lay on cracked sidewalks and buildings leaned at

371

crazy angles. Ridges of rock thrust up through concrete, blocking streets. The few people on the streets ran erratically through clouds of sparkling red smoke.

TJ switched the radio on. Behind a thin veil of static, a calm voice recited the news. "…to your nearest shelter. Current road closures: the 210 is closed between Pasadena and San Dimas. The 10 is stopped in both directions and closed east of Ontario. The 60 is blocked at City of Industry and closed east of Chino. All citizens are advised to evacuate Rancho Cucamonga west of Hermosa Avenue and north of Church Street. In Maywood, avoid Slauson Avenue at the 710 due to a gas main explosion. Safe drinking water is available at fire stations in Glendale, Pomona, Santa Ana and Long Beach. Please report new eruptions to News 8."

Willet whispered, "We're too late."

A man ran along the fence beside the freeway, frantically waving his arms and yelling to them. A smoking swarm of Red Souls descended on him and enveloped his head.

Dean shuddered. "That's bad."

"The poor man," Willet said. "Is there anything we can do for him?"

Audrey flexed her fingers, opened a window, and leveled a glowing ring in his direction with a Frisbee fling of her hand. The ring brushed over the man and landed at his feet. She tossed another ring. This time it settled over his head and onto his shoulders. The red smoke thinned out and drifted away. The man kept running, gesturing to every car until he veered down a side road out of sight.

"The rings can protect people from Red Souls," Audrey said, studying her fingers. "Good to know."

"This is what Augustus warned me about," Willet murmured. "He said the crystal would break out of the ground and crack open, and then all the Red Souls inside would pour out and attack everyone."

Dean squinted against oncoming headlights. Red smoke glittered in the lights, and a reddish haze saturated the air. "We can't pretend to be surprised. Gem told us pretty much the same thing."

"We're the Circle of Augustus," Willet said. "We were supposed to prevent this."

"A longshot at best," TJ observed grimly. "Who are we? Just regular people. What chance do we have without Gem?"

"The big quake might not have happened yet," Dean said. "We know Audrey's rings burn the crystal. We could prevent even more smoke from escaping."

"There's a ton of rock out there, bro," TJ said. "Audrey would have to throw a lot of rings.

"The smoke will drive people crazy," Dean said. "It made me angry and ready to bash someone's face in. We have to do something before people start trying to kill each other."

"I'll throw rings all night, if necessary," Audrey said.

"Great, but we're not going to get far in this car," TJ said. "We're almost out of gas, and the tire's going flat."

"We have the sedan at home," Willet said. "Let's get there, please, please. I need a shower so bad."

*****

Still on the freeway after another half hour, the Jeep tilted to the right on its almost-flat front tire. Traffic barely moved. Audrey threw rings out the back window whenever they saw a person beset by Red Souls.

"We're on empty, folks," TJ informed them in dull voice. "We need a gas station, pronto."

A sign promised gas in five miles, but cars already backed up in front of them. They'd probably run out before they got to the station.

"Six miles to the Hemmings exit, I say we go for it," Audrey said. "If we run out of gas, at least we know where we are. We can start walking if we have to."

"Six miles?" Dean groaned, stretching his arms and legs. "Could this day get any worse?"

The Jeep crawled along on fumes until they reached the Hemmings exit. They pulled off, using the last vapor of gas to roll onto the shoulder. Then the Jeep quit with a huff. A twirling, whooshing cyclone of red smoke immediately descended on the car. Red Souls swarmed every window, faces leering in the smoke.

Willet jammed her hands against her ears and closed her eyes. "They want to burn us," she muttered. "Me, most of all."

Dean wiped the moisture of his breath off the inside of his window and stared at the nightmare of crazed eyes and gaping mouths outside. "They could come in through the vents, couldn't they?" he asked. "Why aren't they doing it?"

"It's the sound prints," Willet said, dropping her hands from her ears for a moment to sample the sounds before clapping them back. "We chanted all the way down the mountain, and the air in the Jeep is still vibrating. It pushes them off. We're in a bubble of sound."

TJ turned blood-shot eyes to his window. "We're trapped in this car, protected by a bubble? How long 'til the bubble bursts?"

"Sound waves do fade over time," Willet said. "The barrier between us and them will disappear eventually."

"I've had those red things in my head. I do *not* want them in there again," Dean said. "If we need to chant, let's do it."

TJ leaned his head back against the headrest. "Okay. Just let me close my eyes a minute. I'll chant later." His eyelids drooped. In five seconds, he was asleep and snoring.

Willet gave his shoulder a sharp poke. "Thomas, you've been driving flat out for over four hours. I get that you're tired, but this is no time sleep."

TJ shook himself awake with a cough.

"It's sure getting warm in here," Dean said. "This seat feels like it's heated."

Audrey ran her palm across her seat. "It does seem warmer." She touched the door handle. "Ow, that's hot!"

"We can't wait any longer," Willet said finally. "We're losing the print."

Audrey started the chant, and Dean and Willet joined her, in long, low tones, but the temperature in the car rose by the second. The metal of the Jeep's chassis glowed dull red. Chatter from the Red Souls grew loud and frantic. Everyone in the Jeep started to sweat.

Dean sat up and away from his seat. Even through a flannel shirt, the leather felt hot. "They're cooking us."

Audrey grasped the door handle from the inside of her backpack and tried to open the door. "I think the lock melted," she said, jiggling it. "It feels like the handle isn't attached to anything."

Feathers of red smoke began to drift in through the vents and circled Dean's head. He swatted at it with both hands. The Circle chanted, and the smoke retreated to the vents, but the air remained suffocating. Their sweat dripped into puddles on the floor, and their voices became hoarse, the chant more of a rasp. One by one, heads nodded. Their lips moved noiselessly, and then stopped.

"Gem," Willet whispered. Her eyes closed and her chin dropped to her chest.

*****

They left their physical bodies behind and floated up above the Jeep. Long beams of light connected each of them to their physical forms like tethered balloons. Thoughts passed telepathically between them in clear, light bell tones.

"Where are we?"

"We're pink. Must be astral bodies."

"Are we dead?"

"No, we're still alive. See those cords of light? They connect us to our physical bodies."

"You know this how?"

"Is someone going to tell me where Gem is?"

Images passed quickly among them – of Gem and Theese, Gem lying on the ground in her own blood, Dora licking her pale cheek.

Willet saw everything they remembered, and drew away from them, horrified.

"That's not true! I just talked to her. She walked with Augustus. They would have told me."

"I wanted to tell you later when we were safe. Theese came after her and shot her. I'm so sorry you have to find out this way."

"We tried to save her. The creep shot her in the head. "Her body dissolved right in front of us. She turned to dust."

"No. No. I don't believe that." Willet's astral form flushed red. She shouted Gem's name with all her strength. The call reverberated to the far reaches of space.

Out of the hollow silence that followed, a dry voice hissed with spite and malevolence. "On our own now, are we?" it whispered. "What a pity." An acrid smell filled the air. The web of crystal in the earth streamed with fire, and blackness spread through the sky like ink in water. The blackness gathered above them and took the familiar shape of a snake. "It is time to face the truth," the voice hissed. "This city belongs to me now."

Chapter 37: Part 1, Confrontation

The body of the snake grew long and thick as the Deceiver took shape. Two appendages sprouted incongruously from its body. Fingers tipped with dagger-sharp claws wriggled at the ends. The Deceiver heaved a dramatic sigh, and then laughed. "The faults of men and planets are ever their undoing." He pointed a claw toward the earth and stabbed at the San Gabriel Mountains like a child poking at a bug. He stabbed at San Jacinto to the east, and at the Malibu Coast to the west. Tremors shuddered under the ground and rolled out from each impact.

"The San Andreas Fault is long overdue for a slip. I apply a bit of pressure, and the crystal explodes. Those big rock plates will slide off in different directions, and voila. Northern California will be free of Southern California. Or, if I poke at the Malibu Coast Fault, we could create new ocean-front property. Malibu is so last century, don't you think? The San Jacinto Fault is near your home, is it not, Listener? A quake there would be very unfortunate."

The Circle looked frantically at each other. Anxious thoughts flew between them like darts.

"He's trying to cause an earthquake!"

"He can't move the ground, can he?"

"Oh no, he's moving it – just look, everything is shaking. What does he want?"

The Deceiver snorted. "What I want is for you to behave, like good girls and boys. I have breached the Gate you guard so zealously. Do you comprehend what the Gate is?"

"It's supposed to keep *you* out of *here*, because you don't belong here."

"The Gate is nothing but a shimmer of energy separating your world from mine. A veil so easily torn that one destructive thought can rip it, one emotion out of control, one dark desire turned to action can bring it down, and I move right in."

"The Guardian stopped you. We'll stop you too."

"Foolishness. It is already too late. My crystal undercuts the city at its weakest points. It swells with the fire of my devoted ones. Rise and see what has become of your city."

As soon as the words were spoken, the Circle rose into the air and floated above the Los Angeles Basin. From the ocean to the desert, crystal veins full of fire riddled the vast expanse. The earth's crust heaved over barely contained geologic pressures. The whole area appeared to be wired with explosives and ready to blow at the slightest spark.

The Deceiver roared. "When the crystal breaks, my legions will devour your world. They will take over the bodies of the living and relish the pleasures of the flesh once more. All will worship me as their god."

Terrified thoughts and images of devastation flashed around the Circle. "What do we do? What do we do?"

"Audrey, we need rings!"

"Do you see all the crystal down there? I can't hit all that!"

"We have to try. Start with one ring."

Audrey formed a ring between her palms and tried to expand it. The ring wobbled, tipped to the side and melted away. She tried another ring, spread it between her palms, tossed it up, and balanced it lightly on her fingers. The large ring flew from her hands and headed straight up.

The Deceiver batted the ring away before it hit him and sent it flying out of sight over the Pacific Ocean. He bellowed in triumph and jabbed his claws into the Whittier Fault. The ground shook. Veins of crystal broke open and red smoke poured out. He smashed a fisted claw into the Newport-Inglewood Fault Zone and then at the Santa Monica Fault. Skyscrapers in downtown LA tilted against each other like dominos. Concrete and steel began to rain down on the streets.

"Auddie, try again! Make it bigger."

Audrey worked her rings, trying for more power, but the process exhausted her. "Help me. Maybe we could boost the energy if we work together.

They raised their hands alongside hers and contributed their energy to help her spin a bigger ring. It stabilized around their joined hands. They heaved it at the Deceiver with force, and he dodged it. The ring dropped somewhere near Whittier and landed on a large patch of glowing crystal. Within twenty seconds, the light in the crystal burnt out.

The Circle created rings as fast as they could throw them, each one bigger than the last. The air whistled with energy. Wherever a ring landed, a large swathe of crystal imploded, fire flared, and the crystal burned down to char and ash.

The Deceiver smashed his fists into the ground next to the Jeep. The cords of light attached to their physical bodies flickered precariously like candles in a draft. Contentious thoughts flew between them.

"If he cuts those cords, we die. We need to go back and protect the Jeep."

"The crystal has to be destroyed, or it will destroy everything."

"Gem isn't here now. It's not her life on the line."

"If we don't do something, there'll be nothing left to go back to."

"We can't fight him if we're not together."

Rings sparked around Audrey's fingers, and her arms snapped up to fling them off. The Circle regrouped around her, supporting her arms for a stronger throw. The rings flew off and exploded in the air. Circular pulse waves shot out to the horizons, decimating all the crystal in the ground for miles. The sky blanched white and the air sizzled. The Circle threw ring after ring, each more powerful than the last and flying farther away.

"The rings have gone nuclear, Aud. Nice work. How are you doing it?"

"No idea. They're scalding hot. I can't stand to hold them."

The snake spun against the white sky, hurling barbs of lightning at the Circle from its claws.

The Circle fired off rings like a machine gun, clutching at each other for balance and aiming in every direction. Lightning ricocheted off the rings at odd angles and struck the ground. LA flashed like a giant X-ray, blindingly bright. All over the city, crystal flared hot, burned down to charcoal, and then collapsed under its own weight.

"You snot-nosed piss-ants," the Deceiver hissed. "I will eat your hearts and leave nothing but empty husks."

"We're knocking out your crystal, asshole. Deal with it."

Time stretched. They traded strikes until near dawn and the explosions slowly faded. Clouds of reddish black smoke drifted out to sea. Sporadic flares from remaining crystal died down and guttered out, leaving large parts of the city grey and silent. Other parts burned from gas and electric fires.

The snake's furious scream shattered the quiet as he descended on them. His shadow passed right through their astral bodies. They shivered with cold dread. "Victory is an illusion, little Guardians."

The shadow of the Deceiver morphed into a giant disembodied mouth. Gaping jaws opened over them and swallowed them whole. His jaws clapped shut. They plunged into the darkness of a long tunnel and slid out at the other end, falling unceremoniously on hard ground. They blinked into a colorless sky. Thoughts raced between them.

"He swallowed us and spit us out."

Chapter 37, Part 2: Transience of Form

"I feel nauseous."

"Where are we?"

A flat, grey wasteland spread out from where they stood. Leaden light, neither day nor night, cast shadows on piles of rock. Wind moaned. In the distance, a mountain rose high above the plain.

"Great, we're back in the dead zone. I *hate* this place."

"There's a skeleton walking out there."

A single stick-thin figure trudged across the horizon with head to chest, stooped under some invisible heavy load.

"We could ask him for directions."

"Directions to what? There's nothing here."

"He looks like he has his own problems."

"Let's head for the mountain. Maybe we can get a better view from there."

Dry dirt cracked under their feet, and small spirals of dust flew up into their eyes and noses. They reached the foot of the mountain and studied the rock surface. It looked dull, almost leathery. The massive peaks rose and fell as if the mountain was breathing. And then they heard the familiar chuckle.

The snake traced lazy figure eights in the sky right above their heads. "Welcome back, little mice. I missed you." His voice rumbled like falling boulders. "You will weep for your lost hope."

"Our hope isn't lost."

"There is no hope for you in the land of Jat," the snake hissed.

 "This mountain looks a lot like Mount Wilson."

"These Temblas Mountains mirror your San Gabriel Mountains, two aspects of the same creation, though I do not understand why you would name mountains after that pansy archangel."

The snake took a dive head-first into the mountain and disappeared. The mountain shook, shifted, and came to life. The head and neck of a dragon emerged above the peaks. The Circle stumbled back, craning their necks to take in the dragon's massive form.

"Few know my true visage." The dragon roared and rose to standing on legs the height of the mountain itself. His dark, leathery skin rippled, and his oblong head wobbled on a long, curving neck. Ebony eyes glittered on each side of a blunt nose, and a red eye burned in the middle of his forehead. The head lowered and the giant mouth opened over them, flicking a tongue between jagged black teeth. "I take any shape that serves my purpose," Jat proclaimed. To illustrate the point, the dragon exploded in a cloud of black smoke and quickly reformed into a lion, balancing lightly on the mountain peaks on huge paws. In the space of a minute, the lion became a gryphon, a sphinx, a gorilla and a battleship before the smoke finally restored the form of the dragon.

A particularly snarky voice came from the Circle. "So how do we know if we're dealing with a flunky or the real thing?"

"You have an ignorant tongue," Jat growled. "Your disrespect will not go unpunished." The dragon's single red eye flashed. A sound like the keening of twisting metal drove everyone to their knees with hands and fists pressed against their ears to ease the cutting sound. "Behold the transience of form!" he said.

He spat a wad of white goo at the ground. The waxy consistency oozed and bubbled, stretched and then morphed into the shape and appearance of a human figure with a masklike face. The face stared at them with vacant eyes, and then melted. Figure after figure rose out of the wax, doll-like and lifeless, only to melt back into the ooze, but then the figures began to animate. They became familiar. TJ's third grade baseball coach, Audrey's roommate from freshman year at college. Willet's piano teacher frowned at her, and the bass player from Dean's band played air guitar.

An older man with greying black hair and a mustache emerged from the wax. A warm light kindled behind his eyes, and the color of blood flushed through his skin. He looked at Dean and gave him a kind but tired smile. "Dad!" Dean exclaimed. "Dad, it's me!" The man nodded, smiled again, and then melted back into the wax. Dean choked back a cry of anguish. "Come back, Dad! Please come back."

"It's not him, Dean," TJ said in a low voice. "It can't be."

"I don't care," Dean said, his voice cracking. "I miss him so much."

The wax bubbled again. An attractive young woman of lithe build rose slowly out of the ooze. She had hazel eyes and a mane of brunette hair down her back.

"Shit, that's Valerie Stanfield," TJ mumbled.

385

The wax girl smirked when she opened her eyes and looked at TJ. "Hi baby, how's life? Still miss me?"

"I haven't thought about you since high school." TJ said through clenched teeth.

"Liar. You were such a puppy, all in puppy love. You never got over me."

"You can get over yourself, you manipulative, stuck-up ..."

"Dude, calm down. Don't let her get to you," Dean said under his breath. "She's not real, remember?"

"She's still the same self-involved bitch," TJ muttered.

Valerie's body melted back into the ooze, and a new figure formed, an older woman, silvered hair, neatly dressed in a Chanel suit. She opened watery blue eyes and looked directly at the sisters. "Girls, remember your manners. And who are these men with you?"

"Agnes?" Audrey said in disbelief.

Willet gulped. "Mom?"

"Willet du Place, are you still embarrassing this family with your scenes and hallucinations? I would have thought you'd grow out of it by now."

"This is the Astral Plane, Mom. We're trying to save LA from earthquakes."

"What nonsense. You'd think you were raised by demented hippies."

"You're not even real, lady," Audrey said. "You're some kind of zombie."

The wax woman sighed. "Audrey, you sound as crazy as your sister."

"I'm not crazy," Willet protested.

"This is why your father walked out on us."

"He left *you*, Agnes," Audrey said grimly. "Not us."

"It is my misfortune to have borne both an ungrateful daughter and a crazy one."

"I AM NOT CRAZY!" Willet shouted at her.

The woman melted slowly, shaking her head at them all the way down into her puddle of wax.

"How sad," the snake sang, turning cartwheels in the sky. "It seems your mother despises you."

"Don't listen to him, Will," Audrey whispered. "He just wants to provoke you."

"You're a liar," Willet growled.

The snake sniffed. "The correct term is 'deceiver.' There is a difference."

"There's no difference. What's the difference?"

"In deception, there is the element of truth. Truth shapes the illusion. That is why it so delicious."

Willet turned every shade of red. "You asshole!" she yelled.

"Many thanks for the compliment, Listener. Now *you* are ripe for the picking."

Willet's light, airy astral body turned to the consistency of something thick as mud. She looked down at the heavy arms hanging at her sides. A white liquid dripped off her fingers. Not mud, but wax. Her whole body started to melt.

Audrey shouted her name. She ran to Willet and grabbed her arm, trying to pull her out of the puddle of wax forming at her feet. TJ pulled on the other arm. Her arms turned to mush in their hands. Her legs collapsed into lopsided mounds of goo. Gurgles came from her throat as she dissolved into the bubbling ooze. Her frantic eyes searched their faces before they spilled out of the sockets.

TJ and Audrey stood helplessly over the puddle. Audrey wailed in fury and lunged at the dragon. "I'll kill him," she screamed. "I'll kill him!"

Dean and TJ pulled her back to a safer distance. "Calm down or we'll all melt!" TJ said under his breath.

"You can't kill him, Audrey," Dean whispered. "He's a force of nature."

Jat dropped his long neck to the wax remains and lapped it up with a long black tongue, and then belched fire and smoke after he consumed it. His lips peeled back in a leer. The wax that used to be Willet's body dripped from his teeth. "Oh, do let her try," he coaxed.

Audrey's arms shot up above her head, spinning rings with all her strength and flung them at the dragon's head with vicious precision. His long neck undulated and dodged. A quick series of rings hit him right in the face. Jat shrieked and lowered his head. Angry fire swirled in the eye on his forehead, and spikes of barbed lightning shot out from it.

The lightening tore through their bodies like hot pokers, leaving their skin smoking. They sagged against each other, cringing at the burn.

The next hit electrocuted them and short-circuited their brains. Their movements grew sluggish.

Dean and TJ entwined their arms with Audrey's. Rings lifted from their fingers, some flying wide, others hitting their mark, but with little affect. "We're not hurting him," Dean murmured in Audrey's ear. "We need to defend ourselves, or he'll reduce us to skeletons again. It will be game over."

"I'm exhausted, Dean," she whispered. "I've got nothing left."

"That's the despair talking. Fight it," Dean pleaded. "Please. You said the rings could be used to defend people. Defend *us*!"

The palms of her hands throbbed with pain. "Defend," she said. She pictured Gem and her sister and that wonderful fountain of fresh water she had tasted, pictured herself dipping her hands into its coolness. New rings twirled on her fingers.

Dean slipped his fingers into the rings with hers and stretched them out between them. TJ helped them lift the rings above their heads. As one, they threw the rings into the air with all the strength they had. Instead of flying off, the rings dropped one by one in a stack around them and melded into a solid capsule. A canopy of light spread over them and hardened into a glass shell the color of milky amber.

Jat's lightning hit the canopy and heated it to a cooking temperature. Inside the capsule it was stifling. "I guess this is it," Audrey gasped. "We've done what we can do. I love you guys."

Dean kissed her cheek and TJ wrapped his arms around both of them. They ducked their heads, waiting for the scorching fire that would surely reach them when the shell burned away. But it didn't happen. They looked up through the glass shell.

The dragon's barrage of lightning flashed on the surface and glanced off. The capsule floated up through the lightning strikes and rose above them. The light around the capsule turned clear and bright, tinged with pink. The air cooled as the capsule rose higher and higher.

"Do you hear that?" Audrey asked. "It sounds like ocean waves."

"Where are we going?" Dean asked.

"I hope we're going where my sister went," she said.

Chapter 38: Soul's Dark Night

Willet had seen the horror in the eyes of her sister, Dean, and TJ, as they watched her body melt. Her nose and cheeks hung off her face in wet blobs and her legs sagged. Her soft ribs no longer held her upright. Her chest cavity caved in, and her torso slumped over. Her lungs became too soggy to absorb air. Her lips melted over her teeth. She felt her stomach and intestines liquefy. She tried to scream, but her trachea had turned to jelly. It buckled and folded. Audrey held her sister's hands until her arms fell off. Her skull caved into her softening brain.

Grim-faced, Dean put an arm around Audrey's shoulders, and pulled her away from the growing puddle of wax. TJ's features twisted in anguish and confusion. He buried his face in his hands. He couldn't bear to look at her. That hurt more than anything.

Willet held on to the sight of her loved ones until her eyes turned to liquid and ran out of their sockets. The remains of her body dissolved, and then the connection between her consciousness and her wax form snapped. Death. She was ready to die, wanted to die. But somehow, she continued to *be. What am I? Just a point of view drifting in the dark.*

Her viewpoint drifted through velvet darkness, darting among stars like a comet and skimming the surfaces of glowing planets. She was everything and nothing, a totality, a speck. Her movement picked up speed. She gave herself up to the exhilaration of freedom, without fear. *What else could happen to me?*

Her forward motion began to slow as the atmosphere grew heavier. LA County loomed below her. The long cord of light that had connected to her physical body still extended out of her midsection and pulled her downward. She dropped at collision speed, heading straight for the freeway, the concrete, the parked Jeep. She surrendered to an even more real death than the one she just experienced.

Instead, she dropped through the roof of the Jeep into the back seat, into her body. The cord of light disappeared. She sat up, shocked and gasping, ready to scream. Then she opened her eyes and looked out the windows. *I'm in the Jeep at the Hemmings exit, just as we left it.* She shifted her limbs, felt their weight. The tight enclosure of skin and heaviness of bone felt strange after the lightness of her astral form. The scream died in her throat.

Audrey, Dean and TJ were sprawled in their seats, unconscious. Their bodies twitched violently, as if they were having lucid dreams. Willet grabbed her sister by the shoulders. "Auddie, wake up. Wake up!" She poked Dean in the shoulder, wrapped arms around TJ's neck and shook him. "Wake up, you guys. Come back!" She got no response, not even the flicker of an eyelid, so she unclicked her seat belt, opened the door and stepped out. Red Souls swarmed her, buzzing and chattering, getting in her face. She had no patience for them. She chanted HU out loud, and they pulled back, but still circled the Jeep, trying to get in.

I need gas to move the Jeep. She locked the car and walked up the off ramp to the local road, looking for a passing car. No traffic. She pulled out her phone and tried to call the caretaker at Pine Siskin House. No service. She started walking. The Red Soul swarm followed her, droning like mosquitos. She didn't give them the satisfaction of grabbing her attention, just chanted HU under her breath as she kept up a brisk walk. After a few minutes, they flew away.

In the east, the sun cracked above the horizon and light the color of rust spread out in a thin line. To the west, smoke mixed with fog lay over the ground like a dirty blanket. Gritty air scraped her nose and throat. She was all too aware of her vulnerable situation – no headphones, no hat, no sunglasses. The sun would soon bake her, and any loud noise would be an explosion in her ears.

A pickup truck finally slowed to her outstretched thumb, and the passenger door swung open. The driver had greasy gray hair under a sweat-stained Dodgers cap. He stared at her through heavy, reddened eyes. It made her uncomfortable, but she had to take the ride. She tried to engage him in conversation. He responded to every question or comment with grunts and shrugs, as if he lacked the energy for complete sentences. She had hoped he could tell her how LA had survived the crystal debacle, but he didn't seem to know much.

He dropped her at the far end of Pine Siskin Road, and she walked the rest of the way home, so tired she could have laid down on the ground and slept. When the roof of her house came into view, she was so happy that she used the last of her energy to run. As she got close, she saw a boxy white RV parked in the circular drive.

Who is this? A squatter? We haven't been gone that long, have we?

Willet walked up to the RV and rapped on the side door. She heard movement inside and stepped back as the door opened. The sight of a familiar face shocked her. "Bart? Bart Johnson!" she exclaimed.

She'd only met him once, but she was sure it was him. It seemed like an eternity since she'd talked to a regular human.

Bart jumped out, barefoot, in faded jeans and a tee shirt, and curled her into a big hug. "Thank God," he said. "I thought you guys might be dead." He held her at arm's length, took in her disheveled appearance and concern clouded his eyes. "What happened to you?" he asked. "Where's Audrey?"

Willet tried to remember the last time she had washed her hair. It had been a while. "She's, uh, staying by the Jeep," she stammered. "What are you doing here?"

"My house slid down the slope in my backyard after a big rock pushed up out of the ground and tipped it. I've moved into the RV until I can get some construction help. The house still has to be hauled up, and no one's available. Then I started calling everyone I knew. You ladies were the only ones who didn't answer, so I came down to see if you were okay."

How do I explain Audrey's current state? Best stick to the facts. Audrey needs gas. She's out of gas."

Bart gave her a quizzical look. "Okay, gas. We'll find some."

He unhooked his truck from the RV, and they drove off in search of gas. The first couple of gas stations were closed, but they found one open east of Hemmings. The price for a gallon of gas was twenty-five dollars. They drove to the end of a ten-car line and waited their turn while the line inched along slowly. Every vehicle got an allotment of ten gallons. After fifteen minutes, they were able to pull up to the pump.

"Truck deliveries aren't on schedule since the Wrath of God hit," the fuzzy-haired attendant told them, rubbing his chin stubble as he pumped their gas. "We're the only station around has any left. I hear there'll be some trucks comin' through tomorrow."

"The Wrath of God." Willet repeated. "Is that what people are calling it?"

"That's what I call it," the attendant replied solemnly. "It's the only explanation makes sense. I was driving home from Chico, and my car almost flipped over by one of those rock things. God's angry."

Willet couldn't really disagree. She nodded sympathetically. What she wanted was gas for Bart's truck AND a full gas can for the Jeep, more than the allotment. Maybe her sympathy helped. The attendant agreed to fill the extra can.

With the modicum of gas in the tank, the truck headed to the freeway exit where the Jeep sat. Bart turned off the ignition, and Willet put a hand on his arm. "Wait," she said. "I need to tell you something."

"What?"

"You may be confused by what you see in the Jeep. Audrey and the guys are okay. They're just asleep, in a way. You could say the whole 'Wrath of God' thing had an unsettling effect on them. We need to get them back to the house so they can rest and recover. What I'm trying to tell you is please trust me."

Bart nodded his head slowly. "Okay...there are guys?"

"Yes. It's a long story."

"I'll bet."

They got out of the truck and walked to the Jeep. Audrey, Dean and TJ were still in their seats, out like the proverbial lights. At least they weren't twitching. Willet unlocked the Jeep and lowered all the windows. A cloud of Red Souls still swirled, trying to get to the unconscious passengers. Willet chanted HU to herself, hoping it would be enough to dispel them. Bart went to the driver's side and looked in at TJ, his mouth slack, saliva dribbling out one side.

"That's my boyfriend, TJ, you met him at our house," Willet said. "He drove a long way yesterday, out of the mountains. He's exhausted."

"Clearly. And the other guy?"

"Dean's a friend of mine. Audrey's too. He's a musician."

"Okay, what's the plan?"

"We gas up the Jeep, and I'll drive them home. You follow me. We move fast."

"A doctor should check them out. This doesn't look normal."

Willet really didn't want to take them to a hospital. "The hospitals are probably very crowded right now, and these guys are going to be fine. If you could help get them out of the car and into the house when we get home, I'd appreciate it."

Bart stared at her and shook his head, went back to the truck and retrieved the gas can. He poured the whole contents into the Jeep.

*****

Audrey, Dean and TJ still sat inside the flying capsule, watching the astral world go by. The walls of the capsule had turned from creamy amber to clear, revealing a glorious 360-degree view of tall pines on mountainsides, sparkling rivers, and a long green valley rolling under a sapphire sky.

The burns on their bodies had cooled and the skin healed. Audrey huddled against the capsule wall, wiping away tears when she

396

couldn't hold them back. Dean sat next to her, his arm around her shoulder. He looked helplessly at TJ, who was sprawled on the floor, staring at the ceiling.

"How am I going to explain this to my parents?" Audrey asked in a hoarse voice. "If she's dead, there isn't even a body to bury."

"We don't know what happened," Dean said. "It could be a trick."

"You saw her, Dean. She was choking to death. I'll never forget the panic in her eyes. It's tearing me apart."

"I'll shoot that reptile if I see it again," TJ muttered.

"Let's hope none of us have to see it again," Dean said. "My skin still remembers the burning. And by the way, I think we're going in circles. The same mountains are going by again and again. If anyone's interested…"

"I don't care." Audrey closed her eyes.

"We're trapped in here, Audrey. If there's anything we *can* do about Willet, it won't happen unless we get out." Dean stood and ran his hands over the capsule wall, knocking his knuckles on it here and there. It sounded uniformly solid.

TJ dragged himself off the floor with a sigh and stood next to Dean. "If we break this wall then what happens?" he asked. "We could fall into one of those rivers or hit a tree."

"We're flying around in the astral plane in a pod made out of Audrey's rings. Physical laws probably don't apply."

TJ kicked his foot hard against a low section of the wall. Small cracks spread through it. He kept kicking until a chink formed. He knelt down and peered through it. "I can't see anything out there. It's dark."

"What about the trees and rivers?"

TJ kicked some more and made a bigger hole. He looked out again. "Negative. No trees, no rivers, nothing."

Dean pounded the wall above TJ's hole with his fists, tearing away broken pieces until a sizeable opening formed. He knelt and looked through it. "This thing is just an IMAX theater with a wraparound screen. We've been watching a movie."

Audrey roused herself and came over to take a look. "It looks like we're in space."

TJ and Dean kicked and tore away pieces of the wall until there was an opening big enough to walk through. The capsule was flying silently through darkness.

"How do we stop this thing?" TJ asked.

"Who knows," Dean shrugged. He looked anxiously at Audrey. "This is the Circle, at least for now. I don't want to be a callous jerk, but can we still make rings…?"

Audrey's head drooped and her shoulders rose and fell. She sniffled and wiped her eyes on the sleeves of her shirt. Dean reached out a hand. She took it, and he pulled her into a one-arm hug.

She stood in front of the opening, staring out at the dark void, and then looked at her fingers. Small rings started to spin around each knuckle. She tossed them out into the dark. They hovered in front of the opening, glittering. "I can still throw baby rings."

"That's something. What do you think, Audrey?" Dean asked.

"Willet would want us to keep trying. So, let's go."

"Go where?"

"Who knows? The rings seem to be waiting for us. Maybe they can carry us."

They considered this idea in silence.

"I'll try to grab one, see what happens," TJ said finally.

"Hold on, T," Dean entreated him. "Think about what you're doing."

"I've thought about it. We can't just stay here."

"We can't lose you."

"I love you too, man," TJ replied. "Now stand aside."

"I was just guessing about the rings, TJ," Audrey cautioned. "What if I'm wrong?"

"Then you two will know what not to do. Give me some room."

They stood aside for him. TJ took a deep breath, ran toward the opening and leaped through it. A ring flew straight into his outstretched fingers. He grabbed it with both hands and hung on, laughing as it carried him away from the pod. "Come on, you wimps," he called to them. "Grab a ring."

They watched him drift away until he was just a small circle of light in the distance. Dean and Audrey looked at each other and paced a few steps back.

"Wait a minute, Audrey," Dean said suddenly, extending an arm in front of her. "Before we take this leap, there's something I have to do."

He pulled her into his arms and kissed her lips, lingering as if they had all the time in the world. She wrapped her arms around his waist and kissed him back. They separated slowly, holding each other's eyes.

"Let's make the jump before we change our minds," she said.

They turned to the opening, bolted forward and jumped. The rings quickly came to their hands and carried them into the vast emptiness of space. The capsule disappeared as soon as their feet left it. There was no going back.

"Do you think these rings know where to take us?" Audrey asked. Her voice sounded small in the infinite quiet.

"They're taking us *somewhere*," Dean replied, "and we're going there pretty fast. Every direction looks the same from here."

"Wait, do you see that pinprick of light far ahead?"

"No. Oh, yeah. It's getting bigger."

In fact, the light got bigger in a hurry, exploding in size as it rushed toward them.

"It's a meteor shower!"

A cloud of sizzling cosmic debris swarmed them. Burning particles, the size of grains of sand, whizzed past their faces and under their noses. Burning hunks of rock rolled by like cannon balls.

"Look, the stuff flies right through me," Dean called out. A cloud of sparkling dust flowed into his chest and out his back. "Feels warm and fizzy and kind of tickles."

"We're in our astral bodies," Audrey said. "Otherwise, we'd never survive this."

"If I collide with one of those big rocks, the shock alone might kill me."

They sailed into blazing light at the heart of the meteor shower. Enormous rocks whistled past, close enough to touch, but nothing hit them. Somehow, the rings found a clear, if narrow, path that avoided collisions. When they emerged from the shower, they began to drop rapidly. The darkness around them lightened to grey. Far below, the gridded features of a city came into view. They hurtled toward the ground, clutching the rings for dear life.

"It's Hemmings! That's the bank building."

"We'll slam right into it if we don't slow down."

The trajectory of their flight veered past the bank, leveled off several hundred feet above the ground and sailed along, out of town into the open desert. Pine Siskin House came into view, closer and closer. They headed for the front door at high speed.

"I hope I'm right about the astral bodies." Audrey closed her eyes and braced for impact.

*****

Bart had been so concerned by Audrey's condition and Willet's refusal to get medical attention that he stalked to his RV, climbed in and slammed the door behind him. Willet hadn't seen him since, but the RV was still parked in their driveway. She would knock on the door in the morning and try to talk to him again, though she didn't know what she would say. *Audrey's been out of her body for a while. Way out.* He deserved a better explanation, but that was the best she could do without sounding truly insane.

It was well after midnight, and she couldn't sleep. She thought she heard Audrey talking to her. Her muscles ached and her headache hurt so badly that it upset her stomach. As tired as she was, all she could do was toss and turn. At 4:00 a.m., she got up, flushed and sweating, and wandered through the house like a wraith. She checked Audrey's bedroom. Her sister lay on the bed, barely breathing.

Willet choked on her anguish and prayed. *Please, God, don't let her die, or melt like I did. Audrey's a good person. She doesn't deserve that.*

She moved on to look in the rooms where Dean and TJ lay passed out. Bart had insisted on carrying Audrey into the house by himself, but it took both of them to hoist Dean and TJ, one by one, out of the Jeep and into the guest rooms. Willet checked for sounds. They lay in the same state as Audrey, unmoving and barely breathing.

What is that snake doing to you?

A blast of cold hit her in the back, and passed right through her, making her shiver. She spun to face the cold. Another wave hit her full frontal and whistled out through her back. *What is going on?* Anxious and unsettled, she fetched slippers and robe from her bedroom, and padded out to the front porch. The door clicked shut behind her in the quiet night. Although the evening air was warm, she wrapped herself tightly in the robe to subdue her chills. She sat on the step, closed her eyes and gave up any effort to think. A heavy weight in her chest made it hard to take a breath. How did things go so terribly wrong?

What if Audrey never returned? What if TJ never kissed her again? What if Dean's affection for Audrey never had a chance to grow? Everyone she cared about – lost. And Gem. It seemed impossible that Gem no longer walked in this world. Willet hadn't had time to mourn, and now it was all she could do. She felt so alone, with no way to escape it. *Why am I the one still here? I don't want to be.* She wished the snake had taken her too. There it was – despair. After all the Circle had accomplished, Jat the Deceiver won after all. Numb and hopeless, she sat staring into the night, waiting for nothing.

Chapter 39: Parts of the Whole

Time passed without her notice until the rising sun warmed her face. Sounds of life drifted over from town. A dog barked in the distance. She shook herself and looked toward the ruddy light of the eastern horizon. Another day dawns. Suddenly she couldn't breathe.

The sun silhouetted two approaching figures. A woman in a flowing skirt walked toward her with a purposeful stride. Morning sun glinted off the blonde highlights in the woman's brown curly hair. A large black dog trotted beside her.

Willet's eye's flooded with tears. She kicked off her slippers and ran toward them. She slowed to a walk as she got close enough to the approaching figures to see them clearly. They were Gem and Dora in form and feature, but they looked strange. Gem radiated energy in shimmering waves. Rainbow colors washed across her eyes. Dora bristled with the same energy. Pure light beamed from the white patch on her forehead.

Willet stopped short, suddenly suspicious. "Gem, is that you?"

"It is," the familiar voice rang out.

She studied Gem warily. "You're glowing. It's weird."

"My body is newly formed from primal energy. It will adjust to the slower vibration of the physical plane and become solid. The shine will fade."

Willet took a single step closer for a better look. The shimmering light made her squint. "Are you really alive, like before, or are you some kind of ghost?"

Gem chuckled. "This is a living body, not created through physical birth, but the results are the same."

"How do I know you aren't one of those wax people that Jat spit out?"

"You do well to test your visions, Listener. The eyes are easily fooled."

That sounds like something Gem would say.

She took another step closer. A small measure of hope bloomed in her heart. "Audrey told me you died. They all said it. I didn't believe them."

"They can be forgiven for that conclusion, after what they witnessed."

"I thought I died too. Yet I'm here. I don't understand what happened."

"Death is a relative term, baby girl. I have died many times. Soul survives the body."

It's Gem.

The glow subsided. Willet mustered the nerve to take a few steps closer and look into Gem's eyes, searching for the essence of the woman she knew, the wry smile and steady strength. A wave of love

404

crashed into her and flooded her heart. She closed the remaining distance between them and wrapped the Guardian in a fierce embrace to assure herself that Gem was really there. "You were gone, but I could still feel you," Willet said. Her quivering voice broke.

"No need for tears, dear one. You were ever in my heart."

"How did you get here? Are you still the Guardian?"

"There is still work to be done. After the Circle destroyed the crystal, many Red Souls were left roaming the city. I know you can hear them. They whisper endlessly in the ears of susceptible people. They must be rounded up and sent back to the Underworld."

Willet let go of Gem's shoulders and bent to stroke Dora's head. Dora snuffled her appreciation. "Everyone is asleep at my house. I don't know how to wake them up. I think Jat has them trapped somewhere."

"They have the means to free themselves."

"It was awful, where we were. The Deceiver is awful. I wanted to kill him myself."

"That is why we must assemble the Circle. Jat's influence is still too strong in this city."

Willet groaned. "But we destroyed the crystal. I thought we were done!"

Gem took a long breath and stretched, fluffed the ruffles on the neck of her white blouse and smoothed the long maroon skirt over her hips. It appeared as if she was settling into her physical form, taking possession of it. The glow around her flickered out. "Someone will try to regrow the crystal," she said.

"What? Why would anyone want to do that after what happened? The city is a mess!"

"The crystal can be used for both good and evil. An unsuspecting person may think to recreate it for good, only to learn the evil that it can do. The Circle is needed to steer the process in the right direction."

"I thought I lost my mind the first time around. I thought *I* died. Maybe I'm not cut out for this line of work."

"You are a free being, Listener," Gem replied with a short nod. "You must live your life as you see fit." She turned on her heel and headed toward Pine Siskin House, with Dora trotting beside her.

Willet hurried after her. Bart had just climbed out of his RV in the circular drive. Willet took the opportunity to speak to him by making introductions. "Bart, this is Gem. Gem, Bart."

"Glad to meet you," Bart said formally with a small bow.

Gem gave him an appraising look that made him blush. "Then you must know we have serious matters to attend to here. What is your intent?"

"My intent?" Bart stammered. "I don't know what you mean. I came to see if Audrey and Willet were okay."

Gem turned to the Jeep in the driveway without replying. "I see the Jeep is here. Excellent…" She squinted at it and then frowned. "What happened to my Jeep? It looks lopsided. Where is the bumper?"

"Yeah, about that," Willet said carefully. "We had kind of a rough ride down the mountain, dodged a few boulders along the way. Some of them hit us. It's a wonder there's any Jeep left."

"Ah, the physical plane, so fragile," Gem sighed and turned to Willet. "If you have any more of that refreshing green beverage, it would be much appreciated. This body needs fuel."

*****

Willet wandered around Pine Siskin House in a sort of fog, trying to find the source of a soft, hissing sound she heard constantly. The house was full of familiar things, but they all looked different, slightly distorted and rimmed with light. The comatose travelers remained in their beds. Within the white noise, Willet heard their voices. She felt confused and off-balance. Most confusing of all, Gem had returned. *Am I on the physical plane or the astral plane?*

She walked up and down the back hallway, stopping at each bedroom to listen for breathing. Audrey's chest rose and fell in a slow, gentle rhythm. Dean snored slightly. TJ was more still than death. It frightened her, but she resisted the urge to go to him and shake his shoulder. She wasn't sure *where* he was in consciousness. He could be in that horrible place fighting for his Soul against that monster. She couldn't bear to say its name: Jat the Deceiver, Creator of nightmares, Lord of Despair.

She was about to walk back to the living room when she heard a snort. TJ's body bounced on the bed as if it had fallen from a great height. He sat up suddenly, gasping for breath, his eyes wild.

"Thomas," she whispered. "You're here."

His eyes slowly focused on her. "You're here. Where am I?"

"We're at my house. You've been out of your body for a while."

TJ sniffed suspiciously. "I don't know this room. And what's that noise?"

"What noise?"

407

"That whispering sound. It's creeping me out. Are there bees in here?"

"You're in our guest room. There are no bees, but I hear the white noise too. It's okay. I think it's astral."

He looked at her sharply. "It's not okay. The astral is not okay. The Deceiver tried to burn us, Will. I didn't think we'd make it back."

Willet shuddered. "Nothing was real in that place. None of it."

"It was real enough. His lightening cooked us even worse than his spit. Audrey spun up some kind of flying contraption that carried us away. We had to get out, so I kicked a hole in the wall and jumped out, floated by myself in deep space, holding on to one of Audrey's rings. I thought I was lost."

Suddenly, Willet couldn't stand the distance between them. She ran to the bed and wrapped her arms around his chest, relishing his warmth and inhaling the scent of his skin. She laid her head against his shoulder. "I was so afraid," she whispered.

He slipped an arm around her shoulders, pulled her closer and pressed his lips to her ear. "Babe, after you left us the way you did, I barely held it together. Audrey was hysterical. Dean kept the only clear head. If it wasn't for him, we'd never have gotten away. They both jumped out of the flying machine after I did. I hope to God they made it back."

"Audrey and Dean are both here, still sleeping. They'll come back to their bodies. I feel sure of it now. And I have a surprise for you."

"No more surprises, please. I might finally have that heart attack you predicted."

"You'll like this one. Can you get up and walk? There's someone in the living room you'll be happy to see."

Willet led TJ by the arm into the living room where Gem was curled up in a corner of the sofa with Dora at her feet. When TJ saw her, he swayed on his feet with his mouth hanging open.

"You. You're here. That's not possible."

"Good to see you too, Warrior." Gem smiled sweetly. "How was your journey?"

TJ dropped into a chair and stared at her. "It can't be. You were dust." The color drained from his face. He looked about to faint.

At that moment, Audrey appeared in the doorway, blinking against the morning light. Her eyes swept over the room. She saw her sister, and then she saw Gem. Logically impossible thoughts flickered across her eyes. Her knees buckled.

Behind her, Dean caught her by the elbows and steadied her with an arm around her waist. "Willet. You're here." Then, he noticed Gem too. "Gem," his voice cracked. "There is NO way…"

*****

Audrey snapped out of her semi-faint and ran to her sister. She pulled her into a strangling hug, hyperventilating and almost choking at the same time. "I thought I'd lost you," she gasped in Willet's ear. "Never scare me like that again."

The sisters stood nose to nose, clasping hands and searching each other's faces for explanations through bubbling tears.

"It was just a trick of that damned monster," Willet murmured. "None of it was real."

"You melted, Will! I held your arms in my hands! It was the worst nightmare I ever had. And you!" Audrey said, turning to Gem. "How can *you* be here? I watched your body turn to dust!" She grasped Gem by the shoulders and kissed her firmly on each cheek before hugging her fiercely and stepping back to look her over.

Dean wrapped an arm around Gem and hugged her to his side. He laid his cheek on her hair with a deep sigh.

Gem nodded and gave them all a serene smile. "The Circle is complete," she said.

Chapter 40: Questions

Bart knocked on the door at Pine Siskin House to check on Audrey and found everyone sitting in the living room. Audrey rushed over to give him a warm hug. He received a fish-eyed glare from Dean.

Bart glared back. "Hey, I carried your ass from the car to the bed, buddy," he said. "You were dead weight. I almost broke my back."

Dean's glare turned a bit sheepish. "Oh, well, thanks. I guess."

Bart received another hug from Audrey and one from Willet before returning to his RV. A subdued mood fell over the house, but body and mind still had to be fed. TJ and Dean escaped to the kitchen to raid the refrigerator. Audrey followed them in to do some cooking.

Gem stood up, went to the window and peered out, came back to the couch and sat down, and then got up again to return to the window.

"Gem, I have questions," Willet said. "Things I have to understand, or they'll drive me crazy."

"Questions only beget more questions," Gem replied with a sigh and retook her seat. "Go ahead, ease your mind." She settled into the couch cushions and took a long sip from the slushy green drink on the coffee table.

411

Willet tried to visualize a list of all the things she wanted to ask. Where to start? She would start with a personal question which she wasn't sure she should ask, but she couldn't hold back.

"How old are you, really? I hope that's not rude."

Gem chuckled. "I entered this form for the first time in the year 1850, born Gemimah Jane Hawkins."

"That would make you almost 170 years old!" Willet marveled. "Were you born like a regular person, with parents?"

"I had parents, of course. We were farmers in Ohio. I had an older brother, Abel. Those were violent times for people of my color. My family helped slaves escape to the north. I used my gift of sight to guide them through areas of danger."

"How many times have you changed bodies since then?"

"Bodies come and go. They are a vehicle for Soul. I have used many vehicles of this appearance."

"Have you always been 'you' – Gem, like you are now?"

"Soul never dies, baby girl, but everything else changes."

The aroma of buttery eggs and toast wafted through the house. Audrey was making her famous huevos rancheros. Willet's stomach gurgled. She couldn't remember the last time she had eaten. At this moment, all she wanted was love, companionship, and food, the simple needs of a simple human. Was that so wrong?

Audrey walked into the living room with a steaming plate of eggs in each hand, followed by Dean. She put the plates on the coffee table and sat on the couch next to Gem. Dean dropped into a chair in front of the plates but did not start to eat.

"Gem," Audrey began, "Why did you let that horrible man shoot you? You could have stopped him, right?"

"I could not let Mr. Theese harm anyone else in the Circle. That is why my darling Dora knocked his gun away. As for me, I had a part to play in his karma, and I played it. He will live with the consequences of his choices for a long time. I will not." Gem looked around the coffee table at the faces focused on her. "Anyone else?"

Dean leaned forward with elbows on his knees. "Yeah, I've got one. Who's the tall woman with the brown ponytail? She said she's a traveler or something."

"I see this is a day for complicated questions," Gem said resignedly and curled her legs underneath her. "Very well. Maria Sonrisa Degas de Megaro is one of the Traveling Masters. She has long served the Circle of Augustus but is seldom seen by human eyes."

"I fell off a cliff in my truck," Dean said. "I knew I was going to die. Next thing I know, I'm sitting in the Jeep talking to TJ. Somehow, she moved me out of the truck and into the Jeep. She saved my life."

"Sonrisa has mastered dimensions of space and time. She folds them in a way that the place and time she wants to go touches the time and place she occupies. The energies of those dimensions mingle and become simultaneous. Then she just - steps through. It *is* rather disconcerting the first time you experience it."

Dean searched Gem's face for any hint of humor and found none. "If I didn't experience it myself, I would say you're crazy."

She gave him a rueful look. "That has been said about me before if I am not mistaken. What changed?"

Dean met her eyes. "Just about everything. I don't know what to do."

"Do? What do you mean?"

"I mean, how can I repay a debt like that? I still can't fathom it. Why me? Why should *I* be saved?"

Gem gave him a kind smile. "Why not you, Warrior? You are loved more than you know. Accept such gifts with gratitude. They come from Spirit itself."

Dean blushed and dug into his plate of eggs, shaking his head.

"We've all seen unbelievable things," Willet said. "I don't even trust my own eyes anymore."

"That seems prudent," Gem nodded.

"I mean, when my body melted, I thought I was dying. I felt myself break into pieces. I couldn't breathe, couldn't scream. I was petrified. And it wasn't real."

"Leaving one state of consciousness and entering another is a type of death. It is very real."

"You've experienced death. Is that the way it feels? Do I have to go through that again when my body dies next time?"

Gem studied the glass in her hand, tracing its frosted surface with her thumb. "I do not linger in death. When my physical body begins to die, I leave the shell immediately. You need not stay until the bitter end to watch your corpse decompose. Once is enough for that experience. Let the body go and move on."

"You make it sound so simple."

"It requires awareness and practice."

"That's what you say about everything. I don't want to practice dying."

414

Gem gave her a puzzled look and shrugged. "Then you will not learn to do it correctly."

"People manage to die successfully without practicing. It happens all the time."

"That depends on your definition of success."

There was no point arguing with Gem. Willet had learned that much, at least. Gem was so often right, that it was difficult to doubt her. *Maybe learning to die correctly isn't as absurd as it sounds.*